Winner's Circle

By Joseph Hayes

Winner's Circle

a novel by

Joseph Hayes

Delacorte Press / New York

Published by
Delacorte Press
1 Dag Hammarskjold Plaza
New York, N.Y. 10017

Manufactured in the United States of America

First printing

Designed by Terry Antonicelli

Library of Congress Cataloging in Publication Data

Hayes, Joseph Arnold, 1918–
  Winner's Circle.

  I. Title.
PZ4.H418Wi [PS3515.A942] 813'.54   79-26844
ISBN 0-440-09538-7

For Marrijane
who makes me feel better
simply by walking into a room

Winner's Circle

Chapter One

RACING *fans and addicts, degenerate gamblers, curious interlopers in these rarified climes, fellow knaves, and wide-eyed marks—it's Derby Week again! This is Wyatt Slingerland, worshiped and despised in the netherworld of racing as Count Wyatt. Olympian oracle, the Count knows all, tells little.*

Today marks the official opening of the spring meeting at Churchill Downs, where on a clear day you can see across the track by slicing through the smog with a machete. For you uninitiated outlanders a meeting, in horsemen's parlance, is a series of racing days at a particular track during which wise men and fools alike endeavor to become millionaires by losing their life savings. Earlier this morning some of you insomniacs may have observed huge gaudily colored balloons, appropriately filled with hot air, drifting above in the ozone. Well, be assured this was not an alcoholic hallucination but a Derby Festival event known as the Great Balloon Race. For today, you see, is the last Saturday in April—which, reasonably enough, signifies that it is one week until the first Saturday in May, as the crow flies. And on that gala (they tell me) occasion the world famous Kentucky Derby will climax a week of spectacle, whoopla, pageantry, and general debauchery. This form of insanity has come to be branded fondly as Derby fever, normally intense but occasionally lethal. It's Mardi Gras, Christmas, Hanukkah, New Year's Eve, and the Fourth of July all rolled unmercifully into one—and all accompanied by the merry jingle of cash registers. It's the cuckoo's nest all week, but the whitecoats are out on strike or out making a bundle stiffing the tourists.

For romantics, if any of that ilk still survive, this tribal rite of spring is only innocent revelry, a time for feasting, gluttony, and certainly dipsomania. For the cynics fouling the nest it's a weak excuse for a bacchanal, an ancient Roman saturnalia—seven days and nights of indulgent excesses, wanton dissipation, open licentiousness, and nymphomania amuck, amuck. In short, a Dionysian orgy without orgasm, climaxed by frustration, a huge head, and a flat wallet.

Millions of dollars will change hands this holy week. It's estimated that as much as five million will pass over the pari-mutuel counters in a single day to flash like fireworks on the pretty blinking tote boards. Millions more will find their way, as money in America invariably does, into the numbered bank accounts of the crime cartels in Switzerland. But no matter—fortunes will be lost, but there's always the magical tomorrow. Another day, another horse, another sure thing, or mortal lock, as horse players morbidly put it. And too, one year from now the delirium of Derby Week will, with the inevitability of Greek tragedy, renew itself in all its gory glory!

It was a rotund little Irish haberdasher with ten offspring to support who turned the seventh race on the first Saturday in May into the most important two minutes in sport. Today, more than a century later, touts, grifts, pickpockets, shills, con men, hustlers of every shade and variety, and hookers of any sexual proclivity you're willing to pay for all descend like starving locusts to turn this old gray minimetropolis of Louisville, lazing on the bank of the storied Ohio River, into scam city, the ripoff capital of the world. Hang onto your teeth if there's any gold in them!

At the epicenter of this earthquakelike phenomenon is an animal. He carries a thousand plus pounds on matchstick-fragile legs, running astonishingly on four single digits, single toes called hoofs—try walking on two single fingers some time, or even four—yet this remarkable creature has a stride of over twenty-five feet, can accelerate from a standstill to forty miles per hour in two seconds and, even with a man on his back, can run a mile or more at that speed. He is

2

the thoroughbred racehorse, the finest athlete in the animal world—
and the fastest animal extant. He appeals to the stunted romantic in
the worst of us: a lithe moving thing of infinite grace and heart-
stopping beauty. And, what only a few realize, he is also an individual with intelligence, loyalty, and personality.

There are those, of course, who look upon him as a dumb beast not
worth the cost of his feed, transportation, and stall space. The dreary
fact is that only one out of nine ever earns enough to pay his board,
let alone repay his original purchase price. To which the quixotic
romanticist replies: "It's the one in nine who wins that really matters,
and that is reward sufficient unto the day." The hardheaded busi-
nessman scoffs and snorts and lays out his bet regardless. Yours
truly, Count Wyatt, has one leg planted firmly in each camp and as
a result suffers a psychological hernia.

What entices a hundred thousand otherwise sane and respected ci-
tizens—and millions of others via television—to witness this two
minutes? Is it that racing is the sport of kings? Is it really a sport at
all? How much of it is already in the hands of ruthless entrepreneurs
who have as much concern for honest sport as they have for ecology
and the health of mankind? How long before the conglomerates glom
onto it? Already there is abundant evidence that organized crime has
its sleazy, not to say bloody, hand in the till. No one was ever
caught fixing a Kentucky Derby—but that doesn't mean that no
Kentucky Derby was ever fixed.

Still, the legends on which the popularity of racing flourishes are
legion—and they seem to have less to do with how fast the mile and
a quarter was run than with the drama itself: two jockeys slashing at
each other with whips and snatching at silks as they cross the finish
line; the venerable Shoemaker himself becoming confused and standing up in the stirrups at the eighth pole and thus losing in the
homestretch the race he had already won; Forward Pass being declared official winner of the '68 Derby after it was discovered that
Dancer's Image, who crossed the line first, had been shot with an
illegal drug—which has since been legalized. What corruption and
chicanery lie hidden here? Fans can only speculate—and speculation
titillates the depravity and cupidity lurking in the souls of all of us.

In spite of the miraculous and instant calculations of the tote boards, what keeps racing blessedly somewhat immune from the computerized idiocy of the modern world is the undisputed fact that, for all the wisdom of expert handicappers like myself, the outcome of any race is never really predictable. No matter how the bettor bets or what he believes, there are no so-called mortal locks. The time, the money, the discipline, the dedication, and the delicate breeding that are devoted to producing a Derby champion stagger even my vast imagination. Breeders search for blood strains as if trying to produce a monarch to hold sway over an empire. Foolish Pleasure was syndicated as a stud at eight million dollars, and the average yearling price at the Keeneland auction this year was over one hundred thousand dollars, and prices are going up, up! Nevertheless, the meek do sometimes inherit the earth. A former Chicago policeman nabbed Elocutionist for fifteen thousand dollars, and he was syndicated for over a million. The literature of racing is wormy with nags-to-riches fairy tales. A former car dealer from Puerto Rico bought Bold Forbes for just over fifteen thousand; he won the Derby and the Belmont Stakes and syndicated his stallion at four million. The saga of Seattle Slew is part of modern mythology—purchased at seventeen-five, he was syndicated at twelve million!

At the same time, even the great Secretariat's progeny have been a disappointment on the track. So why do owners stay in racing? Obviously for the same reason that brings those two hundred thousand hopeful souls to Louisville this week: some with dollar signs in their eyes and a few with stars—those few who feel in their bones that watching this beautiful animal perform is one of the great thrills and satisfactions available to poor old battered mankind. If I may be forgiven a sentimental moment, I would like to quote from a short story by one of America's finest and much neglected writers, Sherwood Anderson: "If you've never been crazy about thoroughbreds, it's because you've never been around where they are much and don't know any better. They're beautiful. There isn't anything so lovely and clean and full of spunk and honesty and everything as some racehorses. It brings a lump up into my throat when a horse runs." So, for some the meaning of racing cannot be seen on the flickering tote board, where odds and hopes are read, but are felt deep inside

*one's own self. For those so blessed the sound of hoofbeats is a sym-
phony in the blood.*

*There's another tricky character omnipresent during Derby Week
too. He is the god of sunshine and rain. He either hovers benignly
above, smiling down, or in a foul mood he lurks scowling in dark
clouds. If your horse runs best on a sloppy or muddy track, you welcome thunder as a triumphant sign from the surly god. If your runner prefers a fast, dry track, you flourish and luxuriate in even a hint
of gold above and heat below. You pays your two dollars and you
takes your chances.*

*Frontside, in the boxes, grandstand, and clubhouse—not to men-
tion at the many parties and dances—this is the week that horse
trainers, four-foot-tall jockeys, and owners of every social caste, who
might be untouchables the other fifty-one weeks of the year, reign as
social lions; and horses with muscled rumps and frail legs become
royalty. Backside—that is, along the backstretch on the far side of
the track, where the barns and horse vans are located—other dramas
are undoubtedly unfolding. These could be and probably are much
more thrilling and provocative than the ritualistic mummery the
public sees.*

*But how shall we ever know? What lies behind those elegant hotel
walls? What really happens on the backstretch? And if we could get
a privileged look at those private, secret tragedies and farces behind
the scenes, how much of it would we—true to our unspoken oath of
allegiance to the con game, the cabal, or if you will, the sport—how
much would we actually reveal? Is there honor among scoundrels?
Alas, we may never know.*

*While we speculate let us bow our heads and take a glance at the
possible field for next Saturday's so-called classic. The field, for a
change, looks vintage. Out of the three hundred and nineteen thoroughbreds nominated in February—it costs only a hundred and fifty
dollars to hope—the list has, as always, shrunk. Or withered, like
the hope. Twelve three-year-olds remain. Of these we have two colts
vying for favorite position and another moving up on the outside.
Vincent Van of Thistle Hill Farms here in the bluegrass country,
winner of six out of eight starts last year and recipient of the Eclipse*

award, has the edge by virtue of the fact that he won the Wood Memorial by looking Ancient Mariner in the eye on a cuppy track and surging ahead to finish in a breath-stopping photo finish. The other favorite is Starbright, carrying the colors of the prestigious Blue Ridge Plantation in Virginia but owned by the princess of racing this year, Miss Kimberley Cameron, who, like her colt, is of impeccably aristocratic ancestry. Starbright is undefeated in three starts in his third year and winner of four out of five as a two-year-old—and could possibly be an odds-on favorite here. Then, moving up heavily is a huge dark bay named Ancient Mariner, who lost the Wood by a hair's breadth and won the Bluegrass by two lengths. His bloodlines are royalty all the way, and his owner, Mrs. Rachel Stoddard of Brookfield Stables, Connecticut, is known as the grand dame of racing. There is at least one other superstar, True Blue, another Kentucky speedster. True Blue is also entered in the Derby Trial on Tuesday next. Owned by bluegrass gentry, the James Oliver family, with an outstanding record as a two-year-old True Blue has not found his stride this season, but he poses a true blue threat in spite of the odds. Possibly we should include Fireaway, from the woolly west of New Mexico, who won both the San Vincente Stakes by seven lengths in February and crossed the wire first in the California Derby—and then proceeded to savage his jockey in the winner's circle.

It's an international race this year—and therefore there are mystery runners. Like the inscrutable Fuji Mist from the enigmatic Orient—owned by a Japanese industrialist and reputed to be a volcano in his native land and in Hong Kong. Out of thirty hopeful females only one filly has ever won the Derby, and that was in 1915. But from la belle France we have Bonne Fete, who has been showing European horses her pretty tail at Deauville and Longchamp and Ascot. And also bucking the statistical odds is Irish Thrall, a gray from Ireland. What his very lovely owner, Mrs. Brigid Tyrone of Innisfree Demesne, County Galway, probably does not know is that only three grays have ever won the big one here. Or perhaps, being red-haired and Irish, the lady prefers to ignore the pedestrian statistics.

In any race the also-rans sometimes come in first. So who knows, the winner could be a gelding named by some wag or other just that: Also Ran. Now owned by ex-big-league ballplayer JD Edwards, who must be warned that only seven geldings have ever won the Derby, Also Ran will probably be just that next Saturday. He'll have company, including a big, clumsy liver bay colt named Prescription, who is owned by—you guessed it—a pharmacist from Indiana. With a more than fair record in the so-called bush or leaky-roof circuit, Prescription just might come up with a magical chemical formula. He'll need it. From Florida comes a small black colt named Hotspur—Nasrullah blood through Nashua—with a somewhat indifferent record except for the spectacular five-length win of the Tropical Park Derby in January followed by a weak fourth place in the Arkansas Derby. Hotspur is the only entry trained by his owner—is this comparable to an attorney representing himself and having a fool for a client? How many blacks have ever taken the Derby cup, Mr. Clayton Chalmers? Don't look it up. I'll tell you. Only four, Mr. Chalmers. And finally—and quite possibly least— there is a poor overworked chestnut named Dealer's Choice. Well, what's in a name? Entered also in the Derby Trial on Tuesday, Dealer's Choice ran fifth in the Bluegrass at Keeneland, will compete in the Stepping Stone today, and appears to this canny observer to be outclassed and alarmingly overworked.

Although these are the probable starters, nothing is official until their names are dropped into the box two days before the Derby. And of course until their owners come up with the necessary four thousand dollars at that time to enter and another thirty-five hundred to start. Much can happen between now and Thursday and even more between now and Saturday—and it usually does.

Meanwhile, looking over the field, ponder, ponder. A ninety-nine-to-one shot once won the Derby. Many horses have won it who never won another race. In 1953 Native Dancer, who had won eleven straight and was an odds-on favorite at seventy cents to the dollar, came in second to Dark Star. It was the only race Native Dancer lost in twenty-two starts, and Dark Star never beat another horse! Remember: Even the formidable Discovery couldn't win the Derby. And Bold Ruler, who later sired seventy-eight stakes winners, couldn't finish in the money, and the great Round Table barely did.

So . . . this year's Derby is the best of all possible competitions— it's wide open! And the gold at stake is outweighed by the glory. Or so they tell me.

Jockey Angel Cordero whispered in Spanish into the ear of his mount before the 1976 running: "If you want to be a star, if you want to be the greatest, you got to win the Derby." And after Bold Forbes did win, his trainer Barrera whooped: "There are horse races and horse races, but you are nothing till you win the Derby."

When the three-year-olds in all their brilliant colors parade down the stretch to the strains of "My Old Kentucky Home" played by the massed bands in the infield and you join in the singing with tears brimming in your sentimental eyes, just try not to remember what you didn't even know until I told you; that Stephen Foster died in the hallway of a flophouse with a losing ticket in the pocket where his watch used to be.

For further edification and more words of wit and wisdom as well as some behind-the-scenery views, tune in daily at this same time, same channel on television and same station on radio. Until tomorrow this is your obedient and not so humble servant, Count Wyatt Slingerland. Tallyho, sharpshooters, handicappers, and suckers one and all regardless of race, creed, color, or current state of moral turpitude.

The Charlottesville-Albemare Airport, where Andrew insisted on keeping the sleek Beechcraft Duke rather than give up any of the Blue Ridge grazing acreage for a private runway, was now miles behind. The ground fog was still heavy in the valleys, but at seven thousand feet the air glittered clear and silver, almost blinding. In the vast fertile land below—a changing pattern that remained always the same: farms and villages and twisting roads—did all those people down there harbor a dream, however foolish, however tawdry or withered or hopeless? It was not like Kimberley Cameron to allow her mind to wander over and around such thoughts; but she was in a strange mood this morning, a Sunday, the country churchyards vivid with color and movement below. Was this mood only a prelude to the week to come? Very strange. Aware of the controls in her hands but not casually fondling them the way Andrew did, she glanced at him in the other pilot's seat beside her. His graying head was slightly tilted and his handsome face—square chin, fixed and not quite jutting, profile sharp—was tranquil. As usual. The gray eyes clear and untroubled and gazing ahead. Unaware of her? Anticipating what? She did not know. His whole being seemed slightly withdrawn, distant—as usual. Damn him. Damn such a father anyway.

She recalled last night. Late. After he had won handily at chess in his study, that tabernacle of trophies—silver cups, blue ribbons, bronze castings of Blue Ridge champions, framed photographs on all sides of fillies and colts and mares and sires and of course herself, Kimberley Cameron, at all ages, all stages of youthful vigor and childish delight—she had stood and walked, slim body taut and legs tensed, to the floor-to-ceiling windows. In the faint moonlight she could see the stables and paddocks and in the distance the hazy shape of the mountains.

"Did you hear that your friend who calls himself the Count dubbed me princess in his telecast this morning?" And then, because Andrew didn't answer: "Do you realize that we missed the crowning of the so-called Derby Festival Queen by not being in Louisville last night? Next year, I understand, the queen may be either male or female." She turned then. To find his calm eyes on her, gazing over the rim of his brandy snifter, his heavy gray-black brows arched in amusement only. "Wyatt Slingerland's a prize prick," she said.

Andrew's face did not change except that his wide straight mouth curled almost imperceptibly at one end. "When you were a child, you could never sleep properly for a solid week before an important race. Of course, you've learned a few impressive words since then."

She resented his amusement. Even at her age, even at twenty-nine, and after all these years together, she despised it, loathed it, could not defend herself against it. "Please, Andrew," she said, "please don't suggest that I take a pill. Because I do take them. Regularly. *Religiously.* Even during Lent."

But he did not respond. Not really. He simply stood up, tall and straight and heavy-shouldered—and far away. "I was thinking of sleep, not pregnancy, Daughter." He stepped to the bar and set down his glass. Then he moved in his easy self-contained stride toward the center hall. Where he paused as if momentarily uncertain. Which gave her quick pleasure. "Kimberley, while that finishing school was trying to finish you—"

"It almost did—"

He turned to face her. "And in the course of almost two years at Bryn Mawr did you ever happen to stumble across an obscure author by the name of Shakespeare?"

"Don't patronize me," she warned. But she knew what was coming. What had not yet come but what had to come sooner or later. "I stumbled across the name, yes, but damned if I fell. Too many *zounds* and *exeunts*. But to answer your question, Hotspur was really named Henry Percy. Who plotted against his king and was killed in the Battle of Shrewsbury, year 1403." Had she said enough? Given away too much? He was frowning slightly now, and she felt a sharp stab of satisfaction, gratification.

"That sounds like the *Britannica* version. You really should read Shakespeare's. Hotspur was a hell-raising sort of youth. Hot blooded fire-eater. He dies saying something like, 'O Harry, thou hast robbed me of my youth.' " There was no smile now. None. And there was a probing sharpness in Andrew's narrowed eyes. "I'd hate to think anyone ever did that to you, Kimberley."

Even his tone of voice, touched by sadness, startled her. He was warning her, wasn't he? Or was he trying to ask her something? If so . . . if so, did it mean that he really was concerned?

He drew the black sash of his smoking jacket—clan Cameron plaid, of course—more tightly over his rock-hard bulk of body and said, in a lighter tone: "Damned pretentious name for a racehorse, isn't it?"

She didn't quite trust her voice. Or know what she really felt or had to say. "Your old friend Mrs. Stoddard's entry is registered Ancient Mariner with the Jockey Club."

"Rachel Stoddard," he said, "is an educated, cultured lady."

"It may come as a shock, Andrew, but Clay Chalmers knows Shakespeare as well as you do." Why? Why did she say it? "Or better." She couldn't stop herself, couldn't. Had to. "If it'll make you feel any better"—why should it, *why*?—"Mr. Clay Chalmers, trainer and owner, will have to find another virgin from Virginia this time round." She began to walk about. Aimlessly. Her tone sounded bitter. Had she made a pledge then? To whom? "That spoiled little Cameron bitch is no longer the easy screw she was when she was twenty-two."

Why lie? Easy? Easier, really. Seven goddamned years. Each making the empty space inside larger, emptier. And fun and games, nothing more—often even less. And all of it less, much less, than it had been with Clay. Whom she had come to hate.

As if reading her thoughts, Andrew said in a low, tight voice very foreign to Andrew Cameron: "Daughter, I don't believe I have ever hated anyone, ever, the way I hate Clayton Chalmers."

Hate. It was a strong word for Andrew Cameron. Very strong.

She took several steps toward him. "I hate him as much as you do, Andrew."

It was true.

It was a lie too.

It was both. And at the same time.

How the hell could that be?

"Possibly," Andrew said, his tone wry and dry and hinting at skepticism, apprehension. "But in a different way perhaps."

So shrewd. So wise, always, *always*! But she understood. She didn't want to say it. "You hate him because of Lord Randolph," she accused. She did not say: *a horse.* She did not say *You hate him because of Lord Randolph, not because of me.*

Gently then Andrew said, "Lord Randolph was not just another stallion, Kimberley. As you know. His get included more than sixty stakes winners even before he died. Before he was killed."

She did not want to talk about this. Or think about it. Now or ever. It was over. Seven years. All that mattered now was standing in the winner's circle with Starbright. With thousands and thousands of eyes on them both. And Clay Chalmers's eyes too, his especially, the bastard—

Then what? Perhaps when that happened, she would feel certain again. Whole and real. Why couldn't she ever be certain of any-

Joseph Hayes

thing? Of anyone? Ever. She was twenty-nine years old, but she was still a child poised for escape, panic threatening—

"Good night, Daughter—and try to sleep. If you do, you'll be in fine enough fettle to pilot us to Louisville tomorrow."

And then he was mounting the wide curving stairway. When had they stopped kissing each other good night? And why? Again she felt like an awkward stumbling foal. Off balance. Damn him. He could do this to her every time. Didn't he know how bitterly she hated being shunted aside, left alone? *Abandoned.* Or didn't he care?

She discovered that tears were hot behind her eyes. But why, why now? She hated tears.

You know, of course.

Go away.

Tears for yourself? For Lord Randolph?

No.

For love then. Seven years wasted.

Not love, no. Hate.

Bullshit, Kimberley.

Oh, please, please—

The only one you really hate is Kimberley Cameron, the girl herself.

Why do you torment me? *You're* the one I hate. Who are you?

You know.

Go away.

You're always sending everyone away. Then wondering why you're alone.

Tell me who are you, tell me!

You hate me and you know who I am.

Yes. She knew. The house seemed vast and cool. Her mouth was dry. Her heart was hammering yet fluttering at the same time. Panic closed over her like a cloud, a breathless cloud—

"Has something happened to the pressure?" she asked—and then realized that she was seated in the dual-control, Andrew beside her, frowning now and interrupting his conversation with the Bowman Field tower to say, "I'll take over, Kimberley."

She released the wheel and sat back. Sweat had gathered cold

12

along her spine, and she could feel dampness at the back of her neck.

She had never tried to explain. To anyone. Not even to that pretentious, cocky young psychiatrist she had visited twice, in secret. Another prick. How could she explain when she couldn't understand it herself? It was as if she were two people. As if there was a shadow always lurking. The shadow of herself. Her other self. It terrified her.

Now, though, the other Kimberley was silent. She was now only part of the evil sleepless night behind. That voice of torture inside was silent. Exeunt all doubts, all shadows. Exeunt, forever *exeunt*, goddamn it!

"The castle lies to windward, Princess."

"Princess *shit*," she said and heard Andrew chuckle and wished she hadn't said it. It did no good. Nothing really penetrated. Speak of castles!

But as she felt the plane banking gracefully under her father's hand she looked down and realized that they were descending.

Through wispy drifts of clouds, tinted gold by sun in the mist, lay the oval of palomino-colored dirt track, harrows crawling on it, combing it out after the morning workouts and before the afternoon races. Frontside, the clubhouse and empty grandstand with its famed twin spires on the steeply slanted roof looked fixed and precise and familiar; whereas backside, along the backstretch fence, the barns appeared to be placed helter-skelter at odd angles one to the other, with only a few figures and horses visible between them at this time of day; while the carpet of grass on the infield was lush and brilliant, a dazzling green. All of it seemed unreal, ephemeral. And as the plane moved on and out over the gray curving river with its slow dreamlike traffic of barges and its graceful steel bridges, which looked delicate and lovely from above in the hazy sunlight, and while Andrew asked for landing instructions from the tower she felt the panic closing in.

Don't land, Andrew, go up, this is not what I want, what I want is not here, oh, Andrew, please, turn, turn the plane, I'm afraid, please, let's go home, let's go home, Andrew!

13

But she said nothing, only sat stiff in the grip of dread and desolation and a kind of wild anticipation at the same time until the wheels touched down.

After completing the cordial formalities at the Fourth Street guardhouse and then at the backstretch office of the racing secretary Clay Chalmers decided to walk through the stable area and to locate barn 27 on his own. He didn't want, or need now, questions from Bernie—such as why in hell did the only owner-trainer in the Derby arrive at Churchill Downs itself in a beat-up half-ton pickup truck, where the hell was the sweet little white MG with no top, *zroom, zroom?* The fact was that Clay had sold the classic MG in Memphis, and the transaction had not netted him enough to do more than pay stall rental and feed and vet's fees and the salaries for a week for Bernie, Elijah, and the exercise boys and girls and hot-walkers. Of course if Hotspur had not picked up that nail in his foot five days before the Flamingo and if the infection hadn't been cooking in him so that he didn't even share the purse in the Florida Derby—if, if, if. The oldest and saddest word in racing. In life, perhaps.

Looked at from the opposite, or Pollyanna, point of view, though, the Spur, in spite of a low-grade temperature, had come in fourth in the Arkansas Derby earlier in the month, netting eight thousand of the hundred thousand dollar purse: more hand-to-mouth expense money to limp along on but no cigar, no kewpie doll. If he had only placed (twenty-seven grand) or if he'd even come in third (thirteen and a half thousand)—more if's. And to hell with it.

It was a quiet time backside. The morning works were hours behind, and most of the activity now was around those barns where the afternoon runners were stalled. A groom was brushing down a chestnut filly, and a vet was examining a colt's foreleg while trainer and groom stood by. There were the familiar smells of coffee boiling and bacon frying and the mingled odors of straw and manure and liniment and the soft musky scent of hundreds of animals. There were also the familiar sounds: the metallic clink of a farrier's hammer somewhere, the nickers and the straw-muffled stomping of hoofs, stableboys and stablegirls humming and whistling as they mucked out stalls, a radio blaring rock in a tack room in the distance. Clay Chalmers felt at home. Two men passed, one a groom in denims, the other a huge, beefy man in a plaid jacket and tie who was speaking: "I come up on her tail and she's wearing blinkers but she *smells* me, her jock don't twist his head, but that mare, she's moving off and away and there I sits." Clay Chalmers smiled inside: To an outsider it must sound strange. The big man was no jockey but probably a jockey's agent, and they always spoke as if they were actually riding; and to a racetrack man a horse always runs in the present tense. The pungent smoke of the groom's pipe drifted back pleasantly. There were small animals everywhere, as always: dogs and cats and chickens, even a goat or two. Elijah had once said: "All them hours by hisself, a horse gets painful lonesome. Why, I knowed one once, Indiana, had a parakeet, talking bird, all he could say, though, was 'No shit? No shit?' " The PA crackled into life and a businesslike voice asked that a blacksmith go to barn 27, said there was a phone message for someone in the racing secretary's office, and gave the names and numbers of the first scratches in today's races. Whenever Clay Chalmers arrived at a track, there was an easing inside him—which was paradoxically also an excitement throughout the whole of his mind and body. And soul too, if soul there be.

Approaching barn 27, he could not see the Spur's head along the line of stalls, but there were several empty spaces above the half-doors along the shedrow. He recalled having read that now that the Keeneland meet was over all stable space at the Downs would be filled by Monday.

Then he heard a familiar whinny of protest and a familiar rough but tender voice: "Just you hold still now. Don't you get fractious with Eli, Eli gets fractious right back."

Hotspur's head appeared, one ear pricked back, the other cocked forward. The lean head turned side to side once, then nodded up and down. The narrow blaze down his forehead looked whiter than ever against the shining, intense black of his coat. Watching, Clay went hollow inside. Then, alongside the head protruding from the stall, Eli's huge dark brown face with the short white beard came into view. He didn't grin. No greetings from Eli. "The colt's on the muscle 'cause he worked this morning. He just wants to run, that's all. That's all that boy understands."

When the stiff-backed elderly groom emerged from the stall, Clay moved to stroke the Spur's head, and the colt nuzzled him. Clay had come home. If he had ever been in this particular stable area before, he had been too young to remember it now, but wherever the Spur was, that was home. Elijah, unsmiling and chewing his tobacco, stalked off on his long, huge legs, carrying a bucket, intent on some chore or other. And then another voice, rasping and mocking, spoke from behind, approaching.

"Well, look who finally shows, will you? Two days before the Derby Trial." And when Clay turned to face him, Bernard J. Golden pushed back the bill of his baseball cap and shook his round cherubic head. "I don't want to break up this romantic reunion, but what happened to your white MG and where'd you pick up that battle-scarred pickup?"

Ignoring his assistant trainer, unsmiling although as usual amused by him, Clay spoke to the very small man with the deeply wrinkled face standing beside Bernie: "You're early, Zach. No more rides at Belmont?"

The tiny weathered face twisted slightly. "Flew in this morning. You can fire your exercise rider, male, female, or double-gaited. I'll work the Spur all week, and my agent can sing for his twenty-five percent of nothing." He moved in quick steps to the barrier of the shedrow and lifted his hand. He spoke in a harsh near-whisper around a black cigar that seemed almost as big as he was. "I got the smell of roses in my nose, Clay." The jockey's small hand was rough and calloused, his grip ferocious, hard. "The Spur worked a half-mile this morning in forty-six and four fifths and breezed five eighths in 1:01."

Bernie waddled closer, scowling. "Yeah, yeah," he acknowledged grudgingly, "he's beginning to look like he might turn into a runner. Up to now, though, anyone asks me, he's always been a little belly down."

"Look who's talking," Clay said, and Zach grunted a laugh.

Bernie rubbed the bulge under his mud-caked sweatshirt. "Didn't I tell you? I got knocked up by a blowsy blonde down there at Gulfstream. Hungry, Clay? Zach 'n me're on our way to the kitchen for our awfternoon tea 'n crumpets."

"Tea, hell," Clay said. "Infection down?"

"Doc Hartwell's convinced it's really gone." His soft face twisted and he shook his head. "Do you realize this is Sunday? Trial race's day after tomorrow!"

For some reason, as usually happened, Bernie's simmering anxiety and sour scorn combined with his irrepressible boyish exuberance awakened the strong feelings of comradeship that Clay had first felt for him four years ago. When they had discovered each other, as strangers, in the lower depths of separate depressions. At Thistledown, outside of Cleveland, the rain slashing down. They had almost come to angry blows before Clay had convinced Bernie that, one, he wanted a drink, needed a drink, but would not *take* a drink and two, that he wouldn't fight either, so fuck off, fatso. "Tell God your troubles, Bernie," Clay said now.

"God and me," Bernie said, chewing the frazzled toothpick that was always between his thick lips, "God and me, we ain't exchanged so much as a word since my bar mitzvah." Then he cocked his head sideways and glared upward. "Fair and sunny, twenty percent chance of showers. It don't rain tomorrow night, and buckets, forget the Trial." Then, abruptly serious, almost pleading: "Clay, let's scratch the Trial. It's not like you have to run it on Tuesday to get into the big one on Saturday."

Suddenly tempted to level with Bernie, Clay decided, again, that it was not the time. No reason to tell Bernie and Zach that if the Spur didn't share at least part of the purse on Tuesday there wouldn't be enough money in the kitty to pay the entry fee for the Derby on Thursday and the starting fee before the race . . . Glancing up, he said, "Mackeral sky, twelve hours dry."

"Clay," Bernie said in a strange level voice, his tone grave, "Clay, nobody knows how you busted your balls to get here, but I

17

always suspected there was more behind it than you ever told me. That kinda scares me, that kinda scares me shitless, you want to know. 'Cause ever since I knew you you been walking wounded. They sucked the marrow, somehow, someone, and I just don't want to see anyone or anything kick it outta you again."

Astonished, Clay couldn't believe he had heard the words. It was the longest speech he'd ever heard Bernie make. Catching Zach's amazement out of the corner of his eye, Clay felt a hot tenderness blaze sweetly in his guts. "This time," he said, "if there's any kicking to be done, I'll do it."

Bernie's round, pudgy face brightened, and his dark eyes glinted with sheer joy. He ripped off the baseball cap and whapped Clay across the arm with it. "Now," he almost shouted, "*now* you are making sense again! Now you have made me a promise I'm gonna hold you to!"

Then he turned away and strode off jauntily. Zach trotted on his short legs and joined him, waving a hand at Clay the way he waved to the owner when, standing in the stirrups, his whip between his teeth, he came in a winner. The two figures, one trim and tight and hard, the other soft and thick and heavy, disappeared around the corner of a barn. Both horsemen to the marrow. And more. Love of horses creates an odd fellowship. Beyond that, Clay wished he could somehow manage not to feel the slow, engulfing compassion that he could not arm himself against. Bernie had eaten himself out of the saddle when all he had ever really wanted was to ride; and now Zach, famous among sportswriters for his love of food, would zestfully consume country fried ham and potatoes and gravy and biscuits—only to retreat to the jockeys' room afterward to induce vomiting. Compelled to eat, he knew the consequences even as he did it. He had become one of the racing world's legendary "heavers" and thus the public butt of public jokes. Good natured, he accepted this, but what of his hidden thoughts, feelings? Walking wounded, Bernie had said. Who was not? Then, turning to Hotspur again, Clay remembered what his old man had said once in one of his infrequent pensive moods: *You're just like your mother was. You suffer for other people like you don't have enough worries of your own.* Good old Toby—Clay hadn't thought of his father in years, except in quick recollections that invariably stirred up confusion that left him in a panic to slam the door even tighter on the past. That part of the past, anyway.

A plane droned above. The Spur seemed to be listening. Everything around him seemed to interest him. A sparrow chirping under the shed, a pigeon fluttering by. Music, rock or classical, from one of the other stables. Only the manure truck upset him, and the insistent siren of the ambulance, here dubbed Invalid Carrier. He was curious about everything, everyone, life itself.

"You black character," Clay said fondly as he let himself into the stall, leaving the door open. "But tell me this, why do you have to be such a character that you only run smooth as glass in the goddamn mud?" He ran a hand down the colt's neck to the withers. Small-boned and standing only fifteen hands two fingers high, head lifted now, nostrils pulsing with pleasure, his coat glinting ebony bright—no denying it, the Spur was one fine handsome animal. The stall smelled of straw, and fine motes glittered golden in the slash of sunlight. "You know, when I got you"—Clay ran his palm smoothly down the back, over the loin, and across the point of haunch—"you were a gangly thing with huge hindquarters. When you galloped, it looked as if you had five legs, all going in a different direction. But you always had a great back and long sloping shoulders and I had a hunch, just a hunch—" He patted the buttock once, smiling now. "And your front legs've finally caught up with your hindquarters."

Hotspur lifted his head higher and bobbed it, as if agreeing, or proud. Clay ran his hand down the stifle and leg and then, sitting back on his heels, wrapped the hock and then the fetlock in both hands. The ice had turned the trick. Doc Hartwell was right: There was no heat. If only Hotspur didn't let them down this week— Elijah and Bernie and now Zach as well. If only Hotspur's trainer didn't let them all down. More if's—

A shadowy movement in the doorway of the stall caused him to look up and turn his head.

He went sick and faint and empty. But, as had happened in so many places, at the most unexpected and unlikely times, he realized almost at once that the woman standing there was not Kimberley.

"Isn't it supposed to be bad luck for a racehorse to be black?" she asked. Her voice was throaty and playful, amused—and confident. "And even worse luck if he has white stockings?"

"The track has its own crazy superstitions." He heard the sharpness in his tone as he straightened. "Like most places. Four blacks have taken the cup."

"In a hundred years." Stepping aside as he came out of the stall, she asked, "Do you really talk to horses?"

"Mostly," he said, "I just listen."

The woman, beside him now as he walked along the shedrow, laughed, but there was only a cold mirth in it. She was wearing a tight skirt and an even tighter sweater with a press pass pinned to it. "My name's Janice Wessell." Her hair, the color of honey, was boyishly short. "You must be Mr. Clayton Chalmers."

"What can I do for you, Miss Wessell?"

"Quite a lot, I imagine. At a different time and in a more intimate setting. I work for a newspaper called *Ask* and a magazine called *Expose*—sometimes pronounced with an acute accent over the *e*. I hope you'll forgive me: I'm snooping."

He was walking between barns now, and she was keeping in step. He shrugged but did not reply.

"Owen Chalmers, who trains Fireaway—is he related to you?"

"Brother."

"You don't exactly exude hospitality, do you, Mr. Chalmers?"

He quickened his step. "Work to do." A lie. Why the hell did he allow this woman to set his teeth on edge? Because she had interrupted? Overheard? Or because of that brief kick-in-the-groin moment when he thought that finally the inevitable had occurred? And he had been tricked again. "Any more questions, Miss Wessell?"

"Is it true you once worked for Blue Ridge Plantation in Virginia?"

He stopped. And faced her. Between the two very prominent breasts a small pin in the form of a butterfly nestled and a wire extended from it to her pigskin shoulder bag. A microphone and a recording device no doubt. "If you've done your homework, why do you ask what you already know?"

Her face, which was childlike and pretty in a boyish, brash sort of way, smiled. "In the hope you'll lie." She shrugged. "My job. If you must know, I'm looking for dirt." Her pale eyes taunted, challenged. "My editor calls them human interest stories. The more salacious the better."

Then Clay himself tried to smile. And failed. She didn't amuse him. He damn well didn't like her. "What's dirty about my having once worked for Andrew Cameron?"

"Nothing. That I know of. Yet."

"Miss Wessell—"

"Yes, Mr. Chalmers?"

He almost said fuck off. Instead, with sweet politeness, he said: "Go to hell." He moved away, his step elastic, smooth, vigorous. What did the bitch know, suspect? What had she heard?

"Be seeing you around, Mr. Chalmers," she called after him, mocking him—or threatening.

And it was then that he decided. He had come this far. He could not escape the inescapable. May as well get it over with. It was now or later, and he had waited seven years. He looked at the hanging signs designating the numbers of the barns, and he changed direction. He could feel the urgency pulling at his legs, the eagerness tightening his gut—and the reluctance like poison weakening his blood.

It had been snowing that night, snowing hard for Virginia, and Andrew Cameron's normally composed face was tight and white with cold fury in the light falling from the tack-room window. *You killed him. You killed that horse as surely as if you'd put a bullet in him. Do you know what you've done, Chalmers? Are you too drunk even to realize?*

Yes. He had been too drunk. He could not remember. And even now, seven years later, he could not be sure. It wasn't in him, sober, to injure a horse. To release a prize stallion like Lord Randolph into the snow in the middle of the night. Even blind drunk he did not think it was in him. To allow such a fine and precious animal to shatter both cannon bones on a paddock fence in the dark—

You've had it, boy. You're out of racing. You're through!

The Derby barn was ahead now. As he should have expected, there was some action around it: press, sightseers, owners. And uniformed Pinkerton guards on campstools at both ends of the shedrow day and night.

Clay halted. She wouldn't be on the backstretch at this time of day. Nor would her father. Jason Arnold, the trainer, might be around. Clay had no quarrel with Jason Arnold. In fact, he liked the husky older man, who had taught him one hell of a lot when he was first assistant trainer at Blue Ridge.

Did he have a quarrel with Kimberley then? Yes. She had not had the guts to go with him. *You ask too much, Clay, you always ask too much!*

Or was his quarrel really with her father? *No stall space, Mr. Chalmers, too bad. . . . Full up, Mr. Chalmers, sorry. . . . Trainer job? Someone must've told you wrong, son; no jobs on this farm.* Oh, polite, polite, nothing official, an almost unspoken agreement between gentlemen. No charges, no hearing, no loss of license or suspension. Above all, no hint or suggestion of scandal. A conspiracy of well-mannered silence. Until he had said to hell with it. If the Eastern tracks were closed to him, he'd find others: Beulah Park in Ohio and Tropical Park in Florida, others not so fashionable perhaps, not so prestigious as Saratoga and the Big A, but even Andrew Cameron's gentlemanly power had limits.

But he was here now. He'd made it in spite of Andrew Cameron. And he had a runner. Hotspur would be three years old for only one year. This year. Now. Clay Chalmers was shooting his wad, this year, because he might never get another shot at the big one.

And when the Spur crossed the wire ahead of Starbright—

He turned and retraced his steps. He passed a lean chestnut having his fetlock trimmed, the swarthy-faced groom purring over the sound of the electric clippers: "You stand still now, damn your hide, you want this high-fashion style job or don't you?"

Hotspur, it's up to you now.

Two men went by, both wearing wide-brimmed straw hats, heading for the track kitchen, which looked like a faded white farmhouse. "Blowout at thirty-three and two, I tell you she'll show the field all the way home." And the other: "She's a morning glory, man, she left her race on the track in the workout."

Track talk. His kind of talk. And then that fine feeling came back. Of being home. The track was the only home he'd ever really known. Tracks all over the country. He located the half-ton truck, faded red and, as Bernie had said, beat-up. Chipped and bruised—like everyone Clay Chalmers knew. Remembering something he'd read somewhere, probably in the *Racing Form*, he climbed in and switched on the engine. It purred with smooth, certain power, and he became fonder of it again and less regretful about having traded away the MG. Was it the great Dr. Fager's trainer, John Nerud, who had once said, after a disappointing day at the track: "Not a good day at the races, right. But I'll tell you one thing—I'd rather have me a bad day on the track than a goddamn good day off it somewheres else."

Smartass. Screw Mr. Clayton Chalmers, screw him but royal, and that's just what Janice Wessell would like to do. She was sipping coffee at the counter of the drugstore diagonally across from the northeast corner of the track. And fuck Churchill Downs too. And this famed hangout for true horsemen and handicappers—well, that's what she'd been told. Local color and who needs it? But that Clayton Chalmers now, he was something else. Not a big man, slim and trim, small-boned like his ridiculous black horse—what the fuck chance did that Hotspur have against the likes of Vincent Van and Starbright and Ancient Mariner?—but his whole body had a kind of tensile strength and hardness, a kind of electric quality. The way he stopped and turned on her when she mentioned Blue Ridge Plantation: those eyes blazing in that neat, smooth, narrow face the color of brass—were they actually black, those eyes? And that nose—had he fallen from a horse or what? It looked smashed, slightly humped, and it added to whatever it was that caused her to make up her mind, here and now, to get to know Clayton Chalmers better and to have at least one balling session before next Saturday. Maybe he could make her come. Foolish hope. As stupid as his, that his black could come in a winner. But worth a try. It was always worth a try. And who knows—out of it could come the kind of story her motherfucking editor could use, and she'd keep her lousy job. Anyway, she'd explore the possibilities. And any others. Matter of pride if nothing else. There were stories here: The job was to dig behind the phony mint-julep-sport-of-kings facade. They wouldn't make it easy for her; they all had too much at stake. But Ms. Janice Wessell was just the one to do it. And she knew the ways too. It was a rough and ruthless world, and a brutal one, but she'd learned how to get what she needed to survive. Which was the name of the game. And it was the only game in town too. Any town.

It's that godawful hour of eleven A.M. *on Sunday, that most godawful of all days of the week, and if tonight you see the sky over Louisville exploding, it will not be a merciful invasion from outer space but only a fireworks display—another of those Derby Festival events calculated to convince the nonbelievers that the week has officially begun. By now most of you know this if you have paid your hotel or motel bill in advance, as demanded. Rates have tripled, restaurant prices have gone astronomical, a hot dog will set you back the cost of a steak in more normal times, and a taxi ride in one of the wired-together wrecks that have been resurrected from the city dump will make you wish you had heeded your doctor's advice and taken up jogging like all the other damn fools. To get even reasonably drunk now you'll have to mortgage the family homestead, and if you want to get really plastered on the watered-down cocktails at the corner pub, let's hope you brought the family jewels. The cash is flowing, and so mesmerized by Derby fever are one and all, scarcely a groan can be heard in the land.*

By now followers of this sport of kings know that Bonne Fete, from

France, appropriately won the La Troienne (for fillies only) yesterday afternoon on a fast track. Miss Mariah, of Mrs. Stoddard's Brookfield Stables in Connecticut, placed second with the renowned Pepe Benitez aboard, and the same team will try again in the more prestigious Kentucky Oaks (also fillies only) on the day before the Derby.

At the risk of stirring the ire of the freedom fighters for women's rights among you, Count Wyatt will hazard the observation that in spite of Bonne Fete's record in Europe and yesterday's win, odds on the pretty prancer are twenty-seven to one for Saturday's big event, when the pretty prancer will try to repeat her triumph in the Derby against an all-male field. Chalk it up to male chauvinistic prejudice or to the cynical handicappers' knowledge of what springtime means in terms of equine female physiology. Facts is facts, girls, so please don't picket the press box whence this broadcast emanates—Count Wyatt loves you each and every one.

The Festival week's program will continue with concerts—symphonic, country-and-western, and rock-and-blare—along with all-star basketball games, the Great Steamboat Race on Wednesday, a minimarathon huff-and-puff, cycling races ditto, and the celebrated Pegasus Parade with flowered floats and female pulchritude exploited, and for the true connoisseur of true sport, daily skateboard exhibitions!

In the bosom of all this rapturous hullaballoo and depressing dementia, try to keep in your reeling minds the homespun homage that Kentucky's native son, the bard of Paducah, Irvin S. Cobb, once wrote: "Until you go to Kentucky and with your own eyes behold the Derby, you ain't been nowheres and you ain't seen nothin'." Recalling this literary rhapsody may buoy you up in your desperation as you watch your life savings being gulped into the coffers of the local merchants with all their old-world Southern charm: "Y'all come back now, heah?"

And tonight—another hurricane of hot air: the annual Owners and Breeders Banquet with the venerable Count Wyatt himself presiding after gnawing his way through more greasy deep-fried chicken. So . . . until tomorrow at this same outrageous hour of the A. and M. this is your obedient servant, Wyatt Slingerland, reminding one and all: Saturday, although scheduled, may never arrive. Tallyho and over!

"I've already been interviewed today," Clay Chalmers said mildly. "She also asked questions when she knew the answers."

Wyatt Slingerland didn't know what the hell to make of this Clay Chalmers and so was intrigued. "We do that," he said, "to see whether the interviewee is a liar. You don't lie, do you?"

"Only to the press," Clay Chalmers said, unsmiling.

"One tonic water uncorrupted by alcohol for the gentleman," Wyatt Slingerland told the short-skirted young waitress, "and a very dry double martini for me with no olive to displace the gin, thank you." Then he watched her retreat. Miss Longlegs. Some pretty piece, that ass. To Clay Chalmers across the table he said, "No need to apologize for not drinking. But you didn't, did you? Every man to his own Achilles heel, to coin an aphorism and screw it up." He looked out the window. Twenty-five stories below a lighted barge passed along the dark river, and the *Belle of Louisville* was docked alongside the belvedere, paddle wheel motionless but the decks brightly lit and restless with dancers. He could not hear the music. Just as well probably. Blare of rock or whine of western, or what they now called country, or bluegrass. What the hell ever happened to the sweet sadness of violin and clarinet, the thumping gaiety of banjos? Chiding himself for the romantic damned fool that still lurked in the mind that he prided for its cynicism, fighting again the encroaching sense of time and loss and age, he brought his attention somewhat regretfully back to the table.

Talkative bastard, this Clayton Chalmers: He hadn't spoken fifty words since Wyatt had invited him to have a drink. And he had volunteered precisely nothing. "Only reason I asked you here, Chalmers, is that you were the only male at the dinner not wearing a dinner jacket. Black tie is de rigueur at the annual Owners and Breeders Banquet. Just as my presence is."

"I don't own one."

"You could have rented one."

No reply whatsoever. Not even the courtesy of that gentle smile. Which, in the few times it had flashed, seemed self-mocking. But without contempt. Independent cuss, this one—stubborn. But there was shyness there too. Clay Chalmers's lean body, of medium height or possibly even smaller, was probably as deceptive as his quiet manner. It took great physical strength to be a trainer, and another kind of strength inside too. There had to be wirelike muscles under that (obviously) new blue suit, just as there had to be grit behind that pleasant but unrevealing expression with which the young man met the world, especially strangers like the Count.

"This promises to be one hell of an interview," Wyatt growled, "unless you break down and say something, Chalmers."

"Or unless you ask another question."

"You wild-eyed romantics with stars in your eyes," Wyatt snarled, "you give me a pain very far up my asshole."

"Have you seen a doctor?"

"How much did you pay for your pint-size black?"

"Six thousand. At a dispersal sale. Ohio."

"Why?"

"Good conformation. Sound. Intelligent. Bloodlines respectable."

"Who taught you all that?"

"My old man, among others."

"Trainer?"

Again that twist of smile. "Among other things. Huckster, horse trader, boozer, gambler—you name it. Mostly gambler—horseshoes, poker, trotters, craps. But he always said, 'Training a thoroughbred's like tuning a fine piano. You go too far, the horse'll be long. He's got to be just at fever pitch that exact right moment.' And then he said, 'You do all that, you work your tail off, then all it takes is luck.'"

"Your father dead?"

Now the shrug. "No idea." Then the smile, faint and distant.

Wyatt was beginning to like this quiet kid, who himself looked so tame but had named his yearling Hotspur. Interesting. The other side of Clay Chalmers's character perhaps? What would it take to expose or rile that side of him to action?

"No need to apologize for entering a bargain-basement colt," Wyatt said then. Aware that Clay Chalmers had not apologized and probably would not. "Bold Forbes was purchased for fifteen-two and wound up '76 champion with more than a million in purses."

Clay Chalmers was looking out across the darkened rooftops. "And Princequillo. Fifteen *hundred* dollar claimer. His blood runs in most of the long distance stayers on the tracks today."

"See!" Wyatt snorted. "You *can* talk."

"Given a chance," Clay said.

This time it was Wyatt who smiled. And Miss Longlegs brought the drinks and withdrew with a big Southern-hospitality smile and a twitch of her tail. "Y'all wan' anything else, y'just wave, heah?"

Wyatt wanted plenty more. But he was never likely to have it now. And if he got it, he wasn't sure what he could do with it. He was too old, it was too late; everything was too late. Sipping the martini, he felt the low mood descend and tried to fight it. Abruptly hostile—who did this cocky kid think he was anyway?—he glared across the table and growled: "How'd you manage to clean up your runner?"

"The Spur was never a dirty horse." A quick, hard flatness had come into Clay Chalmers's tone. "Mettlesome, sure. Spirit. But not mean and never a rogue."

Wyatt always made it a point of honor to be skeptical. "Reason you named him Hotspur?"

"Owners tranquilized him to sell him."

Wyatt shrugged. "Common practice these days of moral righteousness and rigorous honesty."

"All he really needed was gentling. A confidence course, mostly." And then, to Wyatt's astonishment, Clay Chalmers was leaning over the table, dark eyes bright and fixed under black brows, voice rushing on for the first time: "Horses are a hunted animal. Not predators. If a horse doesn't want to leave the gate it's not because he's stubborn or lazy—he's scared. And on the track they feel open to attack. Vulnerable every damned step. All you can do about that is fill their lives with enough positives so they can tolerate the negatives and keep running."

Well, for Christ's sake, and this time of night too! Off balance, Wyatt Slingerland began to feel better, much much better. This was the sort of language he seldom heard these days but which he understood, appreciated. Hearing it, however rarely, was one of the positives that allowed *him* to go on running. "What I say, Clay," he said, using Chalmers's first name for the first time, "is that getting through this goddamned world, it doesn't matter where or whatever name you give it, is really running broken-field around piles of shit and trying not to get your Gucci shoes gummed up or fall flat on your goddamned face."

Clay actually laughed. Wyatt got the idea at once that Clay Chalmers didn't really laugh very often. But with the mirth in his clearing brown eyes and satisfaction lighting his face, his whole personality seemed to change. To relax. He looked positively boyish.

Wyatt leaned back and uttered a warm, contemptuous laugh. "Six thousand lousy dollars," he scoffed. He was beginning to feel good. "You realize that one million dollars changes hands every hour at the Keeneland summer sale?" He was, in fact, feeling great, and no longer tired. "Every *hour*. And some individual animals go for a million and a half." Then, on impulse, he took a shot in the dark: "And you show here with a midget three-year-old without enough bread to pass the entry box and, if that, not enough to pay your starting fee." He'd hit paydirt, and he knew it. "Jesus Christ and his brother-in-law Iscariot!"

Clay's face revealed nothing, but Wyatt knew, so he waited. It was a favorite technique: make a flat statement based on rumor or guess or backstretch scuttlebutt, often wildly unreliable, and then the ball was in the other court. If Clay didn't deny it—

But instead of answering Clay sat back, his eyes challenging now. Clay outwaited him. Wyatt was certain, but he couldn't quite believe it, and in all his years around the track he'd never heard of it. His shot in the dark had paid off, and in spades. Finally he took a large swallow of gin and spoke again: "The hundred and fifty dollar nomination fee for the Derby covers the Trial as well. It'll take two hundred more to enter the Trial—"

Clay shrugged. "Hotspur doesn't have to win, only to place on Tuesday—"

"Then you'll have the seventy-five hundred you still need to start in the Derby. And what if your colt trails in last on Tuesday?"

Clay did not shrug. Did not answer. And Wyatt decided that such reckless optimism, or arrogance, should be rewarded, or punished. He had his story for the Tuesday morning telecast now: It might liven up the last of the prep races since the Derby Trial was not really a trial at all and, with only three Derby contenders running, could be a bore. Until it began. To Wyatt and his kind no thoroughbred race could be a total bore.

"I've been admiring your nose," he said now. "How the hell did you get such a nose?"

"My brother."

"I had a brother like that. Only I was bigger than he was." He drained the glass. Should he have another? He decided against it. This young Clay Chalmers might have a serious drinking problem that Wyatt Slingerland didn't know about. And he had come to like the kid. Better to wait: plenty of booze in the apartment his friend Vilma Solotorovski always let him have during Derby Week—at a nominally exorbitant rental. "This the same brother who trains for Stuart Rosser out West? Flying in tonight, his connections tell me. Piloting Rosser's private plane."

A wry fondness came into Clay Chalmers's face. "Even when he was a kid, Owen always said someday he'd fly a plane."

"Ought to be a mildly ho-hum story in here somewhere. Two brothers. Both trainers. One an owner as well. Might have a certain vulgar appeal. Sibling rivalry, all that neurotic shit."

Clay was grinning now. "This time you struck out, Count. My old man, Owen, and I gypsied the whole country when I was a kid. The bush circuit—two-bit tracks, carnivals, even county fairs. The bullrings. But I took off on my own when I was sixteen. Hell, I don't even know what became of my old man, and except for what I read in the *Form* and *Classic* I don't know a damn thing about my brother. Haven't seen him in eighteen years."

"Now that," Wyatt said, "is the kind of close-knit family everyone should come from." He sighed. "Well, another turn-your-stomach story shot to hell. But . . . that Fireaway your brother trains, he's got an impressive record on the West Coast. It's my learned and slightly drunken opinion that Saturday's race is still wide open."

But his attention had wandered. He was gazing across the room at one of the loveliest creatures to have hit these shores in many a Derby. A proud Gaelic beauty, Mrs. Brigid Tyrone by name. Majestic in her own way: tall, patrician, amply endowed—a twenty-four carat stunner with a crown of glowing red hair, two startlingly vivid blue eyes, and a gown to match the Emerald Isle, where both she and her colt, Irish Thrall, had been bred. She was accompanied by a lively young girl with a saucy wide-eyed manner, who could be any age between fifteen and twenty-five: long black hair, quick dazzling eyes to match, and a tiny doll-like body. Holding Mrs. Tyrone's chair while the maître d' held the girl's, Andrew Cameron stood tall and dignified and as usual somewhat aloof. Then he lowered his heavy-shouldered athletic-looking body into the chair between the two: no wasted motion, masculine grace. Bringing Wyatt to the reluctant awareness that he and Andrew Cameron were roughly the same age. Wyatt silently cursed the softness that had accumulated around his own middle. And who gave a damn anyway?

"I wonder," he said to Clay, "how Andrew Cameron was lucky enough to latch onto the widow lady who owns Irish Thrall. She doesn't look particularly merry, but would to God all widows looked like that." Then he glanced across the table. Something strange, puzzling, had come into Clay's eyes. They had gone flat again; the intense brightness had faded. His head had lifted, almost imperceptibly, and his cleft chin was set. But he did not turn his head to look behind him. Following Satchel Paige's advice, "Don't look back, something might be gaining on you"?

It was then that Wyatt recalled that some years ago now Clay Chalmers had worked for the Blue Ridge Plantation. Count Wyatt, turf journalist, made a mental note. Although he was sick to death of making notes, mental or otherwise. He was tired and growing bored again, and the martinis had caught up with him. Maybe he should order the traditional mint julep—half an ounce of cheap bourbon and green weeds smelling enough so you didn't miss the booze. Fuck Derby Week. Like Christmas, it had to come every year. His mood had plummeted again. And he didn't give a damn.

What was happening to the plane? One moment the sleek Piper Twin Comanche was throbbing steadily through the night, clouds billowing against the windshield, the mountains thousands of feet below, eerie and beautiful and slightly sinister in the moonlight. Her husband in the rear seat, tall but thin and frail, had said that he was going to get some shuteye now but before he went to sleep he did want to thank both of them, his wife and the pilot, for having talked him into going to the Derby. He never thought he'd live to see one of his horses in that one. Then he had mumbled sleepily that if a man was lucky enough to employ a trainer who was also a licensed pilot he might as well go to the Derby in style. Possibly he had slept. Possibly he had not had enough time to sleep. Time had a way of getting lost in Christine's mind when she was drinking. It seemed only a few minutes, if that. Sitting in the seat beside the pilot, she began to feel the odd vibrations. Pouring from the leather-encased flask into a silver cup, she felt the gin sloshing over her hand, and then the plane gave a lurch.

It had slowed. She had not been aware of it. Her mind had been filled with blurring pictures of balls and dinner parties and women in fine gowns, men in dinner coats, as she had known them in her youth, as she would now know them again after the isolation, the deadly monotony of adobe and sagebrush and leather, seventeen years put behind her now, withdrawing behind her as the miles receded beneath.

The plane appeared to be losing more speed. She glanced at the pilot, frowning. The tall, muscular, bearded man behind the controls was grasping the wheel, fighting it, and then the wings shuddered, the pilot began to snarl and curse, baffled and angry, and then the tail began to buffet about, the engines coughing. She heard a sound that puzzled her at first—a steady, insistent beeping over her head—and then she recognized it although she had never heard it before: the stall signal. The whole craft was rocking wildly, as if in a storm, but there was no rain on the windshield. She cried out something about seat belts and struggled to locate and fasten her own as she glanced back. The man in the rear seat was sitting stalk upright, seat belt fastened, eyes gone paler than ever and glistening with fright, his Stetson straight on his head but his thong-and-turquoise tie loose on his pearl-buttoned Western shirt.

Then the plane jolted forward, engines thundering now, her neck snapping with a pain that shot through her whole body, and suddenly there was no engine sound whatsoever, and she heard herself shouting to the man behind to take his pills, place his pills under his tongue, but it was hopeless, of course, he could not hear, and no pill could save him from what was going to happen now. The plane banked to one side. She caught a glimpse of crags and snow-capped crests, canyons and chasms below cliffs, and then it plunged down, the nose like the snout of a shark diving deep.

Thrown backward in her seat, legs braced, she could not shout. She could not move. Through the windshield she saw the mountaintops approaching, the upthrust spires and peaks pale and sharp in the moonlight, spikes of stone waiting—

She knew then. She knew but still could not accept it. She did not want to die. She could not die, not like this. It wasn't fair, not now, not when she had only just begun to live again.

The whine was deafening, unbearable, and above it she called his name. Did she really call his name? Whose name? The pilot did not hear. He was too intent, too silent, too concentrated over the wheel, twisting knobs, leaning back, drawing the wheel back—

And then it happened. The engines spit and growled and then thundered to life.

Her mind refused to believe it.

The nose lifted, slowly, straining, very slowly, and the bellowing became more intense, the wind's whine and the shuddering of the plane itself adding to the din. The beeping sound had gone.

The craft was leveling off. And then was climbing. The shark had decided to surface. Dare she believe it?

She could see dim blue sky obscured by clouds, then no clouds, only the night sky clear and empty. As she tilted forward, wondering whether she dare hope or ask, she knew that, whatever had caused it, it was over.

Thank you, Owen. Thank you.

Then she twisted about. And she screamed.

Her scream drowned out all other sound.

It filled the small cabin and caused the pilot to run a hand through his short but thick rust-colored beard and to take his eyes off the instrument panel and turn his head.

The man in the seat behind was still sitting upright, his spare body locked in his seat belt. His eyes stared blindly ahead. His bony jaw was slack, his mouth open, and the thin leathery face looked bloated. Between his teeth was the red ball of his tongue. The black Stetson was square and firm on his head.

The woman was scrambling into the rear seat while the pilot leveled off and set his course. Impulsively but very hesitantly she reached and touched her husband's shoulder. His neck gave way and his head lolled to one side. Stunned, she began to mutter incoherently, but she did not scream again. In a few moments she was embracing his upright corpse. And in time she was weeping.

But the pilot did not hear or see. He did not want to hear or to see. He had timed it exactly: He had not made his move until the woman was almost but not quite bombed out of her tree and the craft was above the Truchas peaks, passing over the Sangre de Cristo range. If he had waited longer, they would have been over flat country. He had not been certain until he had heard that scream that it would work. Where then was the kick, the relief? He had thought that he'd be drunk with it—crazed with it. He'd chanced it, only chanced it, and it had worked. He opened the throttle all the way. What the hell was wrong with him? To feel this way? Letdown if anything. And why the hell did that iron claw still have hold of his balls?

He changed course and then radioed ahead to Taos that he had an emergency on board and would need a doctor at the airport. As if a doctor could do anything for that thing back there that had once been Stuart Rosser.

Would there be questions? Hell, accidents happen. Downdrafts over the mountains. If a man with a bum heart insists on flying and taking in the excitement of the Kentucky Derby against the advice of his doctor and his wife and his trainer as well, advice repeated over and over—

It hadn't been as rough as he'd expected. Gravy. Smooth. Like his old man used to say, he'd hopped the gravy train. He was sorry, sure, but he didn't feel guilty or accountable. He had liked old Mr. Rosser in his own way. Good boss. Fair man. Paid well and gave his trainer leeway. Hell, he'd even agreed to buy the plane because of Owen's urging—and his forty-six-year-old wife's girlish enthusiasm, which the sick older man could not satisfy in other ways. Finally what sold him was the simple fact that he'd never owned a colt like Fireaway, and Fireaway'd be three years old only once. And what he didn't say but had to think: He might not be around much longer.

It hadn't been Owen Chalmers's doing. Poor old Stu had been marked for this. Doomed already. It had been written in the stars. Or ordained by God. Or fate. Nothing to feel sorry about, or guilty. Dangerous to feel anything like that—especially guilty.

Now a wild, crazy joy was sluicing through his veins. A hot flood. And that iron claw let go, just a mite, just enough. He clicked on the radio, gave the plane's ID number again, location and altitude, and requested landing instructions. His voice sounded flat and cool and efficient. At least to him. Control: That was the secret. In spite of the savage exultancy in his gut, that balloon inflating in his chest—

Luck. He'd lucked out.

Like shit. Like his old man had always said: You don't have luck, you make it. It was funny, looked at a certain way, in a certain light. Ole Toby had never made his own luck; had never been able to make it work for him. Any luck at all. Ever. Poor guy. But he'd taught one son anyway. He'd taught Owen Chalmers. Maybe the truth was that ole Toby just didn't have it in him—he wasn't cold-blooded enough, tough enough. Ruthless. If he didn't make his own luck, his son would. And in spades.

And nothing was going to get in the way. Nothing and nobody.

Especially not that little pisser of a baby brother. If he had anyone to thank—now here's a howler for the record, print it!—if anyone was to get credit, it had to go to that bastard. If Owen hadn't read in the *Racing Form* back in February that Clayton Chalmers, owner, was entering a bangtail named Hotspur—hell, chances are he'd never even have got the idea of pointing Fireaway for Louisville. So, thanks, baby brother, and the foot-long icicle up your gismo.

He, Owen Chalmers, was going to show the old man, and he was going to show Clayton Chalmers, sir, too, you asshole.

"I agree with your trainer," Andrew Cameron said in that soft-edged, unhurried voice that was in such contrast to the rather harsh accents that Brigid Tyrone had heard during the evening at dinner. "Racing *is* a violent and hazardous business."

"And no place for a female of the species, is that it?" To challenge a man old enough to be her father and whom they had met just this night—it was not like Molly at all, at all. Black hair loose and tumbling around her pixie face, Molly went on: "Agh, Mr. McGreevey's a grand trainer for sure, but he frets too much." A twist of neck, hair swishing. "As do you, Aunt Brigid." Then across to Andrew Cameron again: "Did you know that more than *fifty years ago* five females rode in the famous Newmarket Town Plate? And sidesaddle too! And in Britain the Jockey Club itself has just elected three women as members!" Oh, the girl should never have insisted on that mint julep. Which Brigid found delightfully refreshing herself. Molly's dark eyes pinned Brigid in their brilliance. "If you'd allow me to ride in the race itself, away with all the male chauvinist prejudice, you'd have no need to hire a Yank rider who knows nothing of the ways of our Irish Thrall."

Rather than reply Brigid glanced across the spacious room, which was somewhat like the dining saloon of a ship, or like an elegant pub: polished woods and ruby-red leather. The idea of Molly's riding in an actual race was unsettling. And with the thought came that curious foreboding that had been recurring ever since she and

Molly had embarked by ship from Cork. Irish Thrall, her grand gray steed, had come by air, but since that horror on the runway in Shannon nine years back—farewell, Danny, my love, my only love—Brigid Tyrone had refused to board a plane. How Daniel would have scoffed. *Away with such Celtic superstition, Bridgie. Are you, for all your worldly airs, only the bogman's daughter still, in the deeps of you?* She took another sip from the ice-glazed glass blooming with green leaves. And she drew her stole of Kenmare lace about her bare shoulders.

"Mr. Cameron," Molly asked in a whisper now, "that steamboat below there, with the lights—is it a showboat?"

"A stern-wheeler. A very old paddle boat, Molly."

Molly. For the first time, not Miss Muldoon. Brigid heard it and sat back. But his calm gray eyes remained politely remote—withdrawn. Still there was an unconventional note, an intriguing incongruity: With his well-cut dinner jacket he wore a waistcoat and a matching bow tie of Cameron plaid. Brigid looked out the window; the rooftops of the city were visible, and she could see the river, wide and placid and dark, winding mysteriously off into this strange country. Should she have come? Was her decision to keep her colt from the Irish Sweeps and Derby Stakes at Epsom only a foolish whim born of restlessness, boredom—loneliness perhaps?

"It's . . . everything's *magical*," Molly breathed. And as Molly began to speak in a rush of Galway Town at Christmas time, Brigid relaxed: Her pleasure now was to give pleasure to this lass, Daniel's niece, the daughter that she and Danny had never had. "It's a dreary stone-gray sort of city except at Christmas. Then . . . oh, then, it's another place entirely. The streets are packed from side to side, with motorcars coming and omnibuses going, and all honking, and the slow men with the horses and carts and heehawing asses tangling up the traffic. And the gabble of turkeys and the chickens cackling with anger and the blue smoke rising in the cold air, all the faces flushed red with expectancy and cheer. Ah, it's a darling sight. Like this. Like Derby Week! A true glory of a time for sure!"

And Brigid saw Andrew Cameron smile. For the first time. His eyes narrowed, fine lines appearing, the pleasant but reserved mask changing its entire aspect. The smile contagious. A suggestion of grit and power behind that courtly manner. He glanced at her briefly. And she had the strangest impression: that he was sharing with her their delight in Molly's unquenchable exuberance. And that he was no longer performing an expected ritual: making the foreigners feel at home. At the kind behest of Nora McGeehan of Kilkenny and Dublin: *He's an old friend, my dear; and he's had a bad time of it. His wife took a fall going over a fence in a hunt, and she still walks with a cane. But somewhere in the south of France. She's a sad, bitter thing, I hear. Drinking as if she were Irish. And, gossip has it, addicted to the pills they gave her in hospital. At any rate, not a backward glance at the husband and daughter she deserted. But he's a gentleman to the bone. And handsome into the bargain.* It was true too: a remarkably handsome man—square-faced, with thick black hair going iron-gray. And brushed, not combed, with a luster in it. Startled at herself, Brigid became abruptly conscious that the stole had slipped off her bare shoulders. For some obscure reason she didn't adjust it.

Andrew Cameron was leaning across the table slightly and, possibly in response to a question, was explaining to Molly that burgoo was a traditional Kentucky stew sold, he understood although he'd never had it there, at the chuckwagon at street level below: beef, chicken, pork, rabbit, possibly even squirrel, and any vegetable you'd care to name, plus herbs that don't even have names. Molly was smiling, telling him that she had just discovered Texas red chili and cowpoke beans and that if she once tasted burgoo she might *never* go back to Ireland.

"Last night," Andrew Cameron said, his deep gray eyes including Brigid in their sudden warmth and humor, "I was dining in the Fountain Room downstairs, and a gentleman from Texas at the next table ordered Chateaubriand for two, and then he turned to the woman with him and asked, 'And what will you have, my dear?' "

Molly laughed. And, astonished at herself, Brigid joined her. Andrew Cameron's smile included both of them.

* * *

Winner's Circle

Clay Chalmers couldn't decide: Was this Wyatt Slingerland trying to live up to some created but unreal image of himself? The smartly trimmed gray goatee, the old-fashioned stiff collar with wings, the long ebony cigarette holder; above all the scornful, knowing squint of eye—was he a phony or only an aging man struggling to latch onto some image that would see him through? On the dais at dinner and in his television appearance his face had had the benevolence of a sly, cheerful pixie, and his tone was mockingly mellifluous; at the table, though, his manner was challenging, and his grunts and snorts were abrasive as hell. Clay decided he was facing a lonely man, another one; the world seemed full of them. The Count had ordered another double martini, and again Clay wished that he could somehow force himself to care less, or not at all. Who was he to feel this quick sympathy for and even identification with any living thing, man or animal, who betrayed some inner loss or ache? What's Hecuba to him or he to Hecuba that he should weep for her? Christ, didn't he have enough of his own to deal with?

When the fresh drink came, Wyatt Slingerland took a swallow and then glared across the table again. "Wanna bet? That Irish runner's in trouble. Wanna bet you can't name even two grays ever won the goddamn Derby?"

"My father," Clay said, "was the gambler. Not me." Then he said: "Determine in '54 and Decidedly in . . . '62."

To which Wyatt said, in a whisper of gravel: "You, sir, are a sonofabitch."

And, although smiling faintly, Clay felt that ugly wave of shyness break over him. It happened often. He knew that the Count thought him presumptuous, possibly preposterous—and to a degree this was true. If only he could somehow break down the barrier that he had thrown around himself and enter into the spirit of a late night's drunken raillery . . . He liked this man, as he liked people in general, perhaps foolishly, but he felt hobbled. Some private part of himself that he cherished and despised at the same damned time squirmed in discomfort. He longed to escape, to be alone.

But Wyatt Slingerland seemed to have lost interest. Over the glass held in midair his gaze had drifted beyond Clay and along the room toward the huge carved-wood doors leading to the elevators. He made a hissing sound between his teeth and then said: "Thar she blows, sonny. The self-crowned princess of this year's main event."

Clay did not turn.

"She doesn't come into a room," Wyatt said. "She *enters*. As if she were doing the room a great favor. Doing the *world* a favor, for God's sake."

Clay's neck was stiff. He still did not turn his head.

"Now there, sonny, is a thoroughbred who needs no confidence course!"

But the feeling did not come: that shot-away emptiness, that faintness and hollowness that he'd known so many times, whenever he'd seen someone who looked like her or carried her head in that proud arrogant way or walked with that limber horsewoman's ease and grace—

"Andy Cameron's got a lock on all the feminine pulchritude tonight," Wyatt groaned.

Strange. Very strange. Clay Chalmers didn't feel at all the way he had known he would feel. Of course he hadn't really seen her yet. His chest was tight, true, and it was just possible that he wasn't breathing at all and his nerves were taut and his heart didn't seem to be pumping, but damned if he'd so much as twist about to look. He'd waited this long, hadn't he?

His new friend Wyatt's tongue had thickened, but he spoke in a lust-filled purr: "A cool piece of merchandise. What you have to admire about Kimberley Cameron is that . . . even though she wears her stable's colors . . . hell, they're the most flattering on her anyway . . . even despite all that, she's never really gone horsy. You know—all those dry planes and hollows in the face . . . and that tight-ass coldness . . . and spare me please that bluff and hearty manner of the tried and true horsewoman." He tilted his head. "Not Kimberley. Cool, oh, hell yes. Blond. Porcelain. But I wonder. Any man has to wonder. That female specimen suggests fires banked down. And hot as hell itself if they ever erupt."

If all that was for Clay's benefit—which Clay doubted—he decided to ignore it. But just listening he felt fires erupting inside himself. Again.

*　　*　　*

Molly, who was surely nattering away this night, and a drop taken, was saying, "I'm the one who exercises him every morning. I should know how he runs on a dirt course. And better than Mr. McGreevey too!" Brigid was about to explain to Andrew Cameron that Gregory McGreevey, the leprechaun who trained for her, spoke like a guardian angel to the horses but with the tongue of an asp to humankind—but she realized that someone had stopped alongside the round table.

"No juleps, please. I haven't sunk that low." The handsome young woman spoke in a soft voice that sounded agreeably indolent. "But Andrew, a stinger would not be rejected, thank you."

Andrew Cameron was standing then, introducing his daughter Kimberley. She was a slender young woman with slightly slanted and deep-set eyes which appeared to be green. Her features were remarkable otherwise only in that they were classically lovely and delicate. Her fair hair, drawn tight, set them off. Unsmiling and serene, courteous as her father, she accepted the chair that he held. But her manner and even her voice suggested incongruity: hesitation and hauteur, uncertainty and challenge, politeness with hostility. Puzzled, Brigid accepted the introduction.

"Oh, yes," Kimberley said. "You own Irish Thrall, don't you? A beautiful animal."

While Andrew spoke to the waitress Brigid said, "I sometimes think that no one really owns Thrall, Miss Cameron. I've little doubt that this very moment he's awake and regaling his sleepy stablemates with all his past glories and triumphs—not all quite accurate, I'm sure."

While Andrew lighted his daughter's cigarette—his face had returned to its sober remoteness—he explained: "Mrs. Tyrone and Molly and I have been comparing our tracks with those in Europe. Her colt is accustomed, of course, to running on grass."

"And," Molly said, "in the opposite direction."

"Too," Andrew said, "the curves are sharper on our tracks."

"If he doubts the differences," Brigid said, "I've just now challenged your father to enter Starbright in the Prix du Jockey Club in Chantilly. It's only a month away. Or the Arc in Paris in October. That's the most important in the world. And also—"

But Brigid broke off. Kimberley's manner had undergone a sea change. "Well," she said sweetly, "the Arc's the *richest*, of course. If you're in racing for the money."

Brigid felt the muscles of her jaw clenching. "The Arc de Triomphe is the most *challenging*."

"Tell me, Mrs. Tyrone, is it true that the Curragh in Ireland runs downhill? That must be an advantage for some horses."

A moment passed. Brigid refused to reply. And for the first time she saw a frown above Andrew Cameron's salt-and-pepper brows. Molly's small chin was lifted dangerously and her eyes crackled. "As a two-year-old," she said, "Thrall won both the Dewhurst and—" But she subsided at Brigid's darting glance.

Then, into the void, Andrew Cameron asked in a lazy and detached but guarded tone, frown vanished, whether Kimberley had had dinner. "Your friends at the banquet inquired."

"Oh? What friends?"

"Oh," her father said mildly, "you still have a few."

"Couldn't face it," the girl said. "All those tired jokes. Jewish and colored jokes whispered, Polish jokes permitted from the podium. All those loudmouthed, backslapping turds chomping on their cigars. Bourbon-belchers and ass-pinchers."

Brigid saw Molly smile. And heard Andrew Cameron say: "Kimberley, one belch doth not a bumpkin make."

Brigid herself laughed then. And regretted it on the instant when she saw Kimberley's frosty eyes on her. Kimberley continued: "So . . . instead of eating I drank. Pub crawling." Her tone dripped chilled honey. "Do you know that phrase, Mrs. Tyrone? Here we sometimes refer to it as barhopping."

Less disconcerted now, somewhat amused but troubled as well, Brigid said, "Oh, my country's not so backward that we don't have some of the civilized niceties, Miss Cameron."

Their eyes held. Kimberley's were almond-shaped and, yes, green. Brigid felt the blood rising to her face.

Kimberley blew smoke. "Andrew's always terrified that I'll be raped. He has never admitted to himself that that's what all women really want, am I right, Mrs. Tyrone?"

"I would think *all* women is putting it too broadly. I imagine there are a sick few who do, yes."

The girl's eyes flickered, brightened, and went hard. And Brigid had a pang of remorse. It had been a low blow, and there was a suggestion of terror in those eyes now.

Andrew Cameron shook his head and ignored them both. "Molly," he said, "Wyatt Slingerland is quite correct. There's a plague that strikes this city once a year. It's called Derby fever."

"Is it contagious?" Molly asked, face innocent—the pleased, devilish conspirator.

Then Andrew did smile. "Particularly among the females of the species, they tell me. See you don't contract it, Molly. It takes many forms." And after the stinger had been set down on the table: "It gets more virulent as Saturday approaches."

Kimberley, fondling her glass, asked, "Have you ever been raped, Mrs. Tyrone?" She took a sip. Brigid was conscious of a quick angry frown on Andrew's face, swiftly replaced by that seemingly imperturbable composure. "This is on the rocks," Kimberley said. "I like my stingers straight up. Like pricks."

Andrew Cameron stared at Brigid Tyrone then. Behind the quiet gray in his eyes and the twisted self-mockery along his lips she saw, or sensed, a genuine concern, more than compassion, possibly even fear. "You'll simply have to forgive Kimberley, Mrs. Tyrone. I've had to, for years."

Kimberley appeared not to hear. She shrugged the black mink stole from her shoulders, which were startlingly white in contrast to her face, which was very tan and glowed with sun and health. Her clinging gown was the color of coral. "I can't help myself, Andrew. It's that time of month." She then drained the glass in one long swallow. "And Andrew, I do deeply resent anyone apologizing for me."

"Then," Andrew said easily and gently, "do it for yourself. Or preferably, avoid the necessity."

Brigid turned to Molly then. "Haven't you a workout to ride in a very few hours?"

"Agh," Molly protested, "I hear worse than this every day on the backstretch, Aunt Brigid."

"I've small doubt," Brigid said, surprised again at the growing intensity of her feelings—and her confusion. "Enough of this carousing or I'll report you to Gregory McGreevey himself."

Molly was standing. Suddenly shy again, she thanked Mr. Cameron for the *delicious* julep, and then she stooped to kiss Brigid on the cheek, whispering, "I'm an ungrateful wretch, I am," and then, "Good night, Miss Cameron." Brigid watched her, a twisting inside herself: a quick-gaited elf, if elves there are—and as much a daughter as a daughter might have been.

Then she caught an expression of sober questioning in Kimberley's gaze—as if the relationship between Brigid and Molly puzzled her somehow. But then, over the young woman's bare shoulder, Brigid caught sight of the Hautots, Paul and Annabelle, passing by the table. Paul Hautot, darkly handsome, bowed without breaking stride, and Annabelle—who, international rumor had it, was not really his wife—drifted on, eyes vacant, small sylphlike body floating, silver-blond hair a trifle too bouffant. Brigid had been introduced to them several times at Longchamp and Deauville, and their filly, Bonne Fete, had come in only half a length ahead of Irish Thrall in the Prix Morny.

Seeing Brigid's nod, Kimberley twisted her head about. And then laughed. But mirthlessly. "M. Paul Hautot joined me in the elevator after lunch today—pardon me, Mrs. Tyrone, the *lift*. He insisted on buying me a drink so we could toast Starbright. Then, in that devastating French accent, he suggested an afternoon fuck session."

"The French will be French," Andrew Cameron said and pushed back his chair but did not stand up. "Mrs. Tyrone, may I show you to your suite?"

"I suspect," Kimberley said, herself gesturing to the waitress, "that M. Hautot is trying to prove he has two balls."

Dismayed, her anger quick and hot now, Brigid did not rise from her chair. But she did realize that for the second, Irish and all, she was speechless. Which was, of course, precisely what the girl intended she be. And at the same time she was not for the moment absolutely certain whether Andrew Cameron was trying to protect *her* or whether the idea of his daughter's sex life was disturbing *him*. "Most European men have only one," Kimberley went on relentlessly, "which is possibly the reason European women prefer American men."

Brigid decided that she'd be damned before she'd be routed in this fashion. She ignored Kimberley altogether and spoke sweetly across to the girl's father. "I understand that only one filly's ever won the Derby."

Andrew Cameron seemed relieved—and a conspiratorial glint came into his eye. "True. But six others have finished second or third." Then he added: "In spite of the fact that the race is run in the spring of the year."

"Bonne Fete's won her first five starts this year, you know. Three times in France and twice in England."

Kimberley, pretending not to notice her exclusion, ordered another stinger. Double and straight up, like a prick, she trusted the waitress knew that a prick was very similar to a cock.

Before the waitress could flee, Andrew lifted his brows and indicated Brigid's glass. "Why not, Andrew?" she said, "*I'm* not riding at the crack of dawn." Had she used his given name for the first time for Kimberley's benefit? Mischievously, then? Cruelly? For childish revenge?

Whatever, Kimberley was the one who stood up. Abruptly. "Starbright," she said, "is not racing in Europe. Starbright, Mrs. Tyrone, is not owned by Blue Ridge. Have you forgotten, Andrew, you gave me Starbright when he was foaled?" But her words were not edged; they were soft and flowing and polite. "Mrs. Tyrone, perhaps you don't know the gruesome facts. Only three foreign-bred horses have *ever* won the Kentucky Derby."

Then, dragging the mink, she was strolling away. And at that moment it came to Brigid—who was already regretting her quick hostility, however justified—that Miss Kimberley Cameron was in truth a hurting child, tender and even vulnerable behind those woefully inadequate ramparts. Poise and ice and obscenities fired broadside, like cannonballs. It could be that what the lass needed, perhaps desperately, was attention, love. She insisted on the one and fought the other before it could take root—as if she feared rather than ached and hungered for it. Or did she? Was Brigid Tyrone, the bogman's daughter, only romanticizing—her wont, as Daniel had often said?

Yes, Daniel—romanticizing, probably.

Was Andrew Cameron aware that by ignoring his daughter or making light of her audacity he only drove her on? Or was that what he intended? Was his manner possibly his own defense against an enigma that he could not fathom or cope with?

Danny, where are you? I need you. I want none of this. Of them. Strangers. It's all too complex, contradictory—bewildering. Danny, I feel so alone now. It's at times like this that I miss you most.

Wyatt's mood was not improved by Clay Chalmers's silence. He was trying to think of something that might startle the younger man out of his goddamned complacency—or was it timidity, did it conceal insecurity?—when he saw the golden-haired princess rise from her father's table, sling her fur over one bare shoulder, and proceed, head high, toward the doors. Would she pass in all her slim glory or would she deign to pause and greet a lowly turf journalist? Make that serf.

She stopped. Wyatt looked up into her smooth and richly tanned face and was again dazzled. And Kimberley said, her tone silkenly derisive: "I'm sorry I missed the dinner, Count. Were you as droll and tedious as ever?"

"More so." He met her lofty gaze. "In honor of your absence." He did not stand when Clay Chalmers did. "You remember Mr. Chalmers perhaps?"

She lifted pale brows but did not smile. "Of course. I remember Mr. Chalmers when he didn't bother to stand for a lady. Or really didn't know it was expected."

"That," Clay Chalmers said easily, "was before I learned that a man is expected to stand for a lady whether the lady's a lady or not."

Icy is as icy does! This could be interesting. Wyatt slid his bulky body toward the window, making room. "And I," he said, "can remember Kimberley Cameron when she was a dumpy little hellion who tried to tear up the old Brown's Hotel every Derby Week. Would you like a drink, Miss Cameron?"

But she remained erect. Stiff, really, chin set as she smiled. "You're the zillionth male who's tried that ploy tonight, Count. I've discovered that I prefer my own company. But I'm sure Mr. Chalmers will be delighted to have another."

"Make it a double," Clay said, sitting down again, a trace of that by-now-familiar self-mockery in his eyes. Count Wyatt Slingerland was delighted. What the hell had he stumbled onto here?

Kimberley was gazing down into Clay's face. "Good luck on Tuesday, Mr. Chalmers."

"Thank you, Miss Cameron. And on Saturday?"

"On Saturday," Kimberley Cameron said, green eyes taunting, amused, "luck won't do you the least bit of good."

Wyatt was staring up into her face again. What he saw amazed him. A faltering, a slight tremor in the fine firm flesh, like a thin zig-zag crack in her glacial self-possession. And her body reflected it too. Out of nowhere. It was as if she were standing there exuding self-confidence, even disdain, yet was poised for flight—in a panic to escape.

"I wish Starbright the best on Saturday," Clay said. Then he added, his narrow face expressionless: "Second best."

Then Kimberley Cameron changed again: Her lips narrowed, and her eyes. She spoke in a tone of lanquid regret: "Isn't it sad, Count Wyatt, that you simply can't be nice to some fuckheads?"

Then she tossed an object to the table with a metallic clatter. Without glancing down she turned and strolled in loose steps toward the heavy carved doors leading to the elevators. Heads turned. Such superb hauteur could only be admired—envied.

"When I knew her," Clay Chalmers said, "she'd fire a hot-walker if she so much as overheard a word like that." He was staring down at the key on the table; it was attached to a leather plaque in the shape of a horseshoe, on which the number of a room or suite was embossed in silver.

Well, she apparently didn't enjoy her own company *enough*. The key, Wyatt acknowledged with a sharp twist of regret, was not intended for him. What the *hell* had he stumbled onto?

A deep, commanding voice broke in: "The ubiquitous Wyatt Slingerland. Is this where one pays homage?" Mrs. Rachel Stoddard seated herself beside him, all two hundred plus pounds of her, cursing under her breath the inventor of such torture chambers as booths. "Not surprising you resort to such horrendous prose, Wyatt. You never sleep."

"Do sit down, Rachel," Wyatt said.

"Thank you, my dear, I think I shall." And she laughed—a husky young woman's laugh although she was, Wyatt knew, at least eighty-three. Her grand manner was even grander after a few late gins. At a meeting, any meeting—Saratoga, Aqueduct, Hialeah—it was Rachel Stoddard's wont to stay up as long as she could find even semi-amusing company. Or, as she often said, as late as anyone would tolerate her. Shrugging off her floor-length fur cape—sable, no less—she peered across at Clay, who was no longer staring down at the key. "We didn't meet at dinner. Wyatt, do your duties and pretend you're a gentleman." Wyatt saw Clay's quick amusement, instant affection—everyone in racing, especially the press, loved this huge, ugly woman with the great hooked nose, helmet of snow-white hair, and warm but imperious manner. Wyatt started to perform a formal introduction, but she silenced him with a gesture of her bejeweled hand and the clinking of gold bracelets. "I know who he is and he knows who I am." She cocked one white brow. "I trust you're not being corrupted by this illiterate handicapper. Which, speaking of literacy, prompts me to ask: Did you name that black colt yourself?"

Clay was still sizing her up. "Does your Ancient Mariner have a glittering eye?"

She studied him more closely then. "How do you come by your knowledge of poetry and such? Most backstretchers—"

"Some of my best friends are backstretchers, Mrs. Stoddard." But he was smiling, faintly. "My mother, when she died, left behind a complete Shakespeare, an Untermeyer collection of poetry, an old edition of Bartlett's *Quotations*, and very little else."

"When did she die?"

"When I was born. I'm the very little else."

Mrs. Rachel Stoddard of Brookfield Farms, Connecticut, roared with hearty laughter. "My husband, who taught me all I know about this game, always warned me to look out for long shots. My trainer's been clocking your Hotspur's works. Crichton doesn't believe in the *Racing Form*'s times or"—she turned to Wyatt—"the accuracy of turf journalists. Mr. Chalmers, I've decided to bet on your little black beast in the Trial on Tuesday."

Clay reached and picked up the key in his hard-looking nut-brown hand. "Well, if you don't win on him on Tuesday, your Ancient Mariner won't have to worry about that particular long shot on Saturday." He stood and made what might have passed for a bow, a head-only nod, and then, mumbling good night, he walked to the carved doors, key in hand.

" 'Yond Cassius,' " Rachel Stoddard quoted, " 'has a lean and hungry look.' "

Wyatt waved the cigarette holder in Miss Longlegs's direction. "He's wily, not to say cunning." Clay Chalmers had just reminded Count Wyatt of the Trial race story in order, if Wyatt was any judge, to divert his mind from what could be a much juicier and sexier tale. He ordered a gibson, very dry, for Mrs. Stoddard and a martini, even drier, for himself. Across the room, almost empty now, he could see Andrew Cameron and the regal Irish beauty with crown of red. Had Andrew Cameron seen his daughter toss that key to the table? If so, what? And had it been intended that he see it?

They picked up the cold glasses and clinked them together.

"Well, ye old soothsayer," Rachel asked, "what does your crystal ball tell you? Will Ancient Mariner bring home the roses?"

"The Mariner's never been really sound, has he?"

"Two Derby winners in his pedigree."

"Bloodlines can fool you."

"Eight out of sixteen career starts."

"Rheumatic condition right from the beginning."

"Took the Bay Shore by three full lengths. The Calumet Purse. Placed in the Gotham."

"All in pain, Rachel."

"He'll take it on guts alone."

"What does Crichton say?"

"What does Crichton know?"

"I never met an owner didn't think he/she knew better'n his/her trainer."

"Or a trainer who didn't think he knew more than his owner *and* his rider!"

"Or a jock who didn't *think* he knew more'n all the connections rolled together."

"And vice-versa."

"Ditto."

"You said it."

They drained their glasses, and Rachel sat chewing the pearl onion. Far below the lights on the *Belle of Louisville* were going out.

"Is it only a myth," Wyatt asked, "that your colt loves music?"

"No myth. Classical only. Especially violins." And when Wyatt grunted an appreciative laugh: "But both rock and bluegrass drive him right up the wall of his stall."

Wyatt laughed again: Every damned horse he'd ever seen had a character all its own. He was beginning to feel better now, much better; he even felt confident enough to drive across town to the apartment. The waitresses were lounging about, ready to close up.

His mind was drifting pleasantly. "Rachel," he asked, "do you believe in romance?"

"If I didn't, I wouldn't be here."

"Young knight in armor, scorned by his beloved's father, bearing her away in the dead of night—after, of course, winning the jousting match on his black charger while all of royalty cheered."

"You're drunk, Wyatt."

"Conceivably."

"You haven't mentioned Enis."

"No. I never do. Unless someone asks."

"I'm asking, Wyatt."

"You're the only one who ever does."

"I'm the only one with the ill manners and the gall."

"She's all the way over the line now. When I visit her, she has no idea I'm there. She simply sits with a beatific expression on her face. It's a benign world she's in. Possibly even a beautiful one. I'll never know."

"I'm sorry."

"Sometimes I'm not sure. Times when I wonder whether I don't envy her."

He didn't ask about Rachel. *Her* loneliness. He took it for granted. Her husband, Eugene Stoddard III, had died four—or was it five?—years ago. She had carried on with Brookfield Farms. Alone. No—*three* years ago: He had died the week Ancient Mariner was foaled. After many drinks Wyatt Slingerland sometimes remembered more easily than he did with fewer drinks.

Clay stepped blindly off the elevator at ground level. His blood was furious. And scorching. Tossing that key to the table: not an invitation, a royal command. Insolent. Imperious.

He went from the lower lobby into the cavernous parking garage. The truck was conspicuous by its shape and senility. He savored its individuality as he walked toward it.

Odd that the feeling had not returned. That empty, shot-away faintness. During all that time when he knew he would never see her again he had had it over and over. Now it was as though with a gesture she had made it impossible. In its place was fury.

But also desire.

Passion. But hate too. And bitter rage.

If that's what she wants, if that's all she wants—

She had made the decision then. Seven years ago. Now she imagined she could make it again. He didn't want it to start over again, all of it.

You ask too much, Clay.

Are you coming?

Can't you understand? I can't leave him after—

After what? Say it: after what I did. You believe what he believes.

51

Joseph Hayes

It's true I can't remember for sure, but I couldn't have done that to a horse like Lord Randolph, any horse, and you should know that!

Oh, Clay, Clay, darling, can't you see? I can't walk out on him. That's what my mother did.

Now, tongue dry and thick and nerves leaping, why didn't he climb into the truck, rev it, leave, go, go—

Instead, the key burning his palm like a hot brand, he slammed the truck door and turned back to the lighted lobby. There was dust in his mouth. Or ashes.

But why had he come all this way if not to see her? To win, yes, but her, to win over her too—

On Saturday luck won't do you the least bit of good.

Standing at the table only minutes ago, she had been radiant. Challenging. Defiant. She had been so close that by reaching out his hand he could have touched her. But even then that other, that hated but cherished feeling had not returned.

He was in the elevator again now. It was ascending. He was alone. As he had always been. As he had wanted to be.

Did he still want to be alone?

If so, why had he come here?

He was walking along a wide corridor. Closed doors on either side. The fever throbbed all through him. The door stood open a few inches.

So—he did not need the key after all. That had been only a gesture. Contemptuous—and contemptible. Bitch.

He extended his hand and pushed open the door.

But what if it had been a plea? Her own desire. Need.

He stepped into the foyer and stared into the shadows. The sitting room was framed by ceiling-high glass doors, gray and flickering city light beyond, a sky faintly pink.

He stood very still. And silent. Unsure that he was breathing. He was not trembling.

There was a movement. Without sound. Phantomlike. And then he saw her. Her body outlined by the dim glow. All of her. Legs slightly parted. Defiance? Or that sad timidity that always twisted him inside? The giveaway to that other self in her that he had glimpsed from time to time. The silhouette was that of a woman.

52

Not the girl he'd known. Her body, still slender, was more rounded, more definitely feminine somehow—

"You bastard." Her voice was a low-pitched whisper. Not harsh but tinged with a strange, fond accusation, even tenderness. "You made me come to you, didn't you?"

A bitter triumph exploded in him. Then roared all through him. True, true, to that extent he *had* won. To that extent he had already won.

As if sensing his feeling, but not moving, she said, in a child's voice naked of deceit: "I lied when I said I didn't go to the banquet because of the dreadful people."

"Bourbon-belching ass-pinchers, I think you often said—" He was amazed at his own voice: There was actually a bantering amusement in it.

Her tone was tremulous, even apologetic: "I couldn't go because I was afraid of seeing you."

Clay remembered then: Even standing at the table, haughty and self-assured, she had given herself away. To him, at least. The glacier cracking. And he had caught a quick but heart-rending glimpse of the awkward, skittish girl within the facade of ice.

When he spoke again, his voice was strangled: "Why the hell do you think I went to that damned dinner?"

Then she came to him. Fast. She collapsed against him, naked, close and warm, her body's heat and softness like an electric shock stopping his blood. And then her arms were around him and his were on her satin-skinned back, and her voice was murmuring against his face as her lips moved over it: "It's been forever, oh, God, forever, where have you been, eternity, didn't you feel that, *don't* you feel that, where have you been, oh, God, you bastard, so long, where have you been—"

The tenderness in him hardened, then erupted volcanically, and a wildness took over. With one hand he lifted her face, pinching it to open her lips, and while the joy of the kiss overwhelmed him he placed his other hand over her full bare breast.

And in that most unlikely of moments he thought of Andrew Cameron.

And knew with a ferocious jolt of triumph that he had won. So soon. *Already* he had won. Nothing could stop him now.
Nothing.
Nobody.

Chapter Two

THREE deuces take it. And some pot. Past three in the A.M. and Vasaturo winning, like always, and therefore not wanting to call it a day, and what Vasaturo wants, he gets, especially playing with his trainer and two straw-brain bodyguards he calls lieutenants for shit's sake. Vasaturo pays all three in salary, then he wins it back in poker, no surprise he's worth how many millions, all those real-estate holdings, kindling-wood tenements, Florida swamplands, phosphate strip mines. Who's he—sagging beagle eyes, Havana cigars, silk suits, and nothing-but-Chivas Regal paunch—who's this prince to listen to his trainer? The animal's tired. "Dealer's Choice ran the Stepping Stone Saturday, now he's in the Trial on Tuesday and the big D on Saturday—already we got the press on our ass for running hot cripples till they drop and that Count Wyatt taking a sideswipe every shot he gets." Okay, so bet a C-note on a lousy seven showing, what's cabbage like that if you can rent a penthouse like this for all Derby Week? But Vasaturo, you got ears stuffed with cement, telling your trainer to shoot Dealer's Choice with more bute 'cause hardly a one races at Laurel ain't on either bute or Lasix; then not listening, not even listening to: "Bute's not gonna keep Dealer's Choice from breaking down, it never does, it only lets the poor horse run without knowing he got the pain; what he needs is rest, like they did Forego when he was lame." And now Vasaturo asks:

"You seeing me, Calvin?" Hell, yes, seeing you and raising on a pair of fours, one down, one showing, let the straw-brains fold their tents. Which they both do. Vasaturo, he grins and deals—a crummy deuce for Calvin, another seven to Vasaturo to match up showing. So now Calvin folds, fuck it, he has to be backside in less than three lousy hours while his boss screws his pillow until time for Mass—never misses a Mass, even weekdays, that's Vasaturo, devout, devout ex-hit man, races his own stable now.

Even before she spoke, he sensed that now, finally, she was awake. Yet there was no light behind the heavy curtains. But soon. And the Spur's workout was scheduled for 6:15.

"Is it true?" she asked, her tone drifting and langorous. "All of this. Tell me, Clay: Is it really happening?" He could picture her warm honey-hued face and the intense whiteness of her body. Its incredible heat seemed to reach him although they were not now touching. "Is this really you, Clay?"

He was tempted then to roll closer. It was all happening again, and this time it was not illusion. Dreamlike but not a dream.

A movement beside him in the bed cut his impulse, and then another voice altogether, but recognizable, remembered, said: "You didn't write. You didn't call. I didn't know where you were."

"I asked you to come along, Kimberley."

"You didn't understand. You didn't then and you don't now, even now."

True. But how had they come to this? And so *soon.* "I understood that you believed what your father believed." He heard the roughness in his tone.

"I couldn't. I didn't. I didn't *want* to."

"But you did." Hold it now—no time for this. That's over, all of it. "And you still do believe it, don't you?"

"What else can I believe?" Her voice was tight and bitter. "What else is there to believe?"

If the night had been inevitable, so then was this conversation. And the old familiar bitterness poisoning his blood. The chill rage.

Unfair, unfair. But hadn't he learned anything? Hadn't he been taught over and over that nothing was ever fair? Then why go on imagining it must be, insisting?

He stood up in the dim room and felt her movement, a quick swish of blanket and sheet. The door opened, he saw a flash of pale body framed a second, and then a light came on in the sitting room. He flipped on the bedroom lamp and began to dress. The waste was in him: seven years. Goddamned stupid, foolish waste. He recalled the sound of the shot that had killed Lord Randolph. It had echoed over the stables and into the wintry woods. And Kimberley's stricken face and frightened eyes watching. The snow coming down and her father's face no longer composed but frozen in cold fury and then the huge hand exploding in his face, the first blow, and then all the others and the taste of blood, of broken teeth, pain, brain splintering while he stood and refused to attack, even to defend. He had never been sure since why he had not fought back. Just as he had never been able to decide whether he had been drunk enough that night to have done what Andrew Cameron had accused him of doing. Would he ever know?

He heard a door open and then close in the sitting room.

Kimberley had made her choice before it happened. Earlier that same night, not drunk, he had asked her to leave with him, hopelessly aware that it was an outrageous, childish demand: to abandon the immense white house with its octagonal drawing room, its formal boxwood gardens, its two thousand acres of stables, paddocks, track, farmland, woods, and jumps—and for what? For life with an assistant trainer, assistant farm manager? All along, even then, he had been shocked by his own quixotic and unreasonable demand. And when she had hesitated, he had gone roaring into the village and had drunk himself into a stupor, and not for the first time, and then the unthinkable had occurred—or had not occurred. Perhaps he would never know. He had almost given up trying to remember.

"I get the funnies!" She stood naked in the door-frame, and the sight of her in full light was a body blow that all but blinded him. She had changed again. Her voice was light and childlike now—mischievous. And her green eyes flashed delight. "The way we used to." She dashed to the bed and then lifted her body into a dive and twisted it in midair to land on her back in the bed, the newspaper clutched against her bare breasts.

He shoved the past aside in his mind: how, the next morning, subdued and sober, he had given her the choice again. A bleak morning along the fence of the training track. She had been in tears, almost hysterical: *How can I, Clay? How can I go now? After what you—after what's happened?* Pulling on his shirt, he stepped to the bed. "Are you going to the track later?"

Her face changed again, and her eyes widened. "The track? Clay, you can't. Not now. Can't your groom work the colt? Your assistant?"

Gently, recognizing the storm signals, he said: "My rider's come all the way from New York. I haven't been with the Spur for almost a week now. What about Starbright?"

"They'll be paddocking him. Close crowds make him jittery, and the Downs is worse than most. So they keep trying to calm him." But her mind seemed to be elsewhere, and her brows were low over her lids. "I should be there." She gazed up into Clay's eyes. "That horse loves me. He *really* loves me." Then in a quick, sharp movement she knelt, tossed the paper aside. "More than you can say, isn't it? You haven't said it. You can't say it, can you, because you don't!"

The accusation was sharp, and her eyes glittered with a coldness that hinted at hate. But also of fear. And Clay remembered. And remembering, his body went weak with tenderness. He could see the pain, the anticipated rejection in which she already believed, alarm—he saw it all again and wished he could not. Yes, it was all happening again. He recalled Count Wyatt's remark that there were fires banked behind the cool porcelain; they had erupted last night, over and over in reckless, demanding abandonment. What he saw now was something else—something baffling and threatening—and as in the past he did not know how to cope with it. She knelt there naked, totally exposed, but not in body alone.

"I think I do love you, Kimberley," he heard himself whisper. "But I'm due at the track."

"Bastard!" she snarled. "Go on then, you sonofabitch, get out, get the hell out—why did you have to come back anyway?"

Instead of retreating, though, he stooped slightly and kissed her forehead, which was scorching to his lips. She twisted away and threw herself flat onto the bed, head down in the pillow. Would she cry? She had always made it a matter of pride never to cry. If she did, what would he do? Could he go?

Smiling slightly at the tyranny implied, he turned away and picked up his jacket. "I can't very well wear this on the backstretch, can I?"

She did not reply.

At the door he paused. "Are you coming to the track?" he asked again.

"No." She did not move; her voice was muffled. "No. Today or ever. Get away."

"I really ought to give you a wallop across the bottom."

"You touch me and I'll rape you." Then she rolled onto her back. "You're the only one. Does that make you feel good? Does that send you off to the track feeling like a god of some kind? You bastard, you're the only one who can really get to me, really get to me, make me feel completely alive." He waited and her face twisted into a smile that was at once quizzical and derisive. "If only you could explain to me why I say the things I do? Why I *do* what I do? It scares me, Clay, and no one can tell me."

And there she was again: helpless, vulnerable, pleading. But this time, in spite of her mask, she was facing it in simple words, head-on. And somehow this stirred a kind of hope in him, but trepidation too. Suddenly he realized what he should have known: that however much she was the same, she had changed too. Now at least she could admit her weakness, fear.

"Clay"—her hands moved through her pale hair—"Clay, what if *she* wins?"

"She?"

"You've seen her and heard her. Many times. Don't you remember?"

Damned if he did. But there would be time to explore it. Later. After last night Clay knew that they had a lifetime really. "If you do come to the backstretch," he said gently, "Hotspur's in barn twenty-seven."

He turned and went through the sitting room and into the corridor, and as he closed the door behind him he heard her silence
from the bedroom as if it were her voice crying out.

JD's tone was growing angrier as he read aloud: "Only seven
geldings have stood in the winner's circle in the more than one
hundred years since 1875." And then he growled and hit the newspaper with his fist, muttering, "Ten to one that scribbling essobee's
a gelding hisself." Almeta rolled onto her side in the other motel
bed and said, "Listen, shortstop, it's not even daylight. You woke
me to read something, why don't you read it?" Which he then did:
"For the record, though, that seven included two of the greatest
names in American sports: Kelso and Exterminator. Could the
owner of Also Ran and his pretty spouse ask for better company
for the only gelding entered in this year's classic? Could anyone
ask for more?" JD could, and of course did: "Yeah, pisser—how
about telling the folks how shiny black my pretty wife is?" And
then Almeta knew how really mad he was, which meant mean,
and that his knee was paining him again. He read on:
"Never mind that Also Ran came in ninth in the Bluegrass Stakes—
in a field of nine—or that he comes out of the gate like he's being
thrown out of a saloon. Anyone who'd buy a horse named Also Ran
has to have a sense of humor and a thick skin." JD hurled the paper
to the floor. "Thick, turkey, and brown. Essobee gets you up, then
he knocks you down. What tears his balls is that there's a black
owner first time in the Derby. Record books don't show that nowhere, do they?" But Almeta knew better now than to reply. She
also knew why he had bought a horse named Also Ran: It was his
way of saying screw-you-honkies-one-and-all. He was convinced
too, as she was not, that they were cramped here in this motel room
simply because they were, as she knew the locals here would call it,
colored. But hadn't he been the six-foot-three slugger, hero to thousands, with a twenty-five home run season once, a .312 batting
average, and ninety-one RBIs—was all that glory behind him forever? Cheated out of the Baseball Hall of Fame—or had he cheated

himself?—he had to win here. Or lose. Sometimes Almeta allowed herself to suspect that the poor, sweet, lovable baby had to lose. JD stood up. "Think I'll go out there and see what that bastard's doing to my horse this morning." She wanted to go back to sleep, but she sat up. "I'll go too." Pulling on the suede cap that he liked to wear at the track, JD said, "I don't want you going backside." And when she frowned and reached for a cigarette, he went into the tiny bathroom. "I don't go for the way that turkey Haslam looks at you." Still she did not object. Matt Haslam was old enough to be her father and then some. Kind of hail-fellow but nice in a soft sort of way. Man'd never paid any attention to her—probably a white-meat-only man in his day, which was probably past. But she knew better than to cross JD when he was in this mood. From the bathroom JD said, "Someday I'm just gonna have to cream that shithead calls hisself a trainer." Almeta blew smoke. Matt Haslam had recommended that JD buy Also Ran: confirmation, bloodlines, never mind the screwy name. Was it this that had turned JD on him? Or his imagined yen for Almeta? Or his color? Or any and all together, so what. Damn JD, he knew how she hated that locker-room talk. "You do that, JD," she said in spite of herself. "You cream Mr. Haslam." She didn't add: just the way you charged out from the plate to the mound and creamed that pitcher when you got hit on the wrist with a curve ball. That time, JD, you weren't able to make a fist, remember, so you had to get on top of the kid and hit him with your elbow. That time, shortstop, all you got was a hefty fine and a two-week suspension. But what about later? "Acts of conduct not in the best interests of baseball"—wasn't that the wording? As one columnist phrased it: "The end of a career continually marred by controversy." He returned, stooped, kissed her lips lightly, then strode on his long, hard legs to the door. She didn't want to remind him. Couldn't. Not only would it be too cruel, but she didn't want any more trouble. Of any kind. Ever. At thirty she had had enough trouble for a lifetime. Nevertheless she said, "Put two dollars on Number Five in the sixth for me." In the open door JD asked, "What horse?" And she took a deep puff and said, "Who knows? Who cares? He's my mortal lock in the sixth. Blow two bucks for your pretty shiny-black spouse, JD." She could sense rather than see the pain in his eyes when he closed the door. She wished she had not said it. Or anything. Why had he wakened her? He had promised he wouldn't bet in Louisville. Again. It was like an alcoholic promising never to take another drink. She had not quite but almost reached the point of admitting that he was incurably hooked—a gambling junkie. If she ever reached the point of admitting that, then what? The man was to be pitied, and she did pity him. Admired even. He had balls—in more ways than one. God, how he'd tried to go on. Working out so hard that more than once she'd found him sick and vomiting, eyes glazed, using the machines and the ice and the heat—and his own grim determination. But nothing could keep that left knee from swelling whenever he played on a hard surface. Cortisone only puffed his face, and the analgesics made him dizzy. In some ways the Astroturf had licked him. Or was it something else—that volcano seething inside him? And the pain. And the gambling. The losing. Sometimes Almeta Edwards wished that she liked drinking the way most folks did. She could do with one right now. Or two, or three. Stiff ones. JD. Where's it going to end?

Clay clicked the stopwatch in his palm as the Spur passed, Zach aboard, his seat high in the air. One thirty-six and three-fifths for the full mile—not enough to satisfy Bernie or Hotspur himself but exactly what Clay had asked for. Zach Massing always bragged he had a stop watch in his skull, and damned if he didn't.

It was not yet light. A dim silver dawn. Across the backstretch of the track the infield grass had begun to glisten. Beyond, behind the homestretch, the clubhouse and grandstand, twin spires above, were hazy and dreamlike shadows. On the other side of the chainlink fence where he stood the workouts continued, so close that even in the chill air he could smell the dirt raised by the thudding hoofs and the sweat of moving, stretching flesh. He could distinguish the heavy, hurried thump of the gallopers and the muffled *tippety-tah-tah* of those breezing and, mingled in, the broken rhythms of the two-year-olds, unmistakable to a horseman's ear. A frail filly sailed by, the leather of the saddle sighing, her lungs exploding gusts of vapor with each thud of hoof, rider bent low, clicking and chucking and begging. And then a colt, hard on the rail, stretching out, each breath an eruption—was there anything as lovely as the liquid movement of a thoroughbred? It never failed to close his throat, to stir a feverish itch in his flesh, to fill him to the brim with sheer pleasure. At no other time, none, did he feel so completely alive.

He was reluctant even to move. He saw Bernie slouched and bulbous atop his pony—why lead horses of whatever breed or size or state of decrepitude were called ponies on a track, he had never learned—and he watched as Zach, thin shoulders birdlike now, joined Bernie and then, passing through the gate, waved to him with his stick. On target, Zach—to the fifth of a second overall. The Spur looked impatient and curious, lifting his head and stretching his black neck as if to locate Clay and to protest—to hell with the rubdown, the leisurely hot-walk to cool out, the hay and oats; he wanted to go on running.

On the track, close to the fence, an enormous bay was returning from his run: handsome, head high, sweating lightly in the flanks, he had the look of aristocracy. Regal. Clay recognized him: Ancient Mariner. Another favorite. Impeccable pedigree, impressive past performance record, winner of the Bay Shore and the Bluegrass, second in the Wood, owned by the elderly silver-haired lady from Connecticut. The exercise girl, lanquid and pretty, smiled down. And the chill air, the lightening sky, the low fog, all the sounds and smells—it was as if he were mesmerized. His blood was throbbing hot, and nothing seemed impossible. Nothing and no one unattainable. The whole goddamn world was within reach.

"I make it seven furlongs at one twenty-two and change," a voice beside him said. "The mile at one thirty-seven and change."

Clay turned. He resented anyone clocking his horse. "One thirty-six and change," he said. "If it's any of your business."

The face that somehow seemed to materialize was obscured by a gust of mist and its own beard, the color of rust. The lips opened in a laugh, and the tall stranger said, "Y'don't recognize your own big brother after all this time?"

And then, only then, did he realize. No mistaking that laugh—

which was gleeful while it mocked and, as always, somehow infectious.

Almost automatically he shook the hand that the tall stranger offered—a thick, strong hand, like dried leather. And he could feel those sharp blue eyes on him, probing. But he said nothing because he felt nothing. He was damned if he'd say he was glad to see Owen. Because he was not so damned sure he was. He wasn't glad, or otherwise. He felt the iron-vise grip crushing his smaller hand, and then as pain mounted his wrist and arm Owen gave it a final squeeze before releasing it. He pushed the broad-brimmed Western hat back from his sun-wrinkled forehead and lifted reddish brows and spoke in that softly scoffing but friendly tone that Clay now remembered distinctly: "I got my first good squint just now. Y'really think that little bangtail of yours can get aboard the gravy train? This race is one mile and a quarter, lil brother! You still puffing away at that pipe-dream corncob of yours?"

"It doesn't smell as bad as your cigar," Clay said, and Owen put his head back to laugh.

Mounts were being led onto and off the track through the open gate. There was a steady, slow clopping flow of traffic to and from the barns. Exercise riders and hot-walkers, stablehands, jockeys and jockey's agents hustling rides for the afternoon races, owners, trainers, newsmen, and miscellaneous connections and hangers-on, anyone and his uncle who could finagle a backstretch pass—it was a casual but busy world, self-contained. And above it all the PA system continued to blare messages. While all over the city the civilians were turning over in their beds to snatch a few more winks before the alarm, here the workday had begun.

Bangtail. A flash of childhood. One of their old man's words. Like *gravy train*, seldom heard today. And *pipe dream*—another half-forgotten echo. "The Spur doesn't have a shot, Owen," Clay said. "I admit it. That's why I'm here."

Owen slipped his watch into the pocket of his leather vest. "Y'know how many blacks have won the Derby? Ever?"

"Four," Clay said, promptly, "until now," and he moved away from the fence, glancing at the sky. Lighter now, but cloudless. Afternoon showers predicted. "And it's only rained twice on Derby Day too."

Owen laughed again. "Haven't changed a fuck's worth, have you? Facts and figures, what the shit they mean to you?" He reached to place his arm around Clay's back as they walked, grasping Clay's upper arm in a steel grip. "Yeah, yeah, I heard your runner was a mudder."

Mudder. Another of good old Toby's words. *Steer your ass clear of mudders, boys. They narrow down the odds somethin' awful. 'Less you know one of them Indian rain dances that's a sure-fire pisser, take your old man's word, he's been there and back!*

It was several moments, while his mind was searching for questions to ask, before Clay realized that Owen's long, powerful stride was carrying them both in the direction of the Derby barn. Where Clay damn well didn't want to go.

"My boss," Owen said, "was something like you, Clay. Had this one idea—that Fireaway could take the blanket of roses 'cause he took the San Vincente Stakes and the California Derby both." His arm tightened along Clay's back. "I guess you heard what happened."

"I heard it on the radio on my way here," Clay said. Cardiac arrest . . . own private plane . . . history of heart trouble . . . dead on arrival some airport out West . . . age sixty-three.

"Too goddamn much excitement," Owen said. "Stubborn prick, though, got to hand it to him. Guts. Had to come along. Wouldn't listen to his doc, his wife, me, nobody." He released Clay's arm and shook his head. "Had to see Fireaway win." He stopped and faced Clay, taking off his tan-colored broad-brimmed hat. "He won't see it, but dead or alive that's what that sweet old guy is going to get, Clay."

Frowning, Clay watched as his brother, towering above him as he always had, wiped the sweatband of his Western hat with a bandana. Had Owen changed? No—he'd always been capable of a certain loyalty. As toward Toby in spite of everything. And quick emotion. Sentimentality even. Clay turned between barns and passed bales of hay, smelling horse sweat and manure and oats and liniment. A vet was grasping a horse's tongue with one hand while he filed down his teeth with the other, a groom holding the horse's lip with a twitch. Owen had also been capable of sly cruelty and plotted revenge, sometimes for hurts only imagined, and of harsh brutality on the spur of the moment. A jock, yawning atop a sleepy-faced mare, was whining to a plump girl who was leading him: "What you gonna do when she wants to run backwards, what the hell you gonna *do*?" Clay didn't want to remember. Owen was no longer a part of him or his life. By Clay's own choice. Years ago. But Owen was alongside again, and Clay felt a once-familiar anger. His blood has slowed to a sluggish, sullen flow. Where had that good feeling, that throbbing sense of promise and antici-pation—where the hell had it gone?

"You haven't even asked about Toby," Owen said.

It was true. So he asked now. With a dry reluctance.

And the question brought Owen to a halt again. He turned. His blue eyes were sharp and hostile. "You still hate the poor old guy, don't you?"

"I don't think," Clay said softly, "that I ever really hated him, Owen." But was he sure? Had he ever really decided?

"Like shit. Well, I can tell you one thing straight, kid—he loved hell out of you."

Clay almost said he had a strange way of showing it. But he knew that that, too, was only part of the truth. Whatever the truth was. An old confusion settled like an ache through him. "Where is he, Owen?"

Owen's legs-apart stance and his tone were as hard as his stare. "He's dead."

Again Clay said nothing. Again uncertain what he really felt even now. He recalled country roads and dust and public showers and la-trines stinking of urine and a thousand rotting barns and tracks and fairgrounds, and a rusting truck with growling motor hauling a creaking horse van. He remembered small dreary towns and houses set back behind lawns and fields and the ache in him as he stared at the lights behind windows where people sat at tables together or in front of blue-lit TV screens, together, families—

"You even give a goddamn how he died?" Owen demanded, and his voice was tinged with disbelief and indignation.

"How?" Clay asked, bleakly, recalling Toby drunk and sober, good old apple-cheeked Toby. Sober: *I can't look at you, Clay, what I don't think of her,* and at those times his love for her a pain in his eyes, at those times himself kind, gentle. "How'd he die?" Clay heard himself ask. *You even got your mother's shiny black hair, Clay, same brown eyes—*

"You remember how the old man used to gamble. Bet on anything that moved—trotters, dogs, cockfights, cockroaches even—"

"How? *When?*"

"Ten, eleven years ago." And now fondness softened Owen's voice. "Couple of hick turds said he was cheating at poker." Then anger again: "Kicked him to a pulp and hauled him out into a corn field. Two below zero and sleeting ice. They left him. They left him like that! He was almost froze by the time I found him. Coroner said his ribs punctured his lungs."

Clay took a shallow breath. Toby, filled with booze, eyes watering and wild, had been another man: *You lily-livered little bastard, you're the one. Hadn't been for you, Erna'd still be alive. She died birthin' you, every time I look at you I think of that. Owen, fetch ole Toby that whip—*

Unfair. *Unjust!* Clay was shaking inside. Again. All the sick old confusions lurched up in him. He stepped around Owen's tall bulk and moved on, his legs weak. He wanted no more of it, would take no more. The past was dead. Now Toby was dead.

"They got theirs, though—them two turds," Owen said, beside him again. "They got what was coming to them. Your big brother saw to that."

Enough! Years ago, eighteen years ago now, when the outrage and the bewilderment and the fury had become too much, he had quietly and secretly packed what little he owned—including the finger-worn *Complete Works of William Shakespeare*—and he had hopped a freight which happened to be moving south from Minnesota. Toby had already thrown the blue-backed poetry collection into the Missouri River: *You just like her, Clay—hankerin' to be*

what you ain't. Black-haired bitch died thinkin' she was better'n me.
And later, he had swiped a book of poems from the public library in
a town named Texarkana, the loneliness and hunger in him too
great to be denied. It had comforted him to believe that his mother,
whom he had never known except in some strange and mysterious
way, would have approved.

As they approached the Derby barn a brown gelding with a dull
coat was being led in the direction of the track by his elderly trainer,
who looked mild and was shaking his head; a tall, lean black man
walked alongside. The trainer seemed to be trying to explain something, but the other man kept muttering "Shit, just more bullshit.
What you seem to forget, Mr. Haslam, is who is the owner of
this animal."

Owen, chuckling now, his mood changing, threw his heavy arm
over Clay's shoulders again. "Can you imagine what ole Toby'd say
about a thing like that? 'What the fuck is this world comin' to—a
coon actually *owning* a horse in the Kentucky Derby!' Can't you
hear the old man, Clay?"

Clay could hear him all right. *Coon*—another of Toby's favorite
words. He recognized the tall black man from newspaper photographs: a famous ex-baseball player whose colt had the misfortune
to be named Also Ran.

Quietly then, into Clay's ear, Owen said, "I missed you, brother.
No shit. Just like it was never the same to the old man after Ma
died, it was never the same for me after you pulled up stakes."

Stakes? Clay smiled to himself, relaxing slightly. When had there
ever been any stakes to pull? But somehow he knew that Owen was
sincere. Just as Toby had been sincere in his loving moments. And
as he had been equally sincere in his cruel and violent ones.

"Want you to meet my connections, Clay." Owen strode around
the end of the barn with a wave at the uniformed Pinkerton guard
on his campstool. And when Clay joined him on the sloping knoll
of grass behind the barn, with the small white houses of Louisville
visible on the street beyond, Owen stood with his legs wide regarding the muscled roan that was being scrubbed down by a small,
tight-muscled young man with a wind-leathered face and a stubble
of sun-bleached hair. When Owen, without taking his gaze from

the colt, introduced him as Eric Millar, the small tight-lipped face remained impassive, and the narrow pale eyes did not so much as blink. Then a huge lean Doberman stood up from the grass and, not quite baring its teeth, stared at Clay, sullen and hostile.

Owen snapped his fingers and the dog sat back on his haunches. "Some runners gotta have goats, birds, even raccoons. Fireaway's stablemate's Max here." He turned his head. "Well, Clay, what do you think of this pig?"

Fireaway was no pig. A handsome muscled body under a fine coat with a satin strawberry sheen to it. Clay already knew his pedigree, his record out West, particularly in California. Indifferent eyes.

"Trouble all the way from the gate," Owen said. "Chew you bloody, man or beast. Get a chance, hell, he'd savage his own dam, gobble his own foals." Was Owen speaking with fondness, or amusement—or pride? "Chewed the fingers off a groom once, right in front of the stands at Bay Meadows." Pride, Clay decided. Owen stepped in and clapped Fireaway on the thigh, hard, and the colt drew back his lips. Owen laughed. "Can't stand to be rated, and the jock's gotta fight him all the way around the goddamn track."

If Clay had learned anything, it was that no horse was born bad. The bad actors, as he'd discovered, were made—by someone who didn't know how to handle them, or didn't care, or took pleasure in their meanness. It was a weary but true old adage in racing that the animals reflected the personalities of the humans around them. Jason Arnold had first put that idea into words for Clay. Starbright's trainer. And with the thought Clay's mind veered to Blue Ridge Plantation. And to Lord Randolph. And to Andrew Cameron.

Which brought to mind Andrew Cameron's daughter—asleep and warm and soft and waiting.

Clay became conscious of Owen studying him, half-smiling, his head cocked to one side. "How about a shot or two of hooch? Eric's always got booze in the trailer." He rubbed his huge hands together. "Jesus, they freeze your balls off before sunup in this neck of the woods, don't they?"

Clay shook his head once and turned away. "What I need is coffee. And grub." Now by god *he* was using old Toby's lingo. He hadn't said *grub* in years.

Owen fell into step beside him. "Fireaway's a stall-walker. Christ, we tried everything—threw in old tires so's he'd stumble, hung a chain from the ceiling. Finally had to hobble his front feet. Only made him meaner. But, baby brother, fuck that Starbright and Vincent Van and that Ancient Mariner, and fuck your shrimp-sized black too, the colt to beat come Saturday is named Fireaway. Take it from his trainer."

"I'll remember to tell Hotspur and his rider," Clay said. "Maybe they'll slow down on the turn for home."

Then Owen laughed again. "Same old Clay. Same old whistle-in-the-wind Clay!"

Ignoring that, Clay said, "According to the radio, there's some doubt Fireaway will run now."

"No luck there, Clay, sorry. It's up to the widow-lady and the widow-lady will do what her trainer advises. Believe me."

Startled but remembering again—Owen almost invariably had his way—Clay believed him. But he wondered: Would Fireaway run because of the dead man's wishes or because of Owen's?

As they went up the steps of the track kitchen—which looked like a small faded farmhouse on the prairie—a jockey still wearing a colored helmet held the door for a tall skinny girl with freckles. "Know what, Amanda? They trying to accuse me of running into a blind switch at the half-mile pole in the sixth yesterday." And the girl giggled: "They crazy, they just plumb out of their tree." Amused, Owen winked at Clay. In the large single room inside Owen bought a *Racing Form* and joined Clay in the cafeteria line at the steam table. In the clash and clatter and the crush of friendly voices Clay caught sight of Zach hunched over a heaping platter, his ridged mask of face fixed, almost ecstatic with pleasure and anticipation. Most people, he knew, thought flipping—as it is called at the track—was amusing. Clay could not agree. To him eating heavily and then forcing yourself to vomit was sad. Sad to Clay Chalmers and to hell with what anyone else thought. He wished he wasn't as fond of Zach Massing as he was.

Sitting across from Owen at the oil-clothed kitchen table, smelling the sizzling ham and fried potatoes and bitter-black coffee, Clay tried to remember all the boyhood meals they'd shared. But, hell, there'd been so many and in so many different places that no memory had a root. He could not force nostalgia. It was as if, once having put the past behind, his mind now insisted on keeping it there.

But not Owen. Again he had changed. Hat on the chair next to him, rusty hair, like his beard, short-clipped and bright, he sat there, straight and broad, and did not eat. He gulped coffee. His eyes had gone stony, the color of the turquoise that held the leather thongs of his tie.

Clay ate and waited. The food tasted wonderful, as it always did after the chill of the workouts. He saw Zach get up and leave. Nearby a tenor voice complained, "That filly, she acts just like a spoiled chick," and a feminine voice croaked, "When you talk like that, I could spit shoe nails," and farther away someone was comparing the Downs to the Big A.

Finally Owen drained his mug and set it down. "Clay," he said in a strange boyish voice touched with something like a plea in it, "kid, you don't know what kind of a guy Toby was when we were living here in Kentucky and he was managing that breeding farm, before she—"

When he didn't continue, Clay said, "Before she died. I couldn't very well remember, could I, when I wasn't even born yet?" He was tempted to add, "Before I killed her," but he went on eating instead.

Owen's neat beard twisted, he shook his head, and his eyes narrowed around the turquoise marbles. "The old man'd say anything when he was boozed up, you know that."

Breech birth. Feet first. Hours. A kitchen table. Death.

Clay stood up. He wasn't hungry after all. "Owen," he said, "my colt's entered in the Trial tomorrow. I've things to do." He turned, amazed at the tension in his muscles, the sour taste on his tongue. "See you around."

It was light outside now and the air was warmer but not really damp. Beyond the slanting roofs of the barns there were a few low

71

clouds. Not many and not dark, but they held a feeble promise. Anything was possible. Hell, he wouldn't be here if he didn't believe that.

"Let's get that drink now."

Owen. He had followed. He had a long, thin cigar between his teeth, and his Stetson was canted at an angle. Old home week again.

"I don't drink," Clay told him.

"No shit? Since when?"

Seven years. He didn't say it. Not since he'd pulled a complete blank and Jason Arnold had had to shoot Lord Randolph in the snow. *No choice, boy*, Jason Arnold had said. *Canon bone's shattered, no way to set it.* Pain in his voice, his eyes—blame? The past again.

"Everybody drinks," Owen said now, and he stopped walking abruptly, grabbing Clay's arm and spinning him around so that he also stopped and they stood facing each other. Owen hooked his thumbs in his wide studded belt and regarded Clay with a taunting gaze. The cigar moved up and down as he spoke: "Little brother, listen now. Listen good. Nobody refuses to drink with Owen Chalmers twice." He grinned around the cigar. Pleasantly. "Nobody."

Clay realized that his body had gone stiff and that his heart was swollen and quivering. Nevertheless his tone was scoffing, although gentle: "What will you do, Owen? Break my nose again? Well, swing with your left this time, maybe you'll straighten it out."

Owen's eyes flashed amusement. "No, sir, you haven't changed one goddamn iota, have you?"

"I've changed," Clay said evenly, but suddenly he wondered.

"That mean that if we tear ass here, just for old time's sake, you won't go behind the barn afterwards and puke your guts out?"

"I probably would," Clay said, because it had always been so: Any violence, whether he was involved or not, turned his stomach. He had once thought that a weakness. "But we're not going to tear ass because, one, we've no reason to and, two, the TRPB boys would be down on us in a second and we'd both be barred from the track." And then, because he couldn't help himself, he said, "For God's sake, Owen, grow up."

For a split second he thought Owen was going to swing, and instinctively he braced for it. But Owen frowned, and the frown turned into a scowl. "Only trying to test whether you grew balls since I seen you last." Then he turned away and strode toward the parked cars: A tall, heavy, wide-shouldered man, made taller by the high-heeled boots, he walked with the truculent near-swagger usually associated with smaller men.

And suddenly, standing there, Clay felt sorry for his brother. Why? He did not know. He had never known. As a boy he had always been baffled by that contradiction inside: Even when he had hated Owen most, he had somehow pitied him. He swung about now, again angry at himself, and walked slowly in the direction of barn 27. And Hotspur. The chores of the morning. But he was remembering: *Don't ever feel sorry for nobody. You take ole Toby's word. Soon's you feel sorry, they screw you royal. Your ma, she never would believe that. She said if she believed that she wouldn't want to live.*

It was then that the sun broke through. Pale gold light illuminated the barns, glinted on the wet grass and on the coats of the passing horses.

Behold! A grand stallion he is indeed. Born black, now a lovely dove-gray: Age would only whiten that lustrous coat and mane. Thrall, indeed—no lowly slave this one but the proud white steed on which Niam rode in her robe of gold in the fantasies and myths of Brigid's childhood. She watched as the freckled-faced boy named Kevin led the colt from the barn. The guards seated at either end did not bother to so much as glance at the fine beast with the lofty lift of head. She was reminded again of what Daniel had said so often: *As with the human animal, it's a quality of spirit that makes a horse what he is or is not.* Glancing at Kevin as she moved closer to Thrall and took the lead into her own hand, she realized that the

boy's face, usually smiling, was long this morning, in his blue eyes
a mournful look, and she remembered that it had been Molly who
had begged that he come to America with them. She took the cubes
of sugar from the pocket of her short tweed cape. I know, me lad,
it's carrots you prefer, but fine hotels do not serve carrots with the
thin transparent brew they call coffee here. Kevin, wearing the
traditional rumpled woollen suit of his homeland, moved off. All
round her the backstretch area was slowing its activities, and she
pressed her face against the fine hairs of Thrall's lowered forehead.
She wondered whether she would ever quite acclimate herself to the
raw voices and strange accents, the baseball caps and cowboy hats,
straw and felt, and denims everywhere, and yoked Western shirts
and the Greek fisherman's caps, and hunting hats, and bandanas,
along with English motoring caps and jogging suits and shoes—a
wild heterogeneous mélange of attire such as would not be encoun-
tered in England or Ireland or France. Well, lass, it was your idea
to come. And so it had been. Whim or fancy or only restlessness—some aching need in her that even she could not define.
After that terror on the runway at Shannon Airport—good-bye,
Danny, farewell—the responsibilities of Innisfree Demesne had
saved her, or almost. How grateful she would always be. Because of
her absorption in racing and breeding she was here now, wasn't she?
And alive still. Not wholly alive—that would never be so again. But
surviving. And another fine and thrilling race on Saturday. Always
another one ahead somewhere.

"Spoiling the animal before his workout," a whisky-coarsened
and familiar voice growled. The dyspeptic leprechaun, by name
Gregory McGreevey, was circling Irish Thrall. He wore, as always,
a brown wool suit with tie, waistcoat, and a gold watch on a gold
chain, and his frayed tweed hat was pushed back from his wrinkled
forehead, a look of distaste and disapproval in his narrow eyes. "Isn't
he already too friendly by half? How do you reasonably expect him
to lead the bogtrotters to the finish pole if you encourage his soft
ways?"

"How is he, Mr. McGreevey?" she asked. "And good morning to
you too."

"I'm dire tempted to use the blinkers that he hates on him, come

Saturday. As soon as he sees an enemy moving up, he thinks it has to be a friend, so he stops for a bit of palaver and the latest back-stretch gossip, damn his eyes." He stooped to lift Thrall's right foreleg but did not remove the green elastic bandage. "Chronic lesion, so says the veterinarian surgeon, but not so the farrier. Agh, I do wish they'd taught these Yankees proper respect for the mither tongue, it's sich a strain to decipher the accent."

She found herself smiling now. Gregory McGreevey often had this effect. And she cherished it. He had opposed the coming and since arrival had missed no chance to remind her of the odds against Thrall on an American course: the sharp turns, running on dirt instead of his accustomed turf, and to top it off, God forbid, running the course in the wrong direction, just the way they drove their cars on the wrong side of the street here!

Upright and at least a hand shorter than she, Mr. McGreevey took out his watch. "Thit Kevin, where is he? No point inquiring as to the girleen. That barn twenty-seven's become her north star this meeting."

Brigid stepped away from Thrall. She discovered that she was frowning. "Barn twenty-seven?"

Sucking noisily at his pipe, Mr. McGreevey joined her. "Arrh, it happens every meeting. Only this time appears she's taken a fancy to a fat ex-jockey with a gift of Jewish blarney, would you believe it? An assistant trainer, but for some reason the colt's not stalled here but entered in the Darby regardless. A feisty black, Hotspur by name."

But Brigid was not listening. She was amused yet puzzled— alerted. And she reminded herself again that not only was Molly not her daughter but that the girl was twenty years old—a woman now?

Then Molly appeared around the corner of the barn, followed by Kevin, who looked even more forlorn. Molly was dressed for riding—skin-tight breeches and an even tighter blue sweater—and Brigid decided: a woman now, yes, full-grown, blossoming, or already bloomed.

Molly performed a graceful curtsy which was more tease than mockery, and then she placed a helmet—a Tress hunt cap covered in black velvet—over her own gleaming dark hair, leaving only two pigtails dangling behind. "Join me for lunch at the chuckwagon downtown, Mr. McGreevey. You'll love it—hot dogs and a tongue-biting stew called chili and barbeques and a concoction called *burgoo!*" She stepped quickly to Irish Thrall, stroking and whispering softly, and the colt lifted his noble head once, nickered, and then nudged his face against hers. Brigid's own mind flashed for only an instant to Andrew Cameron trying to explain the ingredients of burgoo last night in the rooftop restaurant. Kevin stepped to Molly and boosted her up into the tiny racing saddle, avoiding her eye as he handed up the reins. Then he hoisted himself into the enormous Western saddle on his lazy-looking skewbald pony, ignoring the pommel. High on the huge gray Molly sat with confidence, as she always did in the irons—her small face intent with grave pleasure and anticipation, removed from the rest of the world now. A bonny rider. A bonny girl.

"Land of milk and honey, is it?" Mr. McGreevey followed with Brigid behind the two mounts. "Garbage not fit for the gullet of man or beast. A monstrosity called a Big Mac, tall as a cathedral itself, and gobbled down as if the famine was approaching. And on the telly nothin' but dogs and cats devouring horse food which they call beef and chicken and tuna fish, God forgive them for their lies."

"You'll survive," she reassured him, half-listening.

"And no Guinness, only the pale lager, all bubbles and tickling of the tongue, not stout at all."

"Poor Gregory McGreevey," she cooed, "have I dragged him off, body and soul, to a heathen land to perish? But, please, not till he's won the wreath of roses for me."

" 'Tis not a wreath but a blanket, and I think we've made a mistake in not engaging Tim Kantor to come along. These Yank riders are not to me liking, and on a mount accustomed to more civilized ways and courses."

Brigid did not break stride. "If you wish him still, then have him fly. There's time."

"A jockey like Tim Kantor, he's booked by now."

They passed a sorry-looking black groom sloshing water onto the flanks of a bay and scrubbing him down. A lanky stablehand held the rope with one hand and lit a cigarette with the other. "I am draggin' ass this day," the groom said. The stablehand blew smoke: "Hung?" And the groom shook his head sadly: "Hung? I ain't hung, boy, I is *dayd*." To which the boy replied, "No sheet?"

Smiling, amused at her trainer's quick embarrassed glance in her direction, Brigid reached the gate to the track. The two horses had passed onto the brown dirt, where an outrider in a red coat and black derby helmet sat watching and alert for trouble of any sort. A sign read: Helmets Must Be Worn Beyond This Point.

Gregory McGreevey again produced his watch on the gold chain. And sighed. "Trainers and riders here seem to know little of pace. Only what they can read off the face of a watch. Clockings only." He uttered a sound. "When, truth to tell, it's pace that counts in the reckoning." Then, as if he'd been thinking it all along, he said around his pipe: "I've a notion, Mrs. Tyrone, that if we discharged with the red tape and sich, our Molly herself could qualify for an apprentice-jockey bug and ride our Thrall come Saturday."

The shock was like a blow. Deep and hard. She could not speak.

She was aware of Gregory McGreevey waiting; she was aware of her own silence.

"Rather," the trainer wheedled, "than put the Thrall into the hands of one of these fly-by-night jockeys knowing nothing of his nature and ways."

She did speak then. She recognized the words but not her voice: "In no circumstances will Molly Muldoon ride in a race. Understand that, Mr. McGreevey. Misunderstand it at your peril." There was a coldness through her, and she glimpsed the concern and regret in the man's eyes as she turned away. Where? She wished only to flee now. She moved. Past the ambulance which was always at the track gate: an elongated taxicab in appearance, painted yellow, with the words *Invalid Carrier* printed on the side.

She was conscious of a large woman passing, nodding pleasantly, but by the time she realized that she had met Rachel Stoddard twice last night, the older woman with the crest of shining silver hair was beyond earshot, walking with a cane and heavy dignity in the direction of the Derby barn. A picture of Ancient Mariner flashed in Brigid's mind: deep-chested, forbidding, powerful. The magnificent patrician who loved classical music. And Brigid wondered in that instant whether someday she herself might be walking alone, perhaps with a cane, toward some stable to see a prized horse, the grand dame, a *character*, her life done, her own brilliant red hair faded—and what of the years between now and then? Danny, where are you? Help me. I only *appear* strong and secure, Danny. I'm really only the bogman's daughter you married, a girl still and a victim of ancient and dark forebodings—

"Would you like to sit down, Mrs. Tyrone?"

She recognized the voice before she turned. Somehow she had arrived at the miniature grandstand known in Europe as the guinea stand: only eight or nine aluminum runners in a tier with steps. Andrew Cameron was standing up in the second row. His iron-gray head was bare, and he wore a suede hacking jacket with a waistcoat of Cameron plaid and no tie or ascot, shirt collar youthfully open. Odd—when had she noticed a man's clothes before? Flustered, feeling altogether foolish of a sudden, she heard the lilt in her tone as she asked, "Do I seem so old as to require a seat, Mr. Cameron?"

At once she realized that her words might be construed as coquetry, which she hated, or as a bid for a compliment, or reassurance, which she despised. But Andrew Cameron only smiled and reached with his hand, ungloved, which grasped hers, ungloved, and instantly she felt the confusion and foolishness deepen in her. The seats were only half-occupied. Andrew Cameron had field glasses slung around his neck, but he was not using them. Voices floated back from the track, and the double-echo sounds of hoofs thudding, and one rider singing something about rock-and-roll, rock-and-roll.

She found herself huddled in the seat, her eyes trying to spot Molly and the Thrall on the track. She also found herself, to her own astonishment, explaining to Andrew Cameron the origin of the term *guinea stand*: Dating back two hundred years in English racing to the days when stablehands were paid four guineas a day, it was a stand along the backstretch, across the track from the infield, the homestretch, and the grandstands, from which, free of charge, they could watch the morning workouts and the afternoon races. Then she broke off, her eyes evading his. "You know all this, don't you?"

She turned. Andrew Cameron was gazing through the glasses now, his lips smiling. What had she been doing, nattering away like a schoolgirl, boring the poor man? Her face stinging with childish humiliation and dismay, she felt an impulse to stand up and run.

But Andrew Cameron lowered the glasses then and turned to face her. His gray eyes glinted with amusement, but warmly. He spoke, however, with a certain gravity now: "It did occur to me during the night, Mrs. Tyrone—and I'm sure your trainer is as aware of it as I am—that there's a certain risk in bringing over a colt like yours and then asking one of our native riders to steer him."

Anger came then, and with it, a quick confidence. Chin lifted, she asked, "Mr. Cameron, have you been speaking with Gregory McGreevey?"

Lifting one brow, Andrew Cameron almost frowned. "I'm sorry, I've never had the pleasure of meeting the gentleman."

"With Molly then?"

"Last night. You were there." He appeared sincerely puzzled. "A charming girl."

"She's charmed the two of you, as I see it. Are you trying to convince me that Molly should ride in the Derby?"

Andrew Cameron considered, his solid, rugged face grave again. "I said then and I'll say again: I agree with your trainer. Racing's a violent and dangerous business. I wouldn't want a daughter of mine riding."

Daughter. So . . . he had guessed. Judged by bloodlines alone, Molly was only Daniel's niece. In reality, though, she had become Brigid's daughter. Yes. And if Andrew Cameron had guessed that much, then what more?

Had he divined that after escorting her to the door of her suite— had she really had the audacity to say that it was not necessary as she didn't think she was in danger of being *raped*?—she had entered the sitting room, aware of Molly sleeping in one of the two bedrooms, and had then stood in the open windows for a long quiet time, remembering Kimberley Cameron's obscenities and the way the poor tormented girl had left their table to toss her hotel key onto another, remembering her own decision to remain detached and uninvolved no matter what? It was all too sad, too complex, and already so fixed in an inevitability that she could not decipher—she was herself, alone, and she cherished that. Her aloneness had allowed her to come this far. Last night she had made a firm commitment to herself to *remain* detached, and now, this morning, she had only to cling to her decision.

"Mrs. Tyrone," Andrew Cameron's voice said now, after Molly went thundering by, mouth close to Irish Thrall's ear, "you asked me to call you Brigid last night." She did not turn to him, but he handed her the glasses nevertheless, and through them she picked out the dark gray movement on the far curve. "Also, last night you believed that I was performing a courtesy for a friend." Lowering the glasses, she waited, recalling Nora McGeehan in Kilkenny; if the man denied the obvious, she would have naught more to do with him. "Well, I was doing just that." He leaned closer. "Now, courtesies discharged, I am asking you to dinner. Tonight. And alone. Not to accommodate a mutual friend but to accommodate me. It's why I came here this morning."

She did turn then, her whole body twisting, the track forgotten. That had been hard for him. As difficult as if he had been not a man in his fifties but a schoolboy in his teens. The realization touched something in her. What? She did not know. All she knew was that there was a thumping in her, as hard and fast and thunderous as those hoofbeats on the track.

"I think," she said softly, "I think that I would like that very much."

A sad tallyho this morning, friends and foes. Bad tidings from the West. Mr. Stuart Rosser, owner of the Lazy R Ranch in New Mexico and of the Derby entrant, Fireaway, succumbed last night to what the official coroner's report terms "an acute myocardial infarction." The tragedy occurred aboard his own private plane while he was en route here with his wife, the former Christine Norvelle of this city, and his trainer, Owen Chalmers, who was piloting the plane. Mr. Rosser has had a history of heart trouble, and anticipating the Derby has caused heart failure in lesser hopefuls. The question now is whether Fireaway, heavily favored in some quarters, will run on Saturday next. What will his widow, fondly remembered as a lovely Louisville belle in social circles hereabouts, decide? Fireaway, with an impressive record—winner of both the San Vincente Stakes and the California Derby—is already stabled in the Derby barn at the Downs. If he does run, it will be the first time in the annals of these shenanigans that two horses, trained by two brothers, ever competed against each other. The other is the colt named Hotspur, owned and trained by Clayton Chalmers. Backside scuttlebutt, not always reliable but now confirmed by Clay Chalmers himself, casts some doubt on whether this little black will make it to the starting gate—but more of this in my broadcast tomorrow morning before the Derby Trial. Our condolences, Mrs. Rosser. And forgive us for proceeding now to matters of less import.

The James Olivers and their son Leonard, of the blueblood clan and owners three of True Blue, the only other Derby entry besides Hotspur and Dealer's Choice scheduled to compete in the Trial, are rumored to have engaged fifty-four hotel and motel rooms for more than a hundred guests whom they will entertain in bluegrass splendor throughout Derby Week. True Blue, ever a threat, rarely a winner, may be one to fix in your binoculars tomorrow and on Saturday.

Another fine colt, not a Derby entrant but considered by many (your obedient servant included, please) to be a beautiful piece of horseflesh and already nominated for the Preakness and the Belmont, by name Eric the Red—for some heroic character out of Norse sagas, I am told—will thunder out of the chute for the seven-furlong sprint tomorrow. His owners, an artist and his wife uprooted from Iceland by a volcanic eruption, I understand, are decorating the social scene handsomely this year.

Not to be outdone in the social disgraces, the owners of one of the most prestigious Derby entrants, the respected and beloved Vincent Van—who won the Wood Memorial in a thrilling photofinish—the Harold Johnstons of Thistle Hill Farms are conducting a nonstop house party in their columned mansion in Bourbon County outside of Paris, Kentucky, only a few miles down the pike. Envious word has it that bourbon flows all day and champagne all night, with

81

burgoo, Alaskan salmon from Ketchican and sharkfin soup from Bangkok, take your choice, smoked kippers and sweetbreads always at the bubble, and the voice of the pollywog can be heard hiccoughing in the land. Sheikhs and maharajahs brush oily hems with our domestic doers and shafters, stockbrokers, labor leaders, cabinet members, and other gurus and their ladies. If ladies they truly are. Devoted Moslems, having left their own womenfolk at home, veiled to the sinuses, loll and lech for bikinied beauties who frolic in the pools by day and in the bedrooms by night.

Rain has now been predicted officially—meaning that it is very unlikely. If the scientific soothsayers are correct, your obedient servant Count Wyatt Slingerland's choice in tomorrow's sixth race, the Derby Trial, is the aforementioned Hotspur—but only if the heavens open soon and wide.

Meanwhile, happy skateboarding, one and all, and yoicks!

Through the intricate pattern of dark branches and white locust blossoms and green leaves he could see only a jagged piece of sky: dim, inscrutable, with no hint now of the sun through which they had driven or of the rain which he knew now would fall today or tonight. Kimberley lay stretched out beside him on the long crushed grass, which smelled damp. The surface of the slow moving stream, really a wide pond here, was calm and shadowless. She slept. Again. And, as it had the few times when he had awakened during the night in her hotel bedroom, a longing returned in him: to care for her, to cherish and protect. But, again, his mind was shadowed. He could picture them together driving highways, at tracks, in motel rooms, but he could not imagine her waiting for him in some apartment or house. He could not see them together in a home. Yet it was a home that some deep and vital part of him ached for, probably because it was what he had never really known.

Again aware of all this, he turned his head to look at her. She no longer wore the breeches or the boots or the black turtleneck sweater in which she had appeared backside hours ago. One bare arm curved over her eyes, her pale hair long and loose and sprawling, she was unashamedly naked. No mistaking her womanliness, but now she seemed a child, vulnerable, all defenses lowered, all inner torment and confusions temporarily calmed. He had the unreal and transitory impression that she was free. And that anything was within reach. Possible. But . . . could she ever be his really? He had come this long way, in miles, in time—to claim her, to possess her?—yet the lowering dusk filled him with a dark foreboding that his mind could not throw off, even here, even now. He looked up again at the patch of unreadable sky.

"You listen to Elijah now, son," the old groom had said. "No cause to let that sunshine ruffle up your blood. Gonna rain by nightfall sure."

And then Kimberley, who had surprised him by suddenly appearing at the barn, had looped her arm through his and had laughed in Elijah's direction: "You're right, Elijah." And the stolid black giant had actually grinned. "Listen to your groom, Clay," Kimberley had said. "Look at Hotspur. Look at all those horses, darling!" And he had looked: every other horse along the shedrow was reaching down and out with his mouth. "Almost every one of them is yawning!" she had cried in delight, hugging his arm against her breast. "A sure sign, Clay, you know that!" As they had moved away together he had caught sight of Bernie watching: His eyes, deep in the flesh of his face, looked troubled, concerned—apprehensive. "You take care of that boy now, missie, you hear?" Elijah's heavy voice had followed them as they strolled toward the Derby barn. Imagine the silent Elijah speaking that way.

But that had been hours ago now, and there was no rain in the air. Kimberley still slept, lips parted. He did not move; he did not want to wake her. Time seemed to have come to a halt here. Her loveliness was, for now at least, his and his alone.

"When you didn't come back," she had said on the way to the Derby barn, "I had to come to you. Oh, Clay, I don't believe this, any of it. Can you understand, darling?" And then she had let go of his arm and stopped walking. "Look, Clay"—her voice a stunned whisper now, breathless—"look at him." His eyes had followed her bright blue gaze.

Starbright was out of his stall, surrounded by reporters and photographers, and his magnificence, to a horseman's eye, was astounding. Neither large nor small, his light chestnut coat, almost sorrel, radiant in the sun, his conformation a thing of perfect proportion, his whole body, although quite still with lifted head, seemed to give off an electric power suggesting speed. His manner was serene, princely, not quite disdainful. The single star on his forehead was a white jewel. Even with the clatter and whir of cameras, the shuffle of feet, and the chatter of voices Clay felt that he was alone, choked with a reluctant astonishment. He had seen photographs, he knew the colt's past performance record, he had read the accounts of racing experts; but he had not been prepared for what he saw. And then, with a sharp, ugly pang of guilt, he thought of Hotspur, and a slow foreshadowing of inevitable defeat moved poisonously in his blood.

He saw Kimberley step to place her head with tenderness against the colt's, and he heard more cameras clicking and whirring. He saw Pepe Benitez join her—the jockey with the legendary golden hands, famed for hand-riding, without whip, so many champions to victory, including three Derby winners to date. Another survivor—broken bones, spleen removed, wires inside, hospitals, surgery, indescribable pain—Pepe Benitez was a smiling little man, not only admired but universally loved. His soft almond-shaped eyes looked up at Kimberley as Starbright was led back to his stall. There was fond reproach on his smooth copper-colored face. Shaking his head of silken black hair, he held up one hand, displaying a ring in the shape of a diamond-studded horseshoe. His black eyes glittered, and Kimberley, as if brushing aside whatever he was saying, smiled, teasing, and then leaned down to kiss him on the forehead before rejoining Clay.

Taking his hand, she had led him to the parking area and then among the cars and trucks to a gleaming red Porsche 924 with its sun-roof removed. She had stopped and faced him, a quiet, pleased mischief in her eyes as she released his hand. In his palm were two keys on a gold chain.

"You drive," she said. "It's yours."

He had driven. Furiously, slamming the five-speed transmission into gear. Angry, bewildered—at her, himself, the day, the world. He had understood then what Pepe Benitez had been saying to her; he had been chiding her for giving him the expensive ring on his finger. Clay remembered her gifts in the past: cufflinks that he had never worn, hacking jackets and fine Italian belts and silk shirts and ties. He had recalled his confusion of seven years ago—and his conclusion that she felt compelled. As if she had to buy love. Or, having it, doubted it. As if she had to pay for it in some way. As if he—no one—could love her for herself alone.

He had driven out of the city fast, dangerously, giving in to his fury, risking arrest, risking worse. And then compassion had taken over, so that by the time they were in the country, her hair blowing as they turned off the highway onto a narrow shaded road smelling of fresh air and grass and wood bark and the earth itself, he was actually on the verge of tears for the first time in years.

Slowly, in silence, they had driven between rolling white-fenced pastures, infinite shadings of sea green, where horses grazed and chased and frisked, passing signs with the names of some of the most renowned farms in the country, catching sight every mile or so of huge columned houses and stables and paddocks, and finally he had taken her hand in his. Her hair had settled into a golden spray on her shoulders, and when he turned to her, her face looked as he knew it would: tremulous and baffled. And contrite.

But when she spoke, her voice was a sharp whisper: "Screw you, Clay Chalmers."

He had not explained. Or tried to. It had always been hopeless in the past. What he wanted to tell her was that she had no need to buy his love, now or ever.

"I was too young to remember it now," he said, "but I lived around here once. My old man used to talk about it sometimes. This is the old Frankfort Road, called Shady Lane. He used to boast that horses foaled around here in one year won stakes races somewhere in the world every two days."

"Was your father a bastard too?"

They passed another sign: Thistle Hill Farms. And below that, in smaller letters: Home of Vincent Van. Her hand tightened in his, and she shook hair from her face. "They haven't moved Vincent Van to the Downs yet. But since he won the Wood, I think he's the only one Mr. Arnold's really worried about."

Jason Arnold. Clay had often wondered whether Jason Arnold knew what his employer had done to punish Clay for what had happened to Lord Randolph. Somehow he could not believe that Jason Arnold, who had taught him so much at Blue Ridge, could have been a party to anything as rotten as blackballing. Regardless of which, he was here, wasn't he? He shot the Porsche forward. He was here and he was with Andrew Cameron's daughter.

It had been only a mile or so farther along that for some obscure reason he had slowed and turned onto an even narrower road of gravel. Why? No quick memory of childhood flashed in his mind— only a vague feeling, certainly not recognition. Kimberley did not ask. And in a short distance they reached a placid stream and entered the dusky tunnel of a covered bridge. Its planks clattered under the wheels, and its old wooden walls, slatted with light, seemed to be rotting.

Halfway across, out of nowhere, Kimberley had said, "Let's stop. Let's make love."

And so they had made love. On the bank of the stream, well off the road, in this cove of flowering locust trees. They had made love wordlessly and with abandon but slowly and lingeringly, without desperation. And afterward she had stretched and then slept with thoughtless, childish surrender.

He heard a sound now—a low distant growl as of a bombardment many miles away. Then only the buzz and hum of insects again. He could not trust his ears. He dared not give in to hope. He waited—and it came again, a grumbling in the west, definite this time. Then it was gone.

There was a dazzling zig-zag of light and almost simultaneously the deafening, shattering explosion of thunder, and at once he saw the surface of the water pockmarked with huge splashes. Then came the downpour, drenching and cold, as if the floodgates of the sky had been blasted open. He stood, and Kimberley sat up, uttering a sound, and then she was scrambling to her feet, face streaming, smiling into his face, triumphant and radiant, shouting, "I told you! *They* know. The horses always know!"

When he had rung the room, Brigid had invited Andrew Cameron to have a cocktail before going to dinner, and after an infinitesimal pause Andrew Cameron had accepted in what was for him a positively lighthearted voice: "I'm on my way." Over cocktails in the sitting room—the man drank Scotch—he amused her in his soft-edged accent with tales of races won and races lost because of the wrongheaded miscalculations of trainers and riders who invariably justified themselves by placing the blame on the poor horses. It was a side of Andrew Cameron that she had glimpsed only in snatches the evening before, and he told the stories with such wry humor that she found herself—would you believe this!—laughing aloud.

She had entertained misgivings all through the day since she had accepted his invitation so readily in the guinea stand, and if it had not been for Daniel's teasing voice in her mind she might have rung his room to cancel out the evening. But by the time he had helped her don the long rain cape and they were going along the corridor she was relaxed and at ease—positively expectant.

Going down in the lift Andrew Cameron introduced her to a Mr. and Mrs. James Oliver, a hearty red-faced man and his tall dark-haired wife, who were accompanied by a bearded young man in an automated wheelchair, their son, all three in very high spirits indeed. Andrew wished them luck on the morrow, and she recalled then that the Olivers were owners of a colt named True Blue, a favorite in tomorrow's Derby Trial, and that they were hosting a week-long gala in various hotels all over the city. The Olivers invited them both to join them, but Andrew refused in his best courtly manner.

Then the doors slid open onto the lobby, and rather abruptly they were face to face with Andrew's daughter. She was drenched, her hair darkened and matted, and, of all things, she was barefoot. She held her boots between her fingers, and her face was positively aglow, mischief and gaiety sparkling in her eyes. Beside her was the young man whom Brigid had met briefly at the banquet last night and whom she had seen in the restaurant later. He too was soaking wet. As Andrew stepped aside for her, Brigid remembered seeing Kimberley drop a key onto the young man's table; apparently the invitation had not gone wanting.

"Andrew!" his daughter cried. First names for parents always made Brigid uneasy, and she felt herself bracing inside: what now, what next? But, smiling, Kimberley kissed her wet hand and placed her fingers against her father's cheek in greeting, standing carefully back so as not to dampen his dinner jacket. Then: "Oh, Mrs. Tyrone, may I present Clay Chalmers? He tried to drown me in an open car."

Clay Chalmers nodded pleasantly without speaking, and at once his brown eyes returned, quiet and inscrutable, to Andrew, as if waiting for Andrew to speak first.

Which Andrew did: "How are you Chalmers?" But his voice was sharp, clipped, politely cold. Startled, Brigid glanced at him: A subtle but definite alteration had occurred in his face. It was not only aloof, it was almost glacial. And neither of the two men made any move to extend a hand.

But Mr. Chalmers did say, flatly, without any intonation whatever: "Never better, sir."

Then Kimberley stepped to Brigid. "Mrs. Tyrone, I owe you an apology." The lovely young face was somber now, almost timid, hesitant. "Andrew's too loyal to tell you, but I'm often impossible. I behave abominably sometimes." Then she changed again. She made a quick graceful curtsy that did not *seem* at least to be mocking, only happy and girlish and filled with fun. "So forgive me my trespasses. Please."

Again startled, Brigid said, "We all behave abominably at times, Miss Cameron. It's our way of proving we're human, isn't it?" Then she took Andrew's arm. "You'd better tell your daughter it's a hot tub for her now or pneumonia by morning."

Somewhat quickly, Brigid thought, Clay Chalmers said: "It's on our agenda now, Mrs. Tyrone. A shower." He might as well have said *together*.

Andrew did not speak. He led her through the lobby toward the doors opening onto the indoor parking area, and behind them she heard the lift's doors sliding together. So that's the way of it, is it? Last night's suspicions returned: the perplexed, possibly possessive father, the fractious daughter chafing at her bit. Or was there more to it?

"She's really charming," Brigid said.

"It depends on the circumstances," Andrew said. And no more.

Be done with it now. It's no affair of yours whatsoever, Brigid Tyrone, to be sure. And God willing, so it will remain.

In the elevator—which they shared with two Japanese gentlemen in dark suits—Clay was sick. Remembering again, this time his mind choked and flooding with the memory: Andrew Cameron's face, white as the snow drifting down, covering the ground, the flat wooden-sounding blows, the taste of blood, pain exploding on one side of his face then the other, Kimberley's shrill cries turning into screams of protest as it went on, calling Andrew's name, himself upright, remaining stubbornly upright regardless but not striking back, not even protecting his face, taking the savagery, no, not proud but uncertain, still drunk, not knowing whether he deserved it, whether he *had* unlatched the stall gate, unlocked the stable door—had he done that, had he? why?—still the huge fists crashing, one side of his jaw, then the other, bone against bone, the crunching sound, his mouth filling with blood, and then afterward, alone, retching, whole body heaving, hands braced against the paddock fence, the whisky and the vomit and the blood staining the snow, all the while knowing it was over, all of it, Kimberley, Blue Ridge, racing, love, his life—

But . . . it was not over. Here he was on an elevator in the best hotel in Louisville, Kentucky, Kimberley beside him, the Derby only five days off, and Kimberley's voice, a loud conspiratorial whisper with laughter muted in it—what was she saying?

"I only thought we'd have more room in my suite, darling." Was that what she was saying? What did she mean? "You do need such room when you screw, don't you? And my husband won't be there. The bastard's cheating on me again."

It came to him. He glanced at the two Japanese: one heavy-set with bulbous eyes behind thick black-rimmed glasses, the other thin and tall and younger, demeanor sober, eyes forward, expressionless.

"I can't say I blame your husband," Clay heard himself say in a parched voice, breathing again, relaxing. "If I were your husband, I'd cheat on you too."

"You cheat on me anyway." Kimberley brought her wet body against his, clutching his arm against her breasts. "And afterward," she cooed, "in about two lovely, lovely hours, I know the sweetest little Oriental restaurant for dinner. The saki's not warm enough, but the sukiyaki's heavenly. Only the chopsticks are bent."

"That," Clay said, beginning to enjoy himself again, "probably explains the soy sauce on your bosom."

She stepped back. Her breasts were full and pointed and detailed beneath the clinging black sweater. "I thought," she said severely, "you promised never to discuss my breasts in public again."

"I thought," he said, "that I promised not to discuss either one of them after midnight."

"Do you know your history at all?" she asked. "Do you know that Anne Boleyn had three?"

The elevator glided to a stop. Kimberley stepped out, fluttering her eyelids demurely, and Clay turned to the two Japanese and bowed from the waist stiffly. Both bowed formally in return, faces still impassive. "Sayonara," Clay said, "and may Fuji Mist come in honorable third place after Hotspur and Starbright."

"Starbright and Hotspur," Kimberley corrected, and the doors came together.

Then Kimberley was leaning helplessly against the wall, bent over, whooping with laughter. "We forgot," she said, "Clay, we forgot to say 'Remember Pearl Harbor.'"

And then, still laughing, she went racing down the hall. In the foyer and sitting room she did not pause but crossed swiftly toward the bedroom, pulling the wet sweater over her head. "Don't dawdle now, you heard the lady, it's pneumonia time in Piccadilly."

Clay was alone. Shivering now for the first time. How long after that night in Virginia when his blood had streamed down onto the snow, how long had it taken for the suspicion to take root—the conviction, really—that Andrew Cameron, that chivalrous and charming gentleman who was capable of barbaric violence, had himself unlocked the stall gate and the stable door? Would a man who prized his foundation sire so highly be willing to sacrifice the horse in order to prevent his daughter from going off with his assistant trainer? Was his daughter even more prized? Would he go to any lengths to prevent her from going off with any man?

Any man.

"The water's wonderful, come on in," her voice called.

He began to undress. How much later still—he remembered that he had been mucking out stalls at some bush track in Ohio—how much later had it been that he had made up his mind to have his revenge?

She appeared wet and dripping in the bedroom doorway. Her mood had changed. "Clay," she said soberly, very softly. "Clay, she's gone."

"Who?"

"Her. That other Kimberley. The one I hate. She's gone forever, I think." Then she added in a whisper: "Thanks to you."

And then she disappeared again.

Himself naked now, he was no longer shivering. When Hotspur won the Derby, Andrew Cameron would have no excuse to object. No legitimate excuse. Only that other one, that inner secret one that Clay was now certain, seven years later, had driven the man to kill his own prize stud.

Rain fell in torrents behind the tall windows as he moved, his blood scorching his body, his triumph blazing sweetly in his guts. He went lightly, buoyantly, into the bedroom and crossed toward the hot steaming bathroom.

Proceeding from the elevator toward their penthouse apartment, Hosomoto Takashi asked his traveling companion and assistant, Naomi Yogi, whether he thought the young man and woman who had just disembarked were inebriated. Yogi allowed himself a faint and obscene smile and replied that Americans often played games with each other before, after, and sometimes even during sex. While the younger man unlocked the door his employer ventured the remark that while he had, as Yogi knew, a most appealing wife in Kyoto and while he had experienced all the varied pleasures of the geisha, he sometimes was given to wonder about American women, but he did not have sufficient mastery of the English tongue to make the acquaintance of such creatures. Yogi, known as Georgie at the track here, then understood what was expected of him. But, although Hosomoto Takashi was a man of wealth with many holdings and many racing horses, he was reluctant to spend yen, always explaining that he did not wish the Japanese to be compared to the Arabs in American eyes. He was also very short and very ugly and without his thick glasses almost blind. Yogi, on the other hand, was taller, possibly because his father, whom he had never seen and whom he hated as he hated all white-skinned people, was an American GI during the hated occupation. He stepped aside, held open the doors, and mentioned, almost apologetically, that such an arrangement might involve considerable expense. Hosomoto Takashi waved a hand in such a way as to indicate not only that he was dismissing that part of the matter entirely but that Yogi could inflate the price so as to provide himself with some extra wagering money. Mr. Hosomoto, who could never understand why in this country one's family name and given name were reversed in order, then set out one stipulation, only one: The woman must be blond. True blond, was that understood? In the foyer he warned that if any attempt to deceive him was made, he would surely know in time, would he not? And in that event he would be highly displeased, very highly displeased. Then, beginning to unbutton his coat while Yogi helped, resenting as always the menial aspects of his position, Mr. Hosomoto wondered aloud whether all American women spoke so frankly and in public of their bosoms. Moving to pour himself a Scotch whisky, which he preferred to any Oriental beverage, he asked, "Who was Anne Boleyn?"

*   *   *

The airport had changed. The city had changed. She had changed. Face it, lady, you're not the Christine Norvelle who left Louisville . . . how many years ago? She had tried to figure out the exact number of years on the plane. She had in fact figured it out, bombed as she'd been. But now she was more bombed—they keep *plying* you with the stuff!—and all she was certain of was that she was forty-six, no forgetting that, no evading that odious statistic, at least in your own mind. Forty-six and home again, a widow now, a widow woman and far from merry, very damned far. It was raining, and hard, and she had always hated Louisville when it rained. Some of the streets looked familiar: the small houses, white clapboard and red brick, whitewashed cement porches and walkways. But it'd taken her a while to realize that the street lights and lamp posts were different: very modern, not the kind that once swayed pleasantly with any slight wind. Now that they were on the super-highway, darkness on both sides, it was like being on any such throughway, here or in New Mexico or California.

Owen was wearing one of his finest gabardine suits, Western-styled as usual, with silk darts and yoked back, and the Italian silk tie she'd given him after Fireaway's win at Bay Meadows, one of the wins, San Francisco anyway—she recalled selecting it. It was the sort of gift that she could give a trainer without arousing Stuart's suspicions, or anyone's—although she doubted that the ranch hands had any illusions.

Stuart. He had never really been even remotely distrustful. Or if he had, she'd prefer not to think about it now. Bless the poor man, he'd been a kind one—not lover or husband for the last ten years or so, but through no fault of his. He'd been a kind and generous man, and she had made his life as pleasant and rewarding as it was possible for her to make it in the circumstances.

On the flight she had made up her mind that while in Louisville—and she hadn't the faintest idea what she would do afterward—she would see Owen as little as possible and would sleep with him not at all. Not punishment, although it would be hard; it was just that, strange as it might seem to someone else, sleeping with Owen on the ranch with Stuart always nearby and ill had not been so unseemly as sleeping with him now, only hours after poor

Joseph Hayes

Stuart's death, would be. At least in her mind. She might have shed many of the niceties and civilized rules of living, but at least for a while now she would take refuge in the rules by which she had been reared.

But Owen had looked so tall and handsome waiting for her at the exit ramp, sober and dignified, that her fine resolve had all but dissolved as she shook hands formally and thanked him for coming. He did not inquire as to the arrangements she had made during the day—she shuddered slightly whenever she thought of Stuart cold and alone in that strange city, abandoned until she could decide what to do—and now they were en route to the house in the country which, since it would be vacant except for the caretaker, her old friend Marylou Wohlforth had insisted that she and Stuart occupy for Derby Week. The Wohlforths always took refuge in Paris during Derby Week. Thinking that it would be quieter than a hotel, for Stuart's sake she had agreed, although she herself would have welcomed the excitement and social whirlwind of the city. Now that it didn't matter she felt slightly cheated: The house was obviously miles from town.

After inquiring how she was, his blue eyes touchingly concerned as they roamed over her carefully made-up face, Owen had led her to the black Lincoln, which he had thoughtfully rented and which he drove with the same easy abandon and skill with which he rode a horse. He was speaking of the other Derby entries, and she was only half-listening, the gin beginning to wear off. He would skip, he said, any jokes about a chocolate-brown named Also Ran, and as for the three foreign runners, well, Tomy Lee in 1959 and Omar Khayyam in 1917 were the only Derby winners not foaled in the States, and there was one called Prescription who was likely to trail the field if Also Ran didn't. His own brother had entered a horse named Hotspur, did she know? Well, he'd know more about him and the one called True Blue after tomorrow's Trial, although that race was only seven furlongs, and he doubted that Hotspur could last a mile and a quarter. One of the favorites, Ancient Mariner, had a rheumatic condition among other ailments, but he could spell trouble. Of the two odds-on favorites, Starbright was from Virginia, and only one winner, Reigh Count, had ever been foaled

94

in Virginia, and he had won the Derby back in 1928; and he had not yet seen Vincent Van because he was still stalled at his own farm only a few miles east. Very formal, very correct, Owen might have been any trainer giving his employer a rundown on the probable field. Very likely he had done this with Stuart before every race. Owen had always been a great believer in statistics and calculations. But damned if it didn't seem strange—in fact, Owen himself seemed a stranger. Until she realized that of course he too had decided that it would not be fit and proper to continue their familiar relationship now. The idea left her suspended somewhere between relief and disappointment. How, without Owen, without Owen in bed, was she to get through the next five days?

He leaned now and snapped open the glove compartment. In the tiny light she saw a silver flask glinting, and relief swept through her. Even as she unscrewed the cap she knew that it would be gin. And that it would be cold. It was only faintly flavored with vermouth, and the dry bitter taste filled her mouth, flowed pleasantly down her throat, and at once heated her blood. When she extended the flask, he shook his head and for the first time laughed. The sound filled the car, and it was a good sound, a very good sound, and she knew then how much she had missed it during the endless empty day.

Some time had passed; she had no inkling as to how much time, except that the flask was empty now and a very fine glow had settled over her, and the fields alongside the Lincoln—for they had turned off the interstate and onto a curving country road—looked familiar and very dark green, the way the fields outside Louisville had always looked, the way she had remembered them in the dry, dusty wastes of New Mexico where, for a while, she had been happy and had not missed them because Stuart was young then and she was young too, unimaginably young, and they had been in love. She realized that she had sunk more deeply into the plush seat and her mind was floating and loose again and she was wondering why, once they had been beyond the reach of curious eyes at the airport, Owen had not at least stopped the car and kissed her. Just once, only once, why not, one kiss didn't mean they had to sleep together—

Owen was talking again. But business again. The Minstrel, win-

ner of the Irish and English Derbies . . . syndicated at nine million
dollars. And Seattle Slew, *after* winning the Triple Crown, was syndicated at twelve. "It took a hell of a lot of doing, Chris, but I put it
together. Eight million if we win just the Derby itself, and twice
that if Fireaway can take the Preakness and the Belmont as well.
Sixteen, Chris—sixteen million dollars! And Mr. Rosser agreed it
was one hell of a deal."

Her mind refused to concentrate. But . . . but *had* Stu agreed?
She recalled, though vaguely, that he had said that he was not in
racing for the money anyway and that Owen had laughed, that
night in the dining room after dinner, with the candles bringing out
the wooden shine on the heavy beams and coloring the adobe walls
and the patterns of the Indian hangings on the walls, and said that
everyone was in racing for the money. Then Stu had teased that
Owen's share would be ten percent, wouldn't it, and that would
amount to close to a million if Fireaway won the Derby alone, so
he could understand how from Owen's point of view it was a desira-
ble deal, and—he had shrugged his shrunken, wide shoulders—he
was sorry, but he would prefer to wait and see how Fireaway ran on
the Eastern tracks. Maybe they could keep the horse for more years
of racing and get even more when they sold him to stand at stud;
after all, Stu had said—but not sadly, she recalled—he did not
know how many years he had left, and he would prefer to spend
them racing the only really first-rate horse it had been his luck to
own; he would never have another one like Fireaway in the time he
had left.

It was what she remembered, so that now, with Owen driving
and silent again, as if he were waiting for her answer, she said, "Stu
was against the . . . against the syndication deal, wasn't he,
Owen?"

Very calmly, very reasonably, Owen said, "He was against it
because he wanted to go on racing Fireaway under his colors. But,
Chris, Fireaway's not the only horse *you* can own. I picked him for
you, didn't I? And for a lousy seventy thousand."

It was true. It was reasonable. Still—

She wished she hadn't had so much to drink during the day and
on the plane. She wished Owen had not brought along the flask.

"I can pick others, honey. And you can race them all over the world—"

She wished she could stop drinking altogether, and for good. She was always wishing that lately. And now Owen had even taken care of the future: racing all over the world. She'd never thought of that. But with all that money—

"Hell, honey, you could buy a farm here in Kentucky and to hell with the Lazy R—"

Had she ever told Owen how much she missed—

If she had just one more drink, to clear her mind. Eight million dollars. Maybe sixteen. Million, *million*—her mind couldn't even comprehend such figures. Mama and Papa, in Palm Beach now, they'd always been considered reasonably wealthy but—

"Not tonight, Owen. Please. Let's not discuss it tonight. Please."

"I wouldn't even bring it up, honey, if Kinlay Brown wasn't pressing me. These are big shots. They can pick and choose. They've given us enough time. It's no deal anyway if Fireaway lets us down Saturday. The colt's registered in both your names. All they need is your signature now that—"

He broke off, and her mind refused to finish the sentence. She was lost without Stuart. Her loss swept over her again, as it had on the plane, threatening to engulf her, but her mind hardened. "Not tonight, Owen," she said. "Not now." She did not say please again.

Owen swung the wheel and the car rolled down a long brick-paved avenue between high trees. In the headlights she saw the red-brick structure, breathtaking in its simple symmetry, with verandah and high white columns framing the front entrance. Its gracious loveliness was redolent of her childhood: parties and balls and summer dresses and music playing and laughter in the rooms, among the trees. She felt a tightening all through her body. The driveway curved in a crescent, and Owen brought the car to a gliding halt before the steps. Neither of them moved. Until she turned to him.

His eyes were on her in the dimness, tender and waiting. "It's open and ready, Chris." Then he reached and covered her hand with his, lightly. "I gave the caretaker the week off. It's ours for the duration."

Ours. She had been mistaken then: He did not intend to keep his distance. And why should he? Why should they both deny themselves? Here, miles from anywhere, the house theirs, the week stretching ahead! Owen had decided. *He* had made the decision for them both.

She was flooded with relief as she stepped out of the seat before Owen could come around with the umbrella. Her legs were weak, as if air flowed in her veins, and she missed a step going up to the verandah in the rain, and then Owen was at her side, unlocking the heavy door, which then seemed to float silently open at his touch. The hall was high and spacious with a wide staircase curving delicately upward. And soon she seemed to be drifting, weightless, buoyant, from room to room: the parlor with its small English piano on spindly legs and the Sheraton sofa and Regency chairs, and a formal dining room with a long table and a Sheraton sideboard, and a smaller family dining room, a fireplace with an oil portrait above. The ranch house seemed, not a thousand miles away but aeons away, planets away. She knew that she was quite drunk, had to be, drunk or dreaming, because in some magical and incredible way she had come home again. Then she was in the upstairs hall, standing in the doorway of a sitting room—and she stopped there, appalled. The walnut secretary was stacked with odds and ends of notes and scraps of paper, with *Racing Forms* and condition books; the rug was strewn with more scribbled calculations, and the walls themselves were covered with charts, inked with those mysterious combinations of numerals that she recognized from Owen's Lazy R office and from the hotel bedrooms she had shared with him at the meetings in California. Then she had been amused. Now—

"What the hell do you call this?" she demanded.

Owen was leaning against the wall of the hallway, Stetson in hand, head tilted. "A man has to have a place where he can operate." He shrugged and his rusty brown beard twisted around his lips. "Unless you'd prefer I use the servants' quarters. They're off the kitchen."

She was not sure. All of a damned sudden she was not sure of *anything*. "I need a drink," she said, numb and suddenly desolate.

He came to her then. He pulled her against him, hard. "There's plenty of booze in the bedroom." He didn't kiss her but his heavy stone-hard body was against hers and the breath went out of her and her bones melted and the craving came back as he did kiss her, forcing her lips open wide, then wider still, his beard bristly, his leatherlike lips hurting hers and his arms crushing her back and ribs, her breasts in pain, and she could feel his penis moving insistently against her while his tongue pressed hers until she thought he would choke her, until she came to quick, vivid life in his arms, shameless, avid, twisting, and ravenous.

When he had reduced her so, when he knew—he always knew—he let go and took a single step back, and there was that slightly derisive blue lust in his narrow eyes, that damned promise of more to come, much more, and the certainty that she had to have what he offered, the animal male arrogance that she hated, loved, hated—

"I'm going to rape you," he said. His tone was ugly and cruel.

If only he wouldn't say it, if only he would do it and not say it—

"Go in the bedroom and take off your wet clothes, all your goddamn clothes, and lay down."

If only he would say *lie down*, not *lay*. Or maybe *lay* was the word. Was that what she was? Was that what she had become?

His voice changed to a low throb, no longer nasty, no longer mean: "I'm going to fuck you till your eyeballs fall out, and then I'm going to go down on you. That's what you want, isn't it?"

No, oh, please, God, no. But she nodded her head: yes, yes, yes.

"Now I'm going to call Kinlay Brown and tell him the deal's on. Tomorrow. Ten o'clock." His tone had become a low caress. "That'll give us plenty of time."

It was all happening too fast. She couldn't think. She couldn't even breathe.

"Plenty of time 'cause, honey, till ten o'clock tomorrow morning I'm going to see how many times I can make you come."

Turning as if drugged—no, actually drugged, not herself at all—without looking back, almost blindly, she moved into the bedroom. The light was already on and dim. Mahogany four-poster bed. Thick family Bible on the bedside table. Slowly she did as he wanted. As she wanted. She saw a table set with cut-glass decanters, bottles. When she was naked, she poured gin into a crystal goblet.

And without sitting she sipped it. The bed had not been turned down: It had been stripped of everything but a single sheet. Leave it to Owen. Leave everything to Owen.

Blindly she went into the bathroom. When she turned on the light, she was staring into a full-length mirror. Her body was still good: waist not what she might have wished for, haunches slim and firm, thanks to the riding, legs long and still good, still damned fine, breasts fuller than they had once been but soft, pointed now, face not pretty but well-proportioned and strong. Once she had longed for small delicate features, a petite feminine body. Once, long, long ago—

She pushed back her chestnut hair, gray in fashionable streaks, and studied her face. The sun had taken its toll: Fine lines sprayed away from her flecked, pale brown eyes.

Men still found her attractive. Not a beauty, but Stuart had always said she was a handsome figure of a woman. Stuart—she must not think of Stuart. Owen found her more than attractive. He had stirred depths of passion in her that she had not even guessed were there. Shameless. Demanding. Abandoned. Lust.

Her glass was empty. Through the open door of the bedroom as she poured she heard his voice from below. Her befuddled mind could not quite make out the words. He was cursing, though— would he curse at Kinlay Brown, or the attorneys? All she heard distinctly was "You heard me. Tonight, I said. Before it gets light." Puzzled, she drank. Why hadn't he used the upstairs phone? She had seen one on the hall table. Or had she?

She drained the glass. Owen would take care of everything. Owen knew what he was doing. She went to the bed and sank onto it and then lay back, letting the goblet fall from her fingers onto the floor.

At the entrance the white sign was swaying slightly in the wind, its lettering—Thistle Hill Farms—obscured by the falling rain. On the old Frankfort Road a battered gray Land-Rover was parked at an odd angle at the gate, which stood open wide, even at this time of night. It was between four and five in the morning and not yet light. Except for a dog baying somewhere in the distance and an owl hooting in the elms that formed a dark tunnel beyond the gate, the only sound was the Land-Rover's engine, which was running steadily.

Then, muffled and indistinct at first but moving closer, there was another sound: the unmistakable thudding of hoofbeats on gravel.

In another few seconds a huge, handsome bay colt emerged at a gallop from the tunnel of trees and plunged out the gate. Seeing the vehicle, startled, the horse broke stride, neighed once in panic, rearing slightly, and then swerved and rushed headlong down the narrow road in the only direction left open to him by the position of the Land-Rover.

A very brief few seconds later a man no larger than a child but with a man-size face and a thick soft body came running in a grotesque waddle as if trying to catch the colt. He climbed into the seat and eased the Land-Rover forward almost soundlessly, at the same time dropping an object to the seat beside him and then throwing on the headlights. The horse, already going flat out on the asphalt, was flooded in an abrupt glare.

Spooked, are you, Vincent Van, you royal-blooded sonofabitch, your Princequillo blood pumping good and hot now, is it, your Bold Ruler balls frozen, are they?

The driver—a keen cold excitement glittering in his dark eyes, which were set deep in a bulbous face with thick protruding lips and an enormous hooked nose that looked like India rubber—gunned the motor into a roar. He was in the irons again, a match race with the odds-on Derby favorite only ten, eleven lengths ahead on the clubhouse turn. And the power of four hundred horses under him, under Frankie Voight, the kid himself. All of a sudden he was twenty years younger and thirty pounds lighter, breezing, only breezing.

Lathered up, are you, Vincent Van, reaching for more speed? Won't do you any good. Always have to win, don't you? Nine out of eleven career starts, wonder horse, last year's champion two-year-

old, this year's winner of the Flamingo, Arkansas Derby, Wood Memorial—you sure as shit went up in the air when Frankie shot the
juice to your ass back there, didn't you, lover boy?

Backstretch now, time to go to the whip, time for Frankie to flail
the hide off his mount. 'Cause Frankie knew when to make his
move, he was an old-timer, a veteran, he knew what all these
spoiled thoroughbred pigs had to have, deserved to have, had coming to them—show 'em who's boss!

He was closing in now, only two lengths off, behind the big
pumping buttocks and flying tail and glittering shoes throwing
sparks on the pavement, passing the eighth pole, into the stretch—

This is it, Vincent Van, you've had it now! Listen to that crowd
go nuts! You've had it, you big motherfucker, you'll never see the
pay-off pole!

Hunched over the wheel, he bore down on the foot pedal. The
Land-Rover shot forward like a good mount begging for the final
try. He swung the wheel to the right and pulled up on the outside.
It would be a dingdong battle to the wire. He saw the head alongside turn, once and fast, eyes bulging with terror. His mount was
looking Vincent Van in the eye now. Taking one hand from the
wheel, he clamped the heel of it hard over the horn button. The
colt veered left, gave ground, wheeling off the road toward the
fence.

Eat it, you motherfucking bastard, eat the goddamn rail!

Over the motor's thunder and the horn's steady squawk he could
not hear the horse against the fence. He did not need to. He did not
need to hear the sound of splintering wood, ripping flesh, cracking
bones.

He released the horn and increased his speed even more. He had
done his job. And back there at Thistle Hill, whoever it was had
done *his* job too. Timing on the nose, big house sleeping off last
night's shindig, no watchman within a holler, horse loose in the
paddock—slick shit, slick shit all the way.

He began to whistle between his teeth. Why was he barreling it
now? Nobody'd even miss the big pisser until workout time. Even
then they'd figure he'd been stolen. A thousand pounds of precious
meat, gold in his veins. He slowed down. Should he get rid of the

goad he'd used to juice the big pig into moving his ass? He picked up the small flat instrument from the seat. Hell, no—that was what you might call Frankie Voight's electric keepsake. One of the reasons he'd drawn a lifetime suspension and was barred from every big track in the country, but only because he'd got caught. Plenty of jocks used them. So let the stewards, the commish, the owners, and the TRPB jerks, let 'em all fuck off. Who knows, he might need the joint later. Didn't that Eric Millar hint there'd be more work coming up by the end of the week if he pulled this off without a hitch? *Play it right and keep your lip buttoned, you could make a pile, Frankie.*

On the expressway leading back to Louisville he lit a cigarette. He'd made more bread the last few minutes then he could've made riding in the Derby itself. Unless he wound up with a percentage of the purse and waving his stick in the winner's circle—champagne, kisses, picture on front pages all over the goddamn world, TV, backstretch groupies in T-shirts begging for a hay-roll. But to hell with all that. Frankie boy would settle for this.

Christ, maybe the man, whoever he was and Frankie had his own ideas, maybe the man wouldn't pay so good if he knew what a ball-splitting whang Frankie boy himself got out of a caper like this. Squaring his account with all of them at the same time. He felt like a million. Yes, sir, he felt like he used to feel after one great sensational fuck with a six-foot-tall whore.

Chapter Three

"LISTEN to this," he said as she drifted into the sitting room, the filmy peignoir floating over her small slim body, and he read from the morning paper: "In French *bonne fête* means happy holiday, but in English it means move over, also ran." Annabelle laughed lightly. "I'll wager ten thousand francs he pronounces it Bun Fate." He smiled; she had a way, always, of making him smile. "Not Bun Fate, my sweet—Bonnie Fettie." She frowned. "Bone Fate, probably. Is this the same clairvoyant one who's on television—the fleshy fellow with the gray goatee and the cigarette holder?" Paul shook his head. "This is a local prophet with a long white beard that is stained brown with chewing-tobacco juice." But she had not heard. "What in the name of God are these? They wouldn't have the brazen impudence to call them croissants!" He read: "The horse's name is Prescription but it should be printed on a bottle as a skull-and-crossbones—Poison." Her tone brightened: "Oh, I met the owners—a sweet man with two chins and a nervous wife from a town named Terre Haute." He shook his head. "Terry Hut." Over her cup she allowed her very delicate, very lovely face to become grotesque: "Is this coffee?" He shrugged. "Best hotel in the city of Lo-vul." The displeasure cleared from her face: "Loo-vul, not Lo-vul, Loo-vul!" And again she laughed, so he read on: "Ancient Mariner, on the other hand, steers a very fast ship and is especially seaworthy in storms." To which she snapped: "Bonne Fete won at La Troienne by *three lengths*, right here in their godforsaken Loo-vul!" He didn't mention that the race had been for fillies only and was only seven furlongs in length, but he doubted the Derby was as important to her as she pretended. He gazed out over the gray rooftops; the rain had stopped during the night. Then he looked across the table at her, her silver-blond hair contrasting with her bright black eyes and her grace apparent even as she sat there. Everywhere—in England, at Longchamp, Deauville, and in Monte Carlo—everywhere they traveled people always said they made a handsome couple. Hesitating, really hating to ask, he nevertheless did: "How's the hunting so far?" Without looking up she answered, with a dainty suggestion of a shrug: "So far? Dreary. And yours?" He reflected a moment, then: "It's only Tuesday. The hunting may improve." She did look up then, smiling. "Good luck." To which he replied: "And to you, my sweet."

Eleven o'clock again and time to be charmed by your favorite soothsayer, Count Wyatt, he of the dulcet tongue and scurrilous sagacity. Today's exalted event is the running of the renowned Derby Trial. Outsiders and the uninitiated often take the name to signify a qualifying race for entrance into Saturday's main event. Perish the illusion, please. Like the Stepping Stone, run last Saturday and won by a Derby colt named Prescription, today's competition is only one of several so-called prep races. Traditionally a mile in length, the Derby Trial is now only seven furlongs and, as if you didn't know, favors the sprinters more than the stayers. It's a wet track, officially labeled sloppy, and cloudy skies are threatening more Kentucky dew. Of the field of seven, three are definite Derby entrants.

True Blue, at unofficial odds of three-to-two, is favored here and promises to be a threat on Saturday as well. If True Blue, by all standards a class horse with a fine record and the bluest of blue blood, wins today, it will certainly add zest to the week-long party that its owners, the James Olivers and son, are hosting all over this not-so-fair city. The guests now number more than a hundred, so even more than the usual cheering might be expected from the boxes come five this afternoon.

Even though, we repeat unnecessarily, the Trial is in no sense a qualifying event—the true racing world leaves such to the motorcars zooming around the Indianapolis oval at ridiculous speeds—for one horse and his connections this afternoon's contest is exactly what the name implies. But in a most unusual way and one that should add fresh zest and excitement to the race. Scuttlebutt among backstretchers has it that unless the black colt from Florida named Hotspur finishes in the money today, his owner and trainer, Clay Chalmers by name, will not have the four thousand dollars to pass the entry box and the three thousand, five hundred additional to start in the Derby. The racing surface is a ribbon of mud, and Hotspur has won three stakes races in downpours, and his regular jockey, Zach Massing, is said to like eating muck. According to the expert calculations of your obedient servant Hotspur will have to finish at least second in order to run in the Derby. If he does, Mr. Chalmers will even have enough left over to buy a fancy dinner or two—possibly for a young filly who likes her dinners très fawncy and très expensive indeed. If Hotspur lets his owner down today we shall, all of us, be deprived on Saturday of witnessing the unusual spectacle of two brothers vying against each other in the Derby. Sibling rivalry between horses is not uncommon but between human beings—

The third Derby contender is a colt named Dealer's Choice, registered in the name of a Tidewater Stables—one tired animal in this expert's expert opinion. But tired horses are kept going these days by the use of legal drugs that were illegal a few years ago—including Butazolidin, which figured so prominently in the Derby scandal of 1968, when it was not legal in Kentucky. So, good luck, Dealer's Choice, you've already had a rough life. May you see a winner's circle before they let you out to pasture and sex.

All of which, enemies and friends, is not to say that the Trial lineup, a short field of only seven three-year-olds, is not comprised of nice horses from good families. But not every colt is a Derby contender. Take Eric the Red—of that hue, named for a hero of Norse sagas and owned by as handsome a couple of blond Vikings from Iceland as anyone would ever wish to set eyes on. Eric the Red was bred and trained here in Kentucky, and if he never wins another race, he'll be a pleasure to behold today and is judged to have a bright, bright future. The other three entries are Mainly Books, Sakren, and Mac-Kinlay, all at very long odds against the likes of True Blue. But, as my poor old mother used to say in her cups: Anything can happen in horse-racing and almost always does.

Now . . . sad as the fact makes this reporter to report: Some time during the night the beloved Vincent Van suffered a serious injury in his stall at Thistle Hill Farms, and he has been withdrawn from the Derby. A great horse, valued in the millions, Vincent Van was one of the great runners. His dazzling nine-and-three-quarter-length victory in the Champagne Stakes last fall bettered Secretariat's time in that race and tied Seattle Slew's. Last season's recipient of the Eclipse award for the best juvenile colt, he won the Wood Memorial as a three-year-old by going to the wire heart-to-heart with the great Ancient Mariner. He ticked off the nine furlongs in one forty-seven and a fifth. Well, Vincent Van's racing days are over, alas. He will not have to be destroyed—or put down, as the saying has it—but his owner, Harold Johnston, has decided that he will stand at stud. Some among you might not think this such a bad fate: a life of leisure and mares galore. But, like all of his kind, Vincent Van is a runner first and a sire second. Harold Johnston, who could not be reached for comment, is as perturbed a gentleman as any in the state this day, and the pall that has fallen on the week-long house party at Thistle Hill is hard to imagine. But, as the tritest of all banalities has it, most accidents do happen in the home, don't they?

What will this mean to the Derby? Well, it can be safely predicted now that Starbright will enter the gate as the undisputed favorite, possibly an odds-on favorite. Without fear of contradiction Count Wyatt can now go on record as saying that the two front runners Saturday will be Starbright and Ancient Mariner.

But . . . the question that comes to this observer's superstitious mind is this: Is there some sort of mysterious jinx on this year's race? Recall, with sadness, that Stuart Rosser, owner of Fireaway, died of a heart attack less than forty-eight hours ago, although his horse, because of the courageous and sporting spirit of his widow, will run on Saturday regardless of her grief and loss. And now . . . the in-

*trepid Vincent Van put out to pasture. Why are the gods not smiling
on us this year?*

*May they change their moods by five this afternoon, when the
eighth race of the day, the Derby Trial, with a purse of twenty
thousand and twenty thousand added, will be run in the muck and
slush while an estimated ninety thousand frenzied idiots like you
and me yell themselves hoarse and weary. And may Count Wyatt,
who always looks on the uplifting side of the direst happenstance,
remind whoever stands in the winner's circle today that this is only a
seven furlong race, while the Derby is a long mile and a quarter, and
that in all these many years only five winners who took the Trial
Derby trophy have gone on to sip bourbon from the Derby cup. With
which happy thought I take reluctant leave until tomorrow's fore-
noon, when you will again be blessed by your obedient servant's dour
but beloved presence on this shimmering screen.*

Knowing he was talking too much because he always did when
he got keyed-up, Walter Drake was telling the taxi driver: "He's what
they call a liver bay. A bay has black legs below the knees and what
they call the hocks." What had him keyed-up was the way Susan sat
there beside him on the seat staring out the window. The driver,
having lived all his life in Louisville most likely, probably knew
more about horses than he'd ever know, even if someday he owned
a whole stable. "I heard some strange names for horses," the driver
said, "but yours, yours sure enough takes the cake, Mr. Drake."
Walter shifted in the seat. "I'm a druggist after all." Susan was
staring, but she wasn't seeing anything. Pretty, shaded streets with
pleasant-looking houses and little lawns—once you got off the thru-
way Louisville was a pretty town, especially the residential parts.
Because he'd suggested it, Susan had had her hair dyed. But it
wasn't that thick, rich brown it had once been—that he remembered and tried not to. Her face had always been full—soft and
blooming and so lively—but now it was *too* full. Like her body.
Like his body too. And at that, her face wasn't hung with jowls like
his. "Would you folks believe," the driver asked, "that in all the

years I been driving this cab this is the first time I had the honor to have the owners of a Derby horse in my back seat?" Walter hoped that might perk her up, but she didn't move a muscle. He'd even tried to talk her into having one of those face jobs that some of her friends had had. Now that they had the money. Not that they had that much. Until he got into it, he hadn't realized what it cost to board a thoroughbred, what with the feed and the stable space and the vet bills—and not including the salaries. Eight hundred dollars a week, more some weeks, over a thousand. Then more for her sake than the driver's, hoping he could bring her out of it, he started talking about the record: Prescription had raced five times as a two-year-old and won twice at Finger Lakes and three times at Beulah Park, near Columbus, Ohio, and in only his second start he had beat older horses. The driver whistled, but no response from Susan. The empty-nest syndrome—that's what young Dr. Harmon back home had called it. Happens to a lot of women, sometimes men too, when they reach a certain age and their children have flown the coop. He'd prescribed Librium, then Valium, but her depressions only seemed to deepen. It scared him sometimes. He found himself lying awake nights, worrying. This year, he told the driver, Prescription had won twice at River Downs near Cincinnati, once at Thistledown outside of Cleveland, and again at Finger Lakes. Hell, even living on the wrong side of the tracks, as a fellow might say, he'd earned back his purchase price nine times over! Susan had tried to help herself—she'd got all interested in yoga, transcendental meditation, and even astrology for a time there. He himself had offered to start going back to church again, but she had said no, all of that was so long ago, it *seemed* long ago. He'd known what she meant: Going to church was part of a time when they were all together, and happy, Margo and Terrence and the two of them, kind of all one. Now Margo was living with her husband thousands of miles away in Bogotá, Colombia, way down in South America, and worse, much worse, they didn't know where Terry was. Had not known for more than three years. "You didn't mention the Stepping Stone last Saturday here at the Downs," the driver said. "I try to keep up with the races, especially Derby Week. That Stepping Stone is many times a big step toward the Derby, a big step." And Walter leaned forward, lifting his voice excitedly: "That's what I try to tell my wife. True, like the papers keep saying, our colt hasn't been up against the top competition yet, but like that man on the tube says, you never can tell, you never can tell!" But she didn't move. It didn't cheer her. Nothing cheered her. Damn. He glanced at her again. His annoyance never lasted long. It invariably turned into compassion. Pity, even, that made him feel a little weak and sick all through. And helpless. Hadn't he bought the horse because of her? Hoping it would make her happy, add zest to life, excitement. Hell's bells, he didn't have much hope of really winning, but just to be here, just to be an owner and have seats in a box . . . So he kept on trying; he always kept on trying. "Bold Forbes had no better pedigree than Prescription. His sire was named Irish Castle, and he never won beyond six and a half furlongs. And his dam, named Pretty Nell or something like that, hell's bells, she never won at all! Yet look what Bold Forbes did right here in 1976!" No response. Nothing. Walter sat back. He gave up. This could go on all day, right through the Trial and on into the evening. He had come to wonder whether even winning the Derby itself would make her really happy. So, just to make conversation, he told the driver what he sometimes told the other patrons in Mick's Tavern when he was having a beer or two: how Prescription loved beer. "God's truth. Only he isn't just your everyday beer-swilling horse. All he has to do is hear the lid of a can popping open and he pokes his head out of the stall and starts to salivate. He lays back his ears, nods his head, and paws the ground and whinnies. He'll settle for a Coke, but he's happiest with a can of Michelob, and his trainer places a can between his lips at least once a day. Then, two days before a race, he puts him on the wagon. But if he wins, he gets two cans in a row!" The driver sort of cackled a laugh, but it was Susan who spoke: "Walter, Walter Drake, you never told me that!" He looked at her. Her face was all lit up and her eyes were sparkling with mirth. "You never once told me that!" she cried. "I hate beer myself, but I think I love that horse!" Walter was too astonished, too overjoyed, to say a damn thing. He heard the driver say, "If you got your papers and pass, I can take you in the Longfield entrance. That's the VIP gate." It was Susan who answered him: "That would be just marvelous, just scrumptious!" He hadn't heard her use that word in years—not since they were dating in high school and he called her Susie-Q. "I hope I look all right." She began to adjust her flowered hat. "Everyone here always looks so elegant." As he held the door for her he said, "You look fine, honey." Then he added, "Susie-Q, you look more beautiful than any of them." And then he paid the driver and added a ten dollar bill just for the hell of it, and when she took his arm, he glanced at her, and damned if it wasn't the truth: She did look more beautiful than any of them.

He hated this time before a race. He loved it. There was no sun. It was not hot. He was sweating. He had eaten too much. Bernie Golden, the fat dumbass, always ate too much. The guinea stand was almost empty. The seventh race promised to be a dull one. No race was dull if your horse was in it. His was in the eighth. And his adrenaline was up already, all the juices pumping through his body.

At sunup the Spur had blazed five eighths in 0:57 and 3/5, galloped three quarters in 1:09 and 3/5, and breezed seven furlongs in 1:25 and 1/5 handily. He loved that goddamn mud. Maybe Clay hadn't given him enough work, maybe too much. Hell, Hotspur was no morning glory, he hadn't left his afternoon race on the track. Yeah, but what if, what if—

The backside PA behind him crackled again: Doc Carpenter was needed in the Longview barn. The infirmary barn detached from the fenced-in backstretch area. Earlier in the day Doc Hartwell had gone over the Spur, every inch of him. He had come out of the stall muttering, "I'd bet on him." The sour old vet's highest form of approval. And Clay had said, "Don't. As a handicapper, you're a damn good vet." Now the colt was asleep. Believe it or not: standing up in his stall sound asleep! Bernie recalled Elijah's bald black head appearing in the aperture above the stall door, a warning finger over his two lips. Damnedest thing how that horse could do that. Which he did before every race. Like he knew what was coming and he had to get ready, didn't he?

But could Bernie Golden sleep? You'd think there'd be some

damn thing an assistant trainer could do in the last hour before a race. More than sit and listen to the hubbub in the stands on the far side and to the yells and singing and guitars of the kids in the infield having a jam session or whatever the hell they called them these days. The reason there wasn't anything for him to do was that he'd done it all beforehand, and he'd done it well, the way it should be done if a man takes any pride in his goddamn work at all.

Zach, having tossed his cookies after lunch, was now in the jockey room, in the sweat box or playing checkers or poker. Easing away from barn 27 earlier, he'd snarled: "I'll be in the jock room. Maybe I can shit off another sixteen ounces before weigh-in."

Again the matter-of-fact blare of the PA announcing a late scratch in the seventh, due to start in ten minutes: Number Six, King Richard II, by order of the track stewards. Very odd, very damn strange indeed. A scratch this late always raised questions. Even if sick or injured, a horse could be withdrawn only after a thorough examination by the official track veterinarian. The other cause—and a rare one—would be the discovery of illegal drugs in the runner's urine during the routine identification and examination before saddling. But that was King Richard II's problem; Bernie Golden had his own. Like why Clay hadn't at least tried to scratch the Spur this morning when it just might have been allowed. The Spur might have been what they call a stuck horse if the stewards had denied permission; then he'd have had to run anyway. But as Clay's own brother had said when he offered him the seven thousand five in the track kitchen this morning, "Christ, kid, you could take a crack at it. There's always some excuse." Clay had shrugged, grinning. "I could sneak into his stall with a baseball bat." Owen Chalmers should have known he couldn't push Clay, but he wouldn't let him off the hook. "I didn't tumble to how down on your uppers you actually were till I heard that fancy ass on TV. I'm offering you the mazuma to enter the Derby so you won't have to take a chance running your bangtail this afternoon. What the hell more can a brother do?" To which Clay had replied: "He can say thanks. I'm saying it." Owen Chalmers had just laughed then, shaking his head and tilting back his cowboy hat. "Never change, do you? You know what ole Toby always told you about what goeth before a fall. Well, baby brother, you pays your nickel and you takes your chances. I just don't want to see anything happen to that bangtail of yours before Fireaway gets a shot at him."

A cheer went up from the grandstand, and in the infield the kids stopped skimming their Frisbees and the guitar music went dead. The horses for the seventh had come onto the track. Well, the eighth was that much closer.

On the way back to the barn from the kitchen Clay had asked, "What's chewing away at your corpulent gut, my fine Jewish friend?" So Bernie had told him: "Not that I blame you for not taking the bread. But man, man, couldn't you have lied when that phony count asked you about the entry fees? Backstretch scuttlebutt, he said—shit! No one knew. Now everybody knows. Why the hell can't you ever lie? Join the human race." And Clay had only grinned, as from a distance. And Bernie had said, "Christ!" And Clay had said, "You don't have to call me that when we're alone." Bastard—how could he be so cool? It was always like this on race day, and if you want to know, Bernie Golden had no fingernails from climbing up the goddamn wall.

He could hear the track announcer's voice now: The horses were approaching the starting gate. The noise of the crowd had changed, the way it always did, any race: It was quieter, there was no cheering, only a sort of rippling of anticipation.

Molly was over there. In one of the boxes. She'd come backside in the year or so between the fourth and fifth races. He'd had a hell of a time recognizing her. She'd had on a pale blue dress, filmy, flaring down below, and he'd realized that he'd never seen her in a dress before, any dress. But *this* one! And her hair: the way it sort of flowed and fell, glistening black, not held back in pigtails or stuffed under a helmet. She had been too much. Molly Muldoon—even her goddamn name was too much. "When you win," she had asked, "will you be standin' there in the winner's circle yourself?" But he had said with a dry tongue: "Not when, Molly—if." Her dark blue eyes got even brighter then, only how could they get brighter, and she had teased him in that way of hers that he'd never get used to: "Oh, ye of little faith!" And it had been then that she had first placed her cheek against his, the first time, and then she had kissed him quickly, on the lips, also for the first time. She'd gone without a backward glance, so quick that it had been as if she'd vanished. And soon she would too—after Saturday. But damned if he'd think of that now.

He heard a roar and the clanging of the bell, and he stood up, along with the others in the guinea stand, waiting for the horses to reach the backstretch. Already he could hear the hoofbeats, but not yet loud.

"Are there any Jews in Ireland?" he had asked her, yesterday or the day before. What had she done? What did she always do? She had laughed out loud. And heads had turned. And those others eating at the chuckwagon on the plaza under the hotel downtown—what had they done? They had smiled. And felt better. As he had. And then she'd said, "Jews, is it? Why, me lad, Dublin itself had a Jewish mayor for years and years, and have you never heard of James Joyce and a gentleman named Bloom?" He had not, neither of the two, but also he had not met a girl like this before either, and his feelings flummoxed up his brain and made his blood run backward. But he took a strange satisfaction in the ache he felt inside most of the time now. What really blew his mind was that he hadn't even made a pass at this goddamn Molly Muldoon. Maybe because she could sit on a horse better than ninety percent of the jocks he knew.

The racers passed along the backstretch, strung out now, two in the lead along the rail, neck and neck, and then after five lengths six more, bunched, pounding and straining, and then, trailing, a sad-looking mount with a cursing, disgusted rider flailing hopelessly with his stick. The others in the stand were yelling, and two exercise girls were hugging each other and screeching. When the thudding faded, he got down from the stand. Might as well go see whether Hotspur was finished with his pleasant damn dreams.

As he shambled heavily, slowly between barns he came upon two jockeys, still wearing their silks, walking toward the kitchen, the one in front stepping briskly, the other trying to keep up behind and hissing: "You ever bang me like that again, you're goin' over the rail, you're goin' *through* the fuckin' rail!" And the other snarling over his shoulder: "Screw the Inquiry sign, stewards ruled no foul, didn't they?" And, fists clenched, face savage, the one behind bawled: "Camera missed it. Next time I'll tear off your balls and feed 'em to the squirrels!" He broke into a run then and went on. The other one only shrugged. And so did Bernie: par for the course, happens every day, it's rough out there on the dirt, and sometimes dirty.

Behind, farther away now, he heard the roaring reach full tilt and then slowly subside. The seventh was over, and in a few minutes the official results would be announced.

He turned the corner of barn 27, and there stood Clay. And Miss Kimberley Cameron, the kid herself. They were standing face to face, close, outside the shedrow, and behind them he could see the Spur's lean black head in the stall door. Awake.

Miss Kimberley wore a thin, tight, but frilly dress, with very damn little underneath, if anything, and a wide floppy hat. "You know better than I do, Clay, that everything's a risk"—she seemed to be pleading with him—"even vanning, morning works, but especially a race."

And as Bernie continued to the barn as though he were not really hearing, Clay said, a little tensely for Clay, even on a racing day: "I know, Kimb, that a thoroughbred like mine is infected by any human tension around, especially when he's got to be on the track in less than half an hour."

Her face changed. Stiffened. But she looked a little hurt and sad too. Like a little girl. "Are you saying you won't take the loan?"

"You know it's too late now."

"Even if it wasn't, you'd still say no."

Clay smiled a little and took a step toward her. "I'll try to locate some dope in the vet's office if you'll shoot it in." He reached, but she wrenched her bare arm away. "Only way the stewards would let me scratch this late, you know it."

Her face went ugly, twisting, and her eyes turned to ice. "Fuck you, Clay Chalmers."

As Bernie slipped into the tack room Clay said softly: "I try to protect Hotspur from language like that."

Bernie sank into a wooden chair and heard cheers in the distance: the official results had been announced. Through the open window he heard: "Asshole. I hope you win today. I hope you win so Starbright can beat you by seventeen lengths on Saturday!"

In almost a whisper Clay's voice said, as if more amused than pissed-off: "I'll settle for second today and first on Saturday."

The music started up again in the infield and over in the stands there was only a low babbling, and Bernie could picture the fans tearing up tickets and throwing them into the air and winners clambering to get to the pay-off windows. Outside the window now he could hear Clay's voice whispering to Hotspur in his stall. He continued to sit there. Even if it weren't for all the things he'd done for you—like saving you from the booze and having to muck out stalls the rest of your life—how could you help loving a stubborn bastard like Clay Chalmers?

One half hour to post time.

The announcer's voice, flat and mechanical and without character, sounded everywhere: probably, Brigid had decided, one of those timed mechanical recordings, although she'd much prefer, herself, that it was some gentleman actually watching the time. She was with Andrew in a lounge—very elegant, very plush—which was the domain of members of some club or other. Outside the carved wooden doors there were stand-up bars strewn up and down the passageway and enough drinking to make one think she might be back in Ireland. But Brigid Tyrone was quite content to be precisely where she was, thank you, ensconced in a huge chair, wearing her next-to-Derby Day finest finery, hatted and gloved and sipping her second brandy soda of the day and it not yet half-five in the afternoon. Andrew was engaged in conversation with Harold Johnston, a man with an owlish face and melancholy brown eyes, who—even though he'd already quite many more than one drop taken—struck her as nevertheless a mite too defensively withdrawn whenever the name Vincent Van was mentioned. His wife on the divan beside him was of a type Brigid had seen everywhere: slim and handsome and middle-aged with a horsewoman's firm body and a polite expression which it seemed an effort to maintain. She was speaking of the party at Thistle Hill, which they were determined to continue until Sunday regardless of what she termed last night's dreadful, dreadful accident. "Where else," Amanda Johnston asked, "would the poor dears find a place to put their heads?" Then Andrew, less relaxed himself than he had been during the three races they had watched, was saying, "Around thoroughbreds, Harold, there's no such thing as negligence—only *criminal* negligence." For the quick flicker of a second he reminded her of Daniel: It was an attitude he had always had, but she could not now recall his ever having expressed it. "Well," Harold Johnston said, lifting his glass to signal the waiter, "heads will roll, you may damn well count on that. But, as I told Wyatt Slingerland and the rest of the pesky press, it was an accident." And then he added, "Let me tell you: No greater horse ever looked through a bridle." To which Andrew replied: "Blue Ridge had one once, and if he were still alive, I'd give you an argument." Harold Johnston nodded: "Lord Randolph. Yes, yes, you *could* give me an argument there, I suppose." Lifting her throaty voice then, Amanda Johnston asked, "Andrew, wasn't Clay Chalmers working for you at that time?" It was then that Brigid saw Andrew's eyes lose their luster, go almost opaque as he stood murmuring something about being sure he'd see the Johnstons again during the week.

Twenty-eight minutes to post time.

As they descended the clubhouse stairway Andrew was silent. Not a tall man, he always seemed so when close. Clay Chalmers again: The name was like a bell that tolled him back—

They emerged into a golden brilliance. The sun had broken through at last.

"Behold!" she cried. "Andrew, look! Will you look!"

She had stopped him and taken his arm and she was staring into his face. His eyes were on her, and there was amusement in them, but more, and then she was transformed into a Galway schoolgirl, her face scarlet, she was sure, and her whole body flushed and aquiver.

"You have freckles," Andrew said, as if he'd only on the instant made a world-shaking discovery.

"I've always had freckles," she said, but her brain was humming

117

and her tongue, damn the thing, was no more good than a dried mushroom.

A moment. While they were buffeted by shoulders and voices rose and fell around them. His eyes were soft. She had never seen eyes so soft, and all of a sudden.

Twenty-seven minutes to post time.

He took her elbow then, his hand light but firm, and led her into the garden area. She had seen it first when they arrived before the fifth race, and what had struck her then was the startling color, the lushness and loveliness here behind the grandstand, with a tote board blinking odds and results above and people, all sorts and kinds, dressed in all sorts and kinds of ways, strolling and sitting on the benches along the flowerbeds and between the rich banks of riotous colors. It was like an island of iridescence. She allowed herself to be led, not knowing where, not caring.

They approached a couple sitting alone, somewhat detached from the ebb and flow and looking out of place and even slightly ill at ease. When Andrew brought her to a halt in front of them, the man—who had one of those wind-worn faces that she associated with the fishermen all along the west of Ireland and who looked himself openly surprised—stood up, waiting. "Mr. Einarsson?" Andrew asked, and the youngish man nodded his blond head, his intensely golden brows lifting. "Ye-ess. Yess, I am Gunnar Einarsson." He towered above Andrew, who introduced himself then and presented her in a way that, in spite of its formality, suggested a friendly interest. "My stable, Blue Ridge, has a colt in the Derby, and Mrs. Tyrone is the owner of Irish Thrall." The man's head nodding again. "I know. I know." And then he was introducing his wife, whose name was Malfour and whose hair was even blonder than his and brighter in the sun. Slender but with wide shoulders, she rose, her eyes looking down on Brigid Tyrone, who at this moment was overcome with astonishment: what a kind and thoughtful thing for Andrew Cameron, sensing their isolation, to have done. "Won't you sit, please," Gunnar Einarsson invited in an accent that sounded Scandinavian yet had a different ring to it. And then, seated beside Malfour, Brigid relaxed into a pleasant blather, first commenting on the gardens and saying that it was a tradition in her country to plant flowers wherever they would take root, not only in formal gardens but in clusters around almost every door, even in front of the most modest cottages with thatched roofs. "Aster and geranium and lobelia." And Malfour, herself at ease and her tongue loosened in spite of her occasional hesitation with English words, delightedly reported that the same was true in Iceland. Flowers? In Iceland? And Malfour threw back her head and laughed, a sparkling sound, and said she knew that people thought her country barren and only cold, with ice year round, but not only did they love flowers, they grew their own vegetables, but inside, in structures with controlled temperatures, using the volcanic heat deep down in the earth. "Even in the winter when the sun never shows!" she said triumphantly. And Andrew was telling Gunnar Einarsson that he had seen Eric the Red—good girth, plenty of light under, short back, and fine bone. "We have nominated him for the Derby," the tall man said. "We did it in February. But our trainer vishes not to announce until we see today. Eric was trained here in this state, you know. In Iceland we have only small ponies which never grow high." He laughed a deep laugh. "And I am not horseman, only owner of fishing fleet in Vestmannaeyjar."

Twenty-five minutes to post time.

On their way to their seats after farewells, which were formal but warm, Brigid held Andrew's arm. She held it close and could feel his elbow against her breast. Andrew Cameron was not only a gentleman of courtly manners and worldly charm, he was a true and, yes, considerate gentleman in other, more vital senses of that word.

There were a fair share of gross-looking cigar-chompers about and women with lurid and painfully flamboyant clothes—here and in the hotel public rooms, since racing itself seemed to lure them, in this country as well as in Europe—and as such a group bustled up the stairway she felt Andrew stiffen. Was the man a snob then after all? The feminine cackles floated back along the crowded passageway to the boxes, and the two men charged stolidly on. "Dealer's Choice," Andrew said—as if the two words explained something. Or accounted for the look in his eye: a rather sad contempt.

Twenty-four minutes to post time.

Going down the steps to the box they had vacated earlier, catching sight again of the famous names on some of the boxes on both sides and in the other aisles—Claiborne, Darby Dan, Calumet— she saw that Molly had returned to her seat. But standing in the aisle, blocking it, was a very tall bearded man wearing a white Western suit and a white cowboy hat. With him was a fine-looking woman in her forties, extremely well dressed in black, wearing a small, neat black hat. She and Andrew, it appeared, were old friends, and it also appeared that the lady had been drinking, possibly very heavily. Andrew introduced the woman as Mrs. Christine Rosser and the gentleman as Mr. Owen Chalmers. Brigid recognized both names at once as those of the widowed owner of Fireaway and her trainer. "Christine and I," Andrew explained, "knew each other when her name was Chrissie Norvelle and she was the liveliest dancer at any ball in Louisville." Mrs. Rosser laughed a rather guttural laugh, and then Andrew was saying how sorry he was to read about Mr. Rosser. Christine Rosser's face sobered, and she gave Andrew a grateful hug while Owen Chalmers glanced at Brigid, his blue eyes grave above his beard, which was the color of cinnamon. An impressive, handsome young man and, judging by what she had read, a first-rate trainer. Then Christine Rosser was saying that she'd debated some time before coming, especially since she didn't have a horse running today, but that Owen had convinced her that, after all, she couldn't just stop living, could she?

"Right you are, young lady!" another voice broke in from behind, and Brigid turned to see Rachel Stoddard, whom she had met night before last and had seen in the stable area yesterday, coming down the steps toward them. "You are blocking the way to my box, every one of you!" She stopped and regarded them, her crest of silver hair glinting in the sun and her gold-handled cane, which appeared to be more an imperious staff than aid for her age, poised in midair. Behind her loomed a giant of a man with a square, massive face that exuded dignity; he was wearing a tweed jacket with leather patches at the elbows. He simply stood there as silent as Brigid herself. Nodding to her, Rachel Stoddard passed to shake Christine Rosser's hand. "Chrissie Norvelle, when I phoned to invite you to join me, you sounded so relieved even when you said you probably wouldn't that I expected you. Now if you and this handsome, bearded cowboy will step aside, I'll clamber into my box for the festivities. Oh, this is Alex Crichton. Anyone in racing knows he's the best trainer in the game."

After shaking the man's raw-boned hand, Brigid managed to slither into Andrew's box as Rachel Stoddard set up court in the one across the aisle, saying, "Plenty of room, Chrissie, for the both of you. So you two have the lack of imagination to think your Fireaway can give my Mariner a run for it, do you?"

Twenty-two minutes to post time.

Mammoth apparatus were somewhat hopelessly trying to smooth the track, wheels spinning as they appeared to all but sink into the mud.

"Isn't it a lovely track?" Molly asked, as she had been asking through three races now. "All that lovely goo."

Beside her, herself anticipating the race almost as if she had a horse entered, Brigid reassured the lass that she had never seen a more beautiful track. She did not mention Hotspur's preferences in racing surfaces. But she did recall, not for the first time indeed, what Gregory McGreevey had said about Molly's passing her backstretch time in and around barn 27.

Andrew joined them, winking at Molly, whose eyes glittered with excitement. "It hasn't dried out, I see."

Brigid was trying not to crane her neck as she took in the other boxes with her eyes. She saw the Hautots entering theirs. They were not dressed as they might have been at Ascot—Paul Hautot did not wear his cutaway or top hat, but Annabelle's hat would have graced Chantilly. They shared a box with the unlikeliest of fellow owners: the paunchy pharmacist, who wore a straw hat, and his wife, who wore one with a plethora of artificial flowers.

Mischievously Brigid wished that she might eavesdrop on the conversation in that box, if any. It took some doing to locate the Japanese owner of Fuji Mist. He was in an otherwise empty box with not one but two very tall, very blond creatures, whose silk frocks clung to every curve and crevasse and whose décolletage was so severe as to be all but total.

As the flat-toned man warned in a blare that it was now twenty minutes to post someone entered the box and took one of the seats behind them. There was a great huffing and puffing, and a male voice said, in a throaty purr of discontent: "Why a sane man in an insane world would submit himself to this is beyond me."

Andrew, his lips twitching, stood and turned. "Before I say anything else, Blake, let me warn you that there are ladies present." He extended a hand, and the one that reached to take it—Brigid caught only a glimpse over her shoulder—was liver-spotted, bulbous, and pink. "Blake, when did you get in?"

"I arrived in this hellhole of hilarity only two hours ago," the voice said in a drawl that Brigid recognized as American Southern. Andrew's own inflections only suggested its cadence. "Andrew, this is the seventh time I've come all the way from Virginia to see Blue Ridge win a Derby, and I haven't seen it yet."

"Starbright's running under Blue Ridge colors," Andrew explained, "but he's Kimberley's colt." And then he added: "As she'll be the first to remind you."

Then he was performing the introductions, and Brigid turned her head. What she saw was a man who was not only corpulent but flabbily so. His hair lay in white strands over a round scalp that was almost exposed when he removed his hat. His black eyes seemed lost between shaggy brows and fat puffs of flesh. But they twinkled, and Brigid warmed to him at once.

"Two beautiful ladies," Blake Raynolds said. "It is, as the current lingo has it, too much. Now I do forgive you, Andrew, I do that. As I hope you ladies will forgive an old man for not rising. It's not decrepitude entirely but gout, goddamn it, and I trust you'll pardon the expression."

Resuming his seat, Andrew made sure that Blake Raynolds could hear over the buzzing that seemed now to have increased in volume as the call to post moved closer: "Mr. Raynolds is an old, fine friend but a very indifferent attorney, whom I keep on retainer so he won't starve in the street."

"You, suh, are only too aware that I am a man who makes the rich get richer while feathering my own very comfortable nest, thank you." The voice came closer behind her ear: "Mrs. Tyrone, perhaps you will enlighten this curious man as to the differences between the sport of kings here and in Europe."

Brigid was delighted to report her impressions: that there was a more relaxed atmosphere here—more of a holiday spirit, picnics in the infield—while in England and France things were more formal. Of course the Curragh in Ireland was a different matter altogether. And he then reminded her of the racing courses in Japan, where whole communities actually lived in the stable area, with schools and shops, and of Hong Kong, where, he understood, the entire course was enclosed, with the horses living in a skyscraper above. "Personally," Blake Raynolds concluded, "I despise racing."

Brigid sensed some of Molly's tension evaporating as she laughed. Before anyone spoke again, there was another commotion behind, and Kimberley's voice asked, "Do I have to introduce everybody?"

Andrew stood and took over. Kimberley was accompanied by Pepe Benitez, the jockey whose fame had spread worldwide—the little man with the golden hands who was scheduled to ride Starbright on Saturday and, if Brigid's memory served, to ride a filly from Rachel Stoddard's stable in the Kentucky Oaks on Friday. A smiling, shy-looking creature who nodded often and seemed boylike in spite of his forty years. Kimberley was lovely, but the friendliness with which she had greeted Brigid last evening when she had apologized at the hotel elevator was not a part of her today. Her blue eyes brooded as she slouched down between Pepe Benitez and Mr. Raynolds. She glared a greeting at Blake Raynolds, and he smiled blandly.

"Well, Andrew," she said, "*you* look happy."

Sitting down again, her father said, "Perhaps because I am."

Kimberley snorted. "And you, Mrs. Tyrone, you look disgustingly radiant."

Staring ahead at the red-coated outriders coming onto the track, Brigid said, "Possibly because I'm happy too." She did not risk a glance at Andrew.

"Did you hear, Andrew?" Kimberley persisted. "You've made a conquest."

"I'm delighted to hear it," Andrew said and passed Brigid her program—or, as everyone here called it, the card.

And Brigid Tyrone was the flustered Galway schoolgirl again.

"Fuck," Kimberley said behind her.

She was ignored.

"Pepe," Kimberley's voice said, "I'll lay a hundred dollars that Hotspur takes it by five lengths."

"Miss Kimberley, I never bet on horses." And then in that liquid accent of his he added, "Cockfights now, there it is never a matter of past performances."

"Andrew?" Kimberley asked. "Want to bet?"

"In a few minutes now I am going to place a few dollars on True Blue. At the windows."

"Screw you, Charlie Brown," Kimberley said. "Look at the board. True Blue's still two to one. You always play safe with favorites, don't you?"

But Brigid had made up her mind: Nothing was going to spoil this very lovely, this very puzzling day.

Seventeen minutes to post time.

The James Olivers arrived then, to take the adjoining box beyond Molly. There was a great deal of waving and calling and throwing of kisses up and down and behind, and Mrs. Oliver stood slim and tall to greet her many guests and well-wishers while Mr. Oliver, the man with the flushed face to whom Andrew had introduced Brigid yesterday evening coming down in the lift, ignored the hullabaloo and manipulated their son's wheelchair to make certain he had a clear view of the track from the aisle. He and Andrew nodded, Mr. Oliver looking a trifle abstracted, and Andrew wished him luck.

Brigid consulted the program: True Blue was Number Four (jockey Kyle McCague), and Dealer's Choice (jockey Al Manuel) had post position. She glanced up: On the infield toteboard late changes were blinking, but the odds on Dealer's Choice remained the same as the morning line printed on the card: eleven to one. Both were, by all reports, scheduled to run on Saturday as well.

Sixteen minutes to post time.

Andrew stood up. "It's almost time for mount-up. The bets are on me. Name your choices. Molly?"

Startled at first, Molly smiled across Brigid and up into Andrew's face. "Hotspur, thank you. To win."

"Brigid?"

Slightly startled at his way of doing things, she hesitated a second before saying, "The same, thank you."

"Kimberley? Hotspur?"

"Did you think I was serious? I wouldn't bet on Clay Chalmer's cow at a hundred to one."

"He is six to one at the moment. Who, then?"

"Dealer's Choice," Kimberley barked.

Andrew's expression did not change. "Pepe?" But Pepe must have shaken his head. "Blake?"

"If True Blue's good enough for you, he's good enough for me."

Andrew turned and climbed up the aisle after a nod.

Fifteen minutes to post time.

"Mrs. Tyrone—"

"My friends call me Brigid, Kimberley."

"*Mrs. Tyrone.* Side bet." Her tone was level, tense—dangerous? "You and me. I'll lay one thousand dollars on Dealer's Choice against Hotspur. Win only or bet's off. Well?"

"If it'll make you happy, Kimberley."

Molly was very still. The noise on all sides had grown in volume, but the box was very quiet indeed.

"Balls," Kimberley said in a taut whisper. "Don't do me any favors, Madame Defarge. Fuck off."

And then, her blood suddenly scalding but not so much as a tremor in her voice, Brigid turned her body to face Kimberley, her eyes carefully amiable. "Kimberley, my dear, I am sorry if my presence here upsets you. Or if you've had a row with your young man. I have seats of my own, but I am here at the invitation of your father and"—she felt her lips smiling—"I intend to enjoy myself. But if you mean it, I accept your wager."

Fourteen minutes to post time.

You don't realize it's happening, but it always does. It happens before every race, and you should expect it, but somehow it always takes you by surprise, especially if you're a goddamn fool like Clay

Chalmers, Esq. It starts slowly—a tightening of every muscle and nerve, guts pinching, groin shrinking—and then it spreads, like a fever, and takes over completely. Your head gets lighter and your blood is coursing hotter, and as post time gets even closer your mind is infected too. It focuses and you're with it, in complete control, the way you've schooled yourself, your mind clean and straight and with the moment, glacial control but a volcano underneath, fire and fury way down deep, timed not to erupt until that bell clangs and that gate clatters open and your heart jolts and everything explodes. Now is sheer intensity—when a man knows for certain, not in his mind but in his blood, that he's truly alive. And isn't this, after all, what it's all about?

Here in the saddling paddock you try not to let your feelings get to your horse. He has his own way of passing the time.

Sakren, Number Six, was being led around the walking ring by his groom. Some horses are curious, some need calming—anything now to make them feel comfortable and secure.

The Spur was standing alongside Clay in his paddock stall, the one marked with a 2 to correspond with the program number and his position at the post. He was shorter and lighter than any of the other three-year-olds he'd be up against today. His coat was glistening black, bright as polished ebony, and his whole body, although quiet, seemed to exude anticipation. No cocking one ear back and laying the other forward now, no devilment now. He'd been on the muscle all day because of the way he'd worked out this morning, but now he was dead serious, the impatience there all right but, like Clay's, under control. He wore only the bridle, noseband, racing bandages, and blinkers. He'd already been checked out by the identifier, who'd compared the tattooed number inside his upper lip with the number on the Jockey Club's registration papers. And the track vet had given him the required last-minute once-over to make sure he was sound. MacKinlay, running on the outside in Number Seven spot today, was having his tongue tied to keep him from swallowing it, but not Hotspur. Most of the mounts had their tails braided to keep them from picking up mud and adding weight, but Clay operated on the theory that a long tail flying free kept others off his horse's heels.

The saddling area behind the stands was a roofed structure with shoulder-high barricades on two sides and full walls forming one corner. Above the open sides Clay could see many heads: the eager fans curious to glimpse the horses and if possible to hear the trainer's traditional instructions to his boy in the saddle. On a rectangular island of grass in the center, surrounded by loose clay, the other owners and some press people had gathered, a few taking pictures. Clay recognized the woman journalist who had greeted him on his arrival at the track, a Janice Something-or-other who had asked whether it was true he had once worked for Blue Ridge because she was looking for dirt. She waved, but to hell with her: It was true he talked to his horse but not until they parted company on the track. He also recognized the owners of Eric the Red: the handsome Icelandic couple who towered above most of the others. The ubiquitous columnist for the *Daily Racing Form* was there too, but not Count Wyatt, who was probably in the press box—the bastard who'd make a story out of anything, including an owner's poverty.

Hotspur was now saddled and relaxed, but Bernie was gravely rechecking the surcingle. Elijah ran a dark hand along the Spur's dark back. "He knows," he said. "He's sweatin' a little, just enough, and none down between his legs. He knows what he gotta do." And then he started murmuring into the colt's ear: his special mumbo jumbo that always sounded like a man about to make love.

There was a burst of color at the far end of the enclosure: the jockeys coming out of their room wearing their silks, which today shimmered in the sun. Zach was scowling. Usually cheerful, usually smiling, Zach was a different man before a race. He glared at Clay. "You hear that friend of yours on the TV today? Bastard actually believes I eat mud three meals a day. You tell him for me I don't. Tell him for me I eat horse turd but only medium rare."

Zach Massing was forty-one years old. With his lined face he looked even older. A veteran who'd brought home hundreds of winners but had never ridden in a Derby before. Mildly, very carefully, Clay said, "I'll see he gets your message."

The valet handed Zach his whip, which he used only occasionally but which according to regulations he had to carry. He arranged his goggles. He had three pairs around his neck because of the mud. "Isn't this where you're supposed to give me some wise words of advice and all that shit? That's what all those gawkers expect."

Clay nodded. "It's the Spur's kind of track. Just don't let that Dealer's Choice get in front of you. He's a farter and he'll gas you to death. He's worse on the turns, and we don't want Hotspur puking on the homestretch."

Zach didn't grin but he shook his head. "People don't know it, but you are one wild sonofabitch, ain't you?" He straightened. "Is that all?"

"You know what to do."

"Yeah. Win."

"Today I'll settle for place."

"*I* won't."

Ten minutes to post time.

And the paddock judge called, "Riders up."

Zach placed the stick between his teeth. Clay cupped his hands and gave him a leg up.

Zach touched his hanging goggles with one hand and removed the whip with the other, settling in, but upright. "Is that Count Wyatt a faggot?" he growled.

"I'll ask his wife."

Zach uttered some sort of obscenity between his teeth.

The bugle blared "First Call." To Brigid there was no more stirring sound in racing.

"Blow, Gabriel, blow," Kimberley said.

Andrew was passing out the pari-mutuel tickets. When he gave Kimberley hers, she muttered, "Thank you, *Daddy*."

He ignored her. Brigid ignored her too.

When he handed Blake Raynolds his, the big man said, "If I expire before they get around the track, cut off my right big toe or I'll never rest in peace."

Here they are! The horses are coming out on the track.

Everyone stood. Except, presumably, Kimberley. Brigid handed the glasses to Molly and stood with the others. Cheers and applause greeted each horse, the loudest for True Blue.

"Owee, look at all the pretty colors."

No one but Kimberley spoke. The noise subsided somewhat during the post parade. In the aisle beyond the adjoining box the Olivers' son, binoculars to his eyes, was shouting from his wheelchair: "Show 'em, True Blue. True Blue, we love you!"

From behind: "They all look like cows."

Molly was silent as Hotspur, Number Two, was led by, his jockey in red and black striped silks, upright but looking relaxed. Molly was unnaturally quiet. Brigid longed to reach for her hand, then decided not to. She realized that she really knew nothing of the lad attached to barn 27. And for that matter little of what Molly might be feeling.

Down below, between the grandstand and the track, there was a rush to the fence. Groomed, saddled, mounted, and on display, the horses presented a lovely spectacle, always exciting, always breathtaking. Brigid was aware that Europeans often criticized the Americans for cluttering up the post parade with lead ponies, but she thought that the pony boys and girls, wearing colorful matching jackets or shirts, and the outriders resplendent in their traditional red jackets and black helmets only enhanced the pageantry.

When the horses reached the starting gate, the announcer gave the post positions. Again. Then he was identifying each colt as he entered the gate. At the name Dealer's Choice, Number One, there was small response from the crowd. Brigid knew when Hotspur went into his slot: Molly clutched the binoculars until her knuckles whitened. Eric the Red caused a delay. The blaring voice announced that Eric the Red, Number Three, was being fractious.

"Get your big ass in there, Eric, let's get this shit over with."

The others caused no trouble.

They're at the post!

Then came that waiting hush, as if the crowd were holding its collective breath. It was endless. No one seemed to move.

Then the clanging of the bell, the crowd rising in a single wave of movement, and the voice crying: *They're off!*

The stands exploded with sound, a tumultuous roar that reached such a deafening and furious crescendo that Brigid could not be sure that she heard the voice behind her shouting into her ear: "Hotspur, Hotspur, Hotspur, you can do it, you've got to do it!" Kimberley went on and on, wild and urgent, so loud that she could not make out the words of the announcer, which blared in a breathless, steady stream:

They're running in a line, MacKinlay ahead by only a nose, Hotspur seemed to have trouble in the mud coming out of the chute, it's still MacKinlay by a full head on the straightaway, Sakren second by a quarter-length, Mainly Books and Dealer's Choice fighting for third, Dealer's Choice falling back now, True Blue moving up on him, with Eric the Red behind True Blue, trailing by a length, and Hotspur, Number Two, hitting his stride now, he had trouble back there, he's still well behind but gaining, mud flying, now up front Sakren's challenging MacKinlay as they approach the turn, with Mainly Books—look out, there's a horse down, Number One, Dealer's Choice, three horses directly behind—oh, my God, it's a pileup, Oh, my God—

Christ, two, not one, two, smack in front, going down, Spur, both of us, oh, God, three now, no way around, oh, Christ, three thrashing, *three,* have to go over, baby, Spur, up and over, only way, can't see now, goddamn mud, we're done, kaput, *up,* baby, only way, don't rear, straight ahead, don't swerve, try, try, *try,* Zach won't break your neck, you can do it, you—*now,* only way, only goddamn way, doing it, *flying,* nice, oh, Spur, baby, nice, we're clear, in the fuckin' *air*—now, down, down easy, you can breathe now, don't slip, keep those legs goin', oh, baby, we're off again, believe, believe, lean in there, stretch, *stretch,* it's in you, we're on the track, baby, now go, go, go—can't see, fuckin' goggles, *blind,* who's up there, nine lengths, maybe ten, you can do it, who we got, three down there in back, poor bastards, leaves three to go, who, who *who*—lay it on now, sweet Spur, into the turn, oh, sweet Christ, we'll never, never, have to, *will,* black silks, goddamn mud, slop, dots, white dots under muck, white-on-black, Mainly Books, that's who, fuckin' cow, up yours, cheerio, all that, don't let a hearse run over you—now what, please, baby, please, quarter pole behind, got enough dirt ahead, dirt, *shit*, slop, sorry about stick, baby, got to, *got* to, got to do it, *whap*, you're shook, baby, *whap*—can't see colors, white? white? MacKinlay?—diamonds, black diamonds, MacKinlay, Griffin up, here we are, Griff-boy, here we are, surprise, eighth pole, got you, Griff, how's them apples, what the fuck you doin' standin' still on the stretch, your turn now, eat ours, gag on it—oh, baby, one more, you're a beaut, we got second now, not enough, give it everything, to hell with place, do it for Clay, not me, Clay, goin' home, love, only one length to his tail, one, *hell, half*-length, shh, don't bear out, got plenty room, whole fuckin' track, straight ahead, blue stripes, Sakren, Sakren on the rail, tight, howdy, you mother, what you doin' way up here?—go, go, Spur—surprised Sakren?—only a head now, *your* head, Sakren—listen to those stands, blur, still a fuckin' blur, eye-to-eye now, heart-to-heart, there's the pole—you got second, Sakren, take place, cry your eyes out—go, Spur, *now*, two long ones, *two*, listen to them, all for you, baby, go, GO!

You did it, baby, listen to them, all for you, easy now, easy, oh, how you love that mud, you crazy bastard, you, you did it—didn't know you were a jumper, did you?—why you're a goddamn steeplechaser!

There you have it, folks. It's Hotspur by a half-length, Sakren second, and MacKinlay third by a full two lengths, with Mainly Books trailing across the wire by seven. Those results will not be final until the Official sign flashes on the tote board, but get your tickets ready because from where we sit up here in the press box it certainly appears, unless there's been a foul that we didn't catch, that the winner of the Derby Trial is Hotspur, Number Two, owned and trained by Clay Chalmers, with Sakren, Number Six, in second place, and MacKinlay, who started in the outside slot, Number Seven, finishing third. Mainly Books is fourth and last in a decimated field.

And what a race this has been. Once in a lifetime! Listen to that crowd. There have to be disappointed people among them—and some very worried ones—but you'd never know it from the uproar. Up here we've never seen or heard such a wild and tumultuous climax. That thunder must be heard as far away as Cincinnati and Indianapolis if not Chicago. What started out to be a rather routine running of the Derby Trial, only a preliminary to the main event four days from now, has turned into one of the most exciting come-from-behind victories ever witnessed on this track.

But now I'm told that our cameras and Art Bell are ready on the far side, so while we wait for the results to be made official, let's go over to the backstretch and try to find out what happened almost before the race could really get started. To Art Bell, who's over there trying to sort things out. Art?

Thank you, Jonno Brown. Well, it's still confusion over here if not chaos. An ambulance has just come onto the track. The police and security guards are trying to keep the infield crowd behind the fence, and there are some people from the stable area who have broken through, probably relatives and friends of the jockeys involved. It's hard to sort out, but there are two horses still in the mud. One has gotten up and limped to the backstretch gate. That's Number Three, Eric the Red. He appears to be cut up and he's bleeding, and when he walked, he was sort of carrying one foreleg, which is dangling, so he may be seriously injured. His rider, Davey Jessup, is still on the track, and as far as I can make out he hasn't moved. There's a doctor with him. More on him as soon as we know. Eric the Red was trailing True Blue and Dealer's Choice when Dealer's Choice, going all out, went down in the mud. He did not appear to lose his footing. He may have broken down—snapped a leg.

True Blue, who crashed into Dealer's Choice from behind, is still down, but this horse is moving, he's still very much alive at this point. The extent of his injuries will be determined by the vets, who are kneeling in the mud beside him. Kyle McCague, True Blue's jockey, I'm happy to report, left the track under his own power, not limping. He was mightily shaken up but angry, very angry, shaking off the hands of anyone who tried to help.

Dealer's Choice, who triggered the mishap by collapsing at full gallop, is now being loaded by a crane onto the dead animal conveyance. Al Manuel, who was aboard him, is already in the ambulance, which is now trying to leave the track, its wheels spinning. He was bleeding profusely and had to be lifted on a stretcher into the so-called Invalid Carrier. Good luck, Al, from your many fans.

It was, as some of you saw, a bizarre accident—a melee of precious, crippled horseflesh with legs thrashing in the air. It was a miracle that Kyle McCague managed to leap from True Blue's saddle to safety.

But speaking of miracles and leaps—how about that sensational jump by Hotspur, skippered with incredible split-second dexterity by that quick-thinking veteran, Zach Massing? If Hotspur is the horse of the hour, his rider is the man of the moment today.

They are not yet making any effort to move True Blue, ladies and gentlemen. He is still moving his head, probably in pain, and his trainer is conferring with the vets and with a man who has just arrived, who may be True Blue's owner, James Oliver. It could be bad news.

Now back to the press box on the other side of the track, where the results, which you have already heard, have just been made official and where the ceremonies in the winner's circle will commence momentarily. Come in, Jonno Brown.

The three other horses had left the track, their saddlecloths too mud-splattered to be identifiable to most of the crowd, which had not dispersed as usual to go to the pari-mutuel windows and gardens and bars. The winner's circle was the focus of interest, and in it Clay felt he was standing in a core of sound and turmoil: photographers, television cameras, shouted questions and calls, officials in red sports coats with insignia on the lapels, uniformed city police, track police, and Pinkertons.

Clay's whole body was throbbing—not with excitement and victory but with fury.

Bernie was yelling, "To hell with the cup, let's get this megillah over with—give us the purse, we'll get outta your way!" and in the crowd the little Irish girl was waving and smiling. "Don't let the spill bug you, Clay. Only an accident. Cheer up. We won, man, we *won!*"

It had not been an accident—not to Clay. And they had won, hell, yes, but by a fluke. A criminal fluke.

Kimberley was in that mob somewhere. He'd seen her when Elijah led the Spur into the horseshoe-shaped semicircle of hedge: not lifting her hand but her delicate face, framed in the big hat, subdued, almost shy. Was there pride in those hooded eyes? Satisfaction? Starbright would race against Hotspur now. But not even her beauty and the promise of the night ahead could reach that black, choking poison in him—not only rage but hate.

Clay cupped his hands, and Zach climbed back into the irons, the whip stuck in his belt behind. He'd wiped some of the black from his face and his three pairs of goggles. "We slipped coming out of the chute or we wouldn't have been back there."

"You saved him, Zach." It was hard for Clay to recognize his own voice. "You did one hell of a job and you saved us."

But Zach didn't hear. He was leaning backward in the saddle and running his small hand tenderly over the Spur's haunch and whispering, apologizing: "You was one scared colt, wasn't you? Didn't know what the fuck to do after we come down, did you? Well, Zach had to lay on with the stick, Spur, had to settle you in to run, you understand?" Then, his voice a soothing, loving purr, almost lost in all the racket: "It's over now, boy, stop shakin' now, it's all over, all over."

Clay clapped Zach on the leg. "Glad you're all in one piece, Zach. Not just the Spur but *you*."

The creases in Zach's smeared ugly face deepened and he looked down: "We did it, didn't we? Spur too—his goddamn *instinct* sent us flying like a bird."

Clay nodded. He didn't mention that Davey Jessup had died of a broken neck the instant he hit the wet dirt. Zach'd learn that soon enough.

The kid died for no reason. *None.* Waste!

When Clay joined Elijah, whose bald black head was gleaming

in the late sun, Elijah didn't glance at him but said: "I seen many a horse break down, but I been watching that one, works and Stepping Stone. He was marked for calamity, that's what. Mistreated, shame gonna fall on folks mistreat a animal like that. Dealer's Choice, he well outta his misery."

True. The owner's name was Bruno Vasaturo. The trainer was Calvin Roth. Clay wondered whether he had ever hated two men more.

Bernie was telling him that they wanted him up on the platform. "Smile, man. You look like you could murder somebody."

He could. Bruno Vasaturo and Calvin Roth. Murder.

"No, I guess they want you to stand there by Hotspur first, Clay. For the camera. Listen, we're gonna take the big one now. You know that, don't you?"

They killed a boy. One horse at least, maybe two.

The Spur whinnied softly and pushed Clay's shoulder with his nose. "Just a few minutes more now," Clay told him. "Elijah'll mash all that brown lather off, you'll take a nice slow walk—"

Had he ever really wanted, in his gut, to kill anyone before?

"Hold still now, Spur, let's get this shit over with." They risked my boy. They risked my horse. "Then some hay, lotta oats, and doughnuts for dessert." If they deserve to live, it shouldn't be in racing.

"Now up the steps, Clay, onto the platform, the man says—"

And then he was shaking a flabby hand, looking into a pair of bright but harried eyes, and the man in the red jacket was saying, "Well, Mr. Chalmers, how does it feel to own the horse that won the Derby Trial in such a spectacular way?"

"Great," he said. "Just great!"

You phony bastard. Who wants to win that way?

So he added, "I'm only glad we survived."

"My daddy was a gambling man, my mother was a whore. However much my daddy lost, my mother brought home more!"

"Owen. Where'd you ever hear such a song?"

"My old man. He used to sing it when he was feeling his oats."

"And was it true?"

"What?"

"Your mother—*was* she a whore?"

"I don't remember her too well. Toby always said she was a saint."

"That's sweet. Honest to goodness now, Owen, I do honestly think you believe that. That's dear."

"I'm a dear fella. Owen Chalmers—dear as they come."

"The sun's almost down, *dear* fellow—would you mind turning off the air conditioning?"

"Anything to please, yes, ma'am. That's my motto. There's a flask in the glove compartment."

"Hm. You do mean to please, don't you? And you do indeed, indeed take care of me, dear fellow."

I take care of you good, you hot bitch with the fancy ways. You're with me all the way now, and we're on the homestretch. Almost.

"It's been a lovely day, lovely, lovely. Do you think perhaps I've had enough? . . . Oh, Owen, you remembered. A touch of vermouth does it, always does it—"

"Sure you had enough. Why not? What do we have to do now except go home and fuck?"

"I'm not fond of that word. As you know."

The word. You like the act, though. And more, more than anyone ever gave you before, fancy lady. "Leave it all to Owen. He knows how to take care of you, love."

Luck's riding with me and I'm riding with luck. Take today. Just take this single day. Contracts signed in the morning, wrapped up neat and legal, and then the race. True Blue out now, no True Blue on Saturday, and Owen Chalmers didn't have to lift a goddamn finger. It was like I might've *planned* it. And all I did was watch it happen through the glasses. Frankie Voight took care-a Vincent Van, now Lady Luck herself takes care-a True Blue. Hell, it couldn't have been sweeter if I'd *paid* that Dealer's Choice to break down.

"You took care of me on the plane too, didn't you? You brought us out of that dive just when I thought—"

136

"Only thing that makes me sad is that Mr. Rosser won't be here Saturday."

"Don't talk about that, please. Please, darling, I can't bear to think about that, now when I'm feeling so . . . dreamy."

Luck again, only different. Stuart had to get his or he'da jammed the works. Wouldn't have had to happen if the old fart hadn't refused to sell. Bastard shouldn't have tried to cross Owen Chalmers. Nobody ought. 'Cause Owen Chalmers thinks big. Like ole Toby always said: *Think big.* Joke on you, Pop. You always thought big, but that's *all* you did. Your son, though—he's not only thinking, he's *doing.* And he's just getting into gear, so watch his dust. More mazuma'n you could ever dream of, Pop—drunk or sober, in your wildest!

"You looked so handsome, Owen. In your white suit. Why, even old Rachel Stoddard admired you. All of the women—I saw their eyes, and I was so . . . proud."

I saw their eyes too, honey-bitch. But Owen's gonna be a go-od boy. Got your name on the syndication contract now, but Owen's happy right in that elegant, soft four-poster. Whole thing, house and all, suits Owen fine, just hunky-dory.

"I wonder . . . do you think I should have gone today? So soon after, I mean—"

"It's what he would have wanted. Chris. I'll lay odds on it."

"Ye-es. He did try to make me happy. He did *try,* you know. You want a drink of my nice, nice gin, Owen?"

"No, thanks. I'm high enough."

Get any higher, I'll bust wide open!

"Nominating Fireaway for the Derby even . . . he *let* me convince him, you know."

He let you maybe, but you did it 'cause *I* convinced *you.* And you did that 'cause, maybe you didn't even know it last February, but you wanted what I got, hot-cunt.

"Stuart did always want me to have whatever I set my heart on, as he said. It wasn't his fault he got sick and then couldn't . . . you know."

"Fuck."

"Please don't use that word, Owen. Please."

137

Even Rosser's having those heart attacks—luck again, Owen's luck! Riding high now, riding real high for a snot-nosed kid that had to steal milk off front porches to put something in his gut sometimes—

"It's my fault he's not here with us, Chris. Hell, I know how to handle a plane better'n that."

"No, no, no, I won't have you blaming yourself—"

Dumb bitch. Fancy, fancy, bred in the blue. Ole Toby said that kind'd never *look* at you. Tough you didn't live to see the day, Pop.

"You saved us, Owen. You and me anyway—you really saved our lives."

Just keep thinking that way, bitch. You'll get your reward. I'll have you moaning. I'll make you *scream* tonight! Nobody ever gave it to you like that. I can tell. You're a good lay, big-tit. Starved ones always are.

"I'm beginning to feel sleepy, darling. The sun. And . . . all those old friends . . . and your beard . . . it looks like . . . it looks so bright in the sun—"

You'll like it better in between your legs—

"Oh, I'm so happy. In spite of . . . everything. Like coming home again—after all those years. And everyone calling me Chrissie. Nobody's called me Chrissie in . . . oh, years and years. You feel that way too, Owen? Seeing your brother again—"

Just that way, cunt. Only better.

"Has . . . has he changed much? Your brother."

"Not much. Not a goddamn bit, really . . ."

Turning down seven and a half grand, cash, gambling nothing could happen to his horse before the Derby. Well, fucker almost learned his lesson. Black bangtail almost got it. Twice. Coming outta the gate, then—

"That's nice. That's sweet. You never mentioned you even had a brother—"

No surprise, fancy lady. *Real* reason we're here. Only surprise is he didn't go down in that pileup. Wouldn't want that. Not before Saturday—

"I always wished I had a sister. Or brother. Or . . . I think I'm going to sleep, darling. You'll wake me when we get home, won't you?"

Home. If it was home and if we were married—

"You will wake me, won't you? And . . . carry me in—"

"You can bet on it."

Married. Don't give me any more ideas, cunt.

Appalled, still shaken to the roots more than an hour later, Brigid, God forgive her selfishness, was thinking of Molly. She no longer prayed, but if she could, she would thank God that Molly had not been riding.

Andrew was driving his blue Mercedes in silence. He had become a stranger. It was more than understandable, but the change in him had been bewildering in spite of the circumstances. Before he had left his seat to join the Olivers and help manipulate their son's wheelchair up the steps from their box, he had offered to have her driven to the hotel, but she had insisted—for reasons obscure to herself, possibly because she did not relish being alone—on waiting for him. She had watched the last race of the day, which had been an unexciting and uneventful one, and then, when he had rejoined her, he had been grave and distant. In such sharp and startling contrast to the man she had felt she was getting to know. In the motorcar he had answered her inquiries politely enough, but in a dull, flat voice and without glancing in her direction.

True Blue had a shattered left knee and had to be destroyed. His rider? He had leaped clear.

Eric the Red could be saved. He would never race again but would be sold by Mr. and Mrs. Einarsson and would probably stand at stud. His jockey, a boy of twenty-two, had died instantly of a broken neck. And the Einarssons themselves? They were giving up racing and returning to Iceland before the Derby.

Dealer's Choice? Andrew's tone had not changed: The horse did not lose his footing in the mud, according to the monitoring film. "He snapped a foreleg. He broke down." She had recalled then the coarse-looking men and the overdressed women who had passed them on the clubhouse stairway earlier. She remembered that Andrew had stiffened and she had wondered whether Andrew might be a snob. "The jockey is in the hospital. He'll recover but he won't race again this year."

Andrew's replies had been strictly informational. She had been disconcerted, and now she felt pushed aside and lonely again. She was tempted to invent some silly, empty prattle that might force him to talk to her. Or to take his mind off the tragedy—which, after all, did not involve him directly. But she could not, or would not.

Molly had not returned to the box, so Brigid had assumed that she had gone to the stable area to celebrate with her mysterious new friend, whose name was Bernard Golden: a pleasant-enough appearing chap, excited as a small boy in the winner's circle, but an odd choice for Molly for sure. The lad Kevin, who was here at Molly's plea, was tall and lean, almost skinny; whereas this Bernard Golden was short and—yes—almost fat.

Kimberley had not returned to the box either. Brigid recalled her shouting Hotspur's name when the eighth race had begun and could only assume that Kimberley was with young Clay Chalmers now. Could that be the reason for Andrew's mood? Well, whatever lay between Andrew and his daughter, it was something that Brigid still wanted no part of, thank you kindly. And it was something that she already knew she could not fight. Fight? Whatever on earth put that word into her mind?

But, aloud, she said: "Kimberley should be happy." What was she doing, testing the man, baiting him? "She does want her colt to run against Hotspur, doesn't she?"

Andrew spoke in the same low, flat tone: "Hotspur won by default."

Was there a note of hostility in his voice? Had her intuition about the cause of his mood been correct? Was it this that she wanted?

"Whatever I may have against Clay Chalmers as a man," Andrew said then, "he's too good a horseman not to know that himself."

The life seemed to go out of her. It was all beyond her, and so it should be. She was not involved. Thank the good Lord. Well, if silence was what the man wanted, then silence, so be it, he would have.

The traffic now was lighter, but he did not increase his speed. She was eager to get to the hotel. But Andrew seemed scarcely aware that he was driving.

And then, out of nowhere, to her utter astonishment he was speaking. He spoke her name. Once. "Brigid." In a whisper. And then, not in a whisper, but slowly, very slowly: "I can't talk. Please understand. Brigid, I'm afraid to talk. I might shout. I'm afraid I might yell." He took a deep shuddering breath, still staring ahead. "James Oliver's one of the finest men I've ever known. He's so shattered and furious he'll have one hell of a hard time recovering. His wife Helen has been sober for two years—she's already back on the bottle again. Hard. Their son—you saw him, Leonard—Leonard's been hit the hardest. Jim told me. True Blue is . . . was, in a sense, Leonard's horse. He's crying, weeping like a five-year-old child. He was thrown three years ago in a hunt, and he's a paraplegic for life." The words came faster now and harsher, and his heavy shoulders heaved again. "It did not need to happen. All this destruction. All this grief. It's obscene. None of it should have happened. One man dead—a jockey's a man, he's not a bright toy on top of a horse. Davey Jessup was a twenty-two-year-old *man* with a great future, who wanted to *live* just like the rest of us!" His voice was rising, filling the entire car. "Not to mention Al Manuel in the hospital and the Einarssons. Not to mention two horses wantonly *killed*! Another one maimed. Why? Because a horse was run that should not have been raced today. He was not sound. His owners knew it, his trainer had to know it. They didn't care, they didn't *care*!" Suddenly he was hammering with his fist on the steering wheel. "People like that shouldn't be in racing. They don't *care*! People like that should be punished for their crimes, but the sad part is, the terrible thing is, they don't even know they're guilty, and if they did, they wouldn't *care*!"

Abruptly the explosion was over. He subsided. The interior of the motorcar seemed to echo with the angry, anguished sound.

And just as abruptly Brigid understood. What she had taken for snobbery was not snobbery at all, but outrage. Moral outrage.

The same kind that Daniel Tyrone—gentle Daniel—might have felt.

"Anyone who's in racing because he loves it," Andrew said then in a different tone altogether, "has to be sickened by a thing like this." Then he faced her. His face was white. "I'm sick, Brigid, God's truth, I'm sick."

Reaching, Brigid realized with a soft jolt in her breast that she could possibly—yes, quite possibly—she could love this man.

Chapter Four

"TURN the radio up, Mario. I always liked that song. 'In the Still of the Night' by Irving Berlin. Bruno knows the old-timers. Hey, wake up, Cal, we're comin' into Cherry Hill."

"I wasn't asleep."

"Still whinin'? You got a soft heart, Calvin. I like that in a trainer."

"I been thinking about Al Manuel. Intensive care unit. Broken pelvis. Ruptured bladder—"

" 'While the world is in slumber' . . . so the jockey can't pee for a while."

"Busted right arm, fractured ribs, concussion."

"Name of the game."

"He's lucky to be alive."

"Who ain't?"

"His agent says his boy'll never ride for Tidewater again."

"Jocks're a dime a dozen. Thirty-five clams a throw, ten percent of the purse, if any. You tell his agent for Bruno Vasaturo, if he squawks too loud, they got extra beds, that intensive care unit."

"Two horses dead, including Dealer's Choice. One jockey on a slab."

"Tough shit."

"Yeah."

" 'Oh, the times without number'. . . look, Cal, I lost a bundle on True Blue myself."

"You bet against your own horse and got yours—that's kinda beautiful."

"Calvin—Mr. Calvin Markel Roth, Junior—you been a thorn up my ass all the way from Louisville. Even before."

"All I been trying to do is tell you. A thoroughbred, you pump him full a bute, you kill the pain that'd keep him from going if he could feel it. You shoot him with cortisone, baste the poor bastard in iodine, he'll give you all he's got, he'll run till there's nothing left but dog meat."

"That's what you do for a living, Calvin."

"Yeah. Don't think I don't know it."

"That Berlin sure knew how to write a song. Listen, Calvin, Tidewater ain't a stable, we're a factory. We churn 'em out. You know just what platers to claim, and you know just how to make 'em perform."

"Yeah. And when we're finished with them—"

"We sucker a buyer or they crack. Let the fuckin' writers bleat about ripoffs, that shit, it's business."

"Bruno . . . I think I want out."

"Calvin, baby—you know the rules. Nobody gets out."

"That's it, then, a life sentence?"

"Better'n a death sentence."

"Jesus."

"Don't turn in the driveway, Mario. Pull up here. Calvin, look at that house—nineteen rooms. A Tudor mansion, right? Nice neighbors—nice kids, bicycles, Jags, Caddies. Short piss to the Garden State, Pimlico. Longer piss to Belmont, the Big A. I was born over a candy store in the Bronx. So, Calvin, we both made a pile, right? Them high-toned snobs back there'n Kentucky, Virginia, they think they can shut us out. Hell, we run the fuckin' show."

"Jesus."

"So now, go on in the driveway, Mario. Calvin's got the point, right, Calvin?"

"Jesus H. Christ."

144

"Y'ever hear of that commandment—taking the name of the Lord thy God in vain? You don't wanna burn in hell, do you?"

"I'm already there."

"You oughta go to church, Cal. Like me."

We interrupt your late night listening for a bulletin that has just come into our newsroom—

"Finish the song, you bastards!"

We have just been handed a report that fire has broken out in the stable area of Churchill Downs in Louisville, Kentucky. There is an unconfirmed rumor—we emphasize that it is only a rumor at this time—that the blaze started in the barn where the horses that are scheduled to run in the Kentucky Derby are sequestered. More news as it comes in. And now back to the music of Cole Porter.

A phone was ringing, but when he opened his eyes, it was dark, and it took three or four rings before Wyatt could orient himself: He was not in his flat in Baltimore; this one was still unfamiliar, and for some uncivilized reason there was no telephone in the bedroom. It took another couple of rings for him to locate the light switch in the white-walled living room and another couple before he could stumble his way to the glass-topped cocktail table. The telephone was almost lost among the art books that his friend Vilma Solotorovski had left stacked and strewn there. He lifted the instrument, blinking at the huge abstract paintings hanging on every damned wall, and then he spoke carefully, as usual, not giving his name. Could be some drunk who wanted to object to a broadcast or argue the odds he'd predicted.

Even when the voice spoke, he wondered. Because what the voice said was the sort of thing some wag might try to lay on Count Wyatt. But it was the night sports editor of a Louisville paper, who said he knew Wyatt would want to get over to the Downs because, although he had no details, he'd learned that there was a fire in the Derby barn.

"The Derby barn itself?"

"For all I know, pal, it's a hoax. Or it could be the whole back-stretch is burning."

He thanked his friend, who had once been a drinking acquaintance when he was on the *Baltimore Sun*—and he was a damned thoughtful one. Wyatt replaced the phone and shook his head like a horse whinnying, trying to force the sleep out of his brain. The sleep and the booze.

Hoax? It was always possible in a world of idiots. But another word took over in his mind as he returned, heavy-footed and stiff-jointed, to the bedroom. Jinx. He'd used it himself on the air, and after the tragic fiasco at the Derby Trial only a few hours ago the word had echoed there several times. Good God—if there was one—what next?

And *how* many hours since the Trial? He looked at the figures on the illuminated digital clock: WED/01/03.

When the buzzer sounded in its soft we-hope-we're-not-disturbing-you way, Clay did not reach across Kimberley to pick up the foreign-looking telephone. He placed a hand on Kimberley's bare shoulder and shook it gently. No one was going to catch him answering the phone in Miss Kimberley Cameron's bedroom this time of night, whatever the hell time it was. She didn't waken but made soft sounds of pleasure deep in her throat, almost but not quite as sensual as the ones she had made earlier, more than once.

Another polite buzzing.

No wonder Kimberley couldn't open her eyes. She'd gotten herself amusingly and amazingly sloshed at the victory celebration in Bernie's big trailer—*Congratulations, everyone! Now, Clay, you'll have to run against Starbright!*—and then later, here in bed, she'd been even more playful and exciting in a very different way.

The sound repeated itself. He'd broken down and had one tall, weak bourbon and branch, and only one. He'd been too damn angry to drink, and he was taking no chances. He wasn't going to risk blanking out, ever again. He'd been too angry that night seven years back—angry at her for refusing to leave Blue Ridge with him, and then even angrier at himself later for not being able to remember. He'd probably never get over what he might or might not have done. His life had never been the same. His and possibly hers.

The spurts of buzzing became short-spaced and urgent. He increased the pressure of his hand, and her eyes opened. Partly. She scowled a second, then smiled and turned over to face him. He could feel the soft warmth of her body against his. But she heard the sound then, sighed, made a face, and rolled away. Half-sitting, she muttered into the phone, unaware and uncaring that the fawn-colored sheet, which almost matched her falling hair, had fallen from her back and breasts.

"Yes? . . . Andrew? What—"

Then she listened. He saw the muscles of her back stiffen.

"God." Then in a rush: "What about Starbright? What did Jason say about Starbright?"

Clay waited. Her father's voice had apparently silenced her.

Then: "Not there? Why isn't Mr. Arnold there?" She held the phone pressed against her ear and she was upright as she listened. "He's lying, isn't he, Andrew? Something *has* happened to him. You're lying too!"

Her head began to shake from side to side.

"No, no, you won't have to take me. Clay's here." Then in a louder tone she added: "He's right here in bed beside me!"

Clay shrugged. What the hell, her old man must have known that. Then why'd she have to say it?

"Yes, yes, I'll see you there." She slammed the phone into its cradle and did not move when she said, "Something's happened to Starbright, and they're all lying to me. There's a fire in his barn and . . . oh, my God, I can't believe it, I *refuse* to believe it!"

Even as he reached to take her shoulder, Clay could not control the thought: Thank God Hotspur was in barn 27.

"Incendie?" And then Paul Hautot heard himself repeating the word into the telephone. *"Incendie? Où ça?"* His mind was blurred by sleep, but worse, his body was exhausted. Outside the windows of

the hotel the sky was dark, and he had to force himself to concentrate. He remembered to speak Spanish then, because his groom,
Julio, was from Barcelona and had learned little French, and even
less English. It seemed there was a fire, or there had been a fire in
the stable where Bonne Fete was stalled. He listened: Bonne Fete
had been safely removed, and his trainer was en route to the
Downs. Julio was regretful to disturb Señor Hautot, but he did
not wish that he learn of this event from strangers, thank you, señor.
Paul Hautot shrugged and regarded the American boy still sleeping
in the bed. The smooth-faced one who had insisted on addressing
him, even in the most intimate of moments, as Mr. Huhtot. He
stepped to the bed and spoke: "Robert." When the bland, innocent eyes were open, he apologized in English: "There has been
an accident at the stables, and my horse has been seriously injured.
I shall be obliged to go there at once." And then, after the hulk
had taken his money and departed, Paul Hautot picked up a
stemmed glass and sipped the tepid dregs of champagne—
pronounced by the boy sham-pain. Awake now, he reflected that
the blind Benedictine monk, Dom Pérignon, who was said to have
invented the wine, had then exclaimed: "I am drinking the stars."
Poor fellow, if he ever dreamed in his grave what this California
brew tasted like, he would roll over in profound dismay. Paul
looked out the French windows: not a chimney pot in view, only
gray, flat, dreary rooftops with black puddles. He wondered, not for
the first time, why he had ever left Paris. He returned to the bed,
and in his mind he summoned up the vision of Annabelle with a
man moving on top of her. The picture never failed to excite him.
What a blessed relief to be alone again.

"Molly?"

Do not scream now. Hold yourself in hand. It's a dream.

"St. Elizabeth and Mary's Hospital, Mrs. Tyrone. Do you hear
me now?"

In her mind the words, black on yellow: *Invalid Carrier.* Yes,

Mr. McGreevey, Mrs. Tyrone hears you, but she knows it's only a dream—

"For further examination, the medic said. Sure, the lass was conscious and all—"

"Mr. McGreevey—"

"Agh, 'tis bedlam itself here, a terrible state o' chassis—"

Speak softly now. Speak low. "How?"

"The poor colts, they had to be let loose, with all the smoke that black and billowin'—"

Low. *Quietly!* "How, Mr. McGreevey? *How* did it happen?"

"It's a cruel and dreadful thing t'have to tell ye—"

"*How?*" A scream at last, why not! "HOW?"

"The child was trampled, ma'am."

Trampled?

"Agh, me heart's crackin' in me chest. She come tearin' out from somewhere, as Kevin tells it. Sure, the uproar was somethin' frightful. He thought the lass was at the hotel with you for sure—"

Sirens wailing, some long, some short bursts of sound behind his voice. A bell clanging. Voices shouting and a whistle—

"Trampled in what way, Gregory?"

"The girleen did what she thought she had to do to save the colt. She was tryin' to lead him away but the animal was spooked and—"

"Thrall? Irish Thrall himself?"

"Will you find the route alone? Kevin has the colt in hand, not a cut, not a scratch, only the shakin' and shudderin' in terror, every inch and nerve—"

"I'll find the route, Gregory."

"The good sister'll care for the both of you—"

Irish Thrall himself.

"The poor beast had no thought of what he was doin'—"

"Thank you, Gregory." Gregory—my friend, my true dear friend—

You must dress now. Anything. Not the dinner gown. Andrew? Andrew has his own life. A taxicab.

God, let her live. Whatever else, I'm praying, God, *Our Father who art in heaven*, after all these years, hear me, *Hail Mary, full of grace*, I am praying again, I am begging, let my Molly live, relieve her pain and let her live, please, please—

JD lost his last game of eight ball, that was it for the night, and he left the poolroom in back, where there was no TV but plenty of smoke, some of it grass, and he came into the bar, where there *was* a TV and just as much smoke. The same cat was still sitting on the same stool, watching some old movie and still guzzling beer. He looked as friendly as before, but he was tough and big and mean, no conning JD Edwards with that phony grin, JD knew a fucking nigger-hater when he came across one. Old honky was just waiting to jab the needle back in—and just begging to get that big ugly nose shoved down to his asshole. JD had blown almost a hundred at the table, and he knew he'd been hustled, only he couldn't prove it, and besides, every dude in this noisy hole, white and black, knew who he was by now, so in a way his balls were cut off. What really hacked him was that they tried to act kind of friendly, like they didn't know what to say to someone who owned a horse in the Derby. But there's always some turd around with his questions— like where'd he get that name Also Ran and how many horses without balls ever did win. Seven, that's how many, but screw them, he wouldn't say it. JD still had his pride. Saying it'd only make that one pisser laugh louder. JD'd had a gutful of his wise-ass jive. He told the big-tit white gal back of the bar he'd have another vodka, and he told himself it was his last, he was really getting boozed up, and Almeta'd have nothing to say about that—which was worse than her having *something* to say, way she did it. Hitch being that he really loved that pretty gal, and damned if he knew what'd happen to him if she ever decided to split. The big prick the other side of the horseshoe bar only frowned across, like he was mixed up or maybe trying to think of some new way to lay it on the nigger. Ignore him. But if he hits his horn one more time, come down on him like napalm and ice him. Only while JD waited for his drink the mother didn't come through. What he said was, "JD, you better get your ass down to the Downs. They broke into the

movie a while ago and said there was a fire out there in the barns."
The bar girl set down his glass: "They said they'd have more later,
and the TV crew is on its way, or maybe there by now. I didn't
hear." And then the big guy said, "We didn't know whether to tell
you or not, seeing the way you been spoiling for trouble all
night—"

"I debated whether to disturb you or not, Mrs. Stoddard, but I
didn't want you to hear it from somebody else."

"I appreciate that, Crichton. Is the fire under control?"

"It was a small and limited conflagration, and it was brought
under control in short order. There is still smoke, of course."

"Very good. And Ancient Mariner? . . . Well, Crichton, speak
up. Is he back in his stall?"

"His stall was adjacent to the one where the hay was burning—"

"I trust they intend to move all the animals from the barn tonight. Well, Crichton?"

"It's not good news."

"Mr. Crichton, you are absolutely the largest man I have ever
known, but I can scarcely hear your voice. I've never known you to
shilly-shally before, and you are frightening me. So now I know
something has happened to Ancient Mariner, and my mind is picturing things that are probably far worse than reality, so please tell
me now: what?"

"He has injured two legs. The near foreleg does not concern Doc
Carpenter so much, but the off hindleg has fractures above and
below the hock, and that's very unusual. It's clear that he panicked
and in doing so kicked at the walls of his stall, probably many times.
I'm furious at the security guards, but my own feeling is that they
panicked too, and they are probably terrified of horses, especially
spooked horses, the way most people—"

"I shall be there at once."

"Please, Mrs. Stoddard, I knew you'd say that. There's really no
need. You can't imagine what it's like here. Between the smoke and
turmoil I can't tell one horse from another."

"Of course I can imagine. I've been through my share of stable fires like any other horsewoman. Enough to know, Crichton, that horses respond sensitively to such pandemonium and often long after it is over. And horsewoman enough to realize that I'm going to have to decide what must be done to him or for him. I shall be there just as soon as Joseph can have the car brought round."

"Mrs. Stoddard, I assure you that there is nothing you can do."

"I can be with my horse when he needs me. Thank you for your call, Crichton."

For some time Naomi Yogi hesitated to knock on the bedroom door, knowing that behind it the thick, short body of his employer, Hosomoto Takashi, was sandwiched between, or otherwise intermingled with the long, slim bodies of the two American blondes. What he had to report was outrageous to his mind. A fire, imagine! Such an event would be unthinkable in Japan. Why, some two thousand horses were stabled in the famous Ritto Training Center, but in an orderly, safe, and certainly fireproof manner. From his first glimpse Yogi had found the stable area here an appalling spectacle: bales of hay, often *stacks* of hay, everywhere, in the shedrows, in the walking area between stables, in trucks and other conveyances. And tack rooms with the tack hanging from nails on walls, incredible squalor, some with bunks and cots—they were even used as sleeping quarters for the stable help who were not lodged in trailers and campers parked helter-skelter. And the odors! It sickened him in the stomach. At Ritto, where several thousand employees resided, everything was uncluttered and above all *clean* . . . Nevertheless, he was taking pleasure in this holiday and profiting as well. The difference between the sum of American dollars that Hosomoto Takashi had provided to obtain the services of the blondes and the sum that Yogi had actually paid to the blondes' procurer amounted to more than a sufficient sum of American dollars to enable Yogi to entertain the black-haired American girls who were more to his liking and also more than willing to dine and drink and bed with the tall, handsome young Japanese gentleman for the thrill of it.

Groupies, he had learned they were called here, and so long as they believed that he himself was the owner of a Kentucky Derby contender romantically named Fuji Mist, they were delighted to provide him with the services that his employer had to purchase. Now, though, he did not desire to rouse his employer's displeasure by failing to do what might be expected of him, so he tapped carefully on the bedroom door. When Hosomoto Takashi inquired, sleepily but politely, what he wanted at this time of night, Yogi explained through the door in as few words as possible, making certain to assure Hosomoto Takashi that Fuji Mist was unharmed. He anticipated the reply that he now received: "Did you rouse me to speak of horses?" Yogi apologized formally and withdrew. He heard feminine voices, one giggling and one protesting, so he assumed that, once awakened, Hosomoto Takashi was prepared to return to his nocturnal wallowings.

Fireaway? Was he talking about Fireaway?

"Eric says he heard a commotion and managed to get him out before he could even start to sweat." Christine watched Owen get up from the four-poster bed—so delicious, so deep and soft, did he have to go?—and through a haze she could see his tall, naked body and his enormous penis. Imagine noticing that now. He was picking up his clothes from the floor. "Some crazy creep just started opening stall doors. Probably one of the Pinks as freaked as the bangtails. There must've been a kind of stampede. Wild, man, wild."

She made up her mind. She stood up. Or tried to. "I'm going with you." Her knees threatened to cave in. She was really not sure.

"Like hell, Chrissie." Now Owen was calling her Chrissie. Lovely. So many people, nice people, had called her Chrissie at the track today. Or was it yesterday now? "You're going to go back to sleep." She could see the great strength of his body, the torso and legs long as tree trunks, all covered with thick brown-red hair. "You lay back down there now." *Lay.* She did wish he could learn to say *lie.* "The fire's already out, or almost out, but it must be hell-on-wheels out there. Some exercise girl got trampled." At once she was ashamed of her feelings. She sank down to sit on the bed. Owen, dressing, was frowning. "Goddamn shame somebody had to get hurt. Horses go haywire if they even smell smoke. One of them's been hurt. Ancient Mariner." Ancient Mariner—wasn't that Rachel Stoddard's colt? Old Mrs. Stoddard had been so sweet and kind earlier. "They don't know how bad yet. Some goddamn jerk probably dropped a cigarette butt. Or maybe a match." As he pulled on the black shirt which had looked so fine with his white suit in Mrs. Stoddard's box at the track the long muscles of his arms seemed to ripple with vigor, strength. "Not enough security around there, specially at night." What was he doing? He was bringing the decanter to the bed. "Next thing out, you'll see, they'll start lookin' for mischief." He was pouring gin into her glass on the bedside table. "Like somebody'd do a fool thing like that on purpose. Can't think of any goddamn reason anybody would—unless it was to injure a horse and collect insurance." He set the sparkling decanter on the table within reach and towered above her.

"Thank you, darling." Her tongue was thick and as dry as her throat. Owen knew that she would have to have a drink or two now if she was ever going to go back to sleep.

"I won't even call you, Chrissie. Eric says Fireaway's good as new. It's so late now I might stay there for the works." He stooped down, way down, to kiss her. On top of the head. God, her hair must be a frightful jumble. "You lay back and go to sleep now, like a good girl. Owen's taking care of everything, baby." Then he was moving to the hall in those long beautiful strides, his body heavy but his step light.

She heard the muffled thud of his boots on the carpet of the wide-curving staircase—and panic struck. She couldn't stay here the rest of the night in this big strange house. She reached for the glass under the bed lamp. She simply could not, could not be alone, because then she would start thinking of Stuart. She heard the front door open and close. Why, why had Stuart always been so opposed to cremation? She took a slow sip. Now . . . now, because of that, his stubbornness again, his body would lie out there in a cold vault for days. A whole week at least. And then she would have to go back. She closed her eyes and drained the glass. Owen had been right, though: Stuart would not have wanted her to miss the Derby. Especially if Fireaway won. She poured half a glass. Sweet Stuart. *He* had been handsome too. Once. How long ago that seemed. She drank and then set down the glass and stretched out on the bed. She closed her eyes without turning off the light. Fireaway would win. Owen would see to that. How fortunate she had been to have *Owen*. How fortunate she *was*.

She was warm inside now, all the way down her body to her ankles. The tender part of her flesh between her legs felt bruised and scraped. Owen's beard. Owen could make love for so long and in so many ways. He could extend it forever, tormenting her, torturing her so exquisitely, in and in again and deeper in, deeper, until sometimes she actually felt that she was leaving her own body.

Rachel Stoddard discovered that, after all, she was stunned, and she felt only half-dressed as Joseph drove the dark limousine through the night-hushed streets. In the distance now she could hear sirens, and a single bell clanged forlornly. There was a most peculiar knot in her stomach, and her eyes seemed blurred. Rachel had always prided herself on her eyesight—why, even at eighty-three she could still pretty well make out the action on the backstretch without binoculars. Now her eyes seemed a trifle out of focus. There seemed to be an extraordinary amount of traffic on the streets, and when the long car turned and she caught sight of the twin spires—how shadowy they looked now—she realized that she was sitting forward on the seat, her huge body heavy and strangely stiff. She knew that her crown of silver had to be askew. A fire truck passed going in the opposite direction, its bell sounding in light, spaced spurts and no red light showing. There were people on porches here and there and a few gathered on the curb, most wearing nightclothes. Why, it was the middle of the night, wasn't it?

On the narrow street that led to the stable gate there were more fire apparatus and vehicles along the curb, headlights burning, engines churning. And police patrol cars. And more people plastered against the steel-mesh fence. And cars moving along in a slow, steady stream, faces at the windows, and policemen with lighted batons trying to keep the traffic moving. Uniforms of all sorts and kinds seemed to be everywhere. Withal an atmosphere of chaos only just adequately restrained. There was something ominous and unsettling about the scene—as if havoc threatened.

A guard at the gatehouse, who had waved Joseph through many times, insisted on seeing his identification papers. Within the high fence the entire stable area seemed a snarl and clutter: cars and trucks parked at odd, careless angles, as if abandoned, some with headlights still burning, dust thick in the air and heavy as brown fog in the weird pattern of light, a jumble of voices, shouting and calling, and as they passed slowly along between the track and barns she could hear horses in the various stables stomping and whinnying. People seemed to be hurrying about on all sides, men and women running with cameras dangling from their shoulders. Two police cruisers with revolving blue dome lights were parked nose to nose, blocking further passage to the Derby barn. She could not even see it—only, above the roofs, the glare of a huge floodlight laced by streaking blue and red flares.

"I'll walk, Joseph."

But before Joseph could get out and come round, Alex Crichton's huge face loomed outside the window. But he did not open the door.

She touched the button, and the glass rolled down. "Let me out, please, Mr. Crichton."

"Do you want to talk here, Mrs. Stoddard, or would you prefer to go into the racing secretary's or the TRPB office over there?"

She did not sit back. "I can hear you perfectly well, Crichton."

His face, which was homely and misshapen by nature but touched now by apprehension and tenderness, filled the aperture, brows like brown quills, balding head out of view. "Mrs. Stoddard, he's in shock, but he's sedated and partially anaesthetized, so he's calm and lying down and no longer in intense pain." He spoke as if he had rehearsed the words. "The bone of the near fore pastern has cut through the skin, but Doc Carpenter has it in ice and has stopped the hemorrhaging."

"And the off hindleg?"

"Mrs. Stoddard—"

"Please, Crichton."

"Shattered. Above and below the hock."

"Yes?"

"Doc Carpenter recommends euthanasia."

"But . . . surely, with all the sophisticated procedures developed for fractures—at least surgery must be attempted."

The head shook, once. "It was violent, Mrs. Stoddard. He must have kicked and thrashed, but not only that. He must have crashed his whole body against the stall wall. The wood's splintered and cracked. With all that weight—"

"X-rays?"

"I can have him transported to the Longmeadow barn. It would not be easy on him."

She tried to take a deep breath. "You are saying then that it's the vet's opinion that nothing can be done." It was not a question.

"Yes, Mrs. Stoddard. I'm sorry."

He did not need to say that. She was not breathing at all now, but her heart was exploding, over and over and over. "They almost saved Ruffian."

Again the huge head shook. "Only almost. And Ancient Mariner's a lot like Ruffian. In spirit." He paused and then added: "Do we want to put him through that?"

"Get . . . a second opinion."

"I have." Then, in a whisper: "Doc Hartwell. One of the best surgeons in the business."

She could not speak then. She did not try. She heard a siren's low retreating wail. It sounded mournful. Like a train at night remembered from childhood.

"It's the only humane and merciful thing, ma'am." Crichton only rarely addressed her as ma'am. There was love in his voice. Anguish. She heard the low, rough compassion and knew it was not only for the Mariner but for her. Had he sensed then what this animal, this particular animal, meant to her? Did Crichton, who had been there when the horse was foaled and when Eugene died— did he know why this moment was unbearable?

157

"We must have your permission, you know."

She did not say what had to be said. She only nodded her head. She did not weep. But she collapsed inside, and she knew that something had gone from her. Something had gone from her forever.

Things had certainly quieted down, but it had been as if he had wanted to wait until the last dog died, as they said where he came from. Maybe he just didn't want to go back to the motel. Being here in all this ruckus and hullabaloo, with the TV cameras and the floodlights and the firemen and police, had been exciting, and that was that. Fire engines and cop cars were still pulling away when he came out the gate and went to find the taxi he'd left waiting. Let the meter run, what the hell; wasn't every day a druggist who didn't have anything really world-shaking to watch from year to year could see something like *he'd* just seen. The taxi driver almost sneered when he told him to take him to the Holiday Inn on the Bardstown Road. "I brought you, didn't I?" Walter Drake felt like using an obscene word that he never used, but he sat back and ignored the man, who said, "Cigarette in the hay, way they told me out there— mostly smoke damage, right? Some brouhaha over nothing." On the way there the man had bragged that even though he'd been born here in Louisville he couldn't ever work up any sweat over which horse beat which other horse in a lousy mile and a half. Walter hadn't bothered to tell him that the Derby was a mile-and-a-quarter race. But he had told him about Prescription being so fond of beer, and the man hadn't so much as smiled. "I'm a base-ball freak," he had said. "Cincinnati Reds. I go up there every home game. Horses are for the birds. They're always talking about immortal—hell, they'll all end up dog food, won't they?" People were no longer out on their porches now, and most of the lights in the little houses had been turned out. Walter had been tempted to call Susan and tell her that Prescription was okay, but he didn't want to bother her if she was still asleep. She hadn't wakened when Chip Cardinal, the trainer, had called to report, because she had taken the extra sleeping pill after he'd begged her to. But he'd been lying awake there in the other big bed, thinking of the past again, reliving it in bits and pieces. Margo going off to her first prom, how she looked in her apricot-colored gown—bright and eager. Sentimental things like that. And other things too: Terry's face twisting in pain in the emergency room after the second accident, the one where the car had turned over and he'd almost been killed. Walter had come to hate memory. And especially nostalgia. That was most of Susan's trouble—longing to have back what was gone forever. He closed his eyes: Maybe the driver'd think he was dozing. Well, he'd shot his bolt. He'd phoned Margo in Bogotá on the QT and offered to pay her air fare if she could make it for the Derby, but Margo had said her husband was too busy and she was working at the American Embassy and besides she wasn't feeling well and was thinking of seeing a doctor. No sale. But he'd made the old college try. If a man can afford to own a thoroughbred he can sure afford to spend a thousand dollars to make sure his wife enjoys the race, win or lose. Margo was sorry. And so was her father. He opened his eyes. They were passing the headquarters of the Colonel Sanders Kentucky Fried Chicken chain: a Southern mansion set back in a sea of green lawn, all lighted up. He continued to stare out the window. Remembering Susan a few nights before they left Terre Haute, crying out in her sleep from the next bed: "Oh, Terry, won't you ever learn? When are you going to stop doing these things?" Her words had been very clear, as if she were reliving scenes she should forget. Her voice had sounded so exasperated yet so full of love: "Terry, are you ever going to grow up?" Had he grown up? They didn't know. Imagine that, not even knowing where your only son was. On some skid row somewhere, or in prison. Or in some commune stoned out of his mind. His good mind too. The wrecked cars, the injuries, surgeries, courtrooms, the bitterness in him, and the gentleness at times, even joy, the colleges entered, dropped out of, and the debts piled up that had to be paid by somebody. How was it that the boy had never learned to function in a real world? Whose fault was it? Where had it all gone wrong? There were times when he felt like he'd just have to write the boy off. But how could a man write off his own son? "Holiday Inn, mister." Startled, Walter stiffened. He was, he realized, one tired man. And the excitement had worn off. "Man I'd like to meet," the driver said—"that'll be twenty-three seventy, with the wait," and he lifted the flag—"man I'd like to meet is that JD Edwards, even if he is a dinge. You know him?" Walter, giving the driver thirty dollars as he climbed out, said that up to now he hadn't had that pleasure, sorry. Why was he always saying he was sorry? He went into the lobby, which was usually crowded but empty this time of morning, and walked down a corridor, then made a turn. And heard voices. A drunken all-night party? But when he reached the door of his own room, key in hand, he stopped. A peal of laughter—from inside his own room! And when he unlocked the door and went in, Susan was standing between the beds in her night robe, and Margo was coming out of the bathroom. Margo herself, in a traveling suit, Margo who had always been so easygoing and so delightful and looked just that way now. She came into his arms and she kissed him several times and she whispered, "Poppa, the reason I wasn't feeling like myself was . . . is . . . that I'm pregnant. After four years. What do you think of that, Poppa?" And Susan was saying that there wasn't a room in town to be had, so Margo would sleep in her bed and she would sleep with Walter in his. "We used to sleep in the same bed all the time!" Susan cried, and Margo laughed, the way she always had, and Susan said, "You are a sly one, Walter Drake. Margo told me: You cabled her the money even *after* she told you she couldn't come! You did it, Walter, you did it for me!" He had rarely, and not recently, seen her face the way it looked this morning. Well, what was money for anyway?

Clay decided that he'd given Kimberley enough time to get her act together. The word about Starbright had gone around the backside fast because everyone was curious about the celebrity: He'd been released like most of the others and had been safely returned to his stall. Even so, Clay was reluctant to leave Bernie alone in the trailer in this mood. So he poured another cup of black coffee and took a bitter swallow. Clay'd never seen Bernie this way before: His short, soft body couldn't stay in the chair, his face changed from concern to anger in quick flashes. And he'd resorted to the Yiddish words that he used only when under stress or at his happiest. He'd reported at least three times how he had tried to reach Clay at his motel but when the room didn't answer he guessed where Clay was, so since the Spur was not involved, the hell with it. As Clay had pieced it together, the Irish kid Molly had been with Bernie in the trailer when the first shouting started. "She fell asleep while we was talking" had been the way Bernie had explained it, his jaw suggesting that no one, even Clay, should suggest anything more. Since Clay had arrived Bernie had gone out to the booth to phone the hospital twice, and each time he'd returned with his eyes baffled and skeptical: He had spoken with Mrs. Tyrone and everything was the same, Molly was sleeping, there'd be more X-rays in the morning and they would know more. "That means there's bones broken. I've seen people trampled—there's always bones broken." Then he would leap up as soon as he'd sat down and start swearing again: If he got his hands on whoever the hell started this, whether it was carelessness or not he'd send that schlemiel to the hospital personally and with more than broken bones.

Now, after a long gloomy silence, he stood up again. "I gotta ask Mrs. Tyrone whether anything's punctured the lungs."

While Bernie was digging into his pocket again Clay flipped him a dime and stood up. "Time for works in a few hours. You hang in there."

Outside Bernie said, "If you're not back in time, I know what to do."

"Bernie," Clay said, "if I know anything, I know that."

In the dim light Bernie made a try at a smile but failed, so Clay hit him with his fist in the big breadbasket and moved away as Bernie turned to the booth. Clay made his way through the tangle of parked cars and between barns. The fire trucks and police vehicles had gone, and in the tack rooms the lights were going out. You could hear a whinny or two and the hoofs of the jittery ones, but in general things were returning to normal. Beyond, a glare lit the sky, so he assumed they were keeping a floodlight on the important barn.

"When they took her into the ambulance," Bernie had said, "she had enough goddamn pain to make a man howl, but not that kid. She's got real moxie, that Mick."

He reached barn 27, again thinking what he had thought from the beginning and had been half-ashamed of whenever Bernie said it or it returned to his mind: Damned lucky the Spur hadn't been moved to the Derby barn after the Trial. Lucky they'd all been too busy whooping it up to think of it. Hotspur was standing in his dim stall sound asleep. "Rumpus, ruckus, and hullabaloo," Elijah had said. "It's tuckered him. All this little boy want, he want to go back to sleep, if only everybody'd quieten down here." And Hotspur had lifted his head high and nodded it low: Thank you and good night, gentlemen. Since he'd been a kid, though, it had always puzzled Clay why some horses slept lying down and some slept standing up. He saw a light under the door to the tack room: Elijah was sitting up the night anyway, without mentioning it. It gave Clay a good feeling somehow. A fine feeling.

Without touching the Spur he went along the shedrow and turned toward the light. On the way to the track Kimberley had sat hunched down in the seat, every nerve taut, face set: "Can't you drive faster? You know what this foreign hot rod will do." And he had said, "We're off the expressway now, and that's a redlight behind us." And she had growled, "Fuck him, juice it." And when they'd gone through the gate she had leaped out, muttering, "They've lied to me—"

He'd let her go on alone. He didn't want to see Andrew Cameron. Her father might lie, but he doubted Jason Arnold would.

"Hullo there. Remember me?"

He had company. "Sure. You're the one with the tape recorder in her brassière."

The woman laughed. "Janice Wessell. Sorry, no brassière."

"The vultures have gathered."

"Any theories, Mr. Chalmers?"

"Sure. One of the Pinks knocked out his pipe in a bale of hay."

"You don't subscribe to the conspiracy theory then."

"I didn't know there was one."

She laughed again. She had a pleasant enough laugh, but it hovered on the edge of nastiness. In his book. "Well, there have been a hell of a lot of so-called accidents, haven't there?"

"I hadn't noticed."

"Bullshit. Vincent Van first. Now Ancient Mariner's been . . . what's your phrase for it? Ancient Mariner's been put down. That's it, isn't it?"

He hadn't known. Anger flashed through him. As it had when he first learned of the fire.

"He didn't burn. Fire spooked him. I do have the proper race-track patois, don't I? Spooked."

"There'll be an investigation, Miss Wessell."

"The TRPB, I know. The Thoroughbred Racing Protective Bureau—I have that correct too, don't I? That's their office over there, right?"

"Plenty of others." As before, she had begun to work on his nerves. "Why ask me?"

"Lucky for you your horse wasn't in the Derby barn, right?"

He almost missed a step then. "*Right,*" he growled. "But it wasn't luck. I confess, Miss Wessell. But only to you. I threw a rag soaked in kerosene into Ancient Mariner's stall. You may print it. On your ass."

"Then you couldn't see it. Unless you wanted to."

He stopped walking. "I have better things to look at, Miss Wessell. Now buzz off."

She smiled into his face and cocked her head. "We'll meet again."

"No threats, please, Miss Wessell."

He turned a corner now, and he could see the Derby barn—a sort of stage set in an arena of light, with reporters and sightseers and hangers-on, a few uniforms hovering on the fringe, the security guards on their campstools at each end, and in the floodlight glare, outlined against the barn itself, Kimberley facing Jason Arnold. He could smell the crisp stench of ash and charred wood and smoke as he approached. Two men in business suits came out of the tack room, and then he saw the black cave of burnt-out stall as he passed. It was still smoldering. The stall next to it was also empty, and one of its walls looked cracked and splintered. A night breeze was beginning to waft the smell away.

"It took time, Miss Kimberley," Jason Arnold was saying, his forehead furrowed. "I've said I'm sorry I was so far away, but I'm staying with friends in Lexington and—"

"No one was here, *no one!*" And when he heard her voice Clay realized that she had finally given in to hysteria. "No grooms or stableboys!" She sounded on the verge of tears. "No one, goddamn you, goddamn all of you!"

In a low controlled voice Jason Arnold said, "My assistant was here within minutes. Dickie Florsheim's as fine an assistant as I've ever had." Then he caught sight of Clay and without smile or greeting added: "As good as I've ever had, bar one."

Kimberley turned. Her eyes were red and narrow. "Where the hell have *you* been?" Then, without giving him time to answer, she turned away and rushed to the tack room at the other end of the barn.

As Clay passed Jason Arnold to follow her the older man shrugged his wide lean shoulders and said, "See what you can do, Clay. I'll take a closer look at the colt."

In the tack room, with its familiar smell of old leather and liniment, Kimberley was standing with her back to him, as if she were examining the halters and bridles and leads and coiled ropes and iron stirrups hanging from the wall. But she was, he knew, seeing nothing. "On a night like this no one but muck-out kids and gallop girls and assistant trainers."

Gently, softly, almost amused now, remembering Jason Arnold's words a minute ago, Clay said, "I'm here now, Kimb." He stepped to her and took her arm, but she drew it away fiercely.

"Even Andrew's off with that Irish bitch when I need him!"

"Kimb, what is there to say? Starbright's in his stall and—"

But she swung around to face him in the hooded hanging light. She shook her head numbly, as if she couldn't speak. Then she said, "That's not Starbright." She stopped shaking her head and lifted her chin. "He looks like Starbright. But I knew in a second. I've known for an hour. It looks like Starbright, but it's not." Then she came into his arms, collapsing against him, and she was sobbing, her face against the side of his head, her body shaking against his. "Oh, Clay, they've taken Starbright."

Incredulous—she *had* to be wrong, she was hysterical—Clay whispered: "The stockings—"

"One, yes. The other leg was bandaged. When I unwrapped it—" She drew back and her eyes were furious. "Goddamn it, don't you believe me? The tattoo's the same. They've even tattoed the same numbers in his mouth! Who did they think they could fool?"

"Kimb, I swear to God, you've got to be mistaken."

"Mistaken?" It was not quite a scream. "They can't fool me!"

And then a voice spoke behind him. Quietly. "She's right, Clay." Jason Arnold's voice. He heard the door close. "He's a ringer."

Kimberley's eyes glittered. And then Clay heard the door behind him open, and Kimberley's voice barked: "Where are you going?"

"To report it, of course. The sooner—"

"No!"

"But Miss Kimberley—"

"Not till we see what Andrew says. Wouldn't you know where he'd be when I need him?"

Though it had happened too late for the morning papers, the news services would have it, and it would be on the radio and television before his own broadcast at eleven, but Wyatt had stayed around. There'd be no getting back to sleep now anyway—infuriated as he was by the security people. They should have had Ancient Mariner out of that stall before he could do damage to himself, no question about it in his mind. Damned lazy bastards, not horse people, and probably scared—a spooked horse can be a terrifying spectacle.

"Mr. Slingerland." When he stopped and turned, he saw a small woman with tousled hair, sorrel colored, a press card pinned to her sweater, which, he noted at once, was very tight. Not a regular backstretcher; he'd seen her around. He waited, enjoying the view. "My name's Janice Wessell." So? "I'm not after the usual news story. What I'm interested in is getting a behind-the-scenes feature, not just tonight but a human view of the whole scene. Things the public wouldn't ordinarily see or know."

A mouthful, that. But she didn't appear rushed. He was not accustomed to talking with young women, especially in secluded, half-dark places like this, and he wasn't certain what to say. "A privileged peep at the ins and outs. I dig." Wasn't that the lingo? He decided to continue to the parking area. His throat was dry. "And what have you got so far, little lady?"

"Mostly closed doors." She was walking beside him. "And *no comment*'s by the thousands. Especially tonight." Her breasts were quite full and very distinct. "I work for a weekly published in Florida. But it's a national." Wyatt was aware that he had reached an age himself at which he had a difficult time judging the ages of young women or girls, but he'd put hers in the twenties, maybe early twenties. She carried a leather shoulder bag—possibly or probably with a recording device concealed. She looked windblown in this light, even though there was only a gentle early-morning breeze. "Who do you think started it?"

"Oh, so you hope there's something sinister afoot, is that it? Something amiss that would make you a sensational story?"

"My paper prints practically nothing but exposés of lies."

"Little lady," he said, "this seamy old joint may be a pyromaniac's dream, but every small combustion does not represent arson."

"The public will think so."

"Because it wants to." He spotted his old blue Buick convertible with its frayed top up. "Whenever there's a barn fire, the whole world asks, 'Who did it, who did it?' Now any idiot who wanted to could burn down a stable."

"Bullshit."

He was threading his way to the Buick. "You may rest assured there'll be a full inquiry—police, fire marshals, insurance investigators."

"The TRPB. *Official* bullshit."

He opened the car door. "What a suspicious little mind."

"Hey. The cheap scandal rag I work for can't afford wheels. Can I hitch a lift?"

He looked at her. Her face was close and soft, and her eyes looked eager and young. They were hazel colored and slightly slanted, and there was a green shade of makeup on the lids. "A lift to where?"

Her eyes met his, and she tilted her head. "That's for you to say, Count Wyatt." Now what the hell did she mean by that? "Or maybe it'd be better if I just called you Wyatt—"

"Call me what you like," he said shortly and got in.

"How about Mister Something Else?"

Behind the wheel he became conscious of the car's age and state of decrepitude. He became conscious too of his boutonniere, his cigarette holder, and the cant of his felt hat—his costume, or disguise. He thought to lean across, but she opened the door herself.

Her tone was airy. "You know what Nixon always said—just because you're paranoid doesn't mean they're not out to get you."

When she was settled beside him in the seat, he discovered that he was confusingly conscious of her presence, her physical proximity. "I can't decide," she said, "whether you remind me of a riverboat gambler or a *boulevardier*, or both."

"*Gay dog* was the term in my time. I prefer *bon vivant*." As they passed through the gate, he nodding to the guard, she waving, he said, "I am, alas, one of the survivors of a dying breed—a true lover of the game of racing—and I'm fighting a losing battle to keep it the way I imagine it should be."

"Then you do think there's something not quite kosher."

"Did I say that? Listen, my dear—"

"Wyatt, you're just full of it, aren't you?"

"It is what I get paid for."

She laughed. A rather pleasant sound. "Fantastic!" She settled more deeply into the seat, and in the light of the passing street lamps he saw that her skirt was high above her knees. Knees, hell, it was up to her thighs. "Guess where I was this afternoon before the Trial."

"Entertaining some other old man?"

"Bizarre. I went out to Thistle Hill."

"And?"

"More stonewalling. Lovely word, isn't it? We'll never know what really happened to Vincent Van, will we?"

"*Bizarre* is quite a proper word, little lady. The man you see beside you is not really a turf writer but only a broken-down old horseplayer who has found a way to support his habit. My employers, who are various, do not expect investigative reporting."

"Well, if you honestly think that what happened tonight and what happened to Vincent Van are acts of fate—or, as you said on the air, a jinx—then you have to believe in Santa Claus, the Easter Bunny, and the sweet old tooth fairy."

How the hell did he get into this? What did she think he knew? Come to think of it, what *did* he know? "Next thing, Miss Wessell—"

"Jan—"

"Next thing you'll tell me Dealer's Choice didn't just break down, some sly devil tripped him with an invisible wire just as he started to go all out."

"No. I researched that. Horses do break down, and the scuttlebutt—isn't that the word you use?—has it that he was long overdue, right?"

"That, as I also say, is using the old kidneys."

"Happenstances like that only muddy the waters."

This time he laughed. But she leaned back, very far back, and placed her palms behind her head and kicked off her shoes, and something happened to his laugh. Her breasts were very full indeed, and very pointed.

"If . . . just *if* someone did set the fire and that Irish girl dies, *if,* someone would be guilty of murder, wouldn't he? Or manslaughter in some degree or other."

"I have the hospital's assurance that the girl is not going to die."

"I'm just if-ing." She rolled up the window. "There. Cozier, right?"

Something happened then that had not happened in—how long? Several years at least. He had an erection. His groin tightened and his penis stiffened.

And in that moment, thrown completely off-kilter, he felt a great uprush of vigor and youth sweeping through his fleshy sixty-year-old body. He was stunned.

Hoping his voice didn't sound rushed and breathless, he began to speak of other fires. In '65 there had been a bad one, right here on Derby Day itself. A smoldering cigarette got down between the floorboards of a rooftop where tinder had been accumulating for ninety years, and within minutes the clubhouse end of the roof was on fire, but it was confined to a small area and only a few fans even left their seats. Some inmates of the press box ducked down the tiny elevator since the stairs had been shut off to thwart freeloaders, but most didn't think of that and just stayed put. "Which says something about the intelligence of the people who write those infallible columns for *The New York Times* and such, doesn't it?"

There was no answer, only a movement in the seat beside him, and when he glanced at her, she was drawing the sweater over her head. Naked to the waist, she sat back again without looking at him. The nipples of her breasts were dark-tipped and as upright as his penis, which was throbbing.

He tried to concentrate on the dim, deserted street ahead and told her of the fire at Morehead State University here in Kentucky, where forty-two stalls were destroyed, along with twenty-seven saddlebreds and Tennessee Walkers. She twisted her body to regard him. Her eyes, slightly slanted, were soft and kindled. Taunting. Challenging. She looked incredibly young—he had *forgotten*! The full-flowered flesh of youth—how could a man ever forget?

He was about to describe the conflagration at the Garden State Raceway in '77, when fire broke out in the clubhouse kitchen and engulfed the grandstand, but just then she leaned back and away and yawned luxuriously, stretching her arms over her head.

"I covered a fire in Florida once." She sounded casual, even bored. "In the barn of the famous Lippizan stallions." Then she reached quite suddenly and placed her hand over his penis. She laughed. "Old, you said. You're not *old*." She was delighted.

Swiftly he recalled the last several times he'd been with a woman. Or had tried to be. Humiliating. Ignominious.

Joseph Hayes

"Young lady, you ought to be spanked."

She did not remove her hand, which was moving now. "Would you enjoy that?"

Would he? He couldn't even picture it. His stomach had gone hollow and was burning. But damned if he wouldn't. Hell, yes, he'd enjoy it.

"Because if you would, I wouldn't mind."

He did not answer.

She released him then and deftly pulled her body out of her skirt. Her whole soft, glorious, incredible body. She wore nothing underneath.

Then she asked, "How long since you've had a blowjob?"

He didn't answer. Because he could not.

Again she laughed with delight. "Bizarre, man. I bet you never have."

She shifted her naked body about and threw herself across the seat, her head in his lap, facing up. "Slow down so we'll have enough time." She rolled onto her side and pulled down the zipper just as he sucked in his gut. "My pleasure, *old* man. Jan'll do a job that'll pull your eyeballs right back into your head."

"It's a goddamn waste, that's what."

"Leave it to you, you'd be taking some chick's picture on the backstretch."

"No evidence, I know, I know, but to throw a brand new Polaroid camera in the Ohio River, it's a goddamn fuckin' crime."

"Interstate crime too," Owen said. "This is what they call the Sherman Minton Bridge, and back there, Eric, is Indiana, and now here we are in Kentucky again. And in the morning, when we take the next picture, we buy a new camera, and then we throw that away too. Every day the same. None of that what they call incriminating evidence! How's that for pluggin' all the holes up neat?"

"You're in some goddamn jolly mood. Ain't you even sleepy?"

"One more little job tonight, kid, then hightail it back to the track and get some shuteye before works."

170

"Now *I* take the works, is that it?"

"You got the idea."

"While you go tootin' back to that house in this big, smooth Lincoln and screw the broad again."

"That ain't a broad, that's your employer."

"She didn't employ me tonight. That was a goddamn risk, that was."

"What'd you do? You threw a butt away without stomping it out. Shame on you, Eric, shame on you."

"Christ, this mood, you kill me."

"Cheer up, kid. Everything's chiming."

"What if one of those Pinks'd seen me?"

"They didn't, you got paid, now fuck off. Like my old man used to say: 'When you're ridin' high, ride it!' "

"How'd they make the switch?"

"I don't know and I didn't ask."

"Who are they anyway?"

"I don't know that either. And don't want to. And neither should you."

"Christ, after I got back to the camper, I thought it'd be years before anyone started yelling."

"Will you shut your goddamn mouth up, I mean up, Eric, *shut!*"

"It was just like killing Ancient Mariner, you know that, don't you?"

"Shut."

"And what if that Irish doll croaks?"

"We didn't have anything to do with that."

"Like hell. The shit we didn't."

"I don't want anyone to get hurt." It was the truth too. Owen was damned sorry about that. But he couldn't let that, or anything, put the kibosh on the way he felt tonight. "The horse now, that's a different story. Fact he had to be put down, that's what they call a dividend. But the girl—" He wished to God he didn't feel the way he did about that. And he wished Eric would lay off. He'd soon be rid of his calamity howl. It had all gone like clockwork, and he was goddamn well going to make the most of it. All it meant to Eric was a few hundred extra bucks. To him it meant maybe a million.

A million or more. Dollars.

Don't look back, ole Toby had always said. *I spent mosta my life lookin' back—*

"She dies," Eric said, "I could get life."

"*If* she dies. *If* you get caught—"

"If," Eric corrected, "*we* get caught."

"Listen. Listen good, kid. Andrew Cameron's not even gonna report the horse missin'. Nobody's gonna know it was anything but a little accident, kind that happens all the time. Only Cameron, and I got Cameron's number. Him and all his breed. He won't risk that bangtail's life by squawking. I'm counting on him. And that daughter of his—the way she loves that horse, you'd think it was human. And on top of all that, Eric, look at it this way: Those rich snob bastards, they'd do anything to avoid a scandal. Giving racing a black eye, and all that shit. So relax, for Christ's sake, or you won't be able to take the works, and Fireaway's set for six-thirty. Now—where you want me to let you out?"

"Two more blocks. What they call the River City Mall. In the daytime it's all window-shoppers, but at night, man, it's sin city!"

"You got someone to do the job proper? He's got to look like he belongs in that fancy hotel."

"Pretty little fag, white slacks and a blazer jacket, and thorough as they make 'em. For a hundred bucks and five minutes work he don't even ask questions."

"Chiming," Owen said and brought the car to a gliding halt along the curb. "You got the envelope?"

"What do you think? Owen, sometimes you act like I got the brains of one of those coyotes back at the ranch."

"Listen again. If the wrong hands lay hold to that envelope, it could all blow sky-high, and you and me with it, in little pieces."

"I don't want to know any more'n I know."

"Then don't ask so goddamn many questions . . . Gallop the bangtail around once, then breeze him for a half mile. That's all."

"Fuck you, boss man."

Owen drove on. Tough little punk from Newark, with a fresh mouth sometimes, but he'd done his part tonight, he'd located Frankie Voight too, and the fag to deliver the note now. So little ole

Eric had earned every goddamn peso he was going to get. Chicken-shit—like Toby always got. *You two, both my sons, you'll never see any more mazuma than your old man ever got.* Wrong, Toby—wrong. Watch my dust! Clay now, there's only pipe dreams with him, but Owen, Owen knows how to get things done because he makes them happen. The big difference, Toby.

He'd studied a map of the city. Up onto Interstate 65 now, what they called the Northwest Expressway here, then south, miles south, like you was going to the birthplace of ole Abe Lincoln him-self!

He had maybe a hundred or so dollars in his pocket, and maybe six, seven hundred more at the house, but like ole Toby said, *Think big*!

He was thinking big all the way out of the city and all the miles south. Ten percent of the Derby purse to the winning trainer—that alone would come to about twenty-five thousand. Peanuts. More chickenshit. But ten percent of the syndication deal—now that's real mazuma. Funny, Toby always said *mazuma*—must be where he'd picked up the word, 'cause he never heard it much any more, even around the tracks. Ten percent of eight million if he wins the Derby alone, just the one race—that's eight hundred thousand right there! And if he takes the Preakness, another four hundred thou-sand—that's more than a million there. And if he takes the Triple Crown—and that's no pipe dream, it's happening more and more often now—that'd bring his share to one tenth of sixteen million. More than a million and half for Owen Chalmers, the kid hisself! Christ, he'd never get used to even *thinking* in numbers like that!

And . . . it was only a thought, not part of his plan, not yet anyway—what if the bitch married him! Hell, he could do worse. She was a wild one in the hay. And *she* could do worse too, her and her fancy ways but her hot cunt, she could do lots worse than Owen Chalmers!

He turned off the expressway onto a curving country road with high trees on both sides.

Then he'd own the ranch instead of having to buy a stable of his own. The Lazy R. For Rosser. Which he'd change to the Lazy C, for Chalmers. How's that for thinking big, Toby?

And no gamble. You bet on cockroach races, Toby—Owen never bet a dollar since he was a kid. And got wise. Gambling's a bum's swindle, Toby, a fool's game. All Owen Chalmers'd bet on is what he can make happen.

As he was about to swing into the driveway a black car came out of nowhere, from between the goddamn trees and into the headlight beam, and blocked the road in front of the Lincoln. He cursed and slammed on the brakes. And only then did he realize that it was too late.

He heard the rear door open, and a voice said, "Don't turn around. Please." The voice sounded young and very polite, almost apologetic. "Please. There's a Lüger pointed at the base of your skull."

Chapter Five

PAUL Hautot heard the doors to the balcony opening, so he got up from the bed and went into the salon to find Annabelle standing outside at the iron-grille balustrade nude. He decided not to tell her of the fire; instead he stood a moment taking delight in imagining her moving through the lobby in that state and ascending on the elevator, conceivably in the company of one or more inebriated merrymakers. She may well have done so. The picture in his mind wakened him completely. Sensing his presence, she said, "It's an exquisite city, isn't it?" And at once, because she had so often said she detested it, he knew. "Did you have a good time playing in the snow?" Without turning, she said, "No, not playing in the snow." But her voice had that quick, breathless vivaciousness, so he was positive. "Here is another phrase. Doing up a spoon of coke." And then she did turn. "Do not, if you please, speak of fires. The knowledge is all through the city, and don't tell me of Bonne Fete, Paul, if you please. Nothing could ever happen to her, she is too beautiful." She came into the room, small and fragile and exquisite, her silver-blond hair streaming over her soft shoulders. Her body seemed to drift, but her voice was quick. "Nothing horrendous ever happens to beautiful things." The whites of her eyes were streaked with red, but the pupils were brilliant black, not quite in focus but tiny and intense. Her delicate-boned face was flushed. He had no taste for cocaine himself, but he did take pleasure in what it did to her. "Oh, Paul, my sweet, these American men." She pirouetted and gracefully took up her dancing gown from the back of the divan, whirling it above her head and then around her body in a cloud while she went on, speaking gutturally in English: "They are so lacking in accomplishment, *finesse*. They are so what they call macho, such *he*-men, with the jockey straps." She laughed. "Oh, such *machismo*, such empty jockey straps!" And the laughter moved down her body. She tossed the gown aside, and it floated to the floor as she continued her perambulation. "Why are these Americans all in such a great hurry? Rush, rush here, business, look at the watch, hurry to a party, drink fast, talk fast, look at the watch, rush home, make love, in, out, quick, quick, look at the watch, good night, take a pill, sleep fast. Oh, my Paul, my sweet Paul, what of the poor, poor American women?" He realized that he had returned to bed without donning his pajamas after he had ejected the bland-faced young man. "Oh, it is quite the contrary with the women." She came toward him. "Contrary, Paul?" And smiling, his body coming alive with desire, he said, "With them it is oh, must we, everything is such a bore, you know, but proceed if you will, continue if you must—" Annabelle was standing quite, quite still now. Her eyes went down his body. Then she said, "Look at you, sweet. You're not bored. What an object it is, Paul. For me?" She could always do this to him. "Don't ever let anything happen to it, my sweet. Nothing horrendous ever happens to beautiful things, does it?"

His huge, soft body ensconced in a deep chair, his gout raising bloody hell, Blake Raynolds took a long sip of bourbon and said, "I think it's safe then, in the circumstances described, to assume that the fire was arson and a device or ruse to allow the horse to be stolen in the resultant turmoil. Stolen or horse-napped or whatever the word would be."

"Brilliant," Kimberley said. "Go to the head of the class, Mr. Raynolds, suh."

Ignoring that, Jason Arnold spoke in that clipped New England accent of his: "Only a fool would imagine we wouldn't know that horse in the stall was a ringer. He has the star on his forehead, they saw to that, and the same markings except for one stocking, same tattoo on his lip, similar conformation, sure, but anyone in this business knows no two horses really look alike to the people who know them and there's always an exact description in the Jockey Club's Stud Book. And the night eyes never lie."

"Night eyes?" Blake Raynolds asked, lifting his gray brows.

"Oh, for shit's sweet sake," Kimberley said and got up from the sofa and took still another turn around the sitting room of her father's hotel suite.

"Kimberley, my dear," Blake reminded her, "I'm here at your invitation, and at this ungodly hour of the morning. Please, if you want my legal advice, now and when Andrew arrives—"

"*If* he arrives—"

"—you will have to forgive a layman's ignorance." The truth was that Blake didn't really like horses. Or horse racing. To him the sport, if that's what it was, teetered on the edge of the underworld, no matter how dedicated the aristocratic pillars of the turf might be. He had read that each year more than ten billion dollars were bet legally through the pari-mutuel system and, according to Justice Department figures, another thirty billion plus through bookies, illegally. He had no personal taste for it. But he was curious. "Night eyes?" he prompted.

"Called chestnuts," the trainer explained, sounding as if he were relieved to be talking. "Night eyes are the small horny growths on the inside of a horse's legs, just below the knees and hocks. Photographic records of them are kept—like fingerprints. Only foolproof legal means of identification. No two chestnuts are ever the same."

"Remarkable. Then the only reason for that imposter's presence in the stall was—they hoped—to give them time."

"And damned if that's not just what Andrew's causing us to do," Kimberley said.

"Time to stash Starbright someplace without rousing suspicion," Jason Arnold said, nodding his fringed balding head.

There was a brief silence. The medium-sized young man in the tan suede jacket and turtleneck, whose nose had been pretty badly broken at one time, remained at the windows leading to the balcony, his back to the room. Kimberley had off-handedly introduced him to Blake as Clay Chalmers. Blake recalled having caught a glimpse of him in the winner's circle after the Derby Trial. As yet he had not uttered a word.

The tension in the room had intensified steadily, like gathering electricity, and Blake decided that he had better get matters cleared up as soon as possible before Andrew arrived. "I take it, Jason," he said, "that you're in favor of informing the authorities—"

"The TRPB anyway. Or the stewards if not the police. It seems to me we're wasting time."

"Mr. Arnold," Kimberley asked, her tone low and level, "when you spoke to Andrew at the hospital, did you tell him of the switch?"

This seemed to irritate Jason Arnold. "You instructed me not to, Miss Kimberley."

Kimberley did not so much as nod her pretty head. Grimly she said, "Whoever did this had to have help. We don't know what we're up against." She stepped to where the trainer sat in a straight-backed armchair. "And . . . we don't know what they might do to Starbright if we do the wrong thing."

"All the more reason, Miss Kimberley—"

"Goddamn it," she exploded, twisting the camel's-hair belt on her polo coat, "why are you against me on this? Will you just wait till Andrew gets here? He'll know what to do!"

Blake had been observing Kimberley for years, many years—Kimberley and her father, as, long ago now, he had observed her mother. From a New York social family, Irene had never fitted in, and she had given Andrew an ice-coated difficult time. She had been bored, and she had possessed neither the inner grace nor the good manners to conceal it. Then she had been thrown from a horse, probably having had too many Dutch gins beforehand, and though she had been only slightly injured, she had latched on to that as an excuse to turn her pretty back on the whole of Blue Ridge Plantation. Not only on Andrew but on her four-year-old daughter as well. No matter how petulant and willful and erratic, even crude and cruel Kimberley was at times (at others, God knows, she could

be as soft and appealing and winning as any girl he'd known), Blake
had always sensed that this abandonment was at the root of her in-
stability. He had believed that because of it she suffered from a
deep-seated and harrowing discontent, even unhappiness, that was
very real but which, he often thought, she was not aware of herself.
Whenever he saw the storm signals, Blake wondered what storm
they foreshadowed and whether she'd be able to weather it if and
when it struck.

"Kimberley," he said gently, "may your old decrepit friend point
out some of the legalities here, even at the risk of adding to your
hysteria?"

"I'm not hysterical, damn you, I just don't want some asshole to
make a mistake and risk Starbright's life. If he's not already dead."

At this Clay Chalmers turned and took a step toward them, then
paused, frowning.

"Accepted," Blake said, "accepted. But there are certain . . .
laws. Affecting insurance, for instance."

"Fuck insurance, that's money."

"I don't know how I could possibly perform that act on insurance, Kimberley, and I suspect I'm too old anyway."

"Very amusing. Hear that, Clay? Mr. Raynolds is a sit-down
comic as well as a family attorney!"

Clay Chalmers did not move and his expression did not seem to
change, but regarding Kimberley, his eyes betrayed a certain gentleness as well as concern. She did not glance in his direction.

"Another consideration," Blake said, wondering whether he
should wait to say this to Andrew, "is that a crime has been committed. Grand theft. *Very* grand theft in fact. Of which we all have
knowledge, however limited at the moment. Now I am not too con-
versant with the laws of Kentucky, but in most states to conceal
knowledge of a felony is to commit a felony. Namely, abetting the
original crime."

In a very small, very injured, but very sincere voice Kimberley
said, "You're against me too, aren't you?"

"Against you? My job is to look after your best interests." And he
intended to perform that job, for her sake and especially for Andrew's in spite of her if need be. For his own professional protec-

tion, though, he would have to be very wary of advising a client to break the law.

He finished the bourbon but decided not to have another, much as he wanted it, until Andrew arrived. The whisky went straight to his swollen big toe, and it was throbbing with excruciating pain now. He noticed that Jason Arnold was halfheartedly sipping a very weak Scotch and that Clay Chalmers was not drinking.

"We can be fairly confident," he said into the silence, "that arson was also committed, albeit with slight damage as I understand it, though there will certainly be a thorough investigation by experts." The results of which, he cynically suspected, would be hushed up. Then, to change the subject and to relax Kimberley if possible, he said: "I seem to recall a scandal a year or so ago in racing—something about a respected veterinarian who substituted one horse for another, in an actual race, wasn't it?"

"Shoes and ships and sealing wax," Kimberley growled and threw herself full length on the sofa. Her camel's-hair coat fell away from her leg, and Blake decided that she was probably wearing nothing under it. There were times when Blake wished that he had married and had children, and other times when he was glad he hadn't. Tonight was definitely one of the latter occasions.

"Why not speak of cabbages and kings, my dear?" Then to the trainer: "Weren't there South American horses involved, Mr. Arnold?"

"It happened at Belmont, I think. I don't recall the details."

"The horses," Clay Chalmers said, coming to stand behind the sofa, one hand reaching down to touch Kimberley's pale hair, "were from Uruguay. A first-rate runner named Cinzano was supposed to have been put down because of injuries, and insurance had been collected, but actually he was substituted in a race for a worn-out plodder named Lebon." The young man's face was sober and his voice was hard, almost angry. "The betting coup when the fake Lebon won was called the Cinzano caper, and it involved, among others, the respected vet who had treated Secretariat through the Triple Crown."

Blake was impressed. He was beginning to get a line on this Clay

Chalmers. "Shenanigans like that," he said, "intrigue and underhanded chicanery—they're all part of the public appeal, aren't they? Show-biz, as they say, and amusing."

"No," Clay Chalmers said, "not amusing to anyone who gives a good goddamn about racing."

A key sounded in the door. Kimberley sat up. Andrew came in, holding what appeared to be an unopened letter in his hand.

"Did the Mercedes break down?" Kimberley demanded. "Did you have to hitch a ride on a camel?"

Andrew glanced from face to face, then said, "Mrs. Tyrone is most distraught."

"Who the sweet shit isn't?"

He turned to Blake. "Good morning. Jason told me on the phone he was asking you here." Then to the young man behind the sofa, stiffly: "Mr. Chalmers."

"I'm here at Kimberley's invitation," Clay said, equally polite.

"In your absence," Kimberley said.

"You were very mysterious, Jason. But I gathered it was urgent."

Blake decided to be the spokesman. He described what had happened in as few words as possible and then asked the trainer, "Is that about it, Mr. Arnold?"

"The gist of it," Jason Arnold said.

"I'm sorry, Kimb," her father said. "Has the theft been reported?" He tore open the envelope. "This was handed me by the clerk at the desk as I came in downstairs."

"We were waiting for *you*," Blake said. "At Kimberley's insistence."

"This may enlighten us." He read the message quickly in silence, then held up two photographs and examined them both before he said: "It's not signed, of course. They plan to hold the horse in a safe place until Sunday, at which time they will negotiate for his release—presumably for a ransom. And I'll receive two Polaroid snapshots of him every day. One of these is unmistakably Starbright, and the other is a close shot of his head only, which includes the front page of the Tuesday evening paper with the date circled."

He handed the sheet of paper, plain white, and the pictures to Blake, who examined them. The message was typed in blue and in a type face resembling script—the sort a woman might use for personal letters. He did not read it aloud. The envelope was plain cheap paper and had on it only Andrew's name and the two words *Deliver Personal*, in the same blue type. The wall visible behind the horse's body was of old wood with nails and hooks on it. A barn wall. On one hook rested a pitchfork.

Finally Andrew said, "Would you like a drink, Kimb?" and when she shook her head, he went to the bottles on the sideboard, saying, "I'm sorry, Daughter. I know what he meant to you."

"*Meant* to me? Then you think he's already dead?"

"It's a possibility we must face in spite of the evidence to the contrary, isn't it?"

Clay Chalmers said: "If they killed him or harmed him, Kimb, they won't be able to collect a ransom."

"You're right," Andrew said, pouring himself a whisky. "Hard as I find it to believe, whoever has him wants to make sure, first, that he doesn't run Saturday."

"They damn well know," Jason Arnold said, moving to another chair for no apparent reason, "that we couldn't and wouldn't run that cow they left in the stall."

"I'd suggest," Blake said, "that they want to keep your horse out of competition, that's first, and the idea of a ransom might simply be a ruse to make you think—" But he broke off.

Kimberley spoke sharply: "To make us think they won't do anything to Starbright if we keep our mouths shut—is that what you were about to say?"

Quickly Andrew interrupted: "I can't imagine a thing like this being done by any of the other owners, so it must be a gambling ring out to affect the odds somehow. In that case, Kimberley, they'd want to collect the ransom as well."

"Thank you, Andrew," Kimberley said meekly.

"If they know anything at all, they know they could never race him," Andrew went on. "A thoroughbred like that's like an original painting. The financial advantage to them is to hold him for whatever they can force us to pay." He took a deep drink. "When I think

of a sensitive, high-strung animal like that being treated this way—"
But he did not finish.

Recalling that Clay Chalmers had said something *very* similar
earlier, Blake ran a hand over his almost-bald head, which was
perspiring. "We're up against an organization, that much is damn
clear. Anyone can start a fire in the straw, but it takes know-how
and precision to pull off a theft like this."

Then Jason Arnold spoke again: "It's too big for us, the likes of
us. The TRPB would bring in state police, the FBI perhaps—people
who've had experience. That's what they're paid for."

Andrew was shaking his head. "The note makes it sharply clear,
in its illiterate way, that if the authorities are brought in, the horse
will be destroyed."

"We know that," Kimberley cried. "Any goddamn fool knows
that!"

"They're banking on the fact too that no one wants a public scandal three days before the Derby."

Kimberley took shallow, shuddering breaths and lowered her
head between her knees. "They can bank on that all right. Scandal.
Hush-hush. Honor of racing, all that shit."

"I should inject," Blake said, "that if, on the other hand, no one
is informed, there could be insurance complications if—" But Kimberley did not lift her head and when he realized it he stopped speaking.

Andrew stepped to the telephone in the foyer and asked to speak
to the front desk. Blake heaved himself heavily to his feet and went
to pour another bourbon after all. It could be a long night. He
heard Andrew speaking in the foyer, and he heard Jason Arnold
talking about a mare that had recently been stolen from a farm in
Kentucky, and two fillies who not too long ago had been stolen
from Keeneland itself, and a valuable trotter who had been held for
a large sum in Italy and then retrieved when the owner, who vowed
he would not pay ransom, forked over what he called a reward of
more than a half million dollars. "Where the hell's it going to end?"
the trainer asked no one in particular.

Andrew returned to the room as Blake lowered himself again into
his chair, cold glass in hand, a stiff one this time. "They have two
descriptions downstairs of the young man who hand-delivered the

envelope. Both agree that he was extremely well dressed and very polite, and he might or might not be a guest in the hotel. During Derby Week that's the best they can do, sorry."

"In my legal capacity, Andrew," Blake said, "I must warn you that any cooperation is technically illegal. Now in an ordinary kidnapping case there are always mitigating circumstances that allow the authorities to ignore the technicalities—natural concern of parents for a child or husband for a wife, that sort of thing. But here we have what is, in fact, not a human being but a property—"

"Balls," Kimberley said and lifted her head. Her eyes were narrow and red. "He's a living thing and he's mine, and since I'm his owner, I'll make the decision, and it's been made. Give the bastards what they want. That's final."

Seeing Andrew's gray eyes on his daughter, tortured by compassion and love, Blake was again grateful that he had never sired any children. Andrew crumpled the note in his fist and muttered, "I'd like to meet one of them face to face for only five minutes."

Astonished—Blake had never thought of Andrew as a violent man—he said, "Don't destroy that note, Andrew. It's evidence."

Andrew hurled the wad of paper to Blake's lap and stalked out, but into the bedroom this time. He slammed the door behind him with a resounding jolt.

Blake set his glass on the small table beside him and spread out the note. "Well, I suppose you would all like to hear what it says." He started to read it himself. Then he put on his glasses and read aloud: "Mr. C," he read, "property will be returned sound and in one piece Sunday if no police and you do not try to trace this. You will get a picture of your bangtail every day to show he is alive. Will let you know how much mazuma to pay. If you do not cooperate right, you will have a lame gelding that will not be worth nothing but the glue factory. STAY SHUT OR ELSE." Blake took off his glasses. "It's not signed, of course."

Jason Arnold spoke first. "We always have to live alongside the human riffraff this game attracts, jockeys taking bribes and dishonest trainers, but you can't cooperate with scum like this."

Clay Chalmers came around the sofa and stood in front of Blake's chair. "May I see that, sir?"

"Of course, young man." Blake handed over the note. "The spelling leaves something to be desired. And I thought dead horses were sent to pet-food processors these days, not glue factories."

Clay Chalmers moved out onto the balcony and stood there with his back to the room, studying the strange note.

Andrew returned. His face was pale, but he seemed calm enough now. "I spoke with Harold Johnston at Thistle Hill. He didn't want to talk, but I told him we had a crisis here and that it was important. Vincent Van did not have an accident in his stall. The poor animal was discovered on the side of the road in the morning. At least two gates had to have been opened. No report was made to Lloyd's because the insurance wouldn't have been paid if there'd been lax security. And there sure as hell had been. Harold's discharged twelve of his employees, and he lied to the press for obvious reasons. Including the reason that things like this proliferate and there's no reason to give racing another black eye. Now he has eight guards working round the clock, and he's installing a video monitoring system."

There was a long pause. Finally it was Blake who spoke: "It's more than obvious to this outside observer that someone is trying to sabotage the Derby. Probably one of the owners. I can't see it any other way."

"I'd hate like hell to think it," Andrew said. "Whoever it is has also eliminated Ancient Mariner. Possibly by accident." He roamed away, like a man blinded by shock, stunned. "I still don't believe it could be one of the owners." But he believed it, and Blake knew it.

"What you mean," Kimberley said, and now she seemed less girl, more woman, her head lifted, "what you mean, Andrew, is that you don't *want* to believe it." Then she added, as if—to Blake's amazement—Andrew's pain had reached *her:* "I don't want to believe it either, Father."

Blake tried to remember whether he had ever heard her address Andrew as Father. Surprises on all sides this night.

And then still another: Clay Chalmers came into the room from the balcony. And Andrew said quietly: "It seems that anyone with a registered thoroughbred and a hundred and fifty dollars to spare in February can nominate a horse, doesn't it?"

"Andrew!" Kimberley cried and stood up. "You don't think that Clay—"

"I didn't say that," Andrew interrupted. He was staring across the room at Clay Chalmers. "Nor did I imply it."

Now what? Blake wondered. What the devil was there between these two?

"Thank you, sir," Clay Chalmers said, a note of irony very clear in his tone.

"True Blue's out too," Jason Arnold said then, as if he wished to pass some point of conflict, which only puzzled Blake further. "I wouldn't trust the Dealer's Choice owners from here to the Ohio River down below, but I don't see how they could have arranged to have him crack like that and take out True Blue that way."

"He almost took out Hotspur too," Clay Chalmers reminded him.

"Mr. Chalmers," Andrew said, "no one is accusing you of anything. Please keep that in mind."

"Well," Blake said, considering another drink, "it looks like what one of my colleagues always calls a Mexican standoff. At least for tonight."

Kimberley resumed her seat and murmured: "They've got us where the hair is short."

And Jason Arnold said, "There's only one thing to do."

To which Andrew said sharply, "Jason, I wish to God you would stop saying that. That decision has been made. No police."

Blake decided against the drink; he decided it was time to go back to bed. "All we can do is wait and hope, as I see it."

But then, without moving a muscle, Clay Chalmers spoke again: "There's one other possibility."

"Yes?" Blake asked. "What, sir?"

"Pay the ransom."

The young man was being irrational now. "There's been no specific demand for ransom."

"Pay it anyway." There was no irony in Clay Chalmer's manner now, none whatsoever. "Wherever Starbright's hidden there's someone watching him. Someone who's being paid to do it." His eyes were not on Blake but on Andrew. "Offer the sonofabitch more than he's getting paid by whoever hired him."

"To turn the horse over to . . . to whom, Mr. Chalmers?"

"To me. If Kimberley wishes."

Blake glanced quickly at Andrew and then turned to study the young man, but without expression. "What figure did you have in mind?" Blake asked.

"I don't have any figure in mind. How about a hundred thousand?"

"That," Blake said, standing up to return to the bar after all, "is a nice round tidy sum." He used the cane this time.

"The ransom," Clay Chalmers reminded them, "would probably be in the neighborhood of a million."

Blake poured a stiff one. "How could this offer be made and this . . . uh, transaction be arranged?"

"I'm not sure it could. It's a long shot. Does anyone have any short ones in view?"

"It's a modest enough sum," Andrew said finally, "in the circumstances, but—"

"I'm afraid," Clay Chalmers said, "you'll have to trust me, Mr. Cameron. Unless you honestly suspect that I might be the one behind the whole plot."

Turning from the bar, Blake realized that the two men were facing each other with their eyes locked. Again he was astonished. What the devil was there between these two? Kimberley perhaps? Or did Andrew actually suspect the young man? Unless he was blinded by some other emotion, Andrew was too reasonable a man to think that if Clay Chalmers *had* a horse in his possession that was worth several million he would settle for a hundred thousand. And if he wanted Starbright out of the running, why the devil would he offer to return him? Another idea occurred to Blake, who had had considerable experience in judging and questioning witnesses.

"Mr. Chalmers, do you have some idea who wrote that note? Or might have written it?"

The brown gaze shifted slowly to Blake, but without wavering. "That is, as I think you lawyers say, irrelevant now. I'll need the

187

money in unmarked bills, as old as possible and in small denominations, by ten o'clock this morning."

"That is within the realm of possibility, sir. But what guarantee would Mr. Cameron have that it would accomplish anything whatsoever?"

"None."

"Horseshit!" It was Kimberley who spoke then. She leaped up and dashed to the center of the room, giving her shin a painful whack against the cocktail table and knocking a glass to the carpet. "I'll give you the goddamn money, Clay. Get Starbright for me. I'll give you the money. I trust you if Andrew doesn't, but I don't give a damn if you keep it and stick it up your ass!"

After a moment Andrew spoke. "That won't be necessary, Daughter."

"I had other plans for the money, Kimberley," Clay Chalmers said softly. He handed the note to Blake. "You'll want this, I imagine."

And Andrew took three long strides to face him. "If you fail to get possession of the horse, that's one thing. But if he is delivered and cannot run Saturday, for any reason whatsoever, what I did to you last time will be nothing to what will happen to you from that point on."

Clay Chalmers looked for a moment as though he might smile. But he didn't. He only nodded. "Thank you for admitting that you had me blackballed for seven years."

Then Kimberley stepped between the two men. "Shut up!" she screamed. "Shut up, stop it, both of you! What about Starbright? You're forgetting Starbright, both of you!" Tears came to her eyes and streamed down her face, which looked pale beneath the tan. "Goddamn you both!" Her hands were white fists against her coat, her legs were parted and her shoulders quivering. "Goddamn you both!" she shrilled. "What are you doing to me?"

Lost in astonishment now, plunged into a maelstrom of tangled emotions that only bewildered him further, Blake longed to escape. But the silence in the room held him prisoner.

Clay Chalmers took a single step. "Cameron, your daughter knows I couldn't do harm to Starbright. To any horse. And you

know that I was not the cause of Lord Randolph's being destroyed—"

"You were too drunk to—"

"No matter what you've convinced yourself of over the years, you
know damn well you did it, Cameron, and we both know why."

Then, without giving Andrew a chance to reply, he brushed past
him and went into the foyer and out the door. It closed without a
sound.

Blake set down his glass without drinking. "Well, since I charge
double for my time at four o'clock in the morning, I shall be getting
back to my room."

Andrew, his face stiff and inscrutable, moved toward his daughter, but she whirled away and rushed out into the corridor. Shaking
his head once, Andrew walked to the balcony and went outside.

Blake nodded to Jason Arnold, who looked tired and troubled and
did not get up from his chair. "You may have the right idea, Mr.
Arnold, but let us both remember: You and I are only employees."
Blake was feeling very sleepy now, very weary. He placed the note
and photographs in his pocket. "Assure Mr. Chalmers that I shall
arrange the money somehow." Even if doing so might be construed
as contributing to the obstruction of justice. He shambled heavily to
the foyer and out into the corridor. Who, these days, drew strict
lines?

Using the cane, he moved toward the elevators, relieved to be
alone. Away from the whirlpool—the undertow and eddies and
crosscurrents of human emotions. He had become an attorney because he had once believed that the law imposed a rational pattern
on an otherwise unreasonable society. But he had come to believe
that that too was an illusion. Often now he wondered whether the
law was only poor old mankind's way of pretending that order really
existed and that man's nature was manageable.

It did not seem possible that the long night watch which Rachel
Stoddard was remembering had taken place three years ago, but so
it had indeed—three years ago last month. There had been a cold

April rain riding a gusty wind down the Housatonic River valley when Lady Jane, big-bellied with foal, was led at a matronly pace from the mares' stable into the foaling barn. Scourby, the foaling man at Brookfield Stables, anticipated Lady Jane's delivering early. He flicked on the stall light, creating a small island of brightness in the darkening night. Lady Jane was hot and restless, her neck and mane were damp, her eyes anxious. She rubbed her head roughly and impatiently against the black-bearded man's comforting hand. He slipped into the stall and checked the mare's bag and vagina. The one was full, the other slack. Then Scourby, as apt at midwifery as the vet, Dr. Von Egidy—who would be summoned only if his services should be required—turned to her and spoke: "I was right, Mrs. Stoddard. She's bagged up. It may be a while but there's no way she's going to hold off to morning."

Rachel knew, of course, that she was not in Connecticut but in the bed of her hotel suite in Louisville, Kentucky—but that was only her clumsy old body lying here. In her mind—which was the actual and truthful part of her being tonight—she was reliving that blustering spring night at Brookfield. After Scourby had said that he was certain, she had gone to the main house and up to the bedroom to report to Eugene. Brookfield was not a large breeding farm compared to the ones in Kentucky, where some had as many as two hundred mares in foal at the same time; possibly as a consequence of this, though, each birth at Brookfield took on its own importance. Eugene had always been proud of his foaling barn: It was clean and antiseptic and as well-equipped as an operating room, and the wood facing the stalls was varnished and polished. Eugene heard her when she spoke, but he was too weak to respond beyond a nod of his head and a touch of his hand. The face that had always been beefy and red and bursting with vitality was drawn and pale against the pillow. But it was enough for her that he understood.

So she had returned then to the stables to take up the long night vigil, as Eugene had often done, in the small officelike room between the mares' barn and the much smaller foaling barn. Scourby was sitting on a wooden chair, drinking the first of the endless cups of hot coffee that would keep him awake through the watch. There was music playing. Most stablehands read detective stories or watched portable television sets, but Scourby always played classical music on his small FM radio. (Could this be the reason that, to the amusement of the backstretchers and journalists, music had always calmed Ancient Mariner's nervous nature and he had all his short life stalked his stall imperiously and impatiently when someone forgot to turn it on?)

In the hours that followed, Scourby conjectured after one of his periodic examinations that the foal would be a filly because Lady Jane was a mite bigger on her right side, and then after another examination some time later that it would definitely be a colt because she seemed bigger on the left side now. And Rachel had asked what he would predict if she were no bigger on one side than the other, and Scourby had said without a grin: "Twins." Hours later, during Beethoven's Fifth, Scourby boasted that nine times out of ten he could tell whether it was going to be a filly or a colt when the feet came out: if they were large, a colt, and if tiny, a filly. "Or a gray," he said, and this time he did grin, knowing better. Rachel smiled, listening above the music to the wind whistling over the Berkshire foothills: She hoped that Eugene was asleep and that the wind did not presage one of those savage spring storms that upset the horses and which Eugene himself had come to dislike so much since his confinement.

Scourby had been right: Lady Jane was early, and this satisfied Rachel because she knew that when a birth is late, it often took the foal a long time to gain its strength. But Scourby did need Dr. Von Egidy's expertise after all. Lady Jane had a hard and painful time. When she finally went down on her side, one leg cocked up, her tail flared back and her enormous belly standing up, and then when her strong hindlegs were spread and bent, it took forever before the hoofs came through the distended vagina, covered by the white amniotic sac. Scourby, seeing them, nodded: a colt, for sure. It took another eternity, with Lady Jane straining and groaning and Scourby and the vet tugging and working together and in relays, for the shoulders to emerge, big and wide. Scourby ripped the sac off the handsome head, and the foal was breathing.

But it had a hind leg folded up against its belly instead of stretched out behind. It struggled but could not stand, so Rachel herself, shunting the two men aside, had picked it up from the straw by its hindquarters and nudged it tenderly into place so that it could suckle. She did not have to be told: If the leg was paralyzed, the unnamed foal would have to be put down.

But it did not have to be put down. "Biggest damn two-day-old colt I ever saw!" Eugene had said, looking out the window from his bed, his attention, like hers and Crichton's beside her, fixed on the sleek colt following his dam along the paddock fence. Only the day before he had scampered after Lady Jane on his awkward, incongruously and absurdly long and uncertain legs in the wet grass. But this morning the grass had been dried by the sun, the storm had blown over, and the colt moved with long, reaching strides, strong and confident.

That evening, over a candlelit dinner which they shared on a small table alongside his bed, Eugene had named him. "How about Ancient Mariner?" he had asked. "That's always, for some reason, been my favorite poem." They had toasted the name with a small glass of white wine.

And less than a week later, after suffering a relapse, Eugene had died in the ambulance on the way to the New Milford Hospital.

Ancient Mariner was Eugene's horse. And his alone. Had always been.

Now Ancient Mariner was dead too. It was almost as if Eugene had left her again.

As for Rachel herself, lying awake in the unfamiliar bed so far from home . . . she had begun to wonder whether anything mattered. Anything in the world.

Although it was daylight, there was not enough gray light for Christine to see clearly, so she flicked on the overhead porch light, wishing again that Owen had not taken it upon himself to give the caretaker the week off. The dark-haired young man standing there wearing a suede jacket and turtleneck was, as he had said through the door, Owen's brother. Had something happened to Owen? She unlocked the unfamiliar door and opened it, drawing her negligée about herself.

As he stepped inside she asked, "What's happened to Owen?"

"Nothing. Yet."

What an extraordinary answer. She had seen Clayton Chalmers in the winner's circle at the track—when Owen had said, "Seven furlongs in the mud is not a mile and a quarter on a hard track," but had not offered to introduce his brother. Except for his nose he was quite a handsome young man, although rather ordinary compared to Owen. "What is it?" she asked.

"Where's Owen?"

She pushed hopelessly at her hair—this was the second time she'd been wakened, after all—and said, "Well, he's not here, of course." She was careful not to say that he hadn't returned. "At this time of morning he's usually working the horse."

Clayton was glancing around the hall and up the stairs— suspiciously? "I've just come from the track. The racing secretary's office backside gave me this address."

Damn Owen, couldn't he have been more circumspect? But it would be useless to try to dissemble further. "He received a call about the fire and then probably decided to stay on for Fireaway's workout. But he didn't telephone. Is the fire under control?"

"It was not much of a fire." Without a glance or further word he was moving into the sitting room, then opening the doors to the parlor. What did he imagine, that she was lying?

More irritated than amused—but, thank God, quite sober—she asked, "Were there any casualties?"

He moved down the space between stairway and parlor, toward the dining room. "One horse. A girl was injured." He looked into the dining room and then opened the door to the kitchen, all but ignoring her.

"Oh? Which horse, if you're not too busy to tell me?"

"Ancient Mariner."

At this she felt a jolt of shock. Rachel Stoddard's fine colt. How kind Rachel Stoddard had been to her, only hours ago—making her feel as if she'd never really been away.

"He had a little accident in his stall. Like Vincent Van." Then she realized that Owen's brother was actually going up the stairs.

"Make yourself at home," she said. "Since you're Owen's kin, as we say." And as he continued up the curve: "Is there anything I might help you with?"

He paused and turned. His face was without expression. "I've really come to borrow a typewriter," he said. His tone was not ironic, but there was irony there, and more—but what?

"A typewriter?" Now she was more amused than irked: What a strange fellow he was turning out to be. Cool, casual, polite—but not to be put off. "You're joking, of course. Don't you believe that Owen's not here?"

"Tonight I don't believe anything." Then he turned about and continued up the steps.

"There's a typewriter in the study that Owen uses for an office," she called after him. "The first door on your left."

Might as well humor him. After his victory he was probably tight, or recovering. Hadn't Owen told her that his kid brother must have developed a problem because he'd refused to drink with him? She didn't bother to sit down, but she did take advantage of the time to examine herself in the mirror and make a few quick repairs. She did wish those sun lines on her somewhat weathered face, especially those tiny ones shooting out from around her eyes, were not so pronounced. She had been living in the West too long. Would she be happier—well, more content anyway—if she didn't go back there to live? She was beginning to feel at home here. She heard the sound of a typewriter tapping above. What on earth could the odd young man be doing up there? Was he typing a letter? The sound was steady, as if he were swiftly touching each key in succession. She smiled to herself. He was bombed. It was the only explanation. But she was wide awake now, so what the hell: In a few moments—but after he had, as they said in the West, vamoosed—she would have her first gin of the day. She did wish, though, that Owen hadn't felt obliged to turn Marylou's tiny study into such a shambles. Still, the man did have to have a place for his records and his calculations and such.

She realized that the sound of the typewriter had stopped. She looked up. Clayton did not appear. Now what was the boy doing? What was it Owen had said when they were discussing families? That his brother hadn't changed, "not one goddamn bit." She'd been too pleasantly squiffed and contented to pursue it, but somewhere along the line Owen had said that when they were very young, Clay was always getting into troubles that Owen had to bail him out of. Whatever that meant. She was about to go into the sitting room and pour a gin after all when she heard a step and saw Clayton coming down the stairway.

"Did you find what you were looking for?" she asked, her tone slightly mocking, teasing him.

"More."

Whatever on earth could that possibly mean? "Oh? Such as?"

"Such as this." He handed her a hand-size instrument that she'd seen many times before. Printed on it were the words: *Computerized Performance Rating.*

"Oh, this. Yes, Owen loves to bet." She laughed lightly. "Maybe this gizmo is the reason he loses."

"Owen," his brother said, "never placed a bet in his life. He grew up hating gambling, just the way I did." He did not move—and he did not, to her at least, seem to be a bit muddled or unsteady. "You have a top-notch trainer, Mrs. Rosser, and thorough."

He made it sound more like an accusation than a compliment, but she said, "Thank you."

"Most trainers carry little notebooks like this." He reached into his hip pocket and produced a ratty-looking one. "My brother has detailed files, complete histories, not just past performance records and clockings. Not just the sire and dam but the bloodlines all the way back. And the medical histories, both injuries and ailments. Of every horse entered in the Derby." Then, standing in front of her, and close, he said it again: "Thorough."

She didn't relish the way he said it, and she didn't relish his manner or tone. "Owen's made up his mind Fireaway's going to win. That's what I pay him for." She shrugged. "We'd all like to win it, wouldn't we? Wouldn't you?"

"Not as much, apparently, as Owen. And you."

"Then you probably won't." She had had about enough of this.

"If you've written your letter, why don't you leave now and come back when your brother's here?"

There was no mistaking the irony in his tone now: "Be sure to tell him I called." He stepped to open the door. "And one more thing, if you don't mind. Tell him that if he comes near barn twenty-seven, I'll personally crack his skull. Tell him I'll remove it in pieces from around that clever brain of his. And after that I'll send him to prison. And maybe you along with him."

He went out and closed the door. Softly.

She stood staring at it. What an extraordinary thing to say. Was he really drunk? She doubted it now. What could he imagine that Owen had done? Or that she had done?

She decided to have that gin now. Perhaps it would make the strange incident clear to her by the time Owen returned. She went into the sitting room.

Where is everybody?

Are you crying, Kimberley?

No.

You are, though. Like a little girl.

I never cry.

Liar.

Go away.

You're sobbing because you're alone. If I go away, you'll really be alone.

I hate you. Why do you make me do the things I do? Say the things I say?

They're what you really feel, really know.

What do I know?

It's a crock.

I can't believe that. I won't.

You do, though.

Clay loves me. Clay knows the world's not a crock. He makes me feel it.

Where's Clay now?

Helping me. I'm going to take a warm tub.

You already tried that. It doesn't help.

I know, I know.

Starbright's already dead.

No!

You know that too. He's dead.

He's not, he's not, he's not!

What can Clay do?

You'll see, you'll see.

Andrew thinks Clay took him.

Andrew's full of shit.

He thinks your precious Clay arranged the fire. Now that he has the purse from the Trial.

Clay couldn't do that to a horse.

What about Lord Randolph?

I don't want to think about that. I won't. I will not, cannot, you're trying to drive me crazy!

Did you hear what Clay said? He thinks your father caused Lord Randolph's death.

Why would he, why should he?

You're walking again. You'll wear yourself out.

That's what I want. Why would Andrew . . . what you said?

So he could put the blame on Clay, of course.

But why, why?

So you wouldn't leave Blue Ridge with him.

Andrew wouldn't do that.

Why not, Kimberley?

Because Andrew doesn't love me enough.

Maybe. Probably true. Just like Irene.

Damn Irene! Goddamn my mother forever and ever and ever.

She doesn't even know. Why should she bother? She doesn't love you.

She never did. Not so much as a picture postcard from the fucking Riviera.

That's what I mean.

Go away, go away, I hate you!

Not me. Yourself. I *am* you, Kimberley.

What I need is some grass. I drank all the whisky. Room service
is closed. It's getting light, it's morning—what am I going to do all
alone like this? Will someone please tell me why I am always so
goddamned *alone*?

You forget: I'm here.

All you do is torment me, torture me. You hate me too.

I *am* you. You know what you call me. The other Kimberley. If I
hate you, it's only that you hate yourself.

I wish I could kill you.

Never, Kimberley—not while you live.

If I had some grass, some pills, uppers, downers, acid, anything
to make you go away.

Andrew probably has sleeping pills.

Not Andrew. He never needs them, he's too strong, too—

He just might, though. No harm in asking. Why not ring his
room?

Yes. Yes, I'll do that. He . . . he might even come.

He won't come, Kimberley. Go ahead, try.

I am trying.

He won't even be in his room.

Answer, answer, Andrew, please!

Why go on fooling yourself? He doesn't care. Like Irene.

Father, answer the phone, *please*.

Like Clay.

Clay cares. Don't say that. Clay cares!

You know where Andrew is, don't you?

No—

Yes. You know.

Maybe . . . maybe I do.

You owe her a thousand dollars, Kimberley. Remember? She bet
on Hotspur to win.

It wasn't fair. I forced her into it.

The Irish bitch is a big girl, Kimberley.

You forced *me*. The way you always do!

She won, anyway. Don't you pay your gambling debts?

I don't have that much money here.

Write a check.

Yes. Yes, I could do that.
Put on your coat, take it to her—
I couldn't wake her now—
She's not sleeping—
It's only six-thirty—
You know what she's doing.
No.
With Andrew. You know damn well what they're doing.
I don't believe that.
Why not find out?
I couldn't.
It's the only way you'll know.
Please, please leave me alone. Don't make me.
You always pay your gambling debts.
Goddamn you.
There's your coat. Write the check and put on your coat.
Yes.

"Owen! You look awful!"
He went to the bar. "I'll have one of those."
"What happened to you?"
He poured a whisky. "I've had one hell of a time."
"Poor Owen." She stood up and moved across the sitting room
toward him. She hoped she hadn't consumed too much gin. He
didn't appear to have been injured, but his face! He looked like a
small boy who has been through hell, or had pulled some prank for
which he might be scolded or punished. Whenever he looked this
way, it touched some tender chord in her—one that she cherished.
But then she realized. "You've lost again, haven't you?"

Abashed, he drank. "I guess I'm not the handicapper I think I
am. Too many mortal locks."

"Too many exactas. Honey sweet, knowing as much about horses
as you do, how *can* you go on imagining that you can pick both a
horse to win *and* another horse to place in the same race?"

"I know. It's a sucker bet."

"How can you do it over and over, Owen?"

He shook his head. "Damned if I know, Chrissie."

Chrissie—he had only yesterday begun to call her that. *Owen never placed a bet in his life.* Why would his brother lie like that? Even if he wasn't lying, how would he know?

"Owen, where have you been? Why are you so late?"

He drained the glass. "I'm in deep this time, Chrissie." He heaved a deep breath. "Fifty thousand."

"Fifty thousand!"

"Really plunged. I bet True Blue in the Trial, and I'm betting Belmont too, all over. And they're bearing down. They wanted it now, this morning, last night—that's where I been."

She extended her glass. Her hand was trembling slightly and her heart seemed to be fluttering. "What do you mean, Owen?"

"When I come home from the track, they was waiting for me. Two young kids, looked like college football players." His back was to her now as he poured her drink. "Only one had a Lüger."

"My God."

"They collect rough. They took me to see a gal they call Miss Bette. Not Betty—Bette. She seems to run the show." He faced her—and he looked even more shaken, as if remembering. "She gave me till tomorrow. That's today. Before midnight. Fifty-five thousand, 'cause they charge ten percent interest per day." He handed her the glass. "It goes up every day I don't pay. What do they call it?"

"Compounded." She took a long swallow. He'd forgotten the splash of vermouth. "I don't know, Owen, I don't—"

"Look at it this way. What's fifty thousand against what we stand to make—"

"If—"

"Not if, baby—*when.* Hell, my share of the Derby purse will cover that. I'll pay you back."

"If—" she said again.

"And when we close the syndication deal, my percentage—"

"If."

"Goddamn you!" he exploded. "Will you stop saying that!" His

mouth was contorted, his beard twisting, and his eyes were bright
and terrible and threatening. "You don't know what I been through!
I told you, they play rough!"

"Did they . . . did they hurt you, Owen?"

"Not tonight. They just talked."

"Who is *they*, Owen?"

He whirled away and went to the window and looked out. It was
full morning now. "It's not just them, those three. It's an organization. I don't know *who* they are. Only what." His back was turned
to her, and his wide shoulders looked different this morning: slightly
slumped, slightly slack. "Miss Bette, the bitch, she told me what
could happen. Like getting both kneecaps shot off. Just for open-
ers."

"Don't tell me, Owen," Christine said in a breath.

"Like having my balls crushed—"

"I'll get it, Owen, I'll—"

"Like getting my cock cut off—"

"Don't, please don't, I said—"

He swung about to face her. "They mean business. And they
won't wait till after the race."

"Stop it, I said!" It was not quite a scream—more a harsh plea.
She was shaking all over. "I'll arrange it somehow. I'll have the
bank here phone the bank at home."

"This morning. First thing."

"As soon as the banks open." She was very weak, shattered. She
made it to the loveseat and sank into it. "I'll take care of it."

"It's a big organization, Chrissie. They told me: no place to
hide—"

"Please." The sudden taut strength in her tone surprised her.
"We will not talk about it. Ever again. Do you understand?"

It was, she realized, the first time that she had spoken to him in
this way. He looked surprised too—frowning, eyes pale blue again.
"Sure," he said. "Sure, honey. And it'll never happen again. I'm
done with them."

"Are you hungry?"

"Fact is—I couldn't eat."

Then what? She knew what he'd suggest. Not now. Not like this. She was too sapped of strength, too utterly enervated to stand. To move.

It had been a strange night—or morning.

"You had a visitor a while ago."

"A visitor? Eric? I told that fresh kid never to—"

She managed to shake her head and take a sip. "Not Eric. Your brother."

"Clay? What the hell did—"

"I really and honestly can't say. Does . . . does he drink a lot? You did tell me—"

"He used to." But Owen was not moving. "We both did. Started when we was about twelve or thirteen."

He grew up hating gambling, just the way I did. She thrust the thought from her mind.

"Then that may explain it. He was drunk." She was beginning to breathe normally again. "Something has to."

"Explain what?"

"The way he acted. How'd he get that nose?"

"I did it to him," Owen said. "And I'll do it again if he pokes it where it don't . . . What'd he want?"

"Owen . . . you once told me how you used to take care of him. You don't need this money to save his neck or something like that, do you?"

He took several long steps toward her. "Christine, I asked you: What did he want?"

She took a long swallow, a very long swallow, and said, "He came to borrow the typewriter. Would you believe it?"

"You mean you let him take your friend's typewriter?"

"He didn't take it. He only used it."

"What else?"

"Nothing. Oh yes, he did say that I was to warn you to stay away from barn twenty-seven or he'd crack your clever skull open."

"He'll never see that day."

"If he wasn't drunk, he's crazy."

"Always has been." She could see Owen's mind working desperately behind the scowl that had come over his face. "Born feet first, killed our old lady. Toby always said Clay was never right in his head."

"Well, that explains a lot. He threatened to send you to prison. And me along with you. What kind of wild talk is—"

But Owen was not listening. He was moving. Fast. Into the center hall and then up the stairs, three at a time. Again she waited. More baffled than ever. So she decided to have another drink, with or without vermouth, by now it didn't really matter. It would be hours before the banks opened. And at the bar she remembered what Owen had said when he told Stuart that he really thought Fireaway had proved himself enough to be nominated for the Derby: *Can't let baby brother get out in front of me, can I?* She'd thought little enough of it then, and so had Stuart, who had even been amused in that quiet way of his. Well, whatever there was between the two brothers, it had nothing to do with her, after all. The fresh drink was working its magic; she felt much quieter inside, and warm again. She'd heard and read about the rivalry between brothers. Look at Cain and Abel. But those had been strange threats that Clayton had made—even violent ones.

She went into the hall and up the stairway, her legs weak, her whole body and mind tired. If she could get some rest now—

The door to Marylou's study was open, and she heard Owen thrashing about. She looked in. The room was never neat, but now it was chaos. Owen was breathing hard, and his face, when he saw her, looked murderous. She had never seen him like this before. He was a stranger really.

"Puking little coward," he said. "Making threats." But his eyes were not focused now, as if his mind were refusing to function. He didn't seem to see her although he was speaking to her as if he needed to explain further. "Goddamn that bastard, everything bad that ever happened to me in my whole life, he was behind it! Now he's gonna fuck up everything again, but royal."

She had had too much gin and she was too exhausted to face any more. So she said nothing.

"He'll get his this time. His ass is marked."

She did not ask what Clayton had done. Perhaps he had taken something from the room. It didn't matter. It couldn't be that serious.

"Owen, we're both so tired. Why don't you lie down with me and we'll sleep?"

But Owen had changed again. Very quietly he said, "He did kill our mother, you know—"

No, no, no more—that was not possible.

"She died when he was born."

It made no sense. It was so unreasonable. But Owen looked so beaten and forlorn as he sat down in the desk chair and lowered his forehead to the small blue typewriter. "Poor dear Owen," she heard herself say. "It's over now. Please don't think about the past. Come with me now, darling. Let's rest together and—"

"Toby always loved Clay more, you know." His voice was muffled and boyish—and the strain of anguish in it was genuine. And touching. "Because he was dark and reminded him of Erna."

"Forget him now, dear. I'm sorry I mentioned that he came." She went to him and placed a hand on his shoulder. His flesh was actually quivering under the white cloth of his jacket. "I'd like it, Owen, if you'd come rest with me." What she meant was that this vulnerability that he had exposed had brought them closer together, and in a new, different way. "For me, darling?"

He did not lift his head, but his voice said, in a whisper: "I'll be with you in a few minutes. I have to call Eric to see how the works went without me."

She placed her face against the thickness of his red-brown hair and then turned away and went along the hall toward the bedroom.

His voice followed her: "We can sleep, and then when we wake up, maybe we can make love."

Make love. He had never used those words before. And in that way.

She went into the bedroom and shrugged off the negligée. He had always used such common, such terrible words before.

Strange that after all this time she had come to feel closer to him, as a man, than she had ever felt before. And in such curious circumstances too.

Winner's Circle

Who was that in there with him in the living room, or studio, or whatever the hell it was called? Janice had heard that other voice somewhere. When? Why the hell did he, whoever he was, have to speak so low? Naked, as she had been when Count Wyatt had rolled out and put on his robe—black silk, wouldn't you know?—to go answer the door buzzer, she was leaning against the bedroom door straining to hear. But she could only catch what Wyatt said.

"Flattery at this time of morning, but far be it from me to deny that everyone in racing would perish rather than miss my broadcasts." God, she loved phonies, and Count Wyatt was a prince among phonies. "But . . . *but* I have always made it a solemn rule never, repeat never, to accept a suggestion as to the contents thereof."

The other voice, goddamn his whisper, and then Wyatt's again: "What do you mean, what do you mean, the sport that I *claim* to respect and protect? I'm one of its last feeble extant defenders."

The other voice spoke again, and this time Wyatt only grunted. As if, perhaps, he hadn't minded her hearing before but now was becoming cautious. Why?

She couldn't stand it any longer. She stooped and picked up Wyatt's tattersall shirt from the floor, remembering how he had looked when he dropped it—like a pudgy little boy seeing a naked woman for the first time. She fastened only one button, hearing, "I don't *want* you to trust me. If it's that big a story, I'll break it."

Without tapping on it first, she opened the door. The other man, whose voice she should have recognized, since he'd been so damned insulting not once but twice, was Mr. Clayton Chalmers. Owner, trainer, proud possessor of the steeplechase champion of the day just past. He was standing at the far end of the high, vast room, and he turned, frowning when he heard her.

"Sorry," she said, though not contritely, "but if you two are going to keep me awake, I need a cigarette." She drifted to her shoulder bag, which was on the glass-topped table between where Chalmers stood and Wyatt sat in all his glory, his face actually reddening. His eyes, nevertheless, held a certain masculine pride: Look at *my* conquest, behold the legs, the protruding breasts, see what I have in *my* bed! "I'll only be a sec." She fumbled about in the bag, then her hand came up with a single cigarette, which she held aloft. She smiled at Clayton Chalmers, but he made no attempt to light it. "Remember me?"

His face was actually grim, his brown eyes narrowed. "The journalism graduate. You forgot your press badge."

Far out. His eyes barely glanced down at her legs. So she lit her own cigarette—after giving the sonofabitch every chance. "Why aren't you out there clocking your horse this time of morning?" He did not reply. "Oh? Are ladies persona non grata at this kaffee-klatsch?"

"Non goddamned grata," Chalmers said.

Wyatt looked embarrassed. "Sorry, Jan. Business."

Damned if she cared for that possessive male chauvinist tone of dismissal. "Matters of state," she said and, smoking, strolled to the bedroom door. She'd make Wyatt pay, one way or another. "Wyatt baby," she said, blowing smoke, "I'll never, but never go back to sleep till you put me there." She opened the door. "Take your time, Count. I'll let you spank me again for being such a naughty girl."

How do you like those potatoes, Mr. Clayton Chalmers, shithead sublime? She closed the door, making certain they heard the click of the latch. She went to sit on the bed. The Lotus position—that'll drive him up the wall. She smoked, staring at the geometric-patterned paintings on the walls. Weird. But she knew the painter's name and reputation. The pad made a neat hideout for the Count during Derby Week. Here, he was safe from the likes of her, wasn't he? She shrugged off the shirt. Safe like hell, daddy-o.

Now that she didn't have to concentrate, the voices—both inaudible now, because Wyatt was whispering too—didn't work on her nerves.

She could sit and remember her time with the celebrated and respected Count Wyatt, Superman. And she could even chuckle out loud. In a way all men without their clothes were the same: helpless. She'd had to use every trick in the book to turn him on. And in college and the three years since it had become a very thick book. But he'd gotten it up twice. Three times really, if you counted the blowjob in the car on the way. Fantastic. Once to fuck her straight, just because she was on the bed and naked. And not much later, when she'd remembered how his cock had bounced around when she'd mentioned spanking her in the car, she'd asked him *how* he'd like to spank her—flat on the bed, although no belts allowed, or over his knees—and it had come right up again. What was really grotesque, though, was that when she was draped head-down over his knees and his bare palm was whacking her, harder and harder, and her bare flesh was stinging hotter and hotter with each flat clap of his palm, it had turned *her* on. So the silly idea had paid off double, you might say. She'd remembered how she felt when she was in her teens and her father did it. But then only her butt was bare. After Wyatt had got himself so exhilarated that he was ready to screw her again, she hadn't even minded his prickly gray goatee against her face or neck or the soft thickness of his body. Fan-*tas*tic. This old bastard had stumbled on a way to make her come. So maybe the next couple of nights wouldn't be such a god-damn *chore* after all.

And tonight was paying off already. In the next room. The highly sensitive little tape recorder that she had concealed in her shoulder bag—camouflaged by an empty cigarette package—was spinning away now with silent precision. If it was true that the story the dear old Count had mentioned was so big that he'd have to break it, then it was probably something scandalous as well, the whispering pricks—and if so, the price she'd had to pay out of her own lousy salary for the tiny recorder would probably be worth it.

She'd have every word verbatim, and she'd be able to listen as soon as she had Wyatt back to beddy-bye. Whatever that took. Did the horny old bastard have a fourth shot in him?

Eyeless in Gaza. Who in hell wrote that, who the hell cared, what difference did it make? Blind, blind, *blind.* The fury in Clay was a raging torrent, hot lava running wild. How could he have been so stupid, so short-sighted, dimwitted? The rage, as he drove the pickup along the road in the early morning light, was focused on Owen but directed at himself as well. Why had it taken the words in that note, Toby's words, to make him suspect, *force* him to suspect? *Bangtail, mazuma, glue factory—*

Even now, though the certainty was a knot of iron in his gut, he could not make his mind accept it. Why the hell had it always been so hard for him to recognize, to accept, the duplicity, the deviousness and greed and dishonesty that surrounded him? When are you going to grow up, Clay Chalmers? *Ever?* One of his first memories of his brother, if not actually the first, was of a hot midday behind a barn. Owen smilingly offering to fan sweat and flies away with a cardboard box lid: He had fanned and fanned and then, abruptly, the five-year-old Clay lulled into a pleasant torpor, he had dropped the cardboard, and his fist had exploded alongside the boy's face, knocking him sideways, taking his breath away, and then Owen was on top of him in the dirt, pummeling him with delight, still grinning. Even now Clay could recall that shock of disbelief, which had stayed with him even as he tried to fight back, eyes streaming tears. Shame stronger even than the anger had turned him into a small fighting demon as he kicked and slugged and clawed back hopelessly, always hopelessly against that weight and strength; he couldn't win, he never won—

How long, Clay, how many years will it take you to admit finally and forever that your older brother is a shit?

He considered stopping the truck. His stomach was twisting and sour. He was going to puke.

Like hell. He was going to find Owen. But he knew better. He had decided otherwise. If he faced Owen now, whatever violence came of it, however much he ached for it, it would not return Starbright. It would not return Starbright in sound condition anyway.

He had to stay with his scheme. *Bait the hook well; this fish will bite.* Shakespeare. Sound advice, false hope? *Money talks. It's the only thing that really talks!* Toby now, Toby, not Shakespeare—was *he* the one his son was listening to at last? Dear old sly Toby, he'd know what talked, if nothing else, or damn little else. Had the little bastard been right all along? Toby and Owen: *Get it any way you can, but win and get it.* Toby, who never won. Owen, who was making certain. And stupid little brother Clay: *As if we were villains by necessity; fools by heavenly compulsion.* Well, fool he had been and villain he might be now, but he was finally banking on his own cunning, a stranger's cupidity, and treachery all round!

He was not going to stop the truck. He refused to stand alongside the street and vomit into the gutter. It was what Owen wanted, the despised weakness that he knew of, depended on always. Clay choked down the bilious acid that threatened to rise into his throat and mouth.

Damned if he'd give them the satisfaction, either of them.

His body was burning. His blood was scalding. *When I think of a sensitive, high-strung animal like that being treated this way—* Andrew Cameron only a short time ago. An hour? Two? More? He had lost track of time. But he and Andrew Cameron shared the same outrage. If nothing else. And Clay was sick with it. And with the thought of that Irish exercise girl lying in the hospital—Bernie's friend. And with the thought of a great horse like Ancient Mariner destroyed—

He turned a corner and immediately spotted a phone booth. He parked the truck along the curb.

While he waited for the connection to be made his face throbbed and his whole body was soaked in sweat.

"Yes?" Her voice sounded low, forlorn—lost.

"Kimb."

"Clay!"

"Kimb, did I wake you?"

"Wake me?" Her tone hardened. "Do you think I've been *sleeping*? Where the hell are you?"

A frigid flash went through him. "I'm in a booth. I had to find out how you—"

"Where have you been?"

He stiffened. "Kimb, listen, you have to trust—"

"Answer me. Where have you been, what have you been doing? Is Starbright all right?"

Damned if he knew. He would not know for hours. Possibly never. "I don't know. It's too soon to—"

"You've been gone forever!"

A cold knife turned inside. "Kimberley, for God's sake listen—"

"Are you *vomiting?*"

"*Listen,* I said *listen* to me!" He was clutching the telephone so hard that he could feel pain in his arm. "I have to see Mr. Raynolds, I have to check on Hotspur. Bernie took the works, so I have to get his clocking. I—" But he broke off. The sweat had turned cold. What the hell was he doing standing here in a phone booth trying to tell her what he couldn't tell her, what he didn't *know?* "If you want me to do this, you'll have to let me do it my way."

"Do what? Do what, what are you doing?"

"I'll be there tonight."

"Tonight? It's only—" Her tone turned to stone. "You'll come *now.*"

An icy wave threatened to engulf him. "I'll come when I've done what I have to do!" He realized it was a shout. He slammed the phone onto the hook. It fell and dangled. To hell with it.

He opened the folding glass door and started toward the truck. The bile came up into his throat. Filled his mouth. Bitter on his tongue. Again he choked it down, swallowing it.

Be to her virtues very kind; be to her faults a little blind.

He climbed into the truck and switched on the motor. He was on his way to the track again.

I have heard of reasons manifold why Love must needs be blind . . .

Blind again. And furious again. Chilled to the marrow. And tired. How long since he had slept? It hadn't been that long really, if you could still reckon time by a clock, since her father had phoned her room to report on the fire—

Her gentle limbs did she undress, And lay down in her loveliness.

What he needed was a drink. He remembered the good feeling it gave him inside. That first fine upward lift and then the calm, glowing sense of confidence. Would there be any bars open this time of day? He'd had one weak drink in seven years. Last night. The first and only since that night at Blue Ridge. The night of snow when he had or had not unlatched Lord Randolph's stall, had or had not unlocked the stable door. And Andrew Cameron's cold blanched face had contorted in rage as he struck out, again and again. And Kimberley: *How can I go with you now, Clay? After this, how can you expect it?* Now her father suspected he had stolen Starbright. And a short time ago he had accused Andrew Cameron of having destroyed Lord Randolph in order to keep Kimberley with him. Did he believe that? Had he come to think that, had he convinced himself of that in order not to accept the fact that he had done it himself? Andrew Cameron had accused him last night so that Kimberley would believe it. Or at least suspect. *Did* she? The past, the present, all of it came together when it shouldn't. He had to keep his mind clear now for what had to be done. What had to be done now, today.

He did need a drink. To clear his mind. It was as feverish as his body had abruptly become.

But if he had a drink now . . . if he blew this, even if Hotspur won, he would lose everything he'd really come here to get. Kimberley? Yes. Whereas if he pulled this off—

"The knight on a white charger," Wyatt Slingerland had scoffed when he'd explained his scheme. "Come to save his lady fair."

Christ, he had felt like a fool. And maybe he was.

But no booze. Not today.

Why? Because he had to carry the ball? What he *should* do, what any sane and reasonable man would do was inform the police. Report what had happened. Lay out his suspicions, his proof. What proof, for Christ's sake? A small sheet of correspondence stationery with blue engraving at the top: *Marylou Wohlforth,* and an address, *Hyattsville Road, Hyattsville, Kentucky.* With typing on it: *qwertyuiop* and the rest of the keyboard. Blue ribbon. Script face. Which *appeared*, at least, to match the typing on the unsigned ransom note. But did it? He would soon know, or at least he would soon be able to form an opinion; and Mr. Raynolds should be able to help. But he already knew what the lawyer would say: *Young man, all you have is suspicion.* What about the copy of the contract in his pocket? At a quick glance it had appeared that the Lazy R Ranch would sell Fireaway for eight million dollars if he won the Derby. What percentage of that would be Owen's? *Motive and suspicion, that's all, Mr. Chalmers.* And it was also possible that Owen was working for and with Mrs. Rosser on the whole deal. They were living together. Maybe Owen was looking out for her interests. But Owen never looked out for anyone but himself. Like Toby: *Way it is, boys, whole shebang's nothing but a dunghill, and you get to the top for yourself.*

A convulsion of hate, a paroxysm. He knew why he couldn't go to the police or the TRPB. Not because he had no proof but because if he did, Owen and whoever was working for him would maim Starbright. Or destroy him completely. *That* was the bottom line and he knew it; he was boxed in, he was really boxed in. Unless . . . whoever was guarding the horse was as greedy and corrupt as he'd have to be to do such a job.

He made another turn—into the residential area surrounding the Downs. The fog had cleared. He looked across the lawns. Heavy dew—another pretty good sign of fine weather ahead, probably by evening. On the other hand, if the sun came through hot enough to burn through those clouds up there, it could mean afternoon thundershowers this time of year. The street signs far ahead came into sharper focus. More rain for sure. *The farther the sight, the nearer the rain.* Toby had taught him a few things worth remembering. It was three days to the race, almost four, but now, every hour of every day, the signs would have to be studied. As well as the official predictions. He'd know what they were as soon as he reached the track, and also he'd have a look at the barometer in Bernie's trailer. With the luck they'd had for the Derby Trial they couldn't expect too much mud for the big one. But they could hope. Horse people are always hoping.

He could see the twin spires beyond the rooftops now. He was beginning to feel a bit more normal. Still lightheaded, even dizzy, he was no longer freezing cold or feverishly hot. He'd have to stay as controlled and cool-headed as possible, because there was no damn predicting what the day would bring. Or whether his plot would pay off. One minute it seemed a logical, practical plan, the next it turned into a harebrained pipe dream.

Back there at Wyatt's apartment earlier he'd played it cool enough. After the woman Janice Wessell had gone back into the bedroom, Wyatt had lifted his voice to say, "Do you realize that if

this was made public knowledge, it'd be the biggest scandal in racing, probably ever?" He sure as hell did. That was why he'd placed
a silencing finger on his lips and then gone to reach into the little
bitch's shoulder bag to locate the device that he had suspected was
there. It had been concealed in a cigarette package. He flipped it off
and returned it while Wyatt Slingerland stared. But for some reason
the man hadn't been amused. It didn't matter—since he'd agreed to
do his part: "Against my better judgment but because I think I'm
with you on this, Chalmers, although how do you ever know what's
right?" And in the hallway outside the apartment he had shaken his
gray head and tugged at his goatee: "You're asking me to sit on the
most sensational story that ever came down the pike, so if it does
explode in your face I'll disclaim any knowledge of the facts."
Then he added: "Not that I think you have a prayer in hell anyway." Possibly not. Probably not. But he had to take the gamble
and he'd sure as hell foxed the little bitch from Florida.

The backstretch had returned to normal too. The works were
over, no horses on the track, and the guard waved him through the
gate without asking to see his ID or even glancing at the owner's
pass glued to the windshield. He parked the pickup and walked in
the direction of barn 27. It was that lazy time backside that he had
always enjoyed. But not today. Too damn much on his mind and
too much uncertainty. His step seemed stiff and unfamiliar, and he
realized that his body was taut, his muscles tight and strange.

Then he heard the commotion. Grooms and hot-walkers and a
uniformed guard were running. The doors of the TRPB office burst
open, and two men came tearing out. What now? Then he realized
that they were all heading toward the area of barn 27.

He broke into a run. A fast run, passing others. Voices rose, but
above them he could hear a howl. Of pain. Not a horse. The
horses, when the barn came into sight, were stomping and whinnying, as if in terror, and then he saw the group gathered at Hotspur's
stall.

He ran faster, his hands pulling shoulders aside.

The gate of the stall stood open.

The sound was coming from inside.

He heard a deep, angry growling.

The howl grew louder, inhuman now.

A guard stood at the gate with a drawn gun pointed into the stall. He was moving it in two hands as if to make certain of his aim.

Clay reached him. He knocked the arm up and away, not down, and the gun exploded in the air above their heads. He smelled powder.

He hesitated a split second before looking in. Hotspur was drawn against the wall, not rearing but shuddering and cowering, head up, nostrils flaring, and on the straw a dog had its jaws clamped onto someone's shoulder.

Bernie.

His face contorted in pain, mouth wide, the howl deafening, blood soaking his shirt—Bernie's heavy body was thrashing about violently, helpless, the Doberman refusing to let go, his teeth digging in deeper.

Clay was not thinking. There was no time to think. A girl screamed behind him.

He slid into the stall, paused a brief second, then leaped full length onto the back of the dog. His hands reached for its neck. Grasped it.

But the dog's head twisted, its mouth open, and he lost his grip, and now he was face to face with the animal, its lips curling, jaws wide, teeth dripping blood, the growl turning into a snarl as the teeth came up at his face.

If he rolled clear, he was done. The dog would be on him in an instant.

Instead he reached again and managed to get his hands around the animal's smooth hot neck, their faces close, the dog's breath foul and sickening.

He grasped with all his strength and saw the jaws close, shutting off the snarl. He rolled to one side then and, over the canine face, caught a quick glimpse of Bernie moaning and clutching his shoulder and rolling free, blood everywhere.

He increased the pressure with his thumbs, his hands tight on the neck now, and he could feel the dog's paws hammering and thumping at his chest and stomach, clawing at his groin, but he held on, and now the dog's mouth came open again and he was staring into a cavern of teeth and tongue and blood and throat, and he clutched still harder, wrapping his legs around the desperate squirming body until their two bodies were locked together, his ankles crossed behind the dog's back and his legs tightening in a viselike embrace while his hands refused to let go of the slick hide of the neck that pulsed and throbbed with hate and fury under his palms and implacable thumbs.

Could he break the bastard's neck?

Pain climbed his arms. His legs stiffened and pressed.

The mouth was wide, struggling for breath now.

Die, damn you, *die!*

Harder, harder still, with every muscle straining for more strength, more power, pain up into his armpits, he felt his own teeth clamped together so hard that he thought they would crush in his mouth, but he held on, the animal trying to gasp, the stench overpowering, its jaws gaping wide, teeth sharp and throat a red hell, tongue flapping, eyes bulging, legs and feet powerless now, and still he pressed harder on the throbbing of the gullet and bone, and still harder, die, die, goddamn you, *die!*

And then he realized that it was over.

Several spasms, a convulsion through the whole body, a gurgling, and then the head went sideways, the bulging eyes going glassier still, sightless, and he could feel the dog piss against his own stomach, smell its shit, and at last, while he continued to press, the tongue went slack, and he could feel the dog's body turn into a limp weight.

But he still held on, he found a last shot of strength in his arms and hands and gave it all he had left, and then another final squeeze, seeing the tongue loll from between the jaws, saliva running thin and red with blood. Bernie's blood. He still held on, hate and disgust taking over in him now, raging in him.

He found a foothold in the straw and stood, hands still clasping the hanging body, and then he slammed it against the side of the stall so hard that he could hear the wood splinter.

Then, standing there, gasping for breath, he realized that the

215

sounds he heard were coming from a distance—voices, running feet, the low growl of a siren. The faces in the stall door were wooden, fixed—and silent.

He glanced up. Elijah was standing with his back against Hotspur's quivering flanks and one hand running along the colt's withers and shoulder, over and over. It was as if the black man were shielding the horse from the violence while staring at it himself in total disbelief. There was no blood, no gashes or teethmarks. Bernie had saved the horse. Somehow.

Up and down the shedrow, the stomping and whinnying of frightened animals.

"Get him out of here, Eli," Clay heard himself say. Then he shouted: "Someone get a vet over here fast!"

An unfamiliar voice called, "He's on his way!"

The group at the door parted as he went out of the stall. He saw a young medico inside the Invalid Carrier, about to close its rear door as he approached. "St. Elizabeth and Mary's Hospital," the medico shouted at him and pulled the door shut.

The yellow ambulance moved slowly between the barns, its siren wailing in short spurts.

Chapter Six

SHE emerged from the telephone box and went up on the lift to
Molly's floor. The whole world, for Brigid Tyrone, had changed
aspect. No matter where she was or what she was saying or doing,
she seemed to be living in a cloud of incredulity. Gregory McGreevey had just reported on Irish Thrall—not the best of news, not the
worst. And young Kevin Hunter had sent the girl his regards. She
would convey the messages. But when she arrived at Molly's room,
it was empty.

She had been permitted to see the child only very briefly last
night, and now her bed was—

"They've taken your niece to the labs for more tests." The
woman she turned to face was Sister Grace, the sallow-faced but
pleasant-eyed nun who had been so kind last night. Was it last
night? "X-rays and neurological examinations, Mrs. Tyrone. She
was in such shock earlier, you remember, and she had to be so
sedated—and besides at that time of morning the labs weren't func-
tioning." Sister Grace smiled reassuringly. "There's a coffee shop
on the ground floor and a chapel on the fourth. And the waiting
room's just along the hall."

Brigid nodded—and smiled. At least she thought she smiled.

"We have to make sure there's been no nerve damage, Mrs.
Tyrone. And no fractures that weren't discovered when she was

217

brought in." She looked at her watch. "It may be some time yet."

"Thank you, Sister." She started through the door, then stopped. "I think I'll wait on this floor. So that when—"

"We'll let you know as soon as she comes back." The woman had a warm smile, as sincere and unprofessional as one might ever wish. "There are magazines, although not racing ones, I'm afraid."

For the moment Brigid felt she had had quite enough of racing, thank you, racing and all that went with it. She passed along the corridor, which was bustling with activity now, and took a chair in the alcovelike room, where she was alone. Again.

But she was no longer teetering on the thin treacherous rim of hysteria, as she had been during the night, when she had come here the first time. They had been taking X-rays then too, and afterward it had been Sister Grace who had reported that while there were multiple fractures, no ribs had punctured the lungs. But she had been too stunned even to be relieved. They had allowed her to see the child once—how still she looked, how tiny and vulnerable, only her bandaged head and sleeping face visible above the taut sheet— and then, although Sister Grace had insisted that there was nothing more that she could do because Molly was sedated and would sleep for hours, Brigid had nevertheless stayed on. In the large, hushed loungelike waiting area on the ground floor. The young man named Bernie had telephoned not once but several times, and the nurse had been kind enough to summon her each time, but what was there for her to say? What did she herself know?

And then, after an eternity of sitting and trembling and staring at the darkness outside the windows, a voice had spoken her name. A familiar voice? When her vision cleared, she was staring up into the face of Andrew Cameron. It looked as gentle and concerned as his voice sounded: "When I arrived at the track, they told me. So I came."

So he came. She had the impulse then to stand and to collapse into his arms. But naturally she had not. What would the poor kind man think of such a display? He wanted to drive her to the hotel, but stubbornly she refused. She knew it was irrational. She knew that both he and Sister Grace were right; she was of no earthly use here, and in the middle of the night. Then, to her astonishment—

she had been so stunned and without wit or grace that she could only lapse into silence again—he had sat down on the couch next to her. How long had they sat there together? She had no sense of time. It had still been dark outside, but the comings and goings through the wide main doors had become less and less frequent. Had he been there when Bernie Golden had called the last time? She could not be certain. His presence had somehow added to her sense of incredulity—what a kind, considerate man. He had once, she remembered, broken the silence to say that Irish Thrall had survived the pandemonium and by now was probably asleep in the barn. Had he inquired of Molly? No. But he had known of her condition because he had asked the nurses before joining her. She was not exactly sure how she had come by that knowledge. Perhaps he had told her.

And finally he had leaned closer and in a whisper, not asked but pleaded with her to allow him to return her to the hotel. The fact of her own foolishness—Daniel had always said her will would be her undoing—had penetrated then, and just at the moment when she had allowed herself to be persuaded he had been summoned to the telephone. When he returned, he had explained that his trainer had rung him, and she had assumed that it was to report on Starbright. On the ride through the city's hushed residential streets—how pleasant and natural and safe and secure they looked!—he had not intruded on her dulled but pervasive apprehensions. It had been as if his presence were sufficient. And in some miraculous way, so it had been. As they reached the central city area she had recalled what he had said the first night—was it Sunday, had it been only such a brief time ago?—about agreeing with Gregory McGreevey that racing *was* a violent and dangerous business. And then, perhaps because he was usually so calm and confident, she had also recalled his rage and savage indignation when his fist had beaten on the steering wheel on the drive to the hotel after that catastrophe during the Derby Trial. He was many men, this Andrew Cameron. And by the time they were alone in the ascending lift, she had realized that in some mysterious manner and for the first time since Daniel's death she had come to feel cared for again—protected and even cherished.

When he had unlocked her door and pushed it gently open for her, she had turned in the frame and hugged him quickly, his face warm and harsh with stubbles against her own, which was, she realized, chilled. He had appeared as startled as she herself felt when she entered the sitting room.

She had crossed its dim emptiness, only glancing at the closed door of Molly's empty room, and then, without undressing, she had thrown her body, exhausted and weightless, across the bed. The familiar foreboding had returned to her sleepless, wavering mind—the Celtic dread of the bogman's daughter sure, though now no longer presentiment but the fear fulfilled. A pagan thing for certain, but she should have heeded it while still in Ireland. What was happening to Molly was her fault, her doing: They should never have come here.

Now, waiting again, remembering, she wondered: Was her guilt, which had lingered darkly in her in the hours since, as unreasonable and perverse and uncivilized as her earlier apprehensions had been?

"Good morning, Mrs. Tyrone."

Startled, she lifted her head. For a moment she did not recognize the dark-haired young man who stood there.

"Although," he said with a twisting smile, "I don't know what's good about it." He made a quick gesture. "No, don't get up, please. How's Miss Muldoon?"

Clay Chalmers. Of course. They had been introduced once, and she had seen him with his handsome black colt in the winner's circle yesterday. Time again—now dreadfully confusing. And the way he looked—

"We'll know more later," she said. "They're making tests." And she extended her hand.

Which he refused. "I'm pretty dirty," he said. His tone was as she remembered: soft, almost shy, as gentle as his manner. She peered more closely: His jacket was ripped, there were brown splotches of what appeared to be blood on it, a strand or two of straw clung to his rumpled trousers, and his boots were caked with mud.

He answered the question that she had not asked: "Bernie's here. You may or may not want to tell Miss Muldoon."

"Is . . . is Mr. Golden ill then?"

"He may be. They're making tests too. But not of him. Of a dog."

There was a knife in his tone, and his dark eyes were far from gentle: They flashed murder. He was not the same young man she had met. The change was bewildering—and somewhat terrifying.

"He was bitten by a dog," Clay Chalmers said. Then he corrected himself, the knife now turning in his voice: "Not bitten—attacked." Then, as if he knew that was not sufficient: "A dog attacked our horse. Bernie saw it in time and saved him. The dog turned on him."

"I'm terribly sorry to hear it," she said—and so she was: not sorry but distressed, appalled. "Won't you sit down?"

"Thanks, no. I have to move Hotspur to the Derby barn." The twist of smile again, but grimly ironic. "Where he'll have more security." The smile was bitter, and so was his tone. "Although that didn't do anyone much good there last night, did it?" He nodded and turned and was gone in determined strides.

Now what could he have meant by that? Was he implying that last night's fire might not have been accidental? If so, it might . . . it might explain Andrew's behavior during the hour they had spent together early this morning. And that telephone message summoning him—

Yes, it might. His preoccupation, his banked-down fury and frustration, which she had sensed from the moment their paths had crossed again just before dawn—quite by accident this time, but propitiously.

"I couldn't sleep," she had said when she had met him face to face on the plaza below the hotel, where she had gone to walk in the faint hope that it might tire her so that she could get a few winks before returning to the hospital.

"I suspected as much," he had said, "but I hesitated to go to your room."

"You couldn't sleep either."

"True. Shall we take a stroll?" He did not take her arm, however. "It's not safe for anyone, especially women, to go strolling alone this time of day."

"In Ireland it would be."

"This isn't Ireland."

"I know." It was not Ireland, and indeed in some ways, many ways, she wished that she were there. She and Molly, Molly healed and herself again.

They passed through the area where during the day crowds gathered at long tables to eat the various foods that Molly had come to enjoy—barbeque and chili and other such—and there was the beat and thrum of music and what was here called square-dancing. Not speaking then, they moved toward the cobbled riverfront where the stern-wheel steamboat was docked, dark and silent now and empty of its merrymakers and music. The river stretched wide and flat and motionless in the gray light.

When they did speak—which was seldom—it was about horses and racing. Brigid found herself chattering away about Connemara, where her Innisfree Demesne was situated: the noble crags, the blue-shining bogs, the grass sprouting green and nourishing the horses. Andrew knew of it: the Gulf Stream close to the west coast accounted for the richness of the soil, that and the phosphates and limestone below the surface of the pastures.

"I'd like to see it someday," Andrew said. "As often as I've been to Europe, I've never been to Ireland."

"Come then."

"I might." He took her hand and looped her arm through his. "I'd like to."

"I'd like that too," she admitted, lifting her chin.

Then he was speaking of what was called bluegrass: It was not grass at all really but had been developed from a Eurasian weed so aggressive that it drove out the less nourishing plant life.

As they moved from the river toward the dimness of the central city streets, she wondered aloud whether he knew that the horses pictured on the walls of Lascaux and other prehistoric caves were in all likelihood Connemara ponies. And then he was wondering whether those ponies, so distinct from the thoroughbred horses that he knew, might be similar to the Icelandic ponies that Mr. Einarsson had mentioned in the garden at the Downs before the Derby Trial. Probably, they agreed, not wishing to think of the Trial and of what had happened to the Einarssons' Eric the Red. How long ago that seemed—yet it had been only hours really, less than a day.

They explored the River City Mall at dawn. The wide shop-lined avenue with outdoor cafés and many benches and fountains, a place for leisurely strolling and at midday crowded with shoppers and office workers, was utterly deserted now except for a city policeman and his three-wheeled scooter—which he had backed into a recessed doorway so that he could catch a few winks, his head down over the handle bars. They smiled at each other and crossed to return to the hotel, passing a darkened theater and a strip bar with its unlighted marquee advertising the Riverview Follies. Two establishments were still open, and through the plate-glass windows she saw only men at the bars, some wearing leather jackets and some, it appeared, wearing heavy makeup. Andrew didn't notice, or pretended not to; he seemed preoccupied with the intrusion of crime into his world. He spoke of the use of ringers in the breeding sheds, the clandestine poaching of other people's stallions for breeding purposes, the illegal use of artificial insemination methods. And she told him of the accusation in an interview printed in *Paris Match* that ninety percent of all the trotting races in France are rigged. He seemed strangely troubled then. Did she know that a famous broodmare named Fanfreluche, in foal to Secretariat and worth half a million dollars, had been kidnapped from Claiborne Farm in Paris, Kentucky, several years ago; whether a ransom was paid would never be known.

Going up on the lift, she asked, on impulse, whether he would like a drink. Then, the flustered colleen with a ribbon in her red hair again, she added, "In my country there's no time of day not appropriate and no excuse required."

Even pouring the whiskies, though, she was not certain why she'd extended the invitation. Was it only because she wished to return his kindnesses, to reach and to wither his own mood of discontent and restlessness? Or was it—

The door buzzer sounded. Andrew frowned, questions in his gray eyes. She went to open the door, but he stopped her with a shake of his head.

"In my country," he said, the teasing of his tone not matched by the expression in his gaze, "we always ask before opening the door."

"Who is it, please?"

"It's only me, Mrs. Tyrone. I've come to pay my debt."

Kimberley? Could it possibly be?

She opened the door. And Kimberley indeed it was.

But her manner did not agree with the almost defiant brightness of her voice. "I always pay my gambling losses, Mrs. Tyrone. You'll excuse the time of day, I'm sure." Her face looked, if anything, desolate, and her stance, feet together below the camel's-hair coat, was that of a small child expecting reproach or punishment—abjectly apologetic. "My check in the amount of one thousand dollars. You chose Hotspur and you won, remember?"

Yes, she remembered. But something about the child—something forlorn and even wretched—touched that chord of compassion that Brigid could never control, so she opened the door further and said, "We were just having a whisky. Would you care to join us?"

Kimberley did not so much as glance at her father. "But it's not even sunup, is it? No, thank you, I've had a few." She turned away, then paused. "Unless you have some pot—"

Andrew was silent.

"I'm afraid I don't, Kimberley. Brandy, though."

The long pale hair shook. "Some other time, thanks."

When she was gone and the door closed, Andrew spoke: "She's terribly upset, Brigid."

Yes. Any fool could see that. But why? Because Andrew was here, and with the widow Tyrone? And before sunup!

She discovered that quite abruptly she was angry. She tore the check across, twice, and then again. It had been a strange, strange night, and it didn't promise to become less so.

She crossed to where Andrew stood and took the whisky and soda from his hand. She took a long swallow, her eyes on him above the rim of glass. Waiting. Accusing?

"The fire disturbed Starbright," Andrew explained. "So much so that he may not be able to run."

Then, of course, she was sorry. And said so. And drifted away from him.

"I'd better go to her," he said.

"Yes." By all means. The girl would have that—by whatever means. "Yes, Andrew." But she was grateful too for the hour just past. For all the consideration and devotion he had displayed. Devotion? "She seems to need you."

He drained his glass and set it down, and then he strode to the door. Where he stopped and turned to face her.

"Are you feeling better, Brigid?"

Was she? She *had* been feeling better. Much. But now—

"Yes, Andrew." She moved toward him. "And you?"

"Much. Thanks to you."

It was too much then. It might have been that the whisky had diminished her restraint. Or had she her Irish up? Whatever, she stepped closer, and surprised that she should have to lift herself onto her toes, she kissed him. On the lips. Lightly but firmly.

Then she stared into his eyes. Something exploded in that calm grayness. And he reached and took her into his arms and then he was kissing her, hungrily, a man starved, his mouth intense and devouring, and she was returning his kiss, their arms wrapped and gripping, their bodies close, and closer, then closer still.

In a minute or two, when he had gone, she stood staring at the door. It had been a wild and contradictory time altogether but none of it more astonishing than what she had decided then: that the girl had thrown down the gauntlet and that she, Brigid Tyrone, had done what Daniel would have expected her to do—she had taken up the challenge.

On the way to the hospital later, driving her BMW, leased for the week, she had tried to evade remembering. But now, sitting here in the waiting room after Clay Chalmers's puzzling visit, she was gratified that she had given in to the impulse to recall. She had no idea what the rest of the week would bring and their embrace might have been only a part of what she had heard referred to here as Derby fever, but whatever, once she knew that Molly would be herself again, she would no longer refuse to face her own feelings head-on, come hell or the rising tide of involvement.

In Ireland, she reflected, there were many women—and men too, for the matter of that, unmarried into their thirties or even into their old age, poor souls. A father devoted to his daughter, or vice-versa, was more often than not considered virtuous. But in her own mind, Brigid Tyrone's mind . . . well, one woman's virtue might well be another's—

"Mrs. Tyrone, you may see her now." It was Sister Grace. Her smile and eyes spoke relief before her words as Brigid stood up from her reverie. "The doctors have found no internal injuries of consequence, and no major nerve damage, although the child will be some time in healing." They were walking together along the corridor, the nun's step as brisk as her voice. "Superficial contusions and abrasions, as expected. The collarbone is fractured, but it was not smashed, and the upper left arm seems to have taken most of the punishment." She halted at the door to allow Brigid to pass. "She may thank her Lord, she's a fortunate girl. If you'd like a television set in the room, it can be arranged."

But in spite of the woman's words Brigid's mind had begun to thunder again with last night's apprehension and confusion. She went in with a nod of thanks to Sister Grace.

Under the white sheet Molly's small body lay quite still, and the white plaster cast on her shoulder and arm looked heavy and ugly. The bruised swelling of her tiny face had lost some of its violent color, and the many small cuts on the fair skin above her eyes, which were shut, were no longer that angry blood-red. The bandage covering the many small stitches on her forehead seemed smaller this morning, but . . . it was not Molly. Oh, child, child, what have they done to you?

"Molly." Was that her voice? "Top o' the morning to you, Molly. And from Mr. McGreevey as well, and Kevin." Should she mention Bernie Golden? Mr. Chalmers had suggested she use her judgment.

Molly's lids lifted. Those were not her eyes, those dull and lifeless spots of darkness there. She rolled her head to one side and regarded Brigid without expression. Her lips—pale, so pale—did not smile. Brigid took her small hand; it was not warm.

"Mr. McGreevey says Thrall's sound and healthy." She did not mention that he had also quoted the veterinarian, who had said that it was beyond his ken to diagnose psychological or emotional damage. "They gave him a light workout and missed your riding." What was to be gained by reporting that Kevin had said the colt was off his feed and that he'd worked poorly? "Thrall will miss you too, Molly."

"I don't care."

Had she heard? "Sister Grace says you've had quite a shock and—"

"I don't care whether he misses me or not."

Brigid recalled Gregory McGreevey on the telephone: *The girleen did what she thought she had to do to save the colt. She was tryin' to lead him away but the animal was wild.*

"I don't care whether I ever see him again." Her voice was toneless and flat. "I hope I never see him again."

She believed he'd turned on her. "Molly, you know more about horses than to imagine—"

"Aunt Brigid, I hate him."

And now Brigid was speechless. Oh, how she longed to bend down and, like Niam, drawing her gold robes about her, lift the girl, like Ossian, onto her white steed and take her off to the lovely Land of Youth, where the dark evil of a dark world could not touch them, either one—

If JD was at the track, he was not in the barn with Also Ran for one good reason: No matter how cocksure he acted or how hard he tried to cover it, that big strong shortstop was freaked out by horses. Being near them, especially close, in the stall for instance—it blew the man's mind! Almeta had read in one of the racing magazines that a horse could sense fear, almost smell it. If JD was at the track, what he was doing was gambling. Craps, blackjack, poker, even cockroach races, it didn't matter. What is known as a degenerate gambler, one who gambles just for the doing—and has to lose. She often wished she'd married an alcoholic like her father, or a junkie like her mother. But no, she had to get stuck with the great JD Edwards. She was waiting for her breakfast in the quick-order joint near the motel—because now it was late and Almeta Edwards was one starved chick. He hadn't phoned all night; she didn't even know whether he knew there'd been a fire. Life with JD. And she was getting fed. To the gills, fed. And then there he was, sitting down in the booth across from her, not shaved, his eyes streaked, and that tired shot-away look in them. "He said he tried to get me at the motel. Did he phone you about the fire?" Not so much as a good morning, how did you sleep? Uptight as usual. About Matt Haslam. "He called, sure. How did I know where you were? He told me not to come to the track." JD shook his head: "What right's he got telling *you*?" The tray arrived, and the young white boy smiled down. "I guess," she said, "Mr. Haslam thought he'd protect me from the rumpus out there." JD looked at her plate. "I'm the one he shoulda called, and I told him so." She picked up her juice and drank it. "How was he supposed to know where to find you?" But what good was reason with JD? "I was winning a few bucks, sugar." Liar. "What's that you're eating—grits again?" She explained, again: "I grew up in Manhattan, just like you, but I happen to like grits, and down here I found this place that has them. That's how you knew where to find me. A lot of people like grits, black *and* white." So he ordered eggs and ham and home fries, then said, "You know, Meta, I got to the point where that turkey keeps *sirring* me the way he does, I'm gonna deck him." She was eating. "You do, then where'll we be? You can't run a horse without a licensed trainer." He ignored her: "You heard of Chinese water torture? That's what his *yes sir, no sir* is: a drop of water on the forehead, over and over, till a man thinks he'll go bananas." She drank her coffee and looked out the plate-glass window at the street. "And he's always bad-mouthing our horse. Thinks he's lazy. All niggers're lazy, everybody knows that." He was getting on her nerves again. "JD, get with it. You told me yourself the horse is a glutton. Well, I read Man o' War bolted down twelve quarts of oats a day, plus carrots, all the hay he could get, and all the sugar he could beg. He won a few." JD scowled across at her. "Now you sound just like that mother Haslam. You ask him about running a gelding, and he throws Forego at you, earned almost two million dollars. Or Kelso, biggest money-making champ of all time. You ask him why Also Ran's coat don't shine like all the others, and he sticks more statistics up your ass: Kelso's hide was always dull, and he won thirty-nine outta sixty-some starts, five times Horse of the Year. But you ask him if Also Ran has a chance, and all he says is he finished in the money three out of seven and every horse always has a *chance.*" To change the subject Almeta said: "We've been invited to the Governor's Breakfast on Sunday morning after the Derby." He leaned across the table and asked, "What about the Jordan dinner? Friday night. Out Lexington way. That's the biggest blowout of the week, cream of the cream, sugar, blue blood only, no dinges except in the kitchen, they might order watermelon." His food came and he started to eat. Her voice was light and under control: "I wouldn't know which fork to use anyway. And *I* don't give a damn." But it was not enough for JD. Nothing was ever enough for JD. "I think I'm gonna unload that trainer of ours." Did he mean it? "If you do, sugar, yours truly is going to take a long walk." He stared at her. And he grinned. "Not a chance, baby—we make the magic, you and me." But while she knew he was now speaking the truth and sincerely—they did make the magic and she needed it, and him— still, she meant it. She had had it. If he fired Matt Haslam, there was no way to win. In more ways than one.

Good morning, ladies (if there are any left out there) and gentlemen (ditto). This is your obedient servant, Count Wyatt, reporting at his usual time. As most of you who have heard the morning newscasts know by now, that single most feared disaster around any stable area, fire, broke out in the Derby barn during the night. It was brought under control with dispatch by those intrepid guardians of the safety of horses and man, and damage, I am relieved to assure you, was limited to two stalls and to the single barn. Fire damage, that is. Unfortunately, I am unhappy to inform you, there was a human injury, but not, I hasten to add, a human tragedy. Amidst the resultant turbulence and prevailing hysteria, with much smoke from the straw and horses loose and people running in all directions, a young exercise girl from Ireland suffered multiple injuries. Her name is, melodiously, Molly Muldoon, and in an attempt to get the colt Irish Thrall out of the melee, she was trampled by the panicked horse, the Derby entry of her own stable, Innisfree Demesne, owned by Mrs. Brigid Tyrone. Our collective hearts go out to the stricken child who, I hope, is watching this telecast from her hospital bed. Quick and painless recovery, little one!

Less fortunate was that great and intrepid colt, Ancient Mariner, who in terror injured himself beyond repair in his stall and has had to be destroyed. He was a great one, Ancient Mariner, near winner of the Wood Memorial, with a tremendous record behind him and a spirit to give even strong men pause for admiration. While it is not public knowledge, this powerful offspring of Lady Jane and Count Victor has probably overcome more vicissitudes than any thoroughbred but the beloved Bold Ruler. Alas, he is no more. And every person in racing can have nothing but the deepest sympathy for his owner, that great lady of racing, Mrs. Rachel Stoddard of Brookfield Stables. The Derby has lost a strong challenger, but Rachel Stoddard, whom I count among my personal friends, has many other fine thoroughbreds, including the lovely Miss Mariah, the charming filly who is to run at about six to one in the Kentucky Oaks on Friday, the day after tomorrow. Rachel Stoddard has suffered many losses in her long, full life, and no one who knows her can doubt that she will accept this one with the same fine dauntlessness that made her Ancient Mariner the magnificent colt that he was.

While the investigation is continuing, it can be safely reported now to those skeptics who see evil in all things that there is no evidence of arson or criminal intent. Local fire investigators and members of the Thoroughbred Racing Protective Bureau are on the job now, and they will soon be joined at the invitation and insistence of the Racing Commission and the track stewards by investigators from the state fire marshal's office and by representatives of the insurance companies involved. Oh, yes, Ancient Mariner was insured by that most prestigious of insurance companies, Lloyds of London, Limited, so if any suspicion persists, we the race-going public may rely on the skill and integrity of all these gentlemen to be fully informed. Preliminary indications are that the cause of the small conflagration was accidental—probably some careless fool who failed to extinguish his cigarette properly. And since all stables everywhere are by nature tinderboxes, we can all be thankful that more damage did not result. The other Derby entries have been moved to another barn and are all safely in their stalls. But that is not to say that psychological damage has not occurred. Far be it for this mortal to predict the emotions of a horse, but it can be safely conjectured that an experience such as this is destructively traumatic to some. There is nothing more disturbing to an excitable finebred creature such as a thoroughbred than fire. Nothing. They all have more than three full days to recover, but keep in mind that thoroughbreds, like humans, do not perform at their top capacity when perturbed. But all of this makes horse racing, and accidents do happen, even in the most aristocratic of families.

What was, in the humble opinion of your obedient servant, not an accident was the fantastic fiasco at the Derby Trial yesterday. Reported far and wide for the sensational race that it turned out to be, the Derby Trial would not have degenerated into the gruesome and grotesque spectacle that it was if it had not been for one horse, Dealer's Choice. We are told that he broke down; that he shattered a canon bone. Mind you, he did this on a muddy track, mirabile dictu! *He did more. Through his death and the much more important death of one jockey, the serious injury of another, the destruction of one other horse, and the maiming of another, Dealer's Choice exposed a canker, a growing rot on the hull of what once was a sturdy and honorable ship. Dealer's Choice should not have been allowed to run. His owners had their reasons, and at least on the air we can only conjecture that they were greedy and nefarious reasons. Why did the stewards allow it? Why did the track veterinarians sanction his entry? Why does the Racing Commission, not only here but in every other state, permit horses that have obviously gone wrong to go to the gate? These are the questions that should concern and disquiet all who harbor any lingering respect for our once-proud sport.*

If the gods refused to smile earlier, they are surely scowling down on us now as Derby Week moves inexorably closer to its climax, Derby Day itself. By nature superstitious, horseplayers and horselovers of the world, unite. Summon up your voodoo sorcery. Let the evil spirits hear your voodoo incantations, exorcise the dark diabolical spell of ill fortune that threatens to overwhelm our innocent frivolity—no more catastrophe, please, whoever you are up there, cease and desist, enough, enough!

With Vincent Van and True Blue and now Ancient Mariner out of the running, the Derby field has grown shorter, and the odds are changing fast. The morning line—which to newcomers among us means the odds designated by the track's official handicapper—the morning line shows Starbright the undisputed favorite now, and there's little doubt now that he will go to the gate Saturday an odds-on favorite. Meaning, my children, that for every dollar you slide across the pari-mutuel window, you will, if you win, win less than even money.

While the untimely demise of Ancient Mariner will deprive us of the sidelight pleasure of seeing three horses owned by widows competing on Saturday, the sensational win of that unpredictable little black named Hotspur in yesterday's Derby Trial will guarantee us the privilege of witnessing the friendly sibling rivalry between two trainers whose horses are running against each other. As everyone has seen in the newsreels by now, Clay Chalmers's Hotspur, after an incredible steeplechase jump, came from behind to win in the mud. Consequently his odds have shot from fifteen-to-one to nine-to-one today. Fireaway, trained by Clay Chalmers's brother, Owen Chalmers, remains unchanged at seven to one. These are the so-called human-interest aspects that it is your obedient servant's very pleasant task to report.

In line with which, hear this. In last night's pandemonium in the stable area of the Downs a thing of some value was lost. The owner, who wishes to remain nameless, contacted me at this station and begged me to make this announcement. The object—the exact nature of which he did not describe except to say that it is really not negotiable—is nevertheless highly prized by its owner for sentimental reasons. So highly and emotionally prized, for instance, that he has authorized this reporter to offer a substantial reward for its return—a reward in six figures, in fact, and no questions asked. Anyone, then, who has found anything that might appear to have sentimental value to a rich gentleman and who would like to become rich overnight himself is requested to telephone this number . . . let's see now, where did I put it? . . . This number: 222-1918. To make arrangements for its return directly with the party involved. Now there you are: Again Count Wyatt has done his civic duty. But I do wish people would be less careless, don't you? The number again is 222-1918. And no questions asked. So much for such trivia, but please, no jokesters need apply—bear in mind, one and all, that what might seem trivial to outsiders may be vital to the owner.

And now for that other omnipresent character who haunts all horse races: the weather. Rain off and on all day today and a forty percent chance of precipitation continuing into the night. The long-range prediction holds some slight hope—possible clearing tomorrow. And what of three days hence? Only the gods know, so remember, prayers and incantations and a human offering only if absolutely necessary.

Until Thursday, the witching hour before noon, when post positions will be announced hereon, this is Wyatt Slingerland, the high priest himself. Benedictions and invocations.

Andrew turned off the television set. "So that's the way he thinks he can do it."

Now Blake Raynolds realized why Clay Chalmers, an hour ago—when Blake had given him the money—had suggested that he and Andrew watch Count Wyatt's telecast today. Blake had also, to the young man's astonishment, handed him a revolver. "You might need it," Blake had suggested. "You don't know what you're getting into."

"Chalmers," Blake said, "admitted it was a long shot. He also inquired, if I recall, whether anyone had any short ones in view." Should he mention the gun to Andrew? It had been his own idea. Why burden the man further?

"Marylou Wohlforth," Andrew said, as if struggling to place it in his mind. "It's not a common name."

"No reason you should have heard it," Blake reminded him. It was the name engraved at the top of the sheet of blue stationery that Clay Chalmers had given Blake earlier and that Blake had shown

Andrew shortly before the telecast. The script face of the typing on the stationery and that on the ransom note seemed, to their un-skilled eyes, to match. "Young Chalmers—possibly because he's trying to protect somebody—refused to say where he obtained the stationery." Did Andrew still suspect Chalmers? "He seems deter-mined to play a lone hand." And the legal question now was whether by cooperating in various ways Blake and Andrew were not breaking the law themselves—or bending it damned hard anyway. That note was evidence and to suppress evidence—

"Blake," Andrew said without turning, "I owe you an explanation for my feelings toward Clay Chalmers, I think."

"It might help me to function a bit more efficiently, Andrew." His foot was not paining him this morning, and he had not yet had his first bourbon of the day, but it would appear there was a vigil in front of both of them now, and as when waiting for juries to return, it was not an interval that Blake relished. "If it would help me un-derstand why even now you seem to suspect Chalmers of playing some sort of game here, I should know. On the other hand, if it's purely personal—" He allowed the suggestion to hang in the air. He couldn't rid himself of the idea that Andrew's cool hostility had to do somehow with Kimberley and her feelings toward Chalmers, whatever the devil they actually were, and if so, Blake wanted no part of that tangled web, even knowledge of it.

"Clay Chalmers was responsible for the injury and destruction of the finest foundation sire it was ever my good fortune to own." And now Andrew did turn. "Sire of forty-nine stakes winners and two Derby winners. The grandsire, in fact, of Starbright."

So that was it. Or was it? Blake Raynolds mistrusted un-complicated motives; to do so had become second nature to him. "When he was working for you at Blue Ridge, I assume. Last night you accused him of being drunk at the time."

"That's no excuse. Around thoroughbreds there is no such thing as negligence. Except criminal negligence."

"You discharged him, I take it, and if he was telling the truth last night, had him blackballed. Well, acting in anger, and revenge being the motive it is—" Blake shrugged.

"I did worse, Blake. I'm not proud of any of it. I should have had his license suspended and stopped at that. But I was so outraged, I resorted to violence."

Violence? Andrew Cameron? Now Blake *was* astonished. "Only shows you're human, Andrew." Odd, come to think of it, no one ever addressed him as Andy.

With a wry smile Andrew sat down on the sofa across the cocktail table from Blake. "Did you imagine I wasn't, Blake?"

"There have been times, there have been times—" Truth too: He still couldn't imagine Andrew Cameron fighting physically. And then he recalled that he had been some sort of intercollegiate boxing champion; Blake had seen the bronze trophy in the study at Blue Ridge. But Chalmers looked fit enough, although he was not a large young man.

"Worst thing about it," Andrew said, frowning into space, "was that he didn't fight back."

"Well, if he was drunk—"

"I always took his refusal to defend himself as a tacit admission of guilt."

Was Andrew right? Or was that simply what he had in time come to think? *No matter what you've convinced yourself of over the years, you know damn well you did it, Cameron, and we both know why.* Had Andrew done it himself? And if so, did he know why? Damned if Blake did. Why would a man destroy a horse he valued that highly? Well, it was not today's problem, which concerned another horse entirely, but in the silence Blake's mind, accustomed to reading motives behind motives, wondered whether Andrew were intent on keeping Kimberley away from Chalmers because he didn't think the young man suitable, or for some other conceivable reason— which possibly Andrew did not wish to acknowledge. Kimberley, he recalled, had shouted, *Shut up, stop it, both of you!* as though she were being crushed between the two of them. Knowing how Kimberley would react to the horse's death and his own grief and anger, was it possible that Andrew might actually have used that devious method to—

"You'll have to forgive my . . . hesitations, Blake." Andrew did not actually say *suspicions.* "Chalmers's horse is not stalled in the Derby barn, you know."

Blake made up his mind. It might relieve his friend; on the other hand, it might antagonize him. Nevertheless he said, "It's my impression that Chalmers, for reasons of his own, is not telling us all the facts." He saw Andrew frown, waiting. "But he may have legitimate reasons. Or he may not really be absolutely certain who *is* behind it. Regardless, I think he's operating on the level."

A time passed. Andrew sat in silence. Then he stood up. He was beginning to look tired. "I think he's on the level too," he said at last—almost as if he were making a reluctant admission. "His own horse was attacked by a dog at the track this morning."

Before Blake could absorb this completely, the door buzzer sounded and Andrew went into the foyer to open it. His stride was not quite so vigorous as it had been a few hours ago.

"Come in, Daughter," Andrew said. "Did you get any sleep? Did the pills do their job?"

Kimberley kissed her father on the cheek and came into the sitting room. She was wearing a pantsuit, and her hair was tight against her head and glistening. Regardless of which she looked like a small chastened child, and grave. "They did their job," she said. "Thank you, Andrew." And then: "Good morning, Mr. Raynolds."

Well, well, you could never predict this one. Blake was relieved. "Did you hear Mr. Slingerland, my dear?"

She nodded. "You told me to listen."

Andrew asked, "Have you had breakfast? Shall I ring room service?"

"I'm not hungry," she said. "Here." She held out a white envelope. While Andrew opened it and examined its contents she said, "It was delivered to *my* room this time." And then: "I'm sorry I came to Mrs. Tyrone's room, Andrew." He was examining two photographs. "I don't know why I do those things. Shall I phone her and apologize? I could have some flowers sent."

Andrew stepped to Blake and handed him the photographs and envelope. "That won't be necessary, Kimberley. My guess is that Mrs. Tyrone is at the hospital with the girl." To Blake: "True to his promise, whoever the clever bastard is."

One picture was of Starbright full length and the other a closeup of his head, as before, but this time the paper being held there by an invisible hand was a copy of the *Daily Racing Form* with the date encircled. Today's edition. Proving the horse was still alive this many hours after the first photographs had been taken. The risk, of course, was that whoever had taken those pictures had also heard the telecast. What then? It was, Blake acknowledged grimly, a damn long shot indeed. Personally he had little hope that Clay Chalmers's scheme would work. But transparent and farfetched as that scheme was, it was better than doing nothing and being totally at the mercy of someone who could injure or kill the horse at will.

"I'm not myself sometimes," Kimberley said, her green-blue eyes on her father. It sounded as if she were still trying to make amends for something. "I'm someone else altogether. Someone I hate."

"So I have observed," Andrew said, and Blake decided to make his own apologies and escape as soon as possible.

But Kimberley drifted toward the foyer. "Clay will call me, I think," she said in the same subdued voice. "I'll be in my room." She turned. "Thank you, Andrew, for taking care of me."

No way, man, no way you'll get Frankie Voight to fall for that one.

Six figures. That's bread!

Yeah, but what if it was a trick? What if the fuzz or the fucking TRPB or the Pinks or all of them working in cahoots—what if they'd made a deal with that faggoty old Count Wyatt to trap him, arrest him, take the colt—

A dude could get maybe twenty years for stealing a horse like that one out there in that beat-up old barn, sleeping off the dope, whatever it was they hit him with. *Sentimental value*—bullshit. Not that he'd stole it himself. Them others, whoever the shit they was, they'd pulled it off, clean as ice. They'd done the job, not Frankie. Only there was what they call being an accessory. All his job was was to feed it and take care of it for a few days. Cooling his ass out here in this crummy little farmhouse in Indiana, across the river from the scene. Watching TV and only hoping to get paid for it. Hell, that Chalmers shithead and his boy Eric—they hadn't even settled up for the Vincent Van job yet. And the chances he took on that one, kee-rist.

And if the cops ever tied the two jobs together, they'd throw the goddamn book at him. Life maybe. All the rest of his life in the slammer.

Only . . . if they was so anxious to get the nag back in time for the Derby, what a chance, what a chance to get rich and pay off his score against all of them, both at the same time. Beautiful.

He looked out the window at the big ramshackle barn out back. You can bet your ass they paid the farmer a bundle to make himself scarce the rest of the week. Probably paid him more than they even promised Frankie Voight, that broken down old jock they wouldn't even let show his face at a track, any track.

Six figures. That's a hundred grand, *minimum*. Rock bottom. No questions asked. Never get another chance like this. Where would the likes of a has-been like him get a crack at bread like that? Sure as hell not sitting here in this smelly old kitchen staring at the black-and-white TV—like looking at a snowstorm—and risking his balls for chickenshit.

He stood up. It had stopped raining, but there was dripping and gurgles everywhere, and even the goddamn roof leaked. But . . . no way, you cocksuckers, Frankie Voight's got your number, you're not setting *him* up.

He couldn't find a pencil, but he had the number in his mind. Like clocking a horse—Frankie Voight always had a mind for numbers.

One hundred big ones. A tenth of a million. That's right: one tenth of one million.

And if he didn't make his move—hell, he was forty-five years old and coming into the stretch—if he didn't make his move when he had the chance . . . it was the only one he'd ever get.

But jeez, a double cross like this, he'd have to make himself scarce in these parts, and fast. Like the minute he had his mitts on the bread, the *second* he had it, into the Land-Rover, to hell with the van hidden in the shed, then velvet, velvet all the way! Sure as it rains in Indianapolis, like the song said, he'd never be able to show at any track in the country, ever again. He'd have to bury

himself, out West somewhere, or in some big city, just get lost. But
. . . he'd have the dough to do it.

That Owen Chalmers, out here again a few hours ago, taking
more pictures—he was tough, you could see it in that frame, them
leather paws, them flat blue eyes—no telling what a tough-hide
prick like that'd do if you crossed him.

All he had to do to make his move'd be to go out there into that
ratty hallway and pick up the phone. Two, two, two, one, nine,
one, eight—had it in his mind. Who'd answer? That Count Wyatt
himself, that fruity voice—

If all Chalmers and those other fuckers wanted to do was shut the
favorite out of the Derby, why'd they need him anyway? Could
have killed the nag—one bullet, shot of juice, even a sledge
hammer—and buried it in a pit, bag of lime, fill it in—

He was sick to his stomach.

He could protect himself. He had the hunting rifle he'd come
across in the bedroom. And the bullets. Even one of those fancy
telescopic sights.

All he had to do was pick up the phone—

Then what?

He knew how to tell them to get here—

Then the phone rang.

Let it ring.

If he answered it and it was for the farmer—

It kept on ringing.

Howard Blassingame, that was the farmer's name. What could he
say, he was the butler and Mr. Blassingame wasn't at home?

It did not stop ringing.

It could be Eric. Or his boss.

Maybe he should pick it up.

Not if he was going to make his own call.

It stopped ringing.

Fifty-five thousand dollars is a lot of money.

Christine knew that she was by all ordinary standards a rich woman, and she was aware too that once Stuart's estate was settled and his insurance was paid—oh, how she shuddered to think of all that still ahead of her—she would be very wealthy by almost any standards. Still, she could not get accustomed to thinking that fifty-five thousand dollars was not a lot of money.

She was driving the big Lincoln, the money on the seat beside her in the leatherlike envelope that the bank had provided. They had been very understanding and considerate really, those people at the bank. And the procedure had been so much simpler than she had anticipated: not a single dignified or guarded question as to her need for it or her reasons for wanting it in cash. A single long-distance telephone call to her own bank, discreetly handled in another office entirely, a few papers to sign, no hint of any necessity of opening an account here in Louisville. They had probably assumed that she was going to wager the money on the races. If only all of life could be so easy and uncomplicated.

She loved this country road. It had been drizzling earlier, and the hood of the car and the pavement and the trunks and leaves of the many, many trees, were all damp. She didn't mind the rain, although Fireaway didn't like it, and Owen dreaded it. In New Mexico, where it had rained so seldom, she had come to look forward to it. Everything here seemed so lush and living. She had missed Kentucky over the years—possibly without even being aware of it.

Imagine Clayton Chalmers threatening to put his own brother into prison—and her along with him! What could he have meant by that? And all that business with Marylou's little typewriter—

She turned into the crescent driveway under the dripping trees and was surprised to see the white Corvette that Owen had rented for the week. It *would* be a Corvette, and white: How Owen loved the small luxuries.

She had taken her time because she thought he would be at the track.

The door of the house opened before she could step out of the Lincoln. Owen came down the steps between the pillars.

"Did you get it?"

"Yes, darling, of course. Owen, you look so—"

"Never mind that. Where is it?"

She turned and reached across the seat and picked up the packet with the bank's name printed on it in gold letters. Naturally Owen looked the way he did. The unimaginable things those dreadful people had threatened to do to him—

He took the leatherlike envelope from her hand.

How could she expect him to be his usual confident, swaggering self in the circumstances? Small wonder the poor man wanted to get the whole nasty thing over with. Such people—

"Owen," she said then, "you be careful now. Hear me?"

He only nodded and turned to the Corvette. "I'm handling it," he reassured her curtly and opened the door. "I don't know when I'll be back." His tall frame stooped to get into the bucket seat.

"Owen, I do wish you didn't look so—" Then a terrible thought thrust itself into her mind. "They won't do anything—they wouldn't have any reason to do anything to you once you paid them, would they?"

He was in the seat, slamming the door. "That's not what's bugging me. Would you believe it, Chrissie? That goddamn brother of mine's killed Eric's Doberman."

No. No, she couldn't believe it. "But why?"

Shaking his copper-colored head, he said, "Don't ask me, don't ask me. Maybe to get back at *me* for something." He revved the motor.

"For what? Why?"

"Just the way the bastard's always been." The car shot forward with a hollow roar. "Bats in the bell tower! Teched in the head, our old man used to say!" Then he thundered off under the trees.

She went into the house. No wonder Owen was not his 'usual self, high-spirited and exuberant—the Owen she had come to love. How he had turned heads yesterday at the Downs—feminine heads. A wave of possessiveness passed over her, warmly.

She decided to have a drink. Just one. Why not? The day stretched ahead, and empty. Nothing to do until Owen came back. Oh, she might go downtown again and shop; she'd seen some really charming shops, and the atmosphere of a city, being *in* a city again, intrigued her. She poured the gin over ice, touched it with a whiff of vermouth. She might look up some of her old friends. Who? She took off her hat and sailed it across the sitting room. No one wore hats downtown these days, she'd noticed. The gin tasted very dry, very delicious. Possibly she could give Rachel Stoddard a ring, possibly invite her to tea—did ladies still go to tea these days? Rachel Stoddard would probably be gloomy after losing her horse that way—and reasonably so. Still, she might as well stay here and relax now. She had half-expected Andrew Cameron to give her a ring, just for old time's sake, although she'd never known him well, only as a dancing partner. Oh, well, Owen would do. Owen would do quite nicely. In his own way—and not only in bed—Owen had brought her back to life. But, she had to admit, in bed particularly—in ways she'd never dreamed of in her wildest fantasies.

She was going up the stairway slowly. She'd change into something that Owen would like. She had all the time, all the time in the world. She passed the door of the room Owen had appropriated for his office. The door was open, as usual. And what a shambles. In the chaos on the floor was the hand-size calculator, or was it a computer, that he used to work out his odds. She heard herself laugh briefly, the deep guttural sound that people had commented on. Who? She couldn't recall now. She was about to close the door on the incredible clutter when she hesitated.

Where was Marylou's little blue typewriter?

The phone jangled again. He answered as he did each time, with caution and with a spasm of hope, his gaze shifting from the woman to one of the cubist paintings on the wall: "Two-two-two, one-nine-one-eight." And listened. Then he muttered: "If you really do have a shoe Secretariat wore when he won the Derby, I trust you know what you can do with it."

Janice Wessell, seated with her legs crossed in one of the ultra-modern chairs in the high-ceilinged studio room, blew smoke and laughed. "Offer a reward and give the crazies a phone number, and the weirdos are bound to keep coming out of the woodwork."

How much did she know? How much had she guessed? Certainly that the lost object with sentimental value was a thoroughbred horse. And, suspicious since his visit early this morning, she'd recognized the telephone number when Wyatt gave it on the air. The little bitch had let herself in with a key, saying, "Oh, hello there. I'm living here now. Didn't the Count tell you?" She had made herself at home, and what could he do about it short of picking her up bodily and throwing her out the door? She hadn't removed the leather bag strung over her shoulder, and he knew the tiny recorder was spinning away in there.

The shock was gone now—that rage and incredulity that he'd been afraid might overwhelm him and leave him helpless. No doubt left now: Owen was behind it all—Vincent Van, the fire, that poor girl in the hospital, and Bernie, Bernie with his face twisting in pain in spite of the medicines, and Ancient Mariner dead and Starbright God knows where. He was still fighting down the sickening disgust and dismay and fury that he knew could lick him if he didn't watch it now. So far he'd been able to play it cool with the little bitch, but he didn't know what he'd do when the legit call came through. If, not when, *if*—

The phone rang again. A string of uncultured pearls. He slammed down the phone.

"Well," Janice Wessell asked, "what did that one have to barter for six figures? Hitler's old truss?" He didn't answer. "Nixon's secondhand lie detector kit?"

Nixon. He recalled what the lawyer Blake Raynolds had said when he handed over the briefcase filled with cash: "If this outlandish plot pays off, which I personally doubt, once you've turned this money over to whomever, you and my client Andrew Cameron will both have become co-conspirators. Aiding and abetting in the commission of a felony. You should be aware of the risk." He had felt guilty and dirty then, and he felt guilty and dirty now, thinking of a line from Shakespeare: *But if the cause be not good . . .* Agincourt, the night before the battle.

"Maybe you're a monk, Mr. Chalmers," the girl said, stubbing out her third or fourth cigarette. "Sworn to a vow of silence. The Trappists have a monastery around here somewhere. Maybe you climbed over the wall."

"I can't make up my mind," Blake Raynolds had said, "whether you're doing this for Kimberley or whether you're trying to prove to her father that you're not guilty." And when Clay had only stared at him, briefcase in hand, ready to go: "Or perhaps both. If that girl ever came to believe you'd done anything to her horse, Andrew would win, wouldn't he?"

The phone was not ringing. Maybe he'd struck out. Or maybe Owen had got wise and reached the horse—

The woman stood up and stretched her arms above her head, feigning a yawn. "What about the vow of chastity, Mr. Chalmers? Have you taken that too?"

He didn't answer. He stood up. When she lowered her arms, he took several quick steps and reached to pull down the strap of the shoulder bag, and with it dangling from his hand he moved into the bedroom and to the bathroom. By then he had opened it and removed the tape recorder disguised in the cigarette case. He heard her behind him: "Give me that, you motherfucker, that's private—" But he hurled the bag at her, stopping her in the doorway, and then he dropped the cigarette package into the toilet bowl.

Then he faced her and spoke for the first time: "It won't take more than a few days to dry out, and it can be repaired." She turned away, her face twisting as he returned through the bedroom to his chair by the telephone.

Promptly it rang again, and he picked it up, giving the number and watching Janice Wessell as she came into the room, her face frozen now, the recording device in her hand. He listened and then said politely: "I'm sorry, mister, I've heard those words all my life, but there's a young woman here who might like to borrow a few." He held out the phone. "It's for you, Miss Wessell."

She hurled the wet recorder at him, hard, and it skimmed off his shoulder and crashed against the wall behind. He spoke into the telephone: "The young lady is otherwise disposed." And he hung up.

Janice Wessell was struggling for control now and breathing hard. "Listen, you sonofabitch—if you think, you and Wyatt and all of you, that you're going to get away with a cover-up like this, I'm going to teach you otherwise. If I were a man, I'd break your nose again!"

Owen again—if he got to the horse before Clay even learned where it was, it would all be over. And damned if he had any other cards up his sleeve. The hate and fury focused on the woman now.

"If you were a man, I'd have broken more than your goddamn nose long before this. To put it where it belongs."

"Where it belongs is getting at the truth. The public has a right to know what's going on." She moved toward him, coldly furious, her voice a rasping sound: "The Derby horses have been moved to another barn, yours included."

"I ordered that. Yes."

"And there's not an empty stall. Security's so tight even the press isn't allowed near."

He was relieved to learn it: Security was the reason he had had Elijah move Hotspur to the official Derby barn.

"I know, Chalmers, that there's a conspiracy of some sort, and I'm not so stupid that I can't guess that what's been quote lost end quote is a horse. Sentimental value, bullshit. So whether you and Wyatt and the rest keep stonewalling or not, I'm going to get to the rock bottom and blow the whistle. Loud and clear." She was very close now, and her face was chiseled rock. "So if you give me the straight shit, I might play along till you get the horse back. If you don't, I'll get the whole scene from Wyatt, and I have my ways. Like giving the old man what he has to have and, if not, a fat knee in his jewels."

Clay considered. He recalled her appearing from the bedroom last night, wearing only Wyatt's shirt. She sure as hell had her ways. But what he had to play for was time: If she broke the story after Starbright was back in Jason Arnold's care—

The phone again. This time he snarled into it as she straightened, fumbling for another cigarette, listening.

After he gave the number the voice, which was a man's and very cautious, asked, "I got him, mister. Who are you?"

"Describe him."

The voice hesitated and then described Starbright: color, size, stockings, the star on the forehead.

"Tattoo number?" Clay asked, certain now, the blood up and rushing, his hand gripping the phone.

"Yeah, yeah," the voice said, not quite shaking. "I got it wrote down." And then he gave it slowly, number by number.

Owen had not heard the broadcast, or had not become suspicious, or had not had time to—

"Directions," Clay demanded.

"Indiana. Cross the Something Minton Bridge. New Albany. You got that?"

"I got it," Clay said. "Interstate toward Lexington—"

"Not Lexington, you fucker—*New Albany*, Indiana."

"Then what?"

"Out River Road, two or three miles south—"

"The old Frankfort Road, that the one they call Shady Lane sometimes?"

"You drunk? Who is this?"

"Go on, go on—"

"Listen, mister, you go toward Lexington, you'll never see—"

"Is there a name?"

"Mailboxes on your left, one of them has *Blassingame* on it, only River Road, not Shady—"

"How far?"

"About three miles outta New Albany, Blassingame, you turn right, second driveway on your left, one to two miles off the River Road—long, gravel, all the way to the barn at the end—"

"I got it all," Clay said, avoiding the girl's narrowed eyes. "Two and one half miles down the old Frankfort Road. Name Blassingame on mailbox."

"I got the wrong number. This is some kinda trick—"

"No trick," Clay assured him. "Take me half an hour, and I got the money. You listen now: one hundred thousand dollars, so you get in that barn and wait for me."

He replaced the phone and stood. He turned to Janice Wessell.

"Now, miss, it's your turn to listen." He took the gun out of his pocket, and she stared at it, her mouth tight but her eyes opening wider now. "If you try to follow me, I'll lose you. If I can't, I'll shoot out your tires. And if you get there before me—which you won't—you may get your head blown away. You got that? We're not playing games, any of us, so don't you get hurt trying to protect the precious public's right to know."

Raining again. And the odds on Hotspur already getting shorter. Hotspur. Clay. Always Clay.

What he had to do, especially now that the white Corvette was up on the superhighway, was to watch his goddamn speed. Now he wished he'd rented a less conspicuous buggy—cops get their kicks pinching Corvettes. He knew. He knew cops and the cop mentality.

Eric had let him down. By rights the rain shouldn't matter 'cause Hotspur shouldn't still be in the running. Was everybody going to start letting him down? He didn't think baby brother had it in him—to strangle a Doberman with his bare hands. Wasn't like Clay at all.

But he'd misread Clay in several ways. Who'd have thought he'd march in the house—that goddamn house, why did it have to be so far out and on the opposite side of the city from Indiana?—who'd have thought Clay would get suspicious like that and walk in and use the typewriter and steal Owen's copy of the syndication contract? Well, *up* Clay, it didn't prove nothing. And he'd soon be rid of the typewriter, which was in its case and on the seat next to him. What'd the contract prove? So there was a deal on to sell the bang-tail if he won. That's all it said. Didn't tie him to anything. He wanted to win, yeah, what trainer didn't, what owner?

He sailed past a phone booth. Should he phone out there to the farmhouse again? He'd tried to get through two or three times after he'd heard that fucking broadcast and while he was waiting for Christine to get back from the bank with the mazuma. The cunt sure took her time. Frankie hadn't answered; he could have been out to the barn, or he could've decided it wasn't safe. That dumb jock's not answering didn't bother him so much, but then when he had pulled off to use that phone in the filling station before coming up here on the interstate, he'd got a busy signal. Like maybe Frankie boy, the bastard, was phoning somebody himself maybe, and if so, he could guess what number, and why. He edged the Corvette along five miles faster. In this deep, you got to take chances. But if they stopped him to hand him a speeding ticket, that meant time, time wasted—

He'd doped it all out great. He'd thought it through. No matter how the race went, win or lose, he'd figured on having the horse for ransom, back-up, insurance, you might say. If Frankie didn't try a double cross, if he got to him and talked reason and upped the ante and maybe roughed him up some to make sure he knew it was business, it'd stop Clay in his tracks. Hell, it'd be worth the whole fifty-five thousand in the leather packet in his hip pocket. Miss B. and her friends, they'd just have to wait till he got his share of the purse on Monday. That's when the drug tests would come back final and the purse would be paid. Only . . . his share would only cover what he already owed Miss B. for setting up the Vincent Van job from inside. And what about the hundred and fifty grand more that he now owed her for last night's job at the track—getting Starbright out and stashing him? Deep. That's what he was in. Plenty deep. *We don't care what you do with the horse, Mr. C., that's your business. But we do not gamble. We get paid.* Cold-hearted little cunt, that Miss Bette. Looked like a sweet innocent college girl, but she ran a big organization, or was part of a still bigger one. She did the talking anyway: *If you don't pay on time, you pay interest. Ten percent per day and compounded every day. If you don't pay both when we call it, my friends here will take pleasure in shooting off your kneecaps at very close range and then cutting off your balls and shoving them down your throat. I mean that literally, Mr. C. And if you try to run and hide, we shall find you. If you go to prison, that only makes our job easier. We have a great many friends in prisons.*

Remembering, Owen had begun to shake as he drove. The fifty-five grand and the hundred and fifty grand for last night's job—that came to two hundred thousand plus, with interest compounded daily till Monday . . . His heart was not even beating now. His share of the sale would cover that. But what if Fireaway let him down? Still, he'd figured he'd be covered by the ransom he knew they'd pay for Starbright on Sunday. And Cameron himself was playing it like Owen knew he would: no police. But Clay, Clay, how the hell did Clay figure in this? What kind of game was *he* playing? And why? Owen knew: to get at him, to plow him under, that's all Clay gave a shit about.

He couldn't afford the time, but he pulled off the highway at the next exit and found a booth almost at once. The phone was out of order. He drove into a service station and from an open shell tried the farmhouse number again. He let it ring seven times.

He was not going to pay Frankie the money. He was not going to offer it. He was going to kill him.

Because this was his one big chance, his chance of a lifetime. He'd never get another like it. He'd come this far, he'd do anything, anything—

What if the horse was gone and Frankie too?

He'd kill Clay.

Your own brother?

Yes.

He was up on the highway again. He could see the river and the outline of a steel bridge.

He'd never killed anyone before.

What about Rosser?

Was it his fault the prick had a bum heart? He'd kill anyone who got in his way now.

He was on the bridge and halfway across when he remembered the typewriter. Glancing into the rearview mirror, he eased the Corvette against the curb, picked up the case by its handle, looked up and down both ways, hesitated to allow a huge truck to thunder past, then dropped the typewriter into the water and was back into the seat before anyone could possibly have seen him. Fuck you, baby brother.

He was driving again before he realized that it was no longer raining. He flipped off the wipers and urged the car forward cautiously. A sixteen-wheeler roared by, and then in the mirror he saw the police cruiser. It moved in close behind and followed. He was doing sixty-five. If they stopped him now—

He was tempted to try a run for it. Maybe Cameron *had* reported after all, had brought in the authorities— Was it possible they even had the horse by now? His mind was streaking. Forward. Backward.

Toby'd said it: *They're all against you. No permanent address, you're shit on a stick. So fuck them, fuck them every chance you get.* Toby had learned him to hate the cops. But he was *not* shit on a stick, he was Owen Chalmers, trainer of a Derby horse, he was as much one of *them* as that shithead Andrew Cameron, Clay—

The siren sounded behind him, a low growl, and lights began to flash. It was too late. What if they searched him—fifty-five thousand dollars in cash.

Wasn't he already halfway across the bridge? Wasn't he in Indiana by now?

His body going slack, his breath gone, he slowed down and edged the Corvette toward the curb. The patrol car pulled slowly alongside, then passed and nosed into the curb at an angle, blocking his path.

He waited.

If you go to prison, that only makes our job easier—

River Road. Row of mailboxes on left. Blassingame. Right turn, one to two miles down side road, second dirt driveway on the left. Dirt, hell, it was mud. Two wheel tracks with black-tipped weeds in between. The pickup had the power, and the van hooked on behind was empty. *Osceola Farms, Florida* was painted on its side. All that seemed light years away now.

The savagery was solid inside him, ice, not fire now but contained. And mixed with hate and disgust—but not with reluctance, not now. If he could pull this off, not only would he return the horse she loved to Kimberley but he'd pay off that conniving brother of his. Whom he had, within only hours, come to realize that he hated.

He had driven as fast as the truck would travel safely with the empty horse van. Owen was no fool, whatever else; if he had heard the broadcast, and he probably had, he'd waste no time doping it and moving. Had he come already? Every instinct in Clay was straining, pleading for a face-to-face showdown with Owen, but not now, not until he had the colt safe and sound in his possession. He'd *better* be sound.

It was a long driveway. They had chosen well, whoever chose— probably Owen himself. He could see the outline of a small house in a stand of trees. "I can have the ransom delivered by professionals. Who can be relied on for silence and who will be paid to take the risks," the lawyer had said. Thank you, Mr. Blake Raynolds, but no thanks: *My dismal scene I needs must act alone.* It had been Clay Chalmers's idea, and so far no one knew who else was involved. If he blew it now, it would be his own misfortune. And Kimb's. And possibly Starbright's. The money was in a black attaché case on the seat. "Stubborn fellow," Raynolds had said. And it had been then that he had produced the gun from the bureau drawer in his hotel room: "You don't have any idea what you're getting into. I would recommend against using this in almost any circumstances except possibly to save your own life, and even then self-defense would make a damn flimsy argument." The revolver was heavy in the slit pocket of the Windbreaker that he had changed into after showering. No report yet on the rabies test. He could not think of Bernie now. "Bear in mind, young man, that a horse is a property, however valuable, not a human being." He would indeed try to bear that in mind, counselor.

The small weathered farmhouse—like thousands, millions perhaps, all across the country—did not appear abandoned, only poor, in need of paint and repair. The sort any farmer, needing the money, any amount, would be eager to rent for a week, no questions asked. Wyatt's phrase. Well, if the horse was here, he'd have no need to ask questions.

He slowed down; Should he go to the house? Moving closer, he caught sight of the barn a hundred yards farther on and decided to continue along the mud ruts. The barn was a big one: high and more ramshackle than the house, raw wood, weathercock on its peak, rusty and slanted by the wind. His eyes scanned the upper section of the barn—no windows from which he could be watched—or shot. Still, he was an open target now and knew it. Parked at an angle, facing out, was a battered old Land-Rover, its seats as wet as its hood, and closer to the weed-covered earth ramp leading to the big sliding doors midway along the side of the barn, an unmarked horse van, glistening wet and new-looking. It was, he noted, not attached to the Land-Rover, although, approaching more closely, he saw the Land-Rover's hitch. He stopped the truck.

Now what? Whose move?

A long-range hunting rifle could pick him off from a window of the house behind, from one of the several small beat-up sheds, from the woods beyond.

Would Owen, feeling tricked, be able to kill him?

If he read the setup, Owen had not yet arrived. All the more reason to move, not to sit here like this.

Whoever was guarding the horse, wherever he was, knew he had the money. If the bastard was capable of murder, it would be only a small task to bury the body as if it had never been alive. And no one, not even the little Wessell bitch—who had *not* followed—knew where he was.

Come out, come out, wherever you are, allee-allee-outs-in-free!

He edged the truck forward and then, with care, made a small semicircle so that as the truck turned it formed a right angle to the van. He switched off the motor. Within the corner formed by the two vehicles he was protected from the barn. He stepped out, picking up the attaché case and taking the revolver from his pocket. "Always trust mankind," the lawyer had said, "but don't neglect to cut the cards."

He looked at the barn carefully. He could see the horse inside, beyond the open sliding doors in the space between the two rows of stalls, above which he knew were two lofts. A perfect setup. But not for him. His side view of the animal, which was tethered in some way he couldn't yet see, suggested at first glance that it was Starbright. But if the bastards had used a ringer once, why not again? Peering through the windows of the pickup, he could see three stockings. The conformation was similar. He did not know Kimberley's colt well, but this animal's bearing and general appearance—

Silence. The gurgling and trickling of water in the broken, hanging roof gutters, and in the woods a steady sound of water dripping—as if a misty rain shower were continuing. Otherwise-—silence. A waiting.

But he had no time for waiting. If he was any judge, the colt should not remain in that leaky barn any longer than absolutely necessary—what a hell of a place to store a fine thoroughbred, susceptible to every exposure, every dampness, and only three days before the race. He choked down his anger. No time for that either. If Owen did appear, it would be another ball game altogether—

The revolver felt unfamiliar in his grasp.

If there was someone inside—and he was convinced that there was—the bastard should be in as great a hurry to get this over with as he was. More so, considering what Owen was capable of doing, *would* do to anyone who crossed him—

Why not open the game by making certain the bastard knew he meant business? He took aim and without hesitation fired at the windshield of the Land-Rover. The shot was deafening, but while its echo reverberated in the woods, there was no sound of glass shattering as he had expected.

No reply. Silence again.

He quickly memorized the license tag on the brown aluminum van. Just in case. A New York plate. Signifying nothing.

"I'm here, mister."

As if he didn't know. The voice was high-pitched, harsh, even angry?

"I'm out here," Clay called. Then, standing straighter, he added: "The pot's open. The game's one-hundred-thousand-dollar stud."

"You got it?"

"I always carry that much cash with me."

"Yeah. You're the same nut. You had me goin' on the phone—I didn't think you'd show. I thought you was drunk maybe."

"I am. Didn't my brother tell you?"

Long silence then. Time for the brain to work in there.

Then: "Your brother? Yeah. Now I know who you are."

And Clay knew, as if he needed further proof, who this squeaky-voiced bastard was working for. *Our doubts are traitors, and make us lose the good we oft might win by fearing to attempt.* And fuck you, Bill Shakespeare. If that guy in there was scared enough, or cunning enough—

"Then," Clay shouted, "if you know who I am, you have me at a disadvantage."

"It's gonna stay that way, man. Now, you just come in with the money, nice and slow and easy, and leave the gun out there—" Scared? It was in his tone now, his cocky overconfident tone.

"Listen, *man*," Clay said. "I'm in just as big a hurry as you are, but if you think I'm coming in there without this gun—"

There was another shot. From inside. Clay ducked down and heard the much louder cracking sound as it reverberated in the woods. He moved to look over the wet hood. The horse was trying to rear but was held somehow, neighing in terror and stomping the wooden floor so that straw dust rose in a cloud around his body.

"Just to show you I got one too. A deer rifle, man. And it's got a telescopic sight. And it's aimed right now at the eye of a nag named Starbright. Dig?"

Cold and stiff with rage and hate and that familiar disgust that he'd come to expect, Clay considered. Then he called out: "You kill the horse, *man*, you got nothing to barter with. And no bread. *Dig?*"

It was the other's turn to consider. Clay waited. He glanced along the driveway past the house. No car approaching.

"Keep the gun, you motherfucker. No bullet can get to me where I am. Bring the dough inside, and I'll tell you where to throw it."

If he went inside, he was really an open target and in full view of the scared bastard in the loft, hidden behind, he had no doubt, bales of hay or straw. And, as he said, safe. "I'm coming in, *man*. And I have the money." He moved around the front of the truck and started to run toward the huge opening in the side of the barn. "I'll tell *you* where to put it." He ran up the earth ramp and then plastered himself against the outside wall of the barn, under the eaves, the water from above still dripping. "You hear me in there?"

"Loud and clear, *Mister* Chalmers."

"When I come in there—if you decide to kill me instead of the horse, you ought to know that three people know exactly where I am. If you're willing to commit murder for a hundred grand, this is your chance. But the police are probably on their way here right now. So move and move fast, whatever you're going to do."

Then he waited. That mind in there cranking again, or darting in a thousand directions at once—or considering.

"I don't want to kill nobody. Which don't mean I won't."

Which, translated, Clay took to mean that the whiny-voiced bastard at least preferred not to shoot him unless he had to.

"I'm coming in." He slid his body along the wall several steps, and then he was framed in the wide aperture. "The money's in the case. Can you see it?"

"I can see it." The voice came from above on his right. There was only a suggestion of a quiver in it. "I can see you too, man. I could . . . I could kill the horse and you in two shots, this close. So you do like I say now."

"I will. My brother's due any second."

That got to him. "Here's what, here's what. You throw the case up over the bales, and soon's I count it, I'm off. Dig?"

"You'll get the money once I see the tattoo."

Starbright was standing in wet straw. He was tethered by two ropes running from his halter to the beams over the right loft and by two more ropes attached to a strap around his girth and stretching to the beams above the left loft. He could hardly move. The bastard hiding up there was worse than a double-crossing criminal, he was a goddamn *savage*. And for Owen to place a horse in a barn where light came through between the rotting clapboards and rain could gather in puddles on the floor from leaks in the roof—

For a split second he hoped that Owen *would* come. Now. It was time—

"Look at the fuckin' tattoo. Puts you both in focus, funnyman."

Clay moved to the horse's head, took the halter tenderly in hand, gingerly faced the two eyes, which looked bloodshot and frightened. No mistaking that star on the forehead. Aware that the back of his own head was the target now as he reached to turn back the lip, he was also aware that a horse treated this way might savage a man out of sheer misery or panic. The way the Irish horse had trampled his own gallop girl. He found himself whispering softly, making only soothing, wordless sounds, checking the numbers in the colt's mouth against those in his own head, which he had obtained from Jason Arnold.

It was Starbright. He had been fairly sure before; now he was certain.

He turned to look up. All he saw were wired bales, no sign of a rifle barrel. "All right, come down and get it!" he snarled.

"Not a chance, man, not a chance in hell. You throw it up here so's I can count it."

"And if it's not in the case?"

Why was he calling his bluff? Why did he even want to now? Something perverse in him made him say, "You can count it down here."

"Listen now, listen"—the voice of a shaken, frightened man about to lose—"listen, you do what I say or two shots, you're both dead."

The bastard meant it. Not because he was strong—because he was weak.

Clay did not hesitate. Why come this far and let your own outrage push you into the loser's camp? He hurled the attaché case up and over the bales of hay and heard it clump to the wooden floor beyond.

Now was his chance. The bastard couldn't count money and keep him and the horse covered with the rifle.

And once he had the money in hand, what was to prevent him from shooting them both anyway?

Quickly, working on a hunch, less, an *assumption*, he shoved the gun back into the Windbreaker pocket and took his knife from his pants pocket, snapped it open, and slashed the two ropes to the girth, then ducked to Starbright's head, fast, and cut the two ropes to the halter. He tugged gently on the halter, urging the colt forward, moving with him toward the barn door.

But not fast enough. A bullet slammed into the floor at his feet, and there was another quick explosion and a bullet grazed his left shoulder. Outside Starbright was free and running.

"Hold it, hold it, *hold* it, goddamn you!"

The pain was not intense, but there was blood, and he could feel the effects of the wound down his arm. Trapped—why risk running for it? He saw the colt pull up, bewildered and more frightened than ever, alongside one of the small sheds.

The rage took over then. "The money's all there, isn't it?" he shouted into the vastness of the barn, seeing nothing, seeing nobody.

"I oughta . . . I oughta pick you off just for the hell of it."

And the bastard might.

"What do you want from me?" He heard his own voice now: a plea not for mercy, not for his life, but for *reason*. "You got the dough. I got the horse. Trade's over!"

But was it? Did the bastard, gun in hand for maybe the first time, scared shitless and all of a sudden rich beyond dreams—did the bastard have to have his pound of flesh—as he said, just for the hell of it?

Should he try another trick? What? If he made him believe that Owen was coming along the driveway, or the police—hell, it might be just the thing to cause the finger to tighten on the trigger. "The criminal mind," Blake Raynolds had warned, "is not like yours and mine." He couldn't stand here like this and wait to get killed. "A criminal may be cold-blooded, but his skull's a crater and inside there's bubbling lava ready to erupt."

Clay tried reason again, knowing it was hopeless. The bastard not only wanted blood, he didn't want Clay to see his face. "I'll go out with the colt, and you go out the other side of the goddamn barn and get lost. We both got what we wanted."

Silence. He glanced out the door: Starbright was trying to eat the wet weeds. But he was quiet, thank God, no longer spooked—unless that gun went off again.

The pain, when it came, was like the slash of a hot knife over his collarbone. He could feel the blood soaking through the Windbreaker. Could the bastard see it from up there?

Clay made up his mind. He uttered a small sound of pain and slumped to the floor.

He lay, waiting and helpless, his cheek against the straw-strewn wood, splinters digging into his flesh.

He moaned but did not move.

His eyes were closed. "In my experience," Raynolds had said, "there's absolutely no way to predict what a criminal will do."

He heard a sound then. From above. And then he heard a scurrying and the bastard swearing under his breath. And then a thud against the floor.

Clay opened his eyes.

The attaché case had been thrown down, and now, rifle in one hand, grasped by the stock and pointed toward the roof, a small but heavy-set man was clambering recklessly down the ladder.

Clay moved. Fast. He was on his feet and across the space between them before the other man knew he had stirred.

He caught the smaller man with his uninjured right shoulder, the jolt sending pain in flaming splinters through his body, and then with his right hand he grabbed the rifle by its barrel, pushed it aside, and in the same movement grasped the bastard with his bloodied left arm and caught him in a hammerlock. He was surprisingly heavy for his size, but Clay managed to swing him about with such force, the bastard's feet completely off the floor, that when he released him, the small man sprawled, breathless and muttering.

Then Clay moved close to stand above the grotesque little figure and he took the revolver from his pocket.

The bastard stared in disbelief, in horror.

But he did not move a muscle now.

In that instant all the fury of the day and night broke like an icy wave over Clay. While inside, *fire burn, and cauldron bubble.* To hell with Blake Raynolds's warnings. To hell with law and reason! He took pleasure in the bright eyes flashing fear. He took delight in the little bastard's dread, his own cruel loathing and disgust. The man had tried to kill him. He'd tied a horse like Starbright as if he were carrion in a butcher shop. If he lived, he'd only do more, go on doing more—

Then why not get it over with?

The wrath did not retreat, the hate and disgust did not dissipate, but Clay stood back and aside and lowered the gun. Why?

Because he was not one of them. Not yet, anyway—not quite.

"Get the hell out of here," he said in a harsh, low whisper of revulsion. Then he snarled, shouting: "Hear me? Get away from me!" It was a wild shout.

The ex-jockey—because he could be nothing else—scrambled to his feet in the loose damp straw and backed away toward the opening.

"You're forgetting something," Clay said.

The figure stopped. The mask of pockmarked face twisted, the panic replaced by puzzlement.

Clay stretched out his leg and kicked the attaché case with his foot so that it spiraled across the floor toward the boots of the other man, who stared down at it. Disbelief was in his mean little eyes when he lifted them.

"We made a deal," Clay said. "I stick by my deals." He did not add: unlike you and my brother. "Take it!" he barked. "I have a horse to attend to."

It was misting again. More rain. More luck for that prick Clay Chalmers.

Janice Wessell had driven the compact that she'd rented only this morning—and which she couldn't afford on her salary—up and down old Frankfort Road from one end to the other over and over. No Blassingame. Some of the swankiest horse farms in the history of man. Some of the most famous and prestigious names in the annals of the goddamn sport. But no Blassingame.

She was sick and trembling and weak with fury. Now she knew what the word *livid* really meant.

But she was not giving up. Not Janice Wessell. She'd get to the bottom of it, whatever it was. And make sure it was printed. If it was hot enough, maybe she'd try to free-lance it to one of the dailies, maybe a New York tabloid—get a by-line anyway.

She'd damn well fuck the story out of that phony, horny old walrus. She'd get the facts if it took till Derby Day and she had to let him paddle her butt raw day and night.

And then it would be her turn to give the shaft to that shy-acting sonofabitch Clayton Chalmers, Esq. Nobody, *nobody* shoved the foot-long icicle up hers—and three times in a row! Nobody.

Owen had known it all along as he sped down River Road with the rain starting again. He was too late.

To think he might have made it in time if it hadn't been for those cops and their summons. And for what? For dropping something into the river from the Sherman Minton Bridge. Like a blue portable typewriter would pollute the whole goddamn Ohio River!

The Jesus-bitten hassle had cost him half a million dollars. Minimum. The ransom alone. The back-up insurance just in case Fireaway didn't cross the wire number one. Maybe Cameron would even have paid a million on Sunday. Or more.

Jeesus-keerist, he'd been had. In spades.

If he ever got hold of that flabby broken-down jock, he'd hang him on a nail in some barn and he'd work him over till he was nothing but blood and pulp.

If he had his brother here now, that's what he'd do to him too. Like when they was kids. Only worse. He'd use those dangling ropes, tie him and punch him till he was—

What? Dead?

Yes. Dead.

And if it don't stop raining, they're gonna have to peel Owen Chalmers hisself off the wall!

Chapter Seven

"THE Louisville Downs, according to the map that Andrew and I are consulting, is located at the juncture of Poplar Level Road and I-264. The spring meet there is over, and the summer meet does not begin until July, but Mr. Arnold thinks that the unhitching of a horse van and its transfer to another vehicle in that area will not raise eyebrows or suspicions. Do you think you can find it, young man?"

"I'll find it, Mr. Raynolds. I should be there in roughly half an hour."

"Very good. Mr. Arnold will meet you. He will be driving a Jeep with *Blue Ridge* painted on the door. Andrew is particularly concerned about the health of the horse."

"He's suffering from exposure, and I'll tell Mr. Arnold what else I think."

"And oh, young man—"

"Yes?"

"Andrew asks me to convey his thanks. And although she's not with us, his daughter's too, I'm sure."

"Half an hour."

"Please, not so abrupt. I am curious as to whether you had occasion to use that . . . uh, lethal object that I loaned you—"

261

"It came in handy. Half an hour."

It had taken less than that, and here he was, as in the old times, working with Jason Arnold to unhitch the van from his pickup. The rain had let up, and the sky, damn it, showed signs of clearing altogether.

"His tongue doesn't look too bad, but watch out for glossitis. He was eating weeds before I could prevent it, so don't be surprised if a little cold develops too."

"Thanks, Clay. Doc Carpenter will give him a thorough going over, but is there anything else?"

"He was sneezing and snorting on the way here, and he's got a dry cough, but look for yourself, no sign of pinkeye."

"Yes. Anything else?"

"When he walks, you'll see, he nods his head when his off foreleg hits the ground. I think there's some lameness in the near foreleg. There's no heat yet, but it takes time for infection. My theory is he's got a splinter in the left foot. Mr. Arnold, they had him in a goddamn pigsty!"

The job done, Jason Arnold took off his felt hat and scrutinized Clay. "You better get to a doctor yourself, from the looks of you."

Clay smiled. The pain had almost left his shoulder and arm, but now there was a burning sensation. "I guess you heard: A dog got into my colt's stall this morning."

"I heard." Jason Arnold put on his hat. "Ask me, I'd say that looked like a bullet wound."

"Then I won't ask you, Mr. Arnold."

"My name's Jason. To my friends. Oh, reminds me: Just before I left the hotel, word came on that dog you mentioned. Mr. Cameron's been after the hospital all morning for a report. And he instructed me to tell you: The Doberman you killed was not rabid."

"Thanks, Jason. One more thing: Make sure Doc Carpenter checks Starbright for girth gall. I don't like the way they had him trussed up."

Jason Arnold appeared to be embarrassed, hesitant. "I guess this is as good a time as any to tell you. Thanks, son." He strode away and, with one leg up to climb into the Jeep, paused and turned his head. "Missed you at Blue Ridge, kid."

Clay drove from one downs to the other. He felt spent, dragged-out, even the exhilaration of triumph and revenge drained from him. It was as if he'd used all the energy he had, and now, while he had things to do, he couldn't really face them. But had to. And would.

Hotspur, first. All the Derby colts had been moved to a new Derby barn, some distance from the one with the burnt-out stall. And it was obvious at a glance that security had been beefed up. *Everybody always locks the barn door after the horse has got away.* More Toby wisdom. Elijah told him that Hotspur had acclimated himself to his new surroundings, but he struck Clay as more nervous, more keyed up than he liked to see him this time of day. Zach had a report on the works: "Three furlongs in thirty-six. He tired some, but after yesterday that colt can do no wrong, ever." Elijah had the report on Bernie: "Wouldn't surprise me none if they let him outta that place today or tomorrow. He said tell you that dark-haired little gallop girl, she is in a sad state, but he's working on her. I don't hardly know what that signifies, but Bernie, he fancies that little foreign gal."

And then, the three strolling away from the barn together, Zach said, "Clay, there's been a guy called Erskine asking questions. Lots of questions. He's with the TRPB and they want to see you soon's you show up, he said. Elijah and me, we didn't know what you wanted, so we played dumb."

"I played dumb," Elijah said. "Zach, he didn't have to."

Zach laughed. "The things I take off this nigger."

"Now," Elijah said, "now we got to get you fixed up neat, Mr. Chalmers, suh, because things've been happening to you, that much a blind man can see, so we got to get that blood washed away so they won't ask any *more* questions than they gonna plague you with anyway."

In Bernie's trailer Elijah treated the wound, sterilizing it and asking no questions himself, while Zach played solitaire and fought down his impulse to go to the track kitchen by nibbling on sunflower seeds.

"Now this," Elijah said, "is going to sting and I mean sting, so get your gut ready, not your shoulder."

It stung all right. "Eli," Clay said, "you're so gentle and tender with me you'd think I was a horse."

Walking to the TRPB office, located in the backside area, Clay had to decide what he would say, how much he would reveal. He hadn't yet told even Kimberley or her father what he now knew to be absolutely true about Owen and Starbright. But . . . not only did he have no proof, he had the knowledge of what the lawyer had said: that paying the ransom would have made them accessories to the crime. What about paying a bribe? What about not reporting a gunshot wound? What about not informing the authorities that you know or have goddamn good reason to suspect that someone is trying to sabotage the whole Derby? To hell with his being your brother. If he was not your brother, you'd probably hate him less. The goddamn monster had to be stopped, didn't he? You think you can do it alone? But what about Andrew Cameron, and Kimberley? And Blake Raynolds? And Jason Arnold? You blow the whistle, they're the ones who'll get the short end of the stick. Not Owen. Not Owen. Not Owen.

By the time he had reached the small gray frame building he had pretty much decided that if they asked about Starbright he'd tell the truth. Who the hell did he think he was, Hamlet? Maybe the time had come to take up arms, legal arms, against the sea of troubles and so end them. But . . . *was* that what would happen? He entered and asked at a counter for a man named Erskine.

"I'm Foster Erskine." The man had appeared in a doorway behind the counter. Not tall, not short, he was heavy-fleshed with brown hair and mustache and pleasant but wary eyes under thick brows. "Come in, Mr. Chalmers. I won't take much of your time."

The office was small and Spartan with a desk, metal files, and an atmosphere of quiet efficiency—an impression that Clay quickly got of Foster Erskine as well. Seated behind the desk, Erskine leaned back in his swivel chair and placed his feet on the ink blotter and his hands behind his head.

"Congratulations on that dramatic win yesterday." Yesterday? So much had happened in between that Clay had to force his mind to orient itself in time. "Your Hotspur should really be named Spectacular Bid." He smiled, and it was genuine enough, but a certain mistrustfulness remained in his brown eyes. "I understand you had a little trouble in barn twenty-seven this morning. I hope your assistant is recovering. Damn nasty business."

"He is, and I agree." What was the man getting at? Clay recalled that most members of the Thoroughbred Racing Protection Bureau were former agents of the FBI. "Damn nasty business."

"I once read of a man strangling a Doberman pinscher to death, but I didn't believe it."

"He was mangling my friend."

"So I understand. We've talked with its owner, Eric Millar. He works for your brother, he told me."

So that was it—Hotspur and the dog, not Starbright. Or was there more to come? "Yes, he does. He has an assistant trainer's license, I imagine."

"We're really not interested in lifting licenses or handing out suspensions—unless you have reason to think the dog's presence in the stall was more than accidental."

"Why should I think that?"

"Because if it *was* accidental, someone in your employ must have been pretty careless. Do you agree?"

"Anybody can be careless. You don't expect attack dogs to be running free around the backside. In fact, there are too damn many dogs loose around here in my opinion. They disturb the horses, not only when they're cooling out but on their way to and from the track."

Foster Erskine studied him, unsmiling. "I'll report your complaint to my superiors. I happen, personally, to agree with you, but I'm not what you'd call an experienced horseman. My job's to investigate any disturbance such as this, make a report. More generally, as you know, we try to police the entire track, backside and frontside. We don't like incidents like this, and we don't like the newspapers to make too big a play of them, if you get my meaning."

"The papers," Clay said, thinking of that little bitch Janice Wessell—was she still out there floundering around on the old Frankfort Road?—"make too much of everything. Public eats it up."

"Exactly. But we, who are in this thing together, we can't afford to lose the confidence of the public, right?"

Another one of those *right?* boys. "Right," Clay said. If the TRPB wanted to cover up, join the crowd, what the hell. But he, for some perverse and damnable reason, couldn't resist adding: "Damn shame if business fell off at the pari-mutuel windows, *right?*"

Foster Erskine smiled, and again it seemed genuine. "One way of looking at it." Then he placed his feet on the floor and leaned over the desk, picking up a pipe. "Not too far off the mark, Mr. Chalmers. I take it, then, that you don't wish to make any charges against anyone."

Clay considered. This was his chance. If he was going to speak out—

"As you say, Mr. Chalmers, everyone's careless one time or another. I wouldn't be too hard on anyone in your crew. Right?"

What the hell was the point of opening the whole can of peas now? Starbright was back in his stall. Hotspur was in running condition. Hand this man a string of accusations, even show him the bullet wound, what could he do? More important, what *would* he do? "Right," Clay said and stood up, not very damn proud of himself.

Foster Erskine lit his pipe and drew on it, eyes amused and relieved. "Your friend Bernard Golden—he will be all right, won't he?"

"In time."

"I've had the rabies report. Who thought to take the carcass of the dog to the hospital?"

"I did."

"Did you?" Pipe between his teeth, Foster Erskine rose to his feet. "You're a somewhat resourceful fellow, aren't you? Frankly, I admire a man who can keep his wits about him under stress."

"Will that be all?"

"My official report will be that the incident was an accident, and I'll recommend that dogs be kept leashed at all times, at least until after the Derby. Does that satisfy you?"

If Owen was not stymied, was Clay cutting off his own balls by playing along now? Would Foster Erskine or any of his fellow agents believe him if in the future he was forced to make official accusations in order to stop Owen—if or when he might *need* them to believe him?

"You seem to have some hesitation, Mr. Chalmers."

Thinking then of Kimberley and her father, he said, "I'm satisfied." Damned if he wanted to get into some official investigation that would probably accomplish nothing anyway. "Thanks."

"Thank you, Mr. Chalmers. I feel that we agree on principle, don't you?"

"I'm not sure," Clay said, "that I still believe in principle."

And he went out. How the hell was a man ever to know? Satisfied? Bernie in the hospital, the Irish kid, Ancient Mariner, Vincent Van, Starbright strung up in a leaky barn—

Passing between two stables, where a groom was brushing down a mare, stroke after stroke, he became conscious of someone coming along in the opposite direction. The other man, whose name was Eric Millar, saw him at the same moment and missed a step. Then, as if deciding, he lifted his head and came straight on. Clay halted. Eric Millar's thin face under his blond brush cut took on a friendly but defiant expression as he approached. He came to a stop a yard away, facing Clay.

"Mr. Chalmers," he said, "I'm Eric Millar."

Clay nodded. Waiting.

"I just want to tell you how sorry I am about—"

Something inside Clay exploded. He stepped, and before the other man could move, Clay's right fist shot out, there was that flat wooden sound of bone against bone, and Eric Millar dropped as if the life had gone from him.

Then there were shouts, a horse whinnied, another began stomping, and Clay was kneeling, clutching Eric Millar's collar so that the other man's eyes bulged, and as Clay twisted, Eric Millar made incoherent sounds, which then died into a gurgle as Clay twisted harder. Their faces were close.

Very softly then, very quietly Clay said, "When Bernie's well, he'll probably kill you. For now, just listen. Take a message for me." Blood appeared at the corner of Eric Millar's mouth, which had gone white. "Tell my brother that it's over. It's all over. Hear me, hear me! He made his last move and he's lost." His grip tightened. "Anything else, anything at all, *anything*, and I'll kill him."

Then he let go and stood up. Eric Millar, hand to his face, did not stay. Clay became conscious of figures on all sides, faces staring, voices shouting.

One of the faces was that of Foster Erskine. His eyes were grave, accusing. "This will cost you, Mr. Chalmers."

"How much?" Clay asked in that same still, low tone.

Foster Erskine placed his pipe between his teeth. Neither of them looked down. "Oh, they probably won't suspend you, but you'll be fined."

"How much?"

Foster Erskine's mustache twisted into a slow grin. "Oh, five hundred dollars. That's only a guess."

"Mr. Erskine," Clay said, "it'd be cheap at twice the price."

Foster Erskine shrugged. "It's only a guess."

And then Clay, his stomach turning, hurried away and around the corner of a barn, and then he stopped and vomited.

Kimberley was on her way to the Downs. If no one else would take her, she would go alone. She knew how to be alone. But she was miserable. If only there were some way never to be alone again—

There is, Kimberley.

Go away.

I'm always with you.

Fuck off.

Now you're yourself again. You're me.

She was driving too fast. She always drove too fast. How many times had she been arrested? Only one accident, though—

That's the way, Kimberley. That's the way never to be alone again.

No, never, no!

When Andrew had rung her suite to tell her that Starbright was safely back in the barn, she had suggested he take her there.

"There's nothing we can do, Kimb. Doc Carpenter's with him," Andrew had said.

"He's sick! He's injured, I know—"

"I won't lie to you, Daughter. He has what may turn into influenza. Jason thinks not."

"What else? Something else!"

"Why don't you go out there yourself, Kimb? You can talk with Jason and with the vet."

"Why don't you go with me?"

"I'm not in the hotel."

"Where are you?"

"I'm at the hospital if you must know. Brigid is with her niece, and then we're going to the steamboat race—"

"That's hours away. Imagine you going to the steamboat race!"

"We're going on a late afternoon picnic before that. In lieu of another big dinner."

"A picnic? I don't believe it, Andrew! You?"

"I've had the hotel pack a basket."

"Did you? That's sweet. I know just the place. It's a grove of locust trees alongside a stream. Off Shady Lane. By a covered bridge. Andrew, it's the best fucking place within miles!"

"So . . . you're in one of those moods."

"No ants, no bugs. But it's best when it rains!"

"I'll see you later, dear. Try to get some rest. It's been a trying night and morning."

" 'These are the times that try men's souls.' See! My education wasn't entirely wasted, was it? Clay's always quoting Shakespeare. I guess I can quote whoever it was said that."

"Kimberley, may I help you? In any way? May I?"

"I don't need help. All I need is to see Starbright and—Clay will take me! Happy fucking, Daddy-o."

But Clay wouldn't take her. He refused.

"I've thanked you, haven't I, darling? I've said I'm sorry for the way I talked when you phoned me awhile ago."

"I've just showered, Kimb—"

"I wish I'd been there."

"And I'm on my way out the door. I don't have an assistant

trainer, and there's a hell of a lot to do. I have to see Bernie in the hospital. By the way, since you didn't ask, the dog was not rabid."

"Dog? What dog?"

"Never mind."

"Then how could I ask? Is everybody and his brother converging on the hospital? What happened to Bernie?"

"Kimb, can't we talk tonight? We'll have dinner and a long evening and then a long, long night—"

"I want you now!"

"Kimb . . . are you saying you need me, for some reason?"

"No. I don't need you. I don't need anyone!"

She had thrown down the telephone.

And now here she was at the track, being waved through and bowed through and smiled through the Fourth Street entrance. And what do you know, here she was, as sure as night follows day, on the backstretch. They'd moved the horses. She wouldn't ask. She refused to ask. She drove. Not allowed. Screw you, brother, and your uniform too. Why do Pinks wear blue uniforms? Makes no sense. She was wearing skin-tight breeches, riding shirt, matching choker, stockpin: go riding, wear riding clothes! Go fucking, wear no clothes, naked, nothing.

And there it was, the new Derby barn, with photographers, more paparazzi, don't they ever sleep, out of the way, please, please, please, do you want to get killed!

"Miss Kimberley." It was Mr. Arnold. The man himself. Ever present. Eyes frowning—concern? Worry? She was out of the car and moving fast. "Miss Kimberley, wait. Let me talk to—"

And a face, a strange face, alongside. "Miss Cameron, my name's Buddy Lee, I'm with the *Indianapolis News*, is there something wrong, is Starbright sick?"

"Indianapolis? I've been there. Dreadful place, with that big prick sticking up out of a circle."

A laugh, startled. "The soldiers and sailors monument?" Another laugh.

Oh, she could be amusing, really funny, give her a try. "Shows the way soldiers and sailors think, doesn't it?"

Pepe. Pepe was here! She ran and threw herself into his arms. Bending down. She didn't mind bending down for Pepe.

"Pepe, what are *you* doing here?"

"The tom-toms," Pepe said, placing a finger over his lips and nodding toward the reporters. "The backside grapevine, it works so well. I heard—"

"Mr. Benitez, can you tell us—"

"I have already told you. No interviews! You may write that I am here to visit my two mounts of the week—Lady Mariah in the Oaks and Starbright, who I will ride on Saturday. That is all. They are both in . . . excellent, yes, excellent condition." Then to Kimberley: "Please, now, for me, you come with me, we take a ride and we talk about your so-lovely—"

But she had to see Starbright. She went under the roof and along the shedrow, away from the press, who were being kept back. Jason Arnold was outside the stall, and a groom and the vet were inside, the gate closed.

She reached and touched Starbright's star and ran a hand down his forehead. He lifted his head and lowered it and tried to nudge her, so she went closer and whispered to him. He seemed calm enough and that reassured her, but—

"Mr. Arnold, tell me. Don't *lie*."

"Lower your voice, Miss Kimberley. They will quote every word." Then in a whisper: "He has a girth gall, easily treated."

"Andrew said a cold—"

Jason Arnold shook his head. "It has not developed, but his cough—"

"Cough?"

"Miss Kimberley, if they hear you, they'll put it on the news wires that Starbright's too ill to run. You know that. A cough—we're watching it."

"And?"

"Splinters in two feet, one fore, one hind. Near side. But neither leg has heated, and his temperature remains normal. All we can do is wait to see whether infection develops."

Wait? How could she wait? Andrew! Clay! Someone!

271

Joseph Hayes

"I am here, Miss Kimberley." Pepe—with his gentle almond eyes and his bright smile on the smooth nut-brown face, looking up at her. Kind, sweet Pepe. No one else had ever ridden Starbright in a race. Pepe—

"You leave your automobile here now, and you come with Pepe. He has, this time, a gift for *you*." They were walking away, slowly, not touching but close. "You have give me so many gifts, you know. Too many." A camera clicked, and a young man and woman came closer, more paparazzi. The woman said, "Mr. Benitez—" But Pepe made a firm gesture, suddenly glowering, and they stood away. Then he was saying, "You give me, look, such a beautiful horseshoe ring with ten diamonds—"

"Don't tell your agent," she said. "He'll want two of them."

And the little man threw back his head and laughed, and his eyes glittered with merriment. "It shall be our secret, Miss Kimberley. It will be my good-luck charm, and as long as I wear it, even in a race, nothing bad can happen to me, okay? And now we go to my car and we go out to the country, see how the sun has come out after the raining. We go and along the way, but not here, I have present for you that will soothe your nerves, okay?"

"Okay, Pepe. That's nice, isn't it? Okay, Pepe—it rhymes. Okay, Pepe."

In his cream-colored Eldorado he sat behind the wheel on a pillow, which, he explained, he had had specially made. "Little is good for horses, not good for automobile, okay?"

"Okay, Pepe."

"You smoke?"

Smoke? "Cigarettes? No."

"Not cigarettes, no—grass? You smoke marijuana?"

"Pot? Do you have pot?"

He drove out the gate, nodding gaily and waving. "In the glove compartment, please. All rolled. I have machine. I roll my own. And when I am not calm, like you now, when I am fretting, worry, it helps, it helps."

"It's better if you don't turn on the air conditioner."

Again he threw back his head of tight black curls and laughed

272

deep in his throat and chest. "You tell me how to smoke the marijuana. Okay, Pepe."

She lit two of the neatly rolled joints and after inhaling deeply extended one to Pepe. "Do you smoke while driving, Pepe?"

"Only when I have guest."

They smoked in silence for a time, and soon, very soon, it was as Pepe had said: She began to feel calm, very calm, relaxed.

"How many races have you ridden, Pepe?"

"If you believe the papers, thirty thousand. I have lost count. I think maybe twenty-five thousand."

"That's a lot, that's really a lot." Her voice sounded different already. It sounded fine. It sounded very fine, and easy. "How many have you won?"

"The newspapers—"

"Screw the newspapers."

He shook his head. He did not laugh. "I will tell you if you promise not to . . . speak so. Okay?"

"You don't like my language? Andrew doesn't either. And Clay— he doesn't say, but I know." She had asked a question. What had she asked? "How many have you won, honest-Injun, tell me no lies—"

"Four thousand, nine hundred and seventy-three. And after Friday, four thousand, nine hundred and seventy-four, and after Saturday—"

"Four thousand, nine hundred and seventy-*five*. Okay?"

"Okay, Pepe." And he laughed again. This time his laugh was more high-pitched though—different.

"You know Starbright better than anyone but Mr. Arnold. And me, she said."

"And with Starbright you never go to the whip. Hand-ride him right to the wire. Okay?"

"You're the driver, Pepe."

Again that laugh. "Okay, okay then. You want to go to the Derby Museum?"

"I haven't been to the Kentucky Derby Museum since I was a little girl."

"You won't tell if I confess? I have *never* been. Not once."

This time she laughed and opened the glove compartment. And then she remembered and placed the tip of the joint that was left in the ashtray, and then she took a fresh one. But it was the last one in the small tin container.

"And," he was saying, "I've been in nine Derbys and placed in two, won one. Let's not break my record—and let's not go to the Derby Museum now, okay?"

"Okay, Pepe. But we're out of grass." She reached the lighted joint to him, but he shook his head.

"You need it more."

True. Very true. She had needed it, and he had known. Dear Pepe.

"More grass where I come from," he said. At the next exit he turned, drove the Cadillac with ease under the highway and then up onto it again. "More grass my room, okay?"

It occurred to her then, but vaguely, that maybe . . . just maybe he was getting her stoned . . . for just possibly a very good reason. She twisted to regard him in the seat as he drove. He did not glance at her. She continued to smoke, cupping her hand as she inhaled deeply and holding each puff in her lungs as long as she could.

And then he was talking about his many injuries. How at Bowie one time a horse broke down and threw him, and as he started to get up three horses kicked him, one after the other. Seven broken ribs, punctured lung, ruptured spleen, separated shoulder. She shuddered and recalled reading in some column that he had been "restrung like a necklace of beads." But she'd never heard him speak of anything like this before. Come to think of it, Pepe rarely talked of himself, in private, to her knowledge, or to the press. Recuperating, he said, he developed gas gangrene, and then she thought of the wood splinters in two of Starbright's feet, and she drew on the joint again, not wishing to think of Starbright, or of Andrew, or of Clay, of anything. Pepe had been, he said, paralyzed for three days.

"And my spine was bent like this." He took one hand from the wheel and crooked a brown finger. "It is still so. They couldn't do anything about it."

You would never know it. He was really a handsome man.

Small, true, but with firm, hard flesh everywhere, and jockeys always seemed, when they married, to marry tall women. She had often thought of it. And wondered. Was he small in all his parts or—

"Let's go to your hotel, Pepe." It was as if she heard herself, as if she had not spoken, only heard.

"We're here," Pepe said. "Only it is a motel. I prefer it so because of the people." He was laughing again. "My fans. Groupies. My groupies—they haunt the lobby. Here, we not need go through lobby, okay?"

Then the fresh air struck her, and she blinked, staring down at Pepe, who was holding her door open. She stepped down, only it was more like floating, and that was fine too, very nice.

"I shall show you how I roll them, okay?"

Roll them? In the hay? Why, Pepe!

The hotel room was large, with two wide double beds. And Pepe was turning off the air conditioning, and then he was rummaging in a drawer. He was really a perfectly proportioned man, and quite handsome. With that smooth, swarthy skin that looked as if he had spent days in the sun, months. Was he nut-brown like that all over?

He handed her a lighted joint, and she thanked him. She said, "Okay, Pepe."

"You are feeling soothed. You see, I told you."

"Pepe . . . let's stay here. All the rest of the day. Let's stay here and get really stoned out of our fucking minds and take off our clothes and you take one bed and I take the other and in time the twain shall meet, okay, Pepe?"

But now he was frowning up at her, his head tilted back and to one side and his face just slightly, pleasantly blurred.

"Miss Kimberley"—and now he sounded so sad, so regretful—"Miss Kimberley, my dear, my dear, I thought perhaps you knew. Very few know, but such a secret cannot be—" Oh, he sounded so sad, why did he have to sound so terribly—

"I'm gay."

No, he was far from gay. He—

Then the words reached her.

And she began to laugh. No, not laugh, giggle. It was very

275

funny. No, not funny, hilarious. So hilarious that she fell across one of the beds, hearing the giggles as they turned into chortles, and then guffaws as she rolled over, and then shrieks, shrieks, she had never heard anything so funny in her life, ever—

And then Pepe was sitting on the bed beside her, and he was beginning to laugh too, so she turned over and looked up into his handsome open-mouthed face as his merriment took possession of him until he too was stretched out on the bed beside her, roaring with laughter—

"Do you . . . do you know something, Pepe?" She could not get the words out because of the laughing, but she went on. "Something, do you know something, Pepe, you're the first gay I ever . . . ever met who . . . who was really gay. Happy—gay."

And then they were both lying there shrieking together.

When she heard another sound. They both stopped laughing and sat up together and listened as the telephone shrilled. They stared at each other. And then it shrilled again, and he reached to pick it up. She was about to fall back across the bed when she heard him speak, scowling now, so she didn't.

"Just a moment, please, okay?" And then: "Who is this?"

He listened and then he capped one small hand over the mouthpiece. "He won't say who he is, but he asked for you."

"For me?" She didn't even know where she was. Pepe's room, yes, but she didn't even know the name of the motel.

Slowly, stunned, she took the telephone. "Yes?"

"Miss Kimberley Cameron?"

"Y—es?"

"This is a friend of yours and you better believe it."

"Who, who is this?" She had never heard the voice before. "Who are you?"

"Best goddamn friend you ever had. I followed you and your jock from the track. It's a cinch nobody's tracing calls from *this* phone. Now you listen careful. Between you and me. Scratch Starbright by ten o'clock tomorrow morning. After they draw for post positions, it'll be too late."

"Too late? It's . . . who the hell is this?"

"Ten A.M. tomorrow morning. Scratch your bangtail or take what's coming."

She was grasping the phone now, and her body stiffened as her mind cleared. "Whoever you are," she shouted, "whoever you are, fuck off!"

And she slammed down the phone.

Steamboat Bill, a mighty man was he . . . Try as he might, Walter Drake could not force the other words of the old song into his mind. (Oh well, a pharmacist wasn't supposed to know the lyrics of songs.) The family was sitting on a grassy embankment along the riverfront in Jeffersonville, Indiana, his home state, waiting for the Great Steamboat Race to begin. He could have taken them to a cocktail party on the thirtieth floor of the First National Tower (everyone welcome at ten dollars each) for an excellent view, live music, and the call of the race on loudspeakers; or they could have fought the crowd for a position on the riverfront in Louisville; but it had been Margo's idea to drive over the John F. Kennedy Bridge, stroll through the Howard Steamboat Museum, and then to see whether they might watch from the opposite side of the river. The sloping embankment was not crowded—campers and cars of every color and description, mostly station wagons, and along the shore a row of houseboats—but they could see the river clearly and across it the city's skyline. Leave it to Margo: She had always been a daughter a man could be proud of. People were everywhere: strolling, sprawling on the grass, gathered on the small porches of the houses behind them, perched on the tops of cars and boats, eating ice cream or shaved ices and drinking pop and beer. The place had the atmosphere and feeling of a small-town fair or carnival, and he felt right at home . . . *a mighty man was he, tore up the Mississippi* . . . He almost had it. They could not hear the gun signaling the start of the race, but they heard the blasts of three whistles, and then they could see the three stern-wheelers start upriver, side by side, their smokestacks streaming pale smoke. "Let's bet," Margo cried.

"I'll take the *Belle of Louisville!*" And her mother, her fleshy face in a beautiful, happy smile, said: "The *Delta Queen.*" And then both Terry and his father took the *Robert E. Lee,* causing Margo to scoff, "Male pigs." The family was together again, the four of them. More words came to him: *Burn up the cargo if you run out of fuel!* They stood to watch until the three triple-decked paddle-wheel boats were almost out of view on their way to Six Mile Island, where they would turn and return. "I'm winning, Poppa," Margo said. "Look!" And her father, standing, said, "Why don't we take in the town while we wait?" The suggestion was unanimously accepted, and they strolled, the four of them, up the grass and onto the sidewalk. The four of them. How many times had Walter wondered whether they'd ever spend a day together again. First he had come back to the motel from the track after the fire last night to find Margo there, and then, when the three of them were lunching in the motel restaurant, Terry had appeared. Materialized out of nowhere! He had stood by the table asking, in that shy teasing way of his: "Am I welcome?" Walter had recognized him at once, even with the heavy black beard, and instantly, with guilt, he had recalled his thoughts in the taxi only a few hours earlier: How can a man write off his own son, his own flesh and blood? "I hitchhiked from California," Terry had said while he ate. And when his mother had asked what he had been doing, he had answered: "Trying to get my shit together." And when she had winced, he had then corrected himself: "Trying to get my head on straight, Mom." And had he? Yes. He had spent a year in a drug-rehabilitation center, and he felt whole again. Now, moving up the incline of a street with stores on both sides, Susan was wondering how she could have lived in Terre Haute all her life and never been in Jeffersonville before. "Why, it's only across the state from us!" They passed a tavern, and Walter asked whether anyone would like a drink, and Terry said, "Not for me, thanks, Pop," so they moved on. Taking her son's arm, Susan said, "You know, I have something to confess! I'm scared of horses. And, forgive me, Walter, I don't even *like* them very much!" And they all laughed, Walter included. He couldn't remember when he had seen Susan so happy. He still hoped Prescription would at least

278

make a respectable showing on Saturday but . . . win? Who cared? A couple of teenagers passed, both wearing T-shirts with lettered slogans printed on them. On his: HIRE THE MORALLY HANDICAPPED. On hers: SEX HAS NO CALORIES. Four smiles were exchanged. How times changed, and how fast. They went into various shops—only looking, killing time, being together, not buying. "Derby fever," Margo said. "I read about it in the paper. Is that what we've all got?" And, on the street again, Susan quoted, " 'We were very tired, we were very merry, we had gone back and forth all night on the ferry . . .' Who wrote that?" Walter recalled: When he was dating Susan all those years ago, she had always liked quoting things she'd read. "Don't ask me, Susie-Q," he said, and her head turned and she smiled again. They were stopped by a high-school band strutting by, majorettes twirling batons and the bass drum too loud; they were playing "Dixie." And then, when the band had passed, he saw someone he recognized, or thought he did, and all he could think was: What is *she* doing here, and by herself? She was coming out of a store, and she was wearing a straw hat with a wide, floppy straw-fringed brim, tight jeans, and a red bandana halter top tied above her bare belly button. It couldn't be, but it was: Kimberley Cameron. And, licking an ice-cream cone, she was coming directly toward them. "Hi," she said, tilting her head, her green eyes holding a friendly but glassy happiness. "I know who you are." They stopped and stood together. "You own Prescription, we've seen you at the track." Susan introduced her daughter, Margo, her husband, Walter, and her son, Terry, and said how pleased she was to meet the owner of the favorite. "Would you . . . we're only waiting for the boats to come back . . . would you like to join us?" But the girl shook her head of long blond hair. "No, thank you. Sometimes I can't bear being alone, and sometimes I love it. Will you forgive me?" They understood, Walter told her, and there was nothing to forgive. "I'm delighted to meet all of you," Kimberley Cameron said and continued on her way back to the riverfront. Terry turned his head to watch her. "Well," he said, "I don't understand, and I'm damned if I forgive. Her *or* you. *That's* what I want hanging on my Christmas tree!" They all laughed. But behind his joking tone was something else. "Now if there were more girls like that, there'd be fewer bachelors. Wow, I say." And then they turned into a store with the words *Used Merchandise* emblazoned across the plate-glass window, and below: *Come in and browse awhile.* Walter decided to stay outside, but he could see into the cluttered interior: broken-down armchairs, an old-fashioned coffee grinder with a hand crank, frayed magazines and old books, tools, secondhand clothing. He could see Terry with his mother and Margo off by herself, idly examining the paperback books. What, Walter wondered, was that Cameron girl doing here, alone among the hoi polloi, when her friends were probably all on the crowded decks of the steamboats having cocktails or dancing? Then the words came to him: *Steamboat Bill, a mighty man was he, tore up the Mississippi trying to beat the record of the Robert E. Lee*—or something close to that. Seeing Terry in there with his mother, Walter wondered whether the boy—hell, he was a man now—had really pulled himself together. What had gone wrong? Had he himself been so scared of ever again being poor, as he'd been as a boy, that he had worked too hard, too much, nights and Sundays, and so allowed this thing to happen? He wasn't sure, even now, what *had* happened. And then Margo was at his side. "Remember me, Poppa?" Startled, he looked at her. What could she mean by that? "It's unfair. I never got drunk, I never tore up cars, I never used drugs or yelled at you or Mom. I love Terry, and he's sunny and funny, and he can make you feel so good, but—" And then he recalled again his thoughts of the night: that Terry had *demanded* one way or the other and out of necessity had received their attention, while Margo—"Today, since he came, it's as if I'm a little girl again, and everything's happening all over again." She looped her arm through his. "But I don't really mind. Now. Soon I'll have a family of my own and—" But she stopped speaking and cocked her head to one side. "Listen!" He listened and he heard it too—the unmistakable deep windy tooting sound of a boat whistle in the distance. "They're coming back!" Margo cried and took his hand. "Come on, come on, let's see who's winning!" He was about to call into the store to Terry and his mother, but he decided against it as he and his daughter together ran down the street toward the river.

Winner's Circle

*   *   *

A grand day it had slowly become. Showers off and on, and now, with two steamers vying to reach the finish line first and the third one, the *Robert E. Lee,* left two miles behind, its healthy, pale smoke having turned a sickish black and its paddle wheel stuttering to a stop, the race was between the *Delta Queen,* which was abreast, and the *Belle of Louisville,* which she rode. In the shade of the middle deck, but nevertheless still wearing the great-brimmed white hat, Brigid Tyrone sat in her chair, looking back over the day and wondering about the night ahead. She had loved the whooshes and the sighs earlier as the boat had drawn away from the dock to take its place in line, and now, returning as its whistle sounded with urgent repeated short blasts and the banjos continued to play from the deck below, she looked at Andrew's back as he stood at the rail waving to the crowded deck of their competitor.

She simply could not get the man into proper focus. The closer to him she felt, and the warmer toward him, the more of an enigma he became. The austere remoteness that had put her off at first she had now recognized as a defense—but against what, and why? His innate good breeding—unshared by that daughter of his, who seemed forever in a state of ferment—had made her feel that she was not intruding on his life, and as time passed she had come to feel his warmth, even his passion, as when they had kissed last night after that most curious scene with Kimberley about paying her gambling debts. And, above all, she had come to feel his outgoing sympathy and understanding—as when he had asked her at the hospital to motor into the countryside to share a picnic with him before going on to the steamboat race. But when they were together in his Mercedes, he had seemed abstracted, somewhat distant, and she had been embarrassed, remembering last night's kiss in the foyer of the hotel suite. Was it Kimberley who was on his mind? If so, small wonder. And we are all several people inside really, so getting acquainted meant meeting the various selves of the other person, didn't it?

The whistle had a mellow merriment in it, and she could see, when someone moved away from the rail, that her boat was drawing out in front. Even if she had not been able to see, she would have known by the shouts and cheers of her fellow passengers. Surprising how many people there were on board and how few she recognized. She had not caught a glimpse of the Hautots, for instance, or of the elderly Mrs. Stoddard, whom she had come to like. She had exchanged greetings in the lobby with Christine Rosser, whom Andrew had known for many years, and with her trainer, the wide-shouldered, handsome fellow in the white Western suit and hat, but they had gone aboard the *Robert E. Lee*, which was far behind now, having given up the ghost.

Andrew turned, and making an explanatory gesture—cupped hand lifting and head tilting back to indicate that he was going below to get them another drink—he disappeared into the crowd. The last thing in the world she needed, thank you, but she had to uphold the Irish tradition, she supposed. What with the brilliant sun and the glittering water and the soft rocking of the boat and the water-turning rhythm of its paddle wheel aft, she had come to feel quite lightheaded, even giddy. There were a number of drunks aboard, most conspicuously that sinister-eyed motion picture star, whose Cro-Magnon ugliness was so celebrated but whose capacity for alcoholic consumption left much to be desired, as did his manners.

She herself had, in truth, been less than scintillating company through the afternoon. As they had strolled, touristlike, through a mansion of Franco-American-Victorian architecture and through another built from a design by Thomas Jefferson, her mind had been with Molly in her hospital bed. Molly had become, overnight, a stranger to her. Laying so still in her bed, her dark eyes staring at the ceiling, the girl seemed lost in an alien land. Sister Grace had suggested she might like a telly in her room—*would* she like that? "No." But if she had to stay through Saturday, she'd want to see the Derby, wouldn't she? "No, thank you, Aunt Brigid." And when she'd told the colleen about Irish Thrall—that Mr. McGreevey had said he was off his feed, refusing the oats he always loved, refusing to eat altogether, acting for all the world like a rejected swain— Molly had turned her head away. "I don't care." But . . . Gregory

McGreevey had a fear that if the colt continued in this frame of mind, he would not be in his finest fettle on Saturday. Bleakly then, Molly had said, her voice hollow, that it did not concern her. "I'll never ride again. Or trust a horse." And when Brigid, appalled, had said that surely she could not blame Irish Thrall, Molly had said, "I hate him." Petrified then, Brigid had stood above the girl and stared. Helpless. What could lift the child's spirit from that dark pit of despondency? She did not remind her that the colt had panicked, that he had not even recognized her. But hours later Molly's gloom had not lifted. Would it ever? Might her wounds go deeper than the fractured bones in their cast or the stitched cuts under the bandages on her forehead? As she reluctantly left the hospital with Andrew, Brigid had wondered whether the true scars of last night's violence might be on the child's delicate youthful spirit itself.

Later, in the Mercedes, moving through the rich countryside past the world-famous horse farms, recognizing the name Thistle Hill Farms as the home of Vincent Van, who was no longer scheduled to run in the Derby because of some injury, she had been taken by surprise when after a long silence Andrew had begun to talk, as if some weight were heavy in his mind: "It's really a closed society, this racing world. I've only recently come to realize it. I don't know how it is in Ireland or England, but here we even police ourselves. We appoint our own officials from our own ranks, and most of them are dependent on racing for their livelihood. And the men trusted to represent the public are political appointees, with their own vested interests. We all have our own vested interests."

Was it this then—something about which she knew nothing—was it this and not Kimberley after all that had been troubling him early this morning in her suite, before Kimberley had come to all but demand his attention?

"It's got to the point where winning is everything, and people will do anything to achieve it."

She had recalled his rage of the evening before on the way to the hotel after the Derby Trial. "Daniel used to say that winning is vital, but secondary."

"Really? I think I would have liked your Daniel."

And she knew that Daniel would have liked Andrew Cameron.

Then he had told her of the 1968 Derby here. Which had been won by a colt named Dancer's Image, whose victory had been questioned after chemical tests revealed an illegal drug in his system. Since test results were not revealed until the Monday after the race the pari-mutuel windows had paid off on the basis of his crossing the line first. But the second-place horse, named Forward Pass, was declared the official winner and had received the purse.

Now, on the deck of the *Belle of Louisville* the banjo music stopped and the steam calliope took over, as lively and festive a sound as one could ask for on such an afternoon. And Andrew returned with the drinks: lemonade, tart and quenching. How thoughtful this man was—how did he know? How did he always seem to sense her wishes, her moods?

"The song," he said, "is called 'Sweet Georgia Brown.' "

He was sitting beside her, crossing his legs. He too wore white today, with a black tie. She became acutely but pleasantly aware of his nearness. As she had been in the grove alongside a brook where they had sat on the grass and shared the picnic lunch of cold fried chicken and rich fresh tomatoes and chilled white wine. It had seemed natural then to lie back on the soft grass and stare at the ramshackle but lovely wood-covered bridge over which they had earlier passed. And it seemed natural too that he should stretch out beside her and kiss her; and that she should return his kisses. But the day had grown—to quote one of her favorite heroines—curioser and curioser. Andrew had suddenly stood up and suggested that it was getting late and they had better move if they wanted to see the steamboat race from the deck of the boat. And on the way back to the city he had driven with a chilled abandon that had riled her and at the same time further baffled her.

Beside her now, the calliope tooting triumph, he had changed again. "Brigid, I've been thinking. What race did you say your Irish Thrall was entered in next month, the Irish St. Leger?"

"No, that's in September. The Irish Sweeps Derby at the Curragh and the Ascot Gold Cup next month, a week apart."

"I've decided," he said. "I'm coming over. And take in the English Darby, as you call it, as well."

She did not know quite what to say. His gray eyes were on her, waiting.

"I did invite you, Andrew."

"I know. I didn't know how . . . firm an invitation it was."

"It was very firm. And is."

"I may even stay in Europe into the fall. I've a three-year-old colt named Hale Fellow that Jason and I've been pointing toward some big stakes."

Her voice was shaking, but only a wee bit. "In addition to the Irish St. Leger and the St. Leger Stakes at Doncaster, England, there's the really greatest of all, le Prix Arc de Triomphe at Longchamp in the autumn."

Then they were staring at each other. Gravely. Quietly.

There was a rush of people to the bow and then a great mingling of shouts and cries, and amidst it all he asked, "Dinner in an hour or so?"

"You said no dinner." She shook her head and took off the hat. "You said the picnic would suffice."

"Did it suffice you?"

"I couldn't eat another morsel."

And then, when he did not speak, she said, "But I would enjoy more chilled white wine. In an hour or so."

"So should I, my darling."

"Then . . . I'll order from my rooms."

"I'll come."

"I think we've won the race."

"I think so too."

But she was still not all that sure.

She had slept off and on all day. Now it was evening and Paul had not returned. She had no inkling as to where he might be. And no concern. She was sipping the wine about which Paul always complained. Perhaps it would waken her completely. She had, she admitted to herself, absorbed more cocaine last night than was wise.

It sometimes left her in this black mood. She had also heard too often last night that it would be incredible if a filly should come in even third or fourth in the Kentucky Derby. Then, so be it. Bonne Fete would run in the Irish Sweeps next month and in the King George VI and Queen Elizabeth Diamond Stakes a few days after Bastille Day. And how pleased and relieved she would be to be back in Europe. And then the Arc itself in the autumn—Paris. Home. Maxim's and all their favorite small restaurants and Givenchy's. Oh, heaven, heaven. She heard the door in the foyer open, and then Paul appeared. Or was it Paul? Aghast, she could not rise to her feet. "Paul, Paul, what have they done to you?" But he did not reply; he could only stare. He appeared as if he might collapse. She stood and rushed to him, reaching, but he flinched away, dark eyes widening in pain, as if he feared her touch. Tenderly, mumbling incoherent questions, she helped him move toward the bedroom, where slowly—he cried out once or twice—very slowly she removed his clothes. His body, neck to heels, front and back, was a fretwork of blood-red rising welts. And then she knew: He had been tied down, naked, and carefully and minutely beaten with a leather belt or strap. It was inevitable that such a thing would happen sooner or later. Here and in Europe he insisted on going into those bars where the husky leather-jacketed homosexuals gathered. She was faint with revulsion and compassion and love. She had always told herself that she would prefer he have affairs with males rather than females. Whereas his preference had always been the opposite. She placed him on the bed, and then she telephoned the pharmacy in the hotel, and then, without trembling, she kissed his pale lips and went into the bathroom to be violently sick. The savages, the savages, the savages—did they have to come to the States to meet with such depravity?

Andrew had discovered some time ago that he had come to approach meetings with Kimberley with some reluctance—for fear that a scene might develop. How long ago had it been that the atmosphere between them had been relaxed and casual and uncluttered—not fraught with the potential for an eruption? And now that Clay Chalmers had reentered her life—

The door of her suite stood ajar, so he pushed it open and entered. From beyond the bedroom he heard the sound of a gushing shower. He decided to take a chair and wait. He did wish, though, that she would get into the habit of closing doors securely and locking them.

Once having made up his mind as to what he must demand of her—no, not demand; lately one demanded of Kimberley at the risk of provoking hysteria—he found that he was even more apprehensive. Her love of Starbright had become almost an obsession, and his disappearance and return had done little, he conjectured, but contribute to it.

The sound of the shower stopped, and in a moment the figure of Kimberley darted across the bedroom, nude and dripping. Of course she didn't know anyone was there, but she had left the door open again—

"You have company, Daughter."

"Andrew? Only a second. I didn't know!"

"Take your time, Daughter."

"Did you have a pleasant day?"

Had he? Yes, in fact, he had had a damned fine day. Brigid's vivid eyes darkening and direct beneath the red brows and hair: *But I would enjoy more chilled white wine. In an hour or so.*

"Well, Andrew, did you?"

"As a matter of fact, I did. Thank you. And you?"

She came in wearing a long white terry robe and toweling her hair. "Beautiful. All by myself mostly." She sat on the sofa and lowered her pale hair between her knees and continued to towel it dry. "I saw the steamboat race from the Indiana side! It's a much better view than from the tower or the deck of the boats. And there were so many people—all sorts and kinds I'd never been with before. Why, I even accepted a can of beer from a truck-driver type in a T-shirt. I didn't know I liked beer so much!"

Her elation, which should have pleased him, did not. Kimberley always said she was two people, but he knew better: She was many people. And by now he had observed the pattern: In time—and he hoped after he had gone—the exhilaration would shatter and give way to either fury or depression or both, and more.

"Would you light a cigarette for me, Andrew?" And while he did: "That reminds me, I had a hilarious visit with Pepe. Which reminds me too—do you have my phone bugged?"

Taken by surprise as he extended the lighted cigarette, he asked, "Whatever gave you that idea?"

She threw back her hair, straightened, stared into his eyes, and said mockingly: "Where *do* you get your ideas, Kimberley?" Her eyes had that bright feverish expression, and she puffed at the cigarette furiously, though smiling; even her smoking was a storm signal of sorts. "Well, did you find the place I told you about? By the covered bridge?"

He resumed his seat. "As a matter of fact, I did."

"Clay showed me. He knew about it from his childhood or something."

Clay Chalmers again: Andrew had not yet made up his mind about him, if he ever would. Much as his feelings baffled him, though, he was certain of one thing: Clay was innocent of Starbright's disappearance.

As casually as if she were asking him to light another cigarette, Kimberley said, "I'm pleased you found the place. Did you have a good fuck?"

Her nature, it appeared, was really set for a spell of riot. He did not give in to his quick anger. She would never force him to lose his dignity again. "I'm an old-fashioned fellow, Kimb."

"Really?" She was mocking, but warmly, almost affectionately, as if humoring him quite sincerely. She leaned forward. "Do you want me to rephrase the question?"

"You know that I wouldn't answer it even if you did."

"You've already answered it."

Damn the child. Even though her assumption was dead wrong. And damn his own mind too. In the grove along the stream with Brigid, Kimberley's words, *It's the best fucking place within miles,* had returned to his mind at exactly the wrong moment and his desire had withered, and then, of course, he had fallen back on his stiff dignity, or inherent stuffiness, and the whole picnic had been ruined—for Brigid as well as for himself, he knew. Kimberley had her ways, without even being aware of them.

"Oh, Andrew, don't look so dreary. A rose by any other name. Have you come to take me to dinner?"

"I thought you'd be dining with Clay."

"Are you satisfied Clay didn't take Starbright, hold him for ransom himself, then pocket the hundred thousand dollars?"

"I'm satisfied as to that, yes." What continued to bewilder him, though, was that on that snowy night seven years ago Clay had not struck back. Had it been because of a drunken knowledge of his own guilt? Had he felt he should be punished, perhaps? Or was it because he had too much respect to fight a man who was old enough to be his father? Whatever Clay Chalmers's reason, the memory of the scene invariably filled Andrew with a hot shame. Not that it mattered now: He wished to God Kimberley would stop bringing up the old dead subject, which seemed never to get resolved. "I think," he said now, "you and I should both be grateful to him."

"I am. And tonight I'm going to show him just *how* grateful. Right here, where, you are so right, we are going to have dinner. First. Or between."

Well, her meaning was clear, but at least she didn't use the word again.

Then she leaped up and, childlike, ran to stoop and pick up a strange-looking object from the floor behind his chair. "Tah-*tah!* A present, Andrew. For you!"

It was black and iron and heavy-looking, and he had no idea in the world what it could be. But her face was radiant with delight and triumph.

"I thought of you, Andrew, the moment the funny little man told me what it was. Neither Hans nor Opal can ever make coffee to please you—well, this is your own. You crank it and it grinds the fresh coffee beans just the way *you* decide!" She placed it in his lap, and it was as heavy and awkward as it appeared. "I'll bet it's the first *used* anything you ever owned!"

The gesture was so like the girl—and at the same time so unlike her. But she was in a high-spirited mood, the kind that invariably planted hope in him, although he had to be apprehensive as to what it might portend.

"Thank you, Daughter. I'll cherish it as a memento of Derby Week." And then he hastily added, "And I'll grind hell out of the coffee beans till I get them *just* the way I like my coffee. I'll do it personally."

She laughed. "I want to be there to see it!" And then she lit still another cigarette.

It was time now, past time, to broach the dangerous subject. In the course of the day, even though Starbright was safe, Andrew had made up his mind. "Kimberley, what would you think of the idea of withdrawing Starbright from the Derby?"

Kimberley was quite still then, her pale brows knitting, her eyes more hurt and puzzled than angry. "So . . . so he called you too."

"Who?"

"Whoever he is. He phoned me while I was at Pepe's motel." She stood up very slowly. "He . . . he said he knew that no one would be tracing calls to Pepe's phone number."

"That does it." He stood up too. "Whoever's behind Starbright's theft is utterly ruthless and damn clever, and he means what he says. What did he threaten?"

"Oh, Andrew, cool it. He didn't threaten anything, only that if I didn't scratch Starbright I'd have to take what's coming, some stinking cliché like that, out of the old movies on TV. What can he do to me?"

Andrew preferred not to answer that or to consider it. Now, at any rate. "Jason Arnold and Doc Carpenter are convinced that Starbright's in no condition to run anyway."

"Andrew—" She was smiling, head tilted. "Andrew, you are *lying*—"

"An experience such as he's had is enough to shake up any thoroughbred, and he has contracted a cold, or influenza—"

"I spoke with Mr. Arnold just before my shower. Starbright's not even coughing now."

He knew he shouldn't have risked the lie. But he'd gone this far now, so he said, "He has two infected feet. You remember what happened to Spectacular Bid before he lost the Belmont Stakes—"

But she was shaking her head and smiling again. "Not yet, no infection yet, Andrew, and the girth gall's being treated successfully too."

Then she waited. He gave up on that line. But what occurred to him was even more important. "Kimb, if you don't withdraw him before the drawing for post positions tomorrow morning the only way he can be scratched is by order of the stewards. And if he's as healthy as you say, the track vet wouldn't advise them to allow it."

"I know what the man meant when he said ten o'clock tomorrow morning." She came closer, her eyes teasing now. "I know the rules and regulations, Andrew darling." She kissed him, very lightly, on the cheek. "So I'll tell you what I told him—" She strolled away, fluffing her hair. "Fuck off, Daddy-o."

"The Derby's only another race, Kimberley."

"Like hell. Blue Ridge has had six tries." Her voice took on a hard edge. "This time we win."

He knew that tone. He could not, would not anyway, risk an explosion. Those curious spells seemed to be growing more frequent, and deep inside he had to fight down a recurrent terror.

She was lighting still another cigarette, blowing smoke in short, sharp little puffs. "How is she in bed, Andrew? The Irish bitch." She began to move, aware of course that Andrew would not answer. "Clay's what they call sen-*say*-tional."

Now, suddenly, Andrew could think of nothing but evasion, escape. Before the girl continued to try to cheapen something that he did not consider cheap in the least. Where the hell had he gone wrong? Or had he? He damn well refused to take responsibility, even in his own mind, for Kimberley's personality, or condition—or illness, if that's what it was.

But, turning in the foyer with the coffee grinder in his hands, he said: "Kimberley, I'm going to ask Blake Raynolds to arrange a bodyguard for you."

Her chin was high and she was gesturing sharply with the cigarette. "You do and I'll throw him off the balcony personally."

Quietly Andrew said, "Bodyguards come in pretty big sizes, Daughter."

"Then I'll have Clay do it."

"I suspect," he said, "that Clay knows more of all this than he's told anyone. And I suspect too that he would agree with me."

"First you accuse him, now you defend him!"

He had to go. Somewhat angrily he said, "These people mean business. Men who would steal the Derby favorite off the Derby grounds are dangerous, and they're not afraid to take chances—"

"Daring is the word!"

"Kimberley, I'm trying to protect you, God damn it!"

"You're swearing, Andrew. What *will* you say next?"

He went out and closed the door sharply.

No point in suggesting she consult a doctor. The single time she had agreed the physician had suggested she see a psychiatrist. "He thinks I'm mad. Do you think I'm mad, Andrew, is that it?" she had demanded. Did *she* think it? Was that the fear which she would never acknowledge even to herself? Andrew was facing a dilemma that had become familiar by now. For some years he had clung to the hope that some miracle would come along to change things. And all the while he had suffered such deep concern, such compassion, such pity and apprehension that it had become an ache all through him.

He walked along the corridor and waited for the elevator. A man could be haunted forever . . . afterward . . . by the thought that if he'd done just this at just the right time . . . or thought of something to say, at just the proper moment, he might have prevented—

On the elevator he was, gratefully, alone. Going down only a short time ago, he had been like an adolescent boy, filled with excitement and eagerness at the thought of the night ahead. It wasn't fair. Something in his mind cried out: It is not fair. A man has to live too. A man has a right to his own life!

Stepping off the elevator at his own floor, he decided; he would telephone Blake, he would find out whether he had been able to learn anything about the name on the blue stationery, Marylou Wohlforth, and he would arrange that Blake engage a reputable and experienced bodyguard with instructions not to reveal his presence or function to Kimberley.

He let himself into his own suite. Then he would shower and change and go to suite 1719 to spend the night with Brigid Tyrone.

He had had his share of affairs since Irene had left—all of them basically unemotional, pleasantly physical, fleetingly satisfying—but in the last few hours he had made up his mind, for ill or good, that this was quite different and distinct. And damn it, he had his right to that too.

He went to the telephone and dialed Blake's room.

Chapter Eight

"HE sent me up and down that old Franklin Road till I thought I was chasing my tail."

"I'm the one chasing your tail."

"Count, you are really something else! Weird."

That he was, and more. Here he was in a restaurant about to have dinner with a woman he'd only met early this morning, very early, and had spent only part of one night with, yet being across the table from her made him tremulous with joy, quivering with lust. He'd been used, he'd been taken, he knew it. She'd only gone with him to his place in the hope of getting a story, and she was with him now for the same reason. But in the time they'd spent together she'd become a parasite in his bloodstream. She had come to absorb his existence. And while he drank deep of the cup of humiliation and abasement and self-mockery, nevertheless he had to have that body of hers, again and again. And would, whatever the cost.

"I could kill your friend Clayton Chalmers!"

Four more nights, four more days, and that would be it. She'd be off to Florida, and he'd head back to Baltimore. *Finis.* But he had to have that time between. That much had to be his.

"If they're never going to bring the steaks, I'll have another vodka gibson, Count."

Anything. He waved to the waiter and then showed him two fingers and pointed down at the table. It was a small intimate restaurant, well beyond her means but not his. Anything to please her, anything—

"They're telling it on the backstretch drums, here to Belmont and Hialeah to Hollywood Park, that the little pisser's horse was attacked by a dog. And that he choked the shit out of it, literally. Now don't you think he ought to be reported to the SPCA?"

Then, eyes drifting around the crowded room, she waited. Pretending that she wasn't. Well, that much he could confirm, but once you told her anything, she'd keep it up until she had the whole story. Then what he'd done and what Clay had done would be all for naught.

"Personally I don't believe it. And how come it wasn't in the evening paper?"

Because, Wyatt knew, the stewards and the TRPB didn't want it there. "Maybe because it's only a rumor," he said.

She leaned across the table then and smiled her dazzling smile. "Bullshit, Count. There's a whole juicy conspiracy somewhere, and you're part of it, and nobody, but nobody, can keep me from getting at it and printing it." She sat back. "So, mister, you can screw me all you want, but don't stonewall Janice Wessell."

He had wakened alone in the bed at five minutes after ten. Where the hell had she gone? His stomach pinched, the blood seemed to leave his body, and his testicles shrank. Was she really gone? He had not been himself all day. He'd been a stranger standing off and watching a man who was supposed to be Wyatt Slingerland going through the motions. Such as writing the broadcast text and hitting the air with it on time, but breathless—

"Well, at last!" The food had arrived. And the fresh drinks at the same time. "About time. I'm starving." Then she smiled up at the middle-aged waiter, flirting. "What'll I do first, eat my steak or drink my gibson?"

Wyatt was stricken with a spasm of jealousy. It had been that way all day.

"Well, here's to us," she toasted, for the fourth time. "And tonight."

Joseph Hayes

"And tomorrow night," he ventured.

She shrugged and her breasts moved deliciously beneath her sweater. "Who knows, who knows, Count?"

He drank his pink lady. Not *his* fourth. It seemed he had been drinking all day. He'd tried to phone, and finally he had gone to her motel. No one answered her door. He'd had the quick pain-filled suspicion that she was in there with someone else. Standing there, with maids working up and down the row of doors, he had been stunned at himself. He'd never felt this way before. But he couldn't lose her, not now—

"By the way," she asked, cutting her rare steak, "did you get a chance to read the story I gave you?"

He had read it. What could he say? "I studied it with great care, my dear."

"Was it even close to the truth?"

He tried to laugh. "Not by miles. Sheer fiction."

"That means it was close, right?"

Wrong. Conjecture. No details. Let her think what she likes, though.

From her motel he had gone to the Downs and into the club-house and up on the minuscule elevator to the press room, which was more or less deserted except for activity around the glassed-in PR offices. The row upon row of typewriters in the long room above the track were not being used, except for one. Janice Wessell, the woman herself, hard at work pounding the keys. He sat down, ignoring her, and tapped out the copy for his telecast, and when he was about to retreat to the small studio at one end, she came over and kissed him and then tilted her head and said, "I'll have a present for you when you finish." Mollified, he had then done his eleven o'clock combined radio and television broadcast. When he had finished, he had come out, but she had already disappeared. The guard who examined the hands of reporters under an ultraviolet light to see whether they were properly marked with an otherwise invisible stamp before admitting them to the elevator had given him a manuscript envelope with his name scrawled on it.

"Do you know, Count," she asked, as if making conversation over the table, "that racing is the biggest spectator sport in America?

It's an industry. Billions of bucks. Yet the press never seems to investigate, to probe—just superficial stories about results and such. Or which jockey has one ball or which trainer has the most winners, and things like that. Don't you think the public deserves to know more about what really goes on?"

"Tell the public to listen to Count Wyatt."

"Sure. He'll give them the straight shit, won't he? He won't even give it to the chick he's sleeping with all Derby Week."

There it was—a promise. Clear and loud. He went hollow. He couldn't eat. He didn't even want the drink. Hell, he'd been putting them down all day when he couldn't locate her. What the hell, why not tell her? At least how to *get* to the facts. He didn't have all of them himself—only that a ringer had been brought in during the fire pandemonium and that Clay Chalmers had this wild idea of getting it back and that in the end he had. But if he told her that much, she'd get the rest, and his word to Clay Chalmers would be kaput, and racing'd get another black eye it couldn't afford. Scandal was either the way to kill the goose that laid the golden egg or to make the egg larger—he had never been able to decide which.

On the way back to the apartment from the restaurant she didn't take off her dress or offer a blowjob. Even though he gave her every opportunity, short of unzipping his fly. Instead she pouted and yawned and said he had insulted her at dinner by criticizing her writing.

After he'd closed and locked the door, she turned on the huge television, and then she disappeared into the bedroom. Should he follow? God, he felt the fool. When he'd come back here before dinner, quite drunk in fact, he'd found her dressed and ready to go to dinner. Where had she been all day? Oh, she'd met a reporter for the *Indianapolis News* who'd amused her so much with some tale about what Kimberley Cameron had said about the monument in the center of his city looking like a sailor's prick that she'd gone to his motel with him and watched soap operas all afternoon. Even the casual way she had said it, as if there were no betrayal in it whatever, sent him into a tailspin, and again he had found himself standing off and observing this stranger he had become and even mocking himself, all to no avail whatsoever.

She came out of the bedroom now, naked. And smoking. And moving to turn up the sound on the television—all as if there were no one else in the room. He watched himself as he went to sit beside her on the sofa. All she did was lift her feet to the cocktail table, legs bent at the knees, and continue to smoke as before, saying, "I don't think I'm in the mood, hon. Not yet anyway."

Not *yet*. He pounced on every word, every suggestion of hope.

He went into the bathroom and, avoiding the sight of his paunchy soft body, took off his clothes and put on the black silk robe, which he tied about his body with quivering fingers, its soft smoothness only contributing to the carnal lubricous sensitivity of his every nerve and muscle. He considered taking an ice-cold shower, but the idea caused him to laugh mirthlessly. He returned to the studiolike living room.

She was as before, except that her knees were parted now, and she was lazily watching a baseball game. She was watching with a certain concentration that struck him as grossly lecherous. And he recalled having read recently that the average baseball player was considered too old at around forty.

"Did you know," she asked, at least acknowledging his presence as he sat in a deep chair, away from her, observing, "did you know that they allow girl reporters in the locker rooms now? Even the showers—"

So . . . he had not been wrong. And swift jealousy flowed through him like liquid fire. But, helpless, breathing hard, he heard himself say, "Maybe you're covering the wrong sport."

"I'm not covering a sport. I'm trying to get a human interest story out of an *event*. That's what my editor calls it." Then she sighed and glanced at him. "But I'm not having much luck, am I? Or"—and her voice suddenly rasped—"or getting much goddamn cooperation."

He did not answer. Her entire effort was so transparent, a kind of sexual blackmail, that he ought to be able to ridicule it into absurdity; it *was* in fact just that—absurd. But he was so trapped by his own morbid need and hunger that he couldn't even smile at his totally ridiculous predicament. Four nights and four days—he wanted them all, every minute of every one, every second.

Then why not tell her? Make her promise to hold the story until the Derby was over.

Promise? What would a promise mean?

But . . . after all, whom was he trying to protect? Andrew Cameron? His bitchy daughter? Clay Chalmers? Racing itself?

"Do you know JD Edwards?" Janice asked, out of nowhere.

"I interviewed him briefly." His throat was dry, his tongue thick. "Why?"

"Oh, I was just wondering. Could you introduce me?"

"I could. Why?"

"Don't keep asking why. Watch the fucking game!"

He turned to the screen. A tall lanky black was swinging the bat loosely, with easy grace and slim strength, waiting for the pitch.

"They say," Janice said now in a languid, contemplative tone, "they say jigs have longer cocks. Did you ever hear that?"

He had. Many times. He had also read, or heard, that it was a myth. But the question was like a blow to his midsection.

The black swung, connected, and the camera followed the ball on a short line drive to third, where it was caught.

"I'm staying tonight on one condition, Count—"

"Yes? Yes?"

"Look all you want but hands off the candy."

He did not answer.

"Is it a deal?"

What if he told her what she wanted to know?

"It's a deal," he said miserably.

He wouldn't touch her, but he'd get so blind drunk that in time he wouldn't care whether he did or not.

". . . not yet, not yet . . . oh, God, Clay . . . more, but not yet, and *more*, again . . . oh, God, I can't stand it . . . Clay, Clay, *Clay* . . . no, not quite, not . . . love you, love you, *love* you, Clay . . . love me, tell me, love me . . . ohmigod, ohmi*god* . . . not yet, no . . . but again, again, *again* . . . almost, almost, love, love, almost . . . yes, yes, yes, now, now, NOW—"

She screamed. Her mouth was wide open and she uttered a single scream of pure joy.

He remained on her and within her, and they were both struggling to breathe, gasping, and her eyes were closed and her head still rolled from side to side, and he knew that he had never, never before, felt such intensity and total abandonment in a woman, and he himself was shattered, depleted, his mind and body floating—

The pain had returned to his shoulder where the bullet had grazed it. When had it come back? To hell with it. He was empty, he was full to the brim, bursting yet empty too, he was alive, and so was she, murmuring now: "Too much, it's oh, Clay, it's too much—"

But it was not too much, could never be, never would be. Already, still within her, he wanted her again, now.

But he kissed her lips, closed now, and moist, and then he rolled aside, both still breathing hard, both with that stunned look and feeling, like people who have been lost in a cave and are just now feeling sunlight, blinded in the cave and now blinded again.

"When we come back," she said. "Clay?"

"Yes, Kimb. When we come back."

"I'm—are you hungry?"

He laughed and went into the bathroom, where he'd left his clothes, and he dressed, slowly, without showering because she was hungry, and the long evening lay ahead, and then the long night. In the mirror he saw the suggestion of blood on the white bandage that Elijah had put on his shoulder, where the flesh was stinging now. He glanced at his face in the mirror: narrow with the crooked nose—Owen's gift, but he would not think of Owen now, he would not let black hate move into that vast peaceful place where light was shining—and the dark-weathered skin, from the Florida sun, and the black hair over dark eyes, an ordinary face.

"I bought you a present," she called from the bedroom. "Now don't be cross with me, Clay, it's only a small present." And then, apologizing more, knowing his foolish stubborn pride, or whatever it was: "I had to thank you, didn't I? For what you did for Starbright."

He opened the door. She was drawing an apricot-colored dress down over her body, which was white in contrast to the dress and her face and arms, and then she was stroking her long blond hair with a brush as he passed through into what she called the sitting room but which he always thought of as a living room.

"I hope you'll like it, Clay. Tell me before you look that you'll love it, even if you lie later."

"I'll love it," he lied, because he still didn't like the idea of her giving him gifts, and hadn't she said she wanted to go to bed before going to dinner so she could thank him for Starbright? And *hadn't* she thanked him? In spades.

"It's on the sofa." But before he could cross to it her tone changed, hardened: "Where were you all day? I went to see Starbright after the boat race, and you weren't anywhere on the backstretch."

He picked up the gift and recognized it. "I was at the hospital with Bernie." It was a stereopticon with a photograph inserted, a picture divided down the middle with identical scenes right and left, so that looking through the hooded glass viewer you could slide the card forward and back on a length of varnished wood until the two views became one, with a natural third dimension. He hadn't seen one for years, but his mother had had one which old Toby had carried on their wanderings for a while when he was a kid. "Bernie asked me to thank you for the flowers, Kimb."

"Is he better?" The accusing note had left her tone. "Is he in pain?"

"He's sore as hell that he can't work." He was adjusting the view. And looking at two Eiffel Towers. "And his shoulder's a mess." Hell, yes, he was in pain—another of Owen's gifts. The two towers became one, surrounded by the black-and-white rooftops of Paris. "Where'd you get this thing?"

She appeared: slim, radiant, her hair tight and bright around her face now, and her shoulders soft and bare. "Jeffersonville, Indiana, that's where! For the first time in my life I saw the boat race the way I wanted to see it. Oh, Clay, it was beautiful! All those people, having fun, really having fun. I ate strawberry ices and ice-cream cones and hot dogs, and I'm starving." But she went to the glass-topped bar. "I felt about nine or ten years old again." She was speaking in a rush, her words hushed and fast. "And when I saw that, I nearly went wild. And I saw the Drakes." She poured a stiff bourbon and splashed soda into it, carelessly. "You know, the druggist man and his wife, he owns Prescription, and I hope his horse comes in second." She drank half the glass fast. "No, not second—third, after Hotspur."

He was looking at a view of Niagara Falls. "Thank you." She had begun to puzzle him. Again. "Prescription's workouts aren't exactly mind-boggling."

"Oh, the way I used to love those views when I was a girl. The Wisconsin Dells, have you seen that one, and the Leaning Tower of Pisa and—" She rushed to the balcony doors. "It's suffocating in here! I can't—can you breathe in a room like this?" She threw open two glass doors and, standing between them, put her head back and drank. "I'll be thirty years old in August. Thirty years, Clay. Is that old?"

"Not to me." He put the stereopticon on the seat and stood up. "Kimb, the reason the maid closed the doors is probably that the air conditioning is on."

"I hate it, the air conditioning doesn't *work*, it's stifling, the maid's crazy." She returned to the bar. "Don't you want one?"

Slowly he said: "I'll wait till we get to the restaurant, thanks."

"Oh, yes, I forgot. Well, go on punishing yourself all your life if you want to." She splashed more whisky into the glass, added neither soda nor ice, drank with her back to him. "What's . . . what's happening to me, Clay? I'm frightened."

He went to her and took the glass, which she relinquished without objection, and then he turned her to face him. Gently he said, "Take it easy now, Kimb. Take it easy. Nothing's happening to you." But he was not so damn certain. "If you're starving, let's get some food."

"Sometimes I think I'm just coming unglued, coming all apart, it's happening now. Oh, God, help me, someone help me—"

She went limp and leaned against him and whispered: "Take care of me, Clay. Someone. Please take care of me." Then she kissed his cheek, her lips damp and perspiration glistening on her shoulders. "Then . . . when we come back, destroy me. In that way you have. Where nothing else is, nothing else even exists—oh, Clay, promise me you'll destroy me again when we come back."

Softly, moved, he said, "I promise." And then he added, "The pleasure's mine too, you know."

She smiled into his face then, eyes blinking fast. "Is it that way for you too? When nothing else even exists, not even the room, not the track or tomorrow or Saturday. *Is it?*"

He took her hand and they went out and into the corridor and along it in silence to the elevator. Where she pulled him to an abrupt halt as he reached to jab the lighted button.

"Let's walk." Surprised, he looked at her. And she said sharply, "You heard me, I want to walk!"

The elevator arrived and the doors slid open and she stood staring into the empty cubicle. "I can't get in there, I'll . . . I'll smother!" It was as if she were actually refusing to step into that small enclosed space.

But, frowning, he said, "It's nineteen flights, Kimb."

And she changed again: "It's all downhill, isn't it?" Like a girl excited by the prospect, this time she grabbed his hand and drew him to the stairway door, threw it open herself, and then went in. He followed, but going down the first steel flight in the narrow concrete stairwell, she released him and plunged ahead and down, running sure-footed but fast, very fast, calling, "It's worse, this is worse, hurry, come on, *hurry!*" Her voice echoed and then died, and he could hear the sharp tapping of her heels as she disappeared around a corner of railing. He did not try to follow her with his eyes or to catch up but continued down, two steps at a time, still hearing the rhythm of her hurrying footsteps below him.

When, breathless, he reached the lobby, she had collapsed onto a huge upholstered couch, and her body was heaving as she struggled for breath. He sat beside her.

"Look, Kimb, there's no hurry. You can't be that hungry." But he felt the fool because hunger played no part in this, only panic.

"Those ugly blank walls," she finally managed to say. "So gray, so ugly, didn't you notice? I . . . . I thought . . . they felt like they were closing in."

"Take your time," he said. But the startlement remained: a thousand questions, amazement. "Your car or my truck, take your choice when you get your breath—"

And again she smiled, her face clearing. "I'd rather walk."

"I won the Trial, remember? I'll blow you to a taxi ride."

Then her face was not clear again; her eyes sparked green fire and her pale brows came together over them. "I said—walk!"

Not even annoyed, still bewildered, he shrugged. "Walk it is, child."

Again a change, softly: "Why do you call me that? You never called me that before." She stood up, actually smiling. "I like it."

They walked. They strolled, hand in hand, hers oddly cool and grasping, but otherwise the mood seemed to have passed. Whatever the hell it was. Whatever the hell it signified. She did seem a child, really—but a happy, relaxed one now, a girl of sixteen or seventeen, walking at a leisurely pace with her boyfriend along a city street. They passed between shops and restaurants along the wide mall, which was free of vehicles but busy at this time of early evening. They looked into windows at nothing in particular, and he found himself unwinding, her outbursts of hysteria behind, a momentary mood, her own symptoms of what they call Derby fever perhaps.

She giggled. He followed her gaze. In the lower corner of the window of a bar was a sign reading Male Dancers. One of the gay bars. He had heard there were two on the mall. She tried to look into the smoke-filled room, which was dim but crowded with men, but then she drew him along again, still smiling in an amused distant way.

"I have a secret," she said quietly. "I have a secret from you, Clay."

"I know: You're a Lesbian."

Then she laughed, a pleasant easy sound, but teasing—the laughter of an adolescent. And he realized that she hadn't spoken a single oath or obscenity all evening. "If you don't know better than that, you never will."

And he laughed too. "Checkmate," he said.

"I know someone who's gay, though—"

"I know a few myself. But I keep my distance."

"No, no—this is someone you couldn't guess. You'd never know in a million years. He's famous."

"You *want* me to guess?"

"No, no, I'd never tell you if you did. It's a secret between him and me. So don't guess." She leaned against him, walking. "I'm so glad it's not you."

"I'm a little relieved myself."

"You don't mind my having a secret?"

"Not if you get this much pleasure out of it." Personally he didn't give a damn who was gay and who was not. "Do you know where we're going?"

"Does it matter? I could float along like this all night."

"You're the one who was starving."

"I almost bought you a T-shirt this afternoon. With words on the front. Like *Surfers Do It Better*, or *Sex Now, Pay Later*."

"Some of the exercise kids and hot-walkers wear them."

"What are you looking at?"

The demand came so suddenly, and out of nowhere, and in such a changed tone, that he thought for a split second that he had not heard. She had stopped and she was staring into his eyes with such sharp and angry accusation that, bewildered, he could not think of what to say.

"I saw you! If you want her, go get her."

"Want who? What the hell are you—"

"Don't lie." Heads were turning. "It only makes it worse. It makes me a fool. Don't *lie*!"

"Kimberley, get hold of yourself, for God's sake."

"That's what Andrew always says!"

"What are you talking about?"

"I saw you. You can still catch up with her. Go on, go after the little bitch if that's what you want!"

Still dumbfounded, he snapped: "Stop this, damn it!"

"She's prettier than I am. *Younger*." Her eyes were keen points and her lips were beginning to curl with contempt. "If that's what you want—you can't get enough, can you? Oh, I know that look." She rose to her toes to peer over his shoulder. "She's still back there, go on, go, *get away from me*!"

He twisted his head.

"Take a good look! Do you like green? *I* can wear green!"

In the crowd he saw faces staring, some turned away politely. He saw a large man in a dark suit whom he'd noticed in the hotel lobby. There was a flash of bright green beyond him among the other figures. He uttered a sigh and turned.

She was gone.

He reached the corner in time to see her apricot-colored dress, moving fast, turning into an entrance with a restaurant marquee above it. He had no choice but to follow. In a cloud of astonishment that was beginning to turn to anger inside him he went along the street and into the restaurant. Wondering whether he should.

She was being seated by the headwaiter at a table for two, her face composed. Until she saw him. Then, as if she had been expecting him to join her for dinner, she waved, and when he reached her, the waiter bowing himself away, she began to chatter in a bright satirical tone.

"You're on time. Fancy that. Did you manage to shake that wife of yours?" The false brittleness of her tone suggested fun and games and her eyes were filled with mockery. "Well, aren't you going to kiss me?"

The fool again, the anger taking hold at last, he leaned across the table, tried to kiss her on the cheek casually, but she turned her head and his mouth met hers and as they kissed he felt her tongue darting against his closed lips. Then as he straightened and sat down across from her, her hand reached across the table and lay there, almost beseeching him to take it. Damned if he would.

Knowing the suggestion that she was acting this way because of the drinks was a lie, he said, "Let's not have a cocktail before we eat."

She was leaning over the table then, all hostility gone from her features, her voice soft and pleading, "Forgive me, Clay. Please forgive me. I can't bear to hurt you. Nothing makes me more miserable."

The sincerity and the pathetic candor reached him, and he felt himself go warm and hollow. "Kimb, you're a little fool," he whispered. But he knew better than that too: The two stiff bourbons did not account for her mercurial moods, nor did her being a fool in love. If that's what she was. "Have you eaten here before?" It was a stupid thing to say, and her arm still lay bare and entreating on the table, so he took her hand and felt it close over his with something like desperation, damp and clutching.

But her tone was light again and playful: "Never. But I'm told it's one of the best. Strictly four-star Michelin. But not French." Her voice grew louder. "Tell me now, what kind of a day did you have, my sweet? How many stocks did you sell, how many worthless bonds, how many customers did you rip off?"

Let her have it her way—whatever would pull her out of her mood. "I ripped off a few. One was a ninety-year-old widow with nine million dollars and a cleft palate."

"Delightful! Did she talk like this? Ywong mun, make mu a mullion un make ut in cash so I can take ut wit-me to mu mausoleum?" Her face had been twisting grotesquely, and now she sat back, still clinging to his hand, and glanced up at a middle-aged waiter who was standing at the ready. "Do you have Tennessee walking whisky, young man?"

He nodded his gray dignified head, unsmiling. "Jack Daniel's, miss?"

"Double. With goddamn little soda, preferably that fucking Perrier water."

"And you, sir?" He didn't blink.

"A small glass of Chablis, thank you."

"Very cold, yes, sir? My name is Alexander, and I'll be serving you this evening. *Thank* you."

And when he was gone, Clay said, "I'd suggest you go easy on the booze. It goes straight to cleft palates."

She laughed. "Don't sound like Andrew again, please. I know what I want. Roast duckling, with orange sauce—a huge roast duckling with all the trimmings!"

Over her shoulder Clay caught sight of the same man he had seen in the hotel lobby and later on the street: burly, sallow-faced with red blotches here and there, and graying, thinning hair.

Alerted, he decided to say nothing that might trigger an outburst: No predicting what twist or turn her mind might take tonight.

"I'm sorry, Clay." Her face and voice were soft and abject again. "About what I said. I know you love me. And only me. I know."

"Forget it," he said, knowing he wouldn't, but there was no time to try to puzzle it out now. "Here are our drinks."

She released his hand, and he realized that it was dry again—very dry. She lifted her tall glass across the table to clink against his, and they drank.

Then she said, "I saw an ancient movie on the late-late-late show one night. Charles Boyer—remember him? He was a monk."

Monks again. Clay thought of the bitch Janice Wessell. When he had phoned to thank Wyatt and to report on the success of their deceit, she had answered: "Oh, you. Well, listen, crud, the Count's coughed up the whole story. So screw you." It may or may not have been the truth; he was inclined to think not from the tone of her voice.

". . . jumped over the wall. Somewhere in Africa, I think. Or am I getting it mixed up with some other show with Boyer? Anyway, he'd been locked away all those years, and then, when he's out, he stumbles into a dance hall with this exotic dancer, and he sits there and stares at her body." While she was speaking, Kimberley was gnawing and crunching at carrots, celery, radishes, lifting them from the iced glass tray and devouring them as if she had not eaten for days. ". . . pathetic but at the same time—terrific." That look in his eyes. "Tell me the truth, Clay, don't you sometimes see someone, at a track or in a bar or on the street, and get a sort of overwhelming desire? *Lust.* Doesn't matter who he is—*she* is . . . some total stranger . . . you feel you can't help yourself, you've got to have him—*her.* Don't you?"

Not exactly. And not often. But he said, "Sometimes, sure."

"There! I'm glad you didn't lie. I *hate* people who lie to me!"

"Kimb—"

"When are we going to order?"

After they had and the food had come, she ate in absorbed silence, as if he weren't there. Like a gluttonous child. Washing it down with wine he'd ordered at her suggestion. And then, for dessert, she ordered caramel custards, two, for herself, and asked to see the pastry cart, please.

Astonished, Clay didn't know whether it was safe to comment or not. But he said, "Zach Massing, who'll ride Hotspur, has one hell of a time with hunger. Five hundred calories a meal. Maximum. And no water. Pills to dehydrate, pills to kill hunger. Hours in a steam bath till he's so dizzy and weak he can hardly walk." He didn't mention Zach's practice of placing two fingers down his throat. But she didn't seem to be listening anyway.

Pouring wine from the bottle herself, Kimberley said, "Andrew wants me to scratch Starbright."

Carefully Clay said, "I spoke with Jason Arnold."

"So did I."

"Then you know: No infection has developed, he's been medicated in case it should, and the cough is gone."

A sly and knowing look came into her eyes, and she leaned across the table confidentially. "Andrew knows that too."

One damn shock after another tonight. "Then why does he want to scratch the colt?" He did not add: after all the goddamn trouble I went through getting him back. "I don't understand, Kimb."

"Andrew's envious."

"Envious?" The fool again. And she had changed again. Now she was a conspirator about to reveal a dark secret. "What the hell do you mean by that, Kimb?"

"You don't know Andrew the way I do, Clay."

"Granted."

"Blue Ridge has had six colts in the Derby and not one has won."

"All the more reason to keep him in."

"No, no, no. Starbright's not Blue Ridge. Starbright's mine and mine alone." It was like an announcement from a high place. "*Now* do you see?"

The dessert arrived, and the pastry wagon as well. She chose an enormous slice of black chocolate cake. He asked for coffee and the check. Damned if he'd offer brandy now. They were alone again.

But her mind had moved around another corner. "Don't fret, my sweet. I won't get fat. Not Kimberley. She rides it off." And then, spooning the caramel: "I'll be as good a lay as always."

Her crudity touched a nerve in him, and he looked away. The dark-suited stranger was still there at his table, reading a newspaper. Not the *Racing Form*.

Kimberley laughed. "You look so shocked." It seemed to delight her. "Do you know who you remind me of? Andrew over and over!"

Quietly he said, "I guess I just don't think of you . . . of us . . . as a lay."

Her laugh ran down and her face twisted and her eyes looked hurt and perplexed—lost. "I don't either, Clay. Honestly, I don't either." Then she threw down her spoon with a clatter. "Let's get out of here! Pay the fucker and let's get out of here!"

While they were waiting for the bill Clay asked, because he had to: "What reason does your father give—for wanting you to withdraw Starbright?"

Her eyes drifted away then. "Oh, he claims he's worried about me. What . . . might happen to me."

"Nobody's going to do anything to you, Kimb."

"He doesn't know that. I guess he thinks maybe they'll try to kidnap *me*."

It came to him then, in a quick knowing flash, why the husky man in the dark pin-striped suit was paying *his* bill and folding his paper. It made sense, it's what Andrew Cameron would do: If he even suspected his daughter might be in danger, he'd hire someone to protect her. But why would such an idea occur to the man?

On the street he did not turn to look. Convinced, he did not have to. A taxi stood at the curb.

Clay glanced at her. That same panic had returned to her face as she stared at it. "Do you want me to suffocate?" she demanded.

No. Or even to imagine she might. But he'd never known her to act this way before. Riding in cars and cabs and elevators was a normal part of life and had always been. He'd never seen her in this state, and utterly confounded, he accompanied her in silence as they walked back to the hotel.

Her hand was in his, and icy, almost clammy. And she spoke only once: "Do you think something horrible's happening to me, Clay?"

Did he? He didn't know. But he said, "It's the tension, probably, Kimb. And what you went through last night and this morning."

But was it? Did that explain it? Possibly. Still—

When they reached the riverfront, the *Belle of Louisville* was leaving the dock, its lights pale in the late dusk but its whistle piping in short spurts of steam and sound and an orchestra playing, dancers moving on its decks. They stood and watched its departure.

"I wish we were on it, don't you?" Kimberley asked softly, forlornly. "And I wish . . . I wish it would keep going and going and going—I don't know where."

Was this the time? Should he risk it?

He decided. "On Sunday," he said, "we could fly to New York." She did not move. "We could get a plane or a ship. Anywhere we wanted to go."

"Did I ruin dinner?" she asked, as if he had not spoken. "I'm always ruining things. And hurting people. Have I hurt you, Clay?"

Yes. But not tonight. "Did you hear me, Kimb?" He was in this deep. "After the Derby, no matter who wins, we could go anywhere we decide."

"But . . . we can't, Clay. We both know."

"I don't."

"You never did, did you?"

"No, Kimb. I never did."

She turned to him then. Hysteria was in her face again. Panic. Her eyes were brilliant and miserable. He recalled that same expression seven years ago. *You know we can't now, Clay. After what you did. After what you did to Lord Randolph.* But that was seven years ago. This was now. And the reason he was here.

"Why not?" he demanded, but gently.

She uttered a deep sound in her throat, as if she were choking, and her eyes flashed hate and fury, and she whirled about, and then she was running, holding her dress high, toward the hotel and up the steps and into the lobby.

Should he follow? He had no choice. Not now. He'd come this far, over the years, over the miles—damned if he'd take it again, damned if he'd give up now.

She was entering the elevator by the time he came into the lobby, and he lunged across the space to join her just as the doors were closing. The shorter and older and fleshier of the two Japanese was in it, flanked by two blondes who looked like expensive hookers— Hosomoto Takashi, owner of Fuji Mist. And also along for the ride was the man in the dark pin-striped suit, who did not glance at him. Kimberley had collapsed against the wall, as if all fight, all fury had left her; she looked as if she might sink to the floor, and her face was pale beneath the tan. Her eyes, haggard, were closed.

The elevator rose. He reached to touch the button for nineteen and it lighted. Silence except for the humming of the cables and the muted piped-in music.

At nineteen it glided to a stop, the door slid open, and he turned to her. Her eyes were open now. They were fixed on one of the blondes. She did not move. He stepped out and waited.

"What are you staring at?" Kimberley demanded of the blonde. "Who the hell do you think you're staring at?" And then, moving to disembark: "Am I so odd-looking?" She paused in the aperture. "Well, what about you? Put your nipples back in your dress and fuck off!" She came into the hall. "I'm sick from the stink of Woolworth Number Five."

The doors closed. She ignored him and slouched along the hall in the wrong direction. He stepped quickly and took her arm, which seemed frail and lifeless, and turned her about. She looked up then and seemed to recognize him. She wrenched her arm away, causing pain to erupt in his shoulder, and lifting her head, she made a show of walking steadily in an uncertain path toward her room.

He followed.

In the living room she was pouring whisky. He went to her.

"No more of that," he said, knowing she was not drunk, knowing that but little else. "I'll put you to bed if you'll let me."

Her chin came up, trembling. "You will not tell me what to do. Not ever. You or anyone." Then she caught sight of the windows and darted, catlike, around him and toward the balcony. "She closed the windows, the maid closed the windows. You're all against me!"

She threw open the French doors so violently that a pane of glass cracked and shattered.

"Everyone hates me!"

She was on the balcony then, leaning over the iron-grille balustrade, her back to him, the lights of the city sparkling beyond.

"Why has everyone always hated me?"

Her voice was so filled with pain that he followed her. Again. He stopped in the open doorway.

She whirled to face him, her face twisted, her body slightly crouched, as if she might leap at him. "You want me to scratch Starbright too, don't you? Don't *lie!*"

He heard the level anger in his own voice. "I didn't do what I did to get him back only to have you scratch him now."

"Liar!" It was a snarling bellow. "You know Starbright can beat Hotspur, and you have to win!" She reminded him of a trapped, vicious animal.

He took a step. "Kimberley, that's crazy. I—"

"Crazy. *You* think I'm crazy too. That's what Andrew thinks."

She moved toward him, eyes wild and furious. "You think I'm crazy, you said so! *Don't* you?"

Was that what she really feared? Was it not so much his accusations—for he had not made any—but some torturing doubt inside herself? Was the question in *her* mind?

"Kimberley, let me help you."

"Help me?" Her tone was scathing, her teeth bared. "I don't need your help." She came closer. "Andrew was right. He suspected you last night and he was right!"

It made no sense. None of this made sense. But—

"You took Starbright and took the money and then you brought him back with infection and influenza."

He could see the twisted logic. The sick logic. And his own terror deepened.

"Why didn't you break his foreleg with a baseball bat while you had him?"

"Kimberley, you're going to listen—"

But as he stepped toward her she came to meet him, her hands lashing out at him, fists pounding face and chest and the side of his head. She was muttering incomprehensible sounds of fury and hate, animallike, junglelike.

He slapped her, hard, once, across the face.

She stood blinking at him as the imprint of his open palm reddened one cheek.

Then she said: "See. You hate me."

She turned and in what appeared to be a single movement lifted the apricot-colored dress over her head and tossed it out from the balcony. Naked, she faced him again.

"There. Don't you *want* me? Don't you?" And she whirled about to shout: "Out there, down there, doesn't *anyone* want me?"

He came up behind her, fast but not fast enough, because as he caught her around the body she twisted and brought up her hands, claws this time, her catlike face contorting and ugly. She raked her nails down both sides of his face, hard. He felt sharp, hot streaks down his flesh. But he held on and her face was close.

Suddenly she was kissing him, holding him, still fighting but clinging, and her mouth opened and she bit his lip. He tasted blood and felt the cutting pain but still held on.

And then he was shaking her. He was grasping her by her slender bare shoulders and he was shaking her body, lifting her feet from the floor, so that she was twisting and kicking and snarling all at the same time while he continued to shake her until her head went weakly back and the fight left her entire body and she went limp, and her eyes rolled back into her head, and then her lids closed.

Then he pulled her against him, not sure she was still conscious, and he held her there, his hands still clinging to her shoulders until he released them and placed his arms around her in a complete hug.

He could feel her heart thumping against his chest and her breath against his ear.

Somewhere down below on the river a tugboat whistle sounded.

He released her and, stooping, picked up her body in both arms and carried her into the living room and across it and into the dim bedroom. He placed her tenderly on the bed, which had been turned down by the maid, and he drew the sheet and blanket up and over her body.

Without opening her eyes—was she asleep already?—she rolled

onto one side and drew her knees up. He adjusted the sheet at her neck. He did not kiss her but stood back to gaze down.

She looked like a sleeping child. At peace. But fragile and vulnerable.

"Good night, Clay."

He was not sure he had heard. A whisper. Her lips did not seem to move.

"Good night, my love, my one and only love—"

He said nothing. He did not turn out the lights in the living room.

In the elevator he wondered whether he should leave her.

Then he changed his mind, touched a button to stop the elevator and then another to take him up to Andrew Cameron's floor. But when he buzzed and then knocked repeatedly on the door, there was no answer. Should he wait? So many questions. Would she sleep till morning? If she didn't, would his presence calm her or only stir more wildness, or violence? Damned if he knew. Should he call the hotel doctor?

Then he remembered the man in the dark suit. So he went down again, this time all the way to the lobby.

The man was sitting on a couch, a couch situated so that he commanded a view of the stairway exit and the elevators. There were only a few guests and bellboys in the lobby.

He crossed directly to stand before the man. Who was older than he had appeared on the street and in the restaurant: his hair thinner and grayer, his suit more crumpled, his pale eyes even more lazy and guarded.

"Who are you working for?"

The man looked up from the magazine which he had been paging. He took a lighted cigar from between his thick lips. "Do I know you?" His voice was mild and friendly.

"I think you know who I am. And I think we're both on the same side."

The man stood. He was taller and somewhat heavier than he had appeared to be. "That depends. Whose side are you on, Mr. Chalmers?"

"I'm in love with Kimberley Cameron."

"You're a lucky man. My name's Peter Cowley. Do you want to see my credentials?"

"Yes."

The man reached inside an open pocket and withdrew a wallet and flipped it open. He was a private investigator but not a Pink. "Mr. Andrew Cameron hired me. To look after his daughter."

"Then why aren't you doing it?"

"I been waiting for you to leave."

"I'm leaving."

"Then I'll go upstairs."

"Good idea."

"I figured a guy could kill a Doberman with his bare hands, the kid was in pretty good company. Good night, Mr. Chalmers."

"Are your instructions not to let her see you?"

"If possible—yes."

"Then don't. Good night, Mr. Cowley."

Chapter Nine

"Mr. Haslam—"

"Hello, Mr. Edwards. What you doing at the track this time of morning? We just had a fair workout. You see it?"

"I saw it. Listen, Haslam—"

"Also Ran keeps getting better. Did five furlongs in 1:01 and change, and track's still kind of muddy at that."

"Haslam, you're fired."

"What'd you say?"

"I said I came here to tell you you're canned."

"Mr. Edwards, you're not yourself. You need some sleep and—"

"Get your ass outta here and stay away from my horse, turkey. That plain enough for you?"

"Mr. Edwards, the stewards won't let you run a horse without a licensed trainer."

"Is that a threat?"

"No, sir. It's not a threat, I'm only trying to—"

"Stop callin' me sir!"

"Whatever you say, you're the boss. Only I—"

"Trainers're a dime to the dozen."

"We do have a contract—"

"I'll pay you off, honky."

"It's not the money, sir—Mr. Edwards, I mean. Look, I'll work the next three days, through the race. Then, if he doesn't run in the money, you don't owe me a cent. I can't be any more fair than that, can I?"

"Don't do me any favors."

"I've come this far with you. I don't know what the hell I've done to get your back up, but I'm kind of fond of that gelding of yours—"

"You said he couldn't win."

"I never said that. I said I'd do my best. That's all any man—"

"I was shootin' craps and it just came over me."

"I'm afraid you'll have a hard time getting—"

"Nobody else'll work for this nigger, that what you sayin'?"

"Not because you're black. Hell, JD, I—"

"Some of your best friends are dinges, that it?"

"The other trainers might—"

"Trainers're like jockeys. I see 'em out here hustling jobs. I'll get one."

"That's what I kind of doubt. This late, I mean."

"Man, Also Ran is a *Derby* horse! The Kentucky *Derby*!"

"I wish you luck."

"Got to be somebody don't call me a shine behind my back."

"I never did. But . . . he's your horse. It's your decision."

"Now y'know what that is? That's goddamn *white* of you, honky."

Had enough? It's only Thursday, so don't go away mad, the best is yet to come! This is Count Wyatt who, after braving grave impediments and sly obstructionists, is back at his familiar stand, cigarette alight and eyes red-streaked but aglow. And how is your moneybag holding out? Have you had to cry havoc and telephone Uncle Shekels or your banker? When will they start using American Express and Master Charge cards at the pari-mutuel windows?

The gods, who have not looked kindly on our innocent revelries to date, have been ominously quiet the past twenty-four hours—are they biding their time, are they conjuring up new disasters? Only

*two and a half more days to the big D now—do the spirits that be
have more shocks up their raveled sleeve of malice?*

Meanwhile, business as usual. One hour ago, punctually at ten
A.M., *in the outer office of the racing secretary—where the decibel
count reached outer-space proportions as owners, trainers, imposters,
stewards, officials of every stripe and color, at least three movie stars,
a pickpocket or two, the press in general, and your obedient servant
in particular gathered in perspiring excitement—the drawing of post
positions in this year's Derby was duly endured and consummated.
In the absence of Miss Kimberley Cameron, whose disappearing act
was not explained (shame on you, princess), a very sexy movie star
did the honors, whether she knew what she was doing or not. She was
assisted by the wife of Mr. JD Edwards, known far and wide in
baseball circles and the owner of the colt unfortunately baptized
Also Ran. The motion picture star, who will remain mercifully
nameless, shook the bottle, among other things. The process—just so
you will be able to edify your grandchildren someday—goes something like this. The racing secretary declares the entry box for the
Kentucky Derby officially closed. This morning Mrs. Edwards pre-
sided over that box, containing the eight entry forms. Miss Cinema
shakes the bottle provided and drops out one pellet at a time, each
one numbered, and then she calls out that number. Mrs. Edwards
then draws from the box one entry form and announces the name of
the horse. Thereby the horse is numbered according to the pellet and
this is that entry's post position. What will they think of next? It is
now my God-given duty to pass along to you, the breath-holding
public, the information already known on backstretches as far away
as San Francisco and Paris and Tokyo.*

Position Number One—closest to the rail and with presumably
much less distance to cover where inches are vital and yards are as-
tronomical lengths: Prescription, owned by Walter Drake of Terre
Haute, Indiana. Number Two: Fireaway, from the Southwest.
Three: Irish Thrall, from, you guessed it, the Emerald Isle itself.
Four: Also Ran. Five: Bonne Fete, a frisky filly from France. Six:
Fuji Mist, still wrapped in the clouds of mystery like the volcano for
which he was named. Number Seven: Hotspur, the little black from
Florida and points south. And last but far, far from least, the odds-*

on favorite per the morning line: Starbright himself, prince to the absent princess, who will begin on the outside.

The original field—a possible twelve or thirteen—has been, as fans know, decimated by a series of misfortunes. Eliminated have been: Vincent Van, Ancient Mariner, True Blue, the unlikely Dealer's Choice, and the uncertain Eric the Red. So it's a short field but a respectable one, and after this morning's ceremony no entry can be withdrawn, or scratched, at the will or whim of his owner. Only the track stewards—upon the advice of the track veterinarian, who must certify a horse as unfit—have that option. So . . . there's your field. Take your choice, and may good fortune shine on all of you.

With the off-and-on rain with which we have been favored the track remains somewhat muddy, and the long-range official forecast is for more showers through tonight with a clearing tomorrow. My prediction is that the Kentucky Oaks—post time five-thirty tomorrow P.M., fillies only, no males need apply—will be run on a cuppy track, and then, if we can trust the U.S. Weather Bureau, which we can't, the Derby course will be hard and fast by Saturday. But the weather is even less predictable than a Derby.

Now for a little thissa and thatta and some questions to ponder in your drunken reveries:

The odds on Hotspur and Fireaway, after that sensational Derby Trial day before yesterday, have evened out; both stand at seven to one. Nothing like a little brotherly competition.

The fire in the Derby barn on Tuesday night has been officially declared accidental: No evidence of arson has been uncovered after a most meticulous investigation. Which fact will not quell the suspicion of those who see the devil's handiwork in the falling of a star.

And oh, yes, lest I overlook more trivia: That object of sentimental value lost the night of the fire has been returned to the owner and the reward has been gratefully paid. Your obedient servant has learned that it was a pearl necklace which an owner's wife carelessly wore to bed and then forgot to remove when she made the hurried and frantic journey to the Downs to look in on her runner. She is happy, her husband is happy, and the lucky gallop girl who found it is a hundred thousand dollars richer, and she is ecstatic and considering retirement at age nineteen.

Which official Derby entry has no trainer as of this morning? It's for Count Wyatt to know and you to guess, so there.

Is it true that there's a horse pining away and refusing to eat because someone he loves cannot be with him? Which of the horses named above, and why?

And finally, with time running out, is it true that a man bit a dog on the backstretch? If so, it's news, and that's the reason you didn't read about it in your daily newspapers.

If the gods can't smile, ask your shaman to implore them not to scowl and to keep their distance. Until tomorrow, with news of the Kentucky Oaks and more trivialities, pray for your uncle the Count and remember: When it's all over, you'll still have your hotel bills to pay. Tallyho and all that—what four-letter word? I didn't use a four-letter word on the air, did I?

"I'm sorry, sir. Miss Cameron's room does not answer."

Clay returned to the truck from the telephone booth and continued in the direction of the hospital. Was she still sleeping, as he had left her? Possibly. Or had she simply taken it into her mind not to show up for the drawing of post positions? After last night nothing would surprise him. Or damned little, anyway.

The midday streets were busy but pleasant, and the sun was threatening to come out full blast. Wyatt's long-range forecast was not promising. Hotspur, why can't you be a horse who eats up a hot, dry track? You were bred and trained in Florida, weren't you? You're as contradictory and perverse as Kimberley. And he loved them both, regardless. Because he was a fool.

"Forty-seven!" Zach had called exuberantly to the official clockers in the tower as he turned the Spur about and joined Clay, who was on the pony and waiting. Four furlongs: 47 flat. Zach sure as hell had a stopwatch in his head. But he knew it was a soggy track—what would happen when the sun dried it?

Leading the Spur to the Derby barn, Elijah had said, "You inform that Bernie for me I think he's fakin'! He likes it there in that hospital 'cause that little Irish gal's down the hall. You tell him for

321

Eli that we gets along jus' fine and dandy without his august presence here."

What Clay did not intend to inform Bernie of was that last night he himself had made quite a dent in the bottle of sour mash that Bernie kept in the trailer—on the theory that if he wasn't tempted he couldn't prove he'd licked the habit that had always wiped him out. Well, it had almost wiped Clay out too, but long ago. And never again. It couldn't. Because last night, arriving at the empty trailer after that wild scene with Kimberley in the hotel, Clay had decided to stay at the track instead of going back to the motel room. And he had decided too to tie one on and to hell with it. He didn't want to try to sort things out; all he wanted was to sleep. But the booze had intensified the pain in his shoulder and had inflamed the scratches down his cheek—the girl was part cat!—and after an inch or so of the bourbon he had plopped the cork back into the bottle and replaced it in the cabinet. He was not drunk, but the room was wheeling a little and the feeling of pressure in his head loosened somewhat, and he knew that now, like most people, he could drink or leave it alone. And there was some sort of vague inner satisfaction in that. Then he had stretched out and turned off the light and listened to the night sounds of the backstretch—voices, a whinnying or a snort, some distant stomping, a radio turned low in some camper or tack room: his world. Then he'd slipped off to sleep with a vision of Kimberley in his mind, but not the Kimberley he'd just left, for that Kimberley was too damn baffling and contradictory. And sick? The idea had slithered into his mind just as he drifted off. And this morning, still raw and confounded by her cruel and irrational attack on him personally and still bewildered by the possible implications of that small storm, he had not yet confronted the question head-on: could Kimberley be sick?

He turned into the parking area at the hospital, which was a tall, handsome brick building with white-robed nuns and nurses in white dresses and pantsuits arriving and leaving, few visitors. But Clay discovered that he was reluctant to get out of the truck. Not because he didn't want to see Bernie but because he could not get Kimberley off his mind. He thought of the man named Peter Cowley who was guarding her, but he refused to think of Owen or Mr. Cameron's reasons for imagining she needed a bodyguard. And he was not going to take out and consider the idea that possibly he agreed with Andrew Cameron on this wisdom of his. He had to be satisfied with the idea that Owen had shot his wad and, licked, would go no farther. But doubt shadowed his mind too.

On his way through the waiting room—no Mrs. Brigid Tyrone today—he was remembering breakfast. With Jason Arnold in the track kitchen. At Jason's invitation. He'd met Pepe Benitez's agent, a small thin man named Ansel Vendig, top-rated, a quiet fellow with a quick friendly smile who represented only two of the best jockeys. "With us aboard Starbright," he had taunted with keen dark eyes, "I don't know why you even enter a nag like Hotspur." It always amused Clay to hear a jockey's agent boast: They always referred to their clients in the plural, as if both he and Pepe would be riding Starbright together. "I hear you don't like dogs, Mr. Chalmers." And then, patting Jason on his thick shoulder, he had gone out whistling with a *Daily Racing Form* folded under his arm.

"Son," Jason had said, "you look as if you'd run afoul of a cat, not a dog."

"Animals don't like me. Except horses."

Jason Arnold only nodded—had he guessed? You never knew about this man. "No infection's developed in Starbright's legs," he reported, drinking coffee and studying Clay across the table. "Girth gall's under control and no more limp. I think we're out of the woods. Although he's not sound enough for me to be able—oh, by the way, Miss Kimberley was here earlier."

Kimb? Starbright's workout?

"Clay, the girl worries me. She begged me to tell her for an absolute fact that her horse was going to win. Begged me to say it. I can't. She's got what I'd call an obsession about that horse. Oh, I've seen it before. Usually in women. But it always scares me. And hers is so . . . so damned intense."

Still Clay did not speak. He'd never seen it before himself, at least nothing to this degree.

"Clay, I'm going to tell you something. I like that girl. I've known her almost all her life." And then, as if with some difficulty: "But I love Andrew Cameron. There are times when I can't stand to see what she does to him."

Taken by abrupt surprise then, Clay had not, at first, known what to say. Why was Jason Arnold telling him this? And why now? Then he asked it, just that.

"Because, kid, I'll tell you. I think the best thing that could happen to both of them, whether Andrew knows it or not, is if you'd tie her up, soon's the Derby's over, lose or win, and throw her into the back of that pickup of yours and take her off. Anywhere."

And looking abashed, frowning at himself, Jason Arnold had resumed eating. And he continued to eat when Clay said: "That's really why I'm here, Jason."

The older man had growled, "I'm relieved to hear it. Good luck."

Arriving at Bernie's hospital room, Clay discovered that it was empty. The only other occupant of the room, an elderly man with one leg in traction, said, "You looking for that racetrack fellow got bit by a dog? He listened to that broadcast about the Derby, and then he just disappeared to tell somebody the news, whatever the hell the news was. All Greek to me."

Clay smiled and said thanks and then made up his mind. "Tell him four furlongs in forty-seven flat. You do that for me?"

"More damn jabberwocky. I got it. I got a photographic memory, mister. Cursed with it from birth."

Not waiting for the elevator, Clay went down the stairway, recalling Kimberley's panic and hysteria in the stairwell of the hotel last night. All of a sudden he had to get to her, and fast. But where? Perhaps her father would know—

"In the south," Brigid said, "we have the Catholics and in the north the Protestants, and they're at each other's throats all the time. Ahh, if only they were heathen so they could all live together like good Christians."

And Andrew Cameron threw back his head and laughed. Picture

the like of it if you can! Here was Brigid Tyrone, after a night of delightful sin, lounging at the breakfast table in the sitting room of her hotel suite, and what was she doing, imagine, but telling this grand man who had shared her sin a series of Irish jokes, one after the other! It was a habit she had fallen into with her niece, and Molly was a storehouse of them, as are many Irish minds, Brigid knew. Her late husband Daniel could regale his drinking companions from dinner into the dawn, and often she had heard his fine hale laughter filling their splendid house at Innisfree Demesne. Often too he had come up to the bedroom, his face red with the drop taken, and he would repeat the choice ones, bawdy and clean. And now it was this man, Andrew, he of the Scottish name, who was roaring with laughter, begging for more, and for the devil of it tossing in a few himself, mostly racing stories, although his mind was somewhat sparsely furnished in the joke department, though not in the humor department next door, thank the good and generous Lord.

"Oh, I'm so relieved you're not English," she said, and he reached across the table and took her hand.

"I feel there's another what we call gag lurking in that statement, my dear, dear Brigid, so let's have it."

"You've perhaps heard it. An Englishman laughs at a joke three times. Once when he hears it. Once when it's explained to him. And once when he understands it."

It was, she knew, a typically Irish libel, but Andrew, she also knew, would enjoy it this morning in the unlikely circumstance that he hadn't heard it a thousand times before. It was that sort of morning. They had fallen into a pattern already. The morning paper lay strewn comfortably about, they had heard the racing broadcast (so Thrall would carry the Number 3 on Saturday; he'd won twice with 3 on his saddlecloth), and then they had ordered still more tea—imagine a Yank enjoying tea for breakfast, as she did—and there had been silences, and kisses, and sessions of quick and eager talk and long minutes of silence between them again, none awkward, none a void to be filled.

"It just came to me," Andrew said in that quiet way of his, "I know an Irish story. But I'm afraid it's a pun."

"I love puns!"

"An Irish queer is always Gaelic."

And then they were both laughing so that it took a second or two before they realized that the telephone was buzzing. She went into the foyer and answered.

"Hello," a male voice said. "I'm calling Mr. Andrew Cameron, *please.*"

"Yes?" she said, startled but refusing to lie. "Who may I say is calling?"

"A friend. With an important message."

The voice was polite enough, not familiar, but she hesitated a fraction of a second, frowning, before she said, "He'll be on the line straightaway."

She put down the telephone. Andrew was rising from his chair, eyes puzzled, and at once she knew he was thinking of Kimberley— and quite naturally, of course.

"You may take it in the bedroom," she said. "He, whoever it is, won't give his name." Then she smiled and called after him as he strode into the bedroom: "But he did say he was a friend."

She heard the small click as Andrew picked up the phone and then his voice, filtered through the foyer phone: "This is Andrew Cameron." Quickly, although curious and a trifle disturbed that anyone should ring him here, she replaced the telephone in its cradle. She had been tempted to listen, though only for an extra moment or two, but she had not. How extraordinary—certainly Andrew would not have told anyone, even his daughter, that he was spending the night in her suite. Now she could hear only Andrew's voice, but quite distinctly.

"It might help if you'd introduce yourself." And then after a pause, wryly: "You do have a name, I presume—" And then: "I'm listening."

She strolled to sit and thought of turning on the television again, but did not. Instead, she sipped tepid tea.

"Does this concern my daughter? . . . I see. . . . Starbright's her horse, not mine. . . . I couldn't do it personally even if I wanted to because I do not have such influence. And I wouldn't do it if it *were* within my power. . . . No, you listen a moment. I wouldn't try to do it by using such influence if I had it. Now—*did* you listen?"

A long pause this time. She found herself tensed and waiting.

And then, in a totally different, lower tone: "I heard. . . . Shut up. . . . Shut your filthy mouth, shut up, shut up!" His shout turned into a savage bellow: "*Shut up!*"

While he listened then she could hear nothing. In a moment there was a sharp click.

She was tempted now to run to him. But something held her back. She waited.

Then she saw him coming through the door. He appeared stunned, almost staggered. His eyes wandered in various directions as if trying to focus, and his face had gone not white but a violent angry red. Mumbling something about going, muttering apologies, he moved as in a dream toward the foyer.

She stood and stepped to him. "Andrew."

His name, or her voice, seemed to bring him abruptly around, back to reason.

She asked the usual question, aware of how banal it sounded, but how necessary it was. "Can I do anything?"

His head came up and his chin clenched and the color left his face and his gray eyes met hers, level and steady with decision. "You can kiss me," he said.

She kissed him. His lips were like hard cold iron. But his embrace was gentle and his own.

Opening the door of Andrew Cameron's suite, Blake Raynolds had one thing uppermost in his mind: the inflammation and swelling of his toe. The pain come in waves, and somehow the medication did not control it for long. He had heard that horses suffered something similar, which was called founder. He must ask Andrew.

But when he saw Andrew's pale and stricken face, he decided this was not the time to complain of personal physical ailments. He was making his way, using the cane, to the chair he had marked out as his own when Andrew asked, without civilities or preliminaries: "What have you learned of Marylou Wohlforth?"

Joseph Hayes

"Very damn little, I'm afraid. Lives, when she's here, in an old Georgian mansion of sorts southeast of the city. Caretaker is supposed to be in charge when she's away, but I couldn't raise anyone by telephone." He lowered his soft bulk into the chair, using both arms, and then stretched out his leg. "She's in Europe at the moment and is not involved in racing in any way. She never married and she spends a great deal of time traveling. In short, I've learned damned little. Why?"

"Maybe Clay Chalmers will be able to enlighten us. He phoned me here from the lobby a minute or so ago, and I asked him to come up."

Clay Chalmers again. More suspicions? "I thought you'd more or less concluded that young Chalmers had nothing to do with Starbright's disappearance, since he returned him. And I also had concluded, Andrew, that you preferred to drop the entire matter now that you have the horse."

"Both conclusions correct." Andrew was standing, very stiffly, and his eyes had a putty-gray look to them. "On the other hand, I've an idea he knows more than he's told us."

Did Andrew still harbor his intense dislike, or hatred, of Chalmers? Based on what? His feeling that the young man was not, as they used to say, suitable for Kimberley? Or his conviction that Chalmers was responsible for the fate of Lord Randolph? Or . . . did it go deeper and have darker, more unmentionable roots in Andrew's possessive love for his daughter? It was Blake's habit of mind to consider all possibilities, and this was not the first time that this particular one had presented itself. Unhealthy motives even when unacknowledged often dictated acts. "If the matter of Starbright is closed, why have you asked me here, Andrew?"

"The subject now is Kimberley."

There. Not too far off the mark, was he? "Well, while we're waiting and since it is well past noon hour, would you mind pouring me a drink?"

"Happy to." He went to the bar. "Glad to be doing something with my hands. But I think I should warn you: We're going to need clear heads now, all of us."

"Lesson noted. But you know what they say: Starve a fever, feed

328

an ulcer, bourbon for gout." Taking the glass, he said: "You are a true and upright Virginia gentleman, *suh*. And I thank you." After taking a swallow he said, to pass the time and to occupy Andrew's mind: "They tell me a so-called foundered horse has really got gout—any truth in that?"

"They're somewhat similar, yes. And painful, both. It's called laminitis and in a horse it's an inflamed congestion between the horny part and the sensitive part of the hoof. Don't imagine I'm not aware of what you're going through, Blake."

"I didn't imagine that for a—"

The door buzzer sounded and Andrew went into the foyer. "I didn't want to talk on the phone," Andrew said, without greeting, to Clay Chalmers.

And when they were both in the room Blake said: "Afternoon, Mr. Chalmers. I never did get to congratulate you on your derring-do. You see, one gambles on the lower instincts of man and he has every chance of winning, correct?"

"You wanted to see me," Andrew said to Clay Chalmers—flatly, abruptly.

Clay Chalmers nodded at Blake in greeting, then said, "I wondered whether you knew where Kimberley might be."

"No idea," Andrew said. "One of the reasons I wanted to talk with you. Did you spend the night with her?"

Again the young man darted a glance toward Blake, who held up a palm: "Don't mind me. I've heard of men and women spending the night together. And I'm privy to far more grievous misdemeanors than that."

Clay Chalmers faced Andrew. "Matter of fact, I didn't. Last night she was in a strange mood and I didn't know what the hell to do."

Andrew nodded. "She ate far too much, drank far too much. Panicked in close quarters. Maybe grew hysterical, maybe turned on you, maybe even attacked you physically." He was staring at the young man, and for the first time Blake noticed the clawlike marks down Clay Chalmers's cheeks. "Then she went to sleep. You probably couldn't have wakened her if you'd tried."

Clay Chalmers nodded, as if even more bewildered. "And she's not in her room now."

"I know."

"Jason saw her at the track earlier. Are you concerned?"

"I'm often concerned," Andrew said then and moved away as if trying to arrange his thoughts into some kind of coherent order. "She had a telephone call yesterday—did she tell you about that?"

"No." The young man's tone was edged. "A telephone call from whom?"

"That," Andrew said, "is what we are here to find out."

"What sort of call?"

"She didn't say, specifically. I've had one this morning. It was a threat that if I didn't find a way to scratch Starbright . . . certain things would happen. To Kimberley."

Blake saw Clay's face go white, saw his slim body stiffen, saw his hands clench along his sides. "What things, Mr. Cameron?"

"I prefer not to be specific. Unspeakable things. Which I do not intend to repeat."

There was a long silence in the room. Finally Blake felt that he should say: "This now definitely becomes a matter for the police."

Andrew took several steps toward him. "Does it? Am I safe in assuming that she's safe under the protection of the man you hired?"

No one was ever safe. In any circumstances. But Blake said: "If anything untoward had happened to her, we'd know."

"Too late," Clay Chalmers said. "We'd know *afterwards.*"

"Not necessarily. A bodyguard is charged with protecting the body, as the term implies, and it's his job to *prevent* anything from happening." Then he added: "You had a little conversation with him last night, I understand."

Ignoring this, Clay Chalmers turned to Andrew. "I think it's time for you to be specific."

In a taut level tone, through tight lips, Andrew said: "If he had Kimberley, he would have said so."

"More specific, sir," Clay Chalmers demanded.

"He said Kimberley wouldn't listen to him, that I should. He said he was calling me where I was—which was not here—because he knew no one would be tracing calls from that phone. He said I could scratch even though technically Starbright's a stuck horse now, since ten this morning. Which we all know. He said I had influence with the stewards and I should damn well use it. Which I do not have but which I may nevertheless try to use, depending." Then he took a deep audible breath. "Then . . . he described what *could* happen to Kimberley. Such as an accident with an eighteen-wheel rig on the highway. *Like,* as he put it, the plane could blow up in the air on our way back to Virginia. *Like* she gets gang-raped. *Like* she gets her pretty face slashed up with knives. *Like* she gets her breasts cut off. *Like* she gets—" But he broke off and turned away, then in a whisper concluded: "Worse, that's all, even worse." Then, as if he had to say it all: "He said he was calling the tune and if Starbright runs, any or all of this could happen at any time. Before or even after the Derby." He straightened and his gaze took in both of them. "The damned trouble is: I think he means it, whoever he is. He sounded almost frantic. He sounded like a man with his back against the wall and I think he means it!"

Slowly Blake said: "I think he means it too. There's nothing unimaginable anymore." He stood, with difficulty. "Shall I phone the authorities now, Andrew?"

"No," Clay Chalmers said.

Andrew said then: "To hell with the scandal, to hell with the Derby—do we have any choice, Clay?"

It was the first time, Blake realized, that he had heard Andrew address the young man by his first name. "We have no proof," Blake said, "but we do have—"

"We maim the horse and force the track vet to certify him unfit to run."

It was a shocking and terrible thing to hear Andrew Cameron, of all people, say.

But Clay Chalmers nodded his head as if he understood. Nevertheless, he said: "Doing anything to that colt, anything, might be just the thing to push Kimberley over the line." And then, moving closer to Andrew, he said: "I don't know how much more she can take, Andrew. She's on the thin edge of something I don't understand and apparently you don't either. We can't risk anything, can we—anything that might push her over?"

Andrew shook his head, dumbly, blinking. Then he managed to say: "Even answering a lot of police questions could do it, possibly. How the hell can you know?"

The younger man took a folded sheaf of papers from the inside pocket of his jacket. He stepped forward and handed it to Blake. "The longer she stays away now, the safer she is," he said. Then to Andrew: "He won't do anything until the last minute, you can count on that, I think. Meanwhile, I'll have a brotherly chat with the bastard."

Brotherly. Before the word could quite register in his mind, Blake realized that it had registered very clearly in Andrew's. He stood staring blindly at the closed door, frowning, beginning to scowl.

Blake unfolded the sheaf of papers and was about to study them when the telephone rang, and since Andrew didn't move, Blake made his way, using the cane, into the foyer and picked it up.

The message was a report from the detective agency: Peter Cowley had lost track of Kimberley Cameron on the interstate highway leading west into Indiana—

He knocked on the door twice, pushed it partway open, then said, "It's only me, Father Bernard Golden, your Yiddish pastor come to hear confession."

Behind him Sister Grace, rolling an empty wheelchair, laughed.

Molly turned her head, looked, said nothing. Her face was as white as the sheets and the cast on her arm and the bandages on her face and head; and her dark eyes looked dull and lifeless.

"I been hearing confessions up and down the line," Bernie said, "and the things people want forgiven, you wouldn't believe!"

Sister Grace said, "I've given . . . uh, Father Golden here permission to take you down and outside providing you don't use the energy to walk."

Molly did not protest that the injuries were in her arm and shoulder and rib cage and that she could walk perfectly well. This was what Bernie thought he had a right to expect—some sort of rebellion. But this was not the Molly he had come to know. And—he admitted it—in his own way, to love.

"You, young fellow, stop being sacrilegious," Sister Grace said with mock severity, and she started to leave the room.

"Oh, Sister, " he said, "will you take a message to the kitchen for me? For supper I'd like matzoh ball soup and pastrami, and if you can't convince them, tell 'em a bowl of chicken soup will work wonders on a poor injured man like me."

"Molly," Sister Grace said from the door, "pay the lad no heed. He was bitten by a mad dog, you know." And then to Bernie: "She's in your hands now."

"Anyone who can handle a thousand pound horse can handle a hundred pound girl."

"Don't be too sure," the nun said, and went out.

Then Bernie stepped to Molly, careful not to touch either her or the bed. "I know one Irish joke," he told her. "The rest are Jewish. Now, get out of there under your own steam and into the chair. I'll wheel you down to the garden."

"I don't wish to see the garden."

"You don't wish to do anything, that's your problem, Irish. Now, move." And while she, to his surprise, complied, he said, "There was this fellow Leo who was in a confessional in Belfast. 'Father, sir, I have sinned,' he said. 'I've gone and blown up three hundred miles of English railroad.' And the priest said, 'All right, my son, for penance do the stations.' "

Her tiny body was in the chair and the faintest hint of a smile flickered along her wide lips, but her eyes remained as before—unseeing. The shock, they had told him: But there was more, and her aunt knew it, because she had confided her worry, and he knew it too, because he had come to know Molly. Or thought he had. Well, even for a laughing girl, a faint smile was a hopeful sign, wasn't it?

On the elevator, which was crowded, he asked whether, being Irish by accident of birth, she knew what an Irish lottery cocktail was? She did not shake her head or look. "An Irish lottery cocktail," he said in a loud whisper, "is one glass and bingo!"

Wheeling her somewhat awkwardly with one arm to the doors

leading to the brick-floored patio with shrubbery and shade and benches, he offered to autograph her cast if she'd sign his. She said nothing.

There were no other patients there, and some distance away, across a field, he could see kids playing on a backyard swing and teeter-totter and he could hear their fun-filled voices. He and Molly seemed to be surrounded by flowers here, some in full bloom.

He looked up at the sky, which was brilliantly clear now. "You'd have to know a horse like Hotspur to make yourself hate sunshine," he said. "What sort of track does Irish Thrall like?" No reply. "Does he prefer dirt or turf?" Still no reply.

Languidly, dark eyes open but unseeing, she sat there as if wrapped in a white cocoon, shut off from the rest of the world. If ever he'd seen a change in a girl—

"Listen," he said, sitting on a concrete bench. "Listen, Miss Lassie, who used to be sassy, listen to Uncle Bernie now. You got your aunt worried sick, you know that, don't you? You're aware that you are causing untold suffering in various directions? You know, don't you, that your trainer, Mr. Gregory McGreevey, is about to throw in the towel? And you've got me, Uncle Bernie hisself, climbing the goddamn wall. Scratch that goddamn—I meant to say bloody. The bloody goddamn wall." He leaned closer, still careful not to touch her or the chair now. "And what about your Thrall? Now, I ask you, is this any way to treat a horse? An aunt maybe, a trainer maybe, me maybe—but a *horse?*"

"Even if I wanted to visit Thrall, they wouldn't let me."

"Ahh, she speaks! She has a tongue, lips, what lips, and a voice box hidden somewhere. The girl is human! She can talk. Like people, real people!"

She turned her head away and lapsed into silence again.

"Face it," Bernie growled. "You think I give a damn about you? It's that gray colt I'm thinking of. There he is, lonely and not eating and doing workouts slower than I can run. How is Hotspur going to win the Derby fair and square if he don't beat Irish Thrall in an even race?"

"It's so sunny out here," she said listlessly.

"You love the sun. You told me! What are you, some kind of liar on top of being a selfish little spoiled brat?"

She faced him. Her eyes, very narrow, sparked darkly, just once. "Take me inside."

"I haven't got the strength."

She reached with one hand and tried to operate the chair, but all she managed to do was to turn it in a half-circle, so that her back was toward him.

He stood and went around and bent his heavy body to put his face fairly close, but not too close, to hers. "Tricky, aren't you? Never know what you got up one sleeve, do I? You want to hear another story?"

She shook her head from side to side.

"Good, then I won't tell it. It seems that this girl—we'll make her Irish just in your honor, Miss Muldoon—it seems this girl walked up to the information desk in this hospital right here and asked to see the upturn. And the nurse says, 'I think you mean intern. What seems to be the trouble?' To which the girl replies, 'I want to have a contamination.' And the nurse says, 'Examination, yes, for what?' The girl says she thinks she belongs in the fraternity ward. And the nurse says she must mean maternity ward. So the girl begins to yell, 'Upturn, intern; contamination, examination; fraternity, maternity—what's the difference? All I know is that I haven't demonstrated in two months and I think I'm stagnant!' "

A long silence. The calls of the kids reached them from a distance and they could hear a siren wailing far off. Bernie waited.

Then Molly said, her face a pale mask, her dark hair, parted down the middle, a brilliance of ebony in the sunlight: "That's a naughty story and I knew it anyway. And many more. And funnier."

"Tell me. Tell me just one. I dare you."

Without hesitation she said, "Little Sammy was playing with little Timothy and suddenly Timothy exclaims: 'My priest knows more than your rabbi!' And Sammy replies: 'Why shouldn't he? You tell him everything.' "

Bernie laughed. Bernie broke his goddamn back laughing,

whapped his knee with his good hand and danced about as if the world would collapse if he didn't keep on laughing.

"It's not that funny," Molly said, almost disgusted.

Bernie sat down on the bricks and folded his thick legs yogi-fashion and said, "Here's one about the track. Sid Solomon met Ansel Marx at the thoroughbred track and Sid says, 'How is it you win all the time and I always lose?' And Ansel brags: 'Because before I come to the track I always go to the temple and pray.' And the next Saturday they meet again and Sid is shaking his head. 'I don't understand it. I went to the temple and I prayed and now I lose every race.' Ansel asks, 'Which temple?' So Sid says, 'Beth Israel.' And now Ansel shakes *his* head. 'You idiot, that's for trotters.' "

And Molly laughed then, out loud, and Bernie leaped to his feet, but Molly said, "Take me in, please."

Bernie stood there petrified a second and then his voice tightened and his body began to move as if pulled from all sides at once by strings. "What does the girl *want* from me? My curses upon you, missie! May the fleas from a thousand camels infest your armpits! All your teeth should fall out except one and that should have a toothache!"

And Molly then began to giggle. It began deep inside and bubbled up, first a tittering, then a lusty laugh, and he thought maybe he had won this one, but to make sure, he knelt alongside her chair and began to talk in a low earnest voice.

"Let me tell you a real story now, Molly. A true story. There was this guy, see, who wanted to be a jockey. All his childhood all he cared about was not really growing up so he could be a jockey. Win, lose, bush-league tracks, big-time—just to sit up there and *ride*! And what happens? He gets double-crossed. He gets double-crossed by his glands, his goddamn pituitary gland, his *thyroid*. He gets fat. He starves. He takes pills to pee, pills to stop eating. He goes the route, and what happens? He gets fatter. So what does he do? He hits the sauce. He becomes a goddamn leeching drunk! The skids. Down the tubes. Then along comes a guy, also on the booze, and what happens? This other guy, he makes him see what kind of louse he is—feeling sorry for himself, blaming the world, hating the world. He quotes Shakespeare at him. So then what? He discovers in all that blubber he's got a spine. This other guy shows him by using his *own* spine. And what happens? He don't ride, but he's assistant to the owner and trainer of a horse in the big one, the really big one, the Derby itself." He stood up. "So stop feeling sorry for yourself and stand up straight and stop hating a horse that got scared and happened, just *happened* to kick you a few times because he didn't know what he was doing! He didn't *choose* you. You tried to help him and he lost his head because he didn't *know* that! Horses are smart, for God's sake, but they can't read minds, and when they're spooked they're not theirselves, just the way you're not yourself now—but you can be if you try to be. I fell in love with a girl and that girl got hurt, same's I got hurt, only she turned her goddamn back on *me* and I don't like it!"

A long silence. Her face was tilted back and she was staring with her dark bright eyes up into his. They were moist.

And finally, while he waited, not breathing, she said in a small strangled voice, "Bernie—"

"Yeah?"

"Did you say love?"

The sour taste was still in his mouth. As if his blood were poisoned, contaminated by the hate that he had for his brother. No incredulity was left, though. Whatever Owen threatened, he was capable of doing. The rage and frustration were like a steel-hard shaft driven deep in him. And there was, regardless, that uncertainty—the knowledge that he was so furious now that, at any second, beyond his conscious control, he could erupt. He was not the same man who had arrived at the track, who had driven through these same gates only a few days ago. Someone had changed that. Owen had changed that.

He had been to the house with the fine white columns south of the city. No answer to his ringing, his knocking, his insistent hammering. Mrs. Rosser could be inside, possibly passed out from the booze. Even Owen might have been in there, refusing to face it out—not scared, not Owen, but determined to play out his game by his own rules. He had to know, though, that sooner or later he would have to meet Clay face to face. Well, the time had come.

Eric Millar was not in his trailer; the door stood open, but it was empty. At the Derby barn he did not even pause to greet Elijah or Hotspur. He inquired, and one of the Pinks said that Mr. Chalmers—by now Clay had come to hate his own name because it was shared—had been around a few minutes ago, he was probably in the track kitchen. Or watching the races. For the afternoon running had begun—Clay had forgotten. But Owen was not in the guinea stand or along the backstretch fence. So Clay decided to try the kitchen.

All along, since leaving Andrew and Mr. Raynolds at the hotel— how damned long ago that seemed now—he had not been able to decide exactly what he could say to Owen. What he could threaten him with. The bastard had to be stopped—but how?

It was not until he was opening the door to the track kitchen that it came to him. Another longshot. Only a suspicion, really. But if he could use it—if he could turn up the one down card, what would he discover? That it was the one that paired up and made him a winner, or a joker? It was the only card he had, anyway. He'd play it if and when the time was right, then let the damned chips fall where they would.

The kitchen was almost deserted, but Owen was there: sitting alone at a table, reading the *Racing Form* and drinking coffee. Seeing him—the Western hat tipped back, the pearl-studded shirt, the casual lazy look of the man—Clay realized that the scene he had been picturing in his mind on the way would not be the scene played here at all. If he blew his cool, Owen had him. So he choked down the rage and sick disgust and went toward Owen, who looked up, first frowning, then grinning.

"You want company?" Clay asked, his own voice sounding strange and controlled and almost, but not quite, friendly. A brotherly chat, he had said at the hotel—and that was the key. He drew back a chair across from Owen. "Anybody sitting here?"

The look of surprise on Owen's face satisfied something perverse in him. He sat down.

"Well," Owen said, "if it ain't my baby brother. I was just lookin' at the official word on Hotspur's works yesterday. He done better today, didn't he?"

"I'm saving him for Saturday. Maybe a blowout."

Owen, an expression of waiting puzzlement in his pale blue eyes, nodded as he folded up the *Racing Form*. "You go your way, I go mine, right? No coffee?"

"No, thanks. Just a visit. Like old times."

"I got a message from you. From Eric."

"Yeah, I remember telling him to pass the word along."

"That you was gonna kill me, wasn't it?"

"I may have said something like that. I get kind of riled when somebody sets a dog on my horse."

"Can't blame you. But kill—that's a big word." He tilted his chair back on two legs. "Don't feed me that. You ain't changed that much. You didn't mean it."

"Sure I meant it." He managed to say it as if he were shrugging it off. "I mean everything I say, don't you?"

"Never tell the truth if a lie'll get you what you want."

"Dear old *Toby*. Right?"

"Right, little brother." He was peering across at Clay, as if trying to follow the drift of this and decide what Clay was up to. "So . . . you choked Eric's Doberman with your bare hands. Could be you have changed."

"Could be. Speaking of messages, did you get mine from Mrs. Rosser?"

"That about sending me and her both to prison?" He shook his head. "Not like you to go round makin' empty threats."

"Nothing empty about it."

"Takes a lotta proof t'send a man to prison—"

Clay said, "True. But proof's not as hard to find as you might think. Not when there are typed ransom notes and contracts, phone calls—"

The legs of Owen's chair came down, flat and hard, on the wooden floor and he leaned forward. "Brother, you are travelin' in some fancy circles these days."

"So are you."

"Never could have pictured you and Cameron in cahoots."

"Cahoots—good word. Toby's, isn't it? Takes me back."

"Didn't figure you carrying the ball for Cameron. That 'cause you're ballin' his daughter?"

Clay made certain that his face did not change and he broke the impulse to move, to swing. "You guessed one thing right, Owen: I did do Andrew Cameron a kind of favor yesterday. And Starbright's fit to run. No thanks to you."

"Where'd I get the idea he might be scratched?"

"Search me. As of ten this morning, he's a stuck horse."

"I don't know. There're always ways."

"People like Andrew Cameron won't use those ways."

"His funeral."

"Seeing you makes me remember—you always hated to lose, didn't you? Even at marbles."

"Built into my nature, I guess."

"Used to drive you up the wall, now that I come to think of it."

"True, baby brother, true. Only one reason to play and that's to win."

"Well, Starbright's got double security on him now. And he's sound as he ever was, according to his trainer. And his owner also has double security on her."

"What the shit's that supposed to mean?" For the first time a glitter came into Owen's eyes. "I been wantin' to ask you. Why? What's in it for you? With Starbright out, you got that much better a shot at the purse, you yourself, right?"

"Right. Only . . . I guess I just didn't listen to Toby. Somewhere along the way I got the idea racing's a sport, or even a business maybe, but with rules."

"You're gonna get screwed, thinkin' that way."

"Yeah. It's a kind of disease. Andrew Cameron has it too."

"Only one rule, kid. Like in business. Same rule."

Clay nodded. "Win. I know."

"That what you fuckin' around for? Why you have to get in the way? I got nothin' against you, personal. What you got against me?"

Clay shook his head. "You've got plenty against me, and *very* personal. All I have against you is what you are. That's enough."

Now Owen was grinning. "You come here with some other kinda message for me?"

"Not me. I'm just shooting the breeze. Isn't that what Toby called it?"

"Shit."

"Yeah, he called it that too."

"Get to it."

"Get to what?"

"You wanta gloat, that it? You screwed me by paying off that shithead jock and stealing the bangtail back, so you gotta try to rub it in, right?"

"Wrong."

"Then what?"

Clay managed another smile and shrugged. "If you want me to go, if I'm interrupting something, just say so."

"Whatever's stickin' in your craw, spit it out."

"You know, Owen—you shouldn't always talk in clichés. It gives you away sometimes. Just a friendly warning from your kid brother."

"Like what?"

"Like that ransom note."

"That's what tipped you! *That's* how you got wise it was me. *You* got wise. Always *you*."

"Oh, I'm against you, Owen. I've been against you all your life. All my life, anyway. That's because I'm a bastard."

Owen leaned across the table. His lips, framed in his rusty beard, hardly moved. "What you are is a *meddlin'* motherfucker."

"I don't see how that could be. Our mother died when I was born. If I recall correctly, I killed her."

"Goddamn you, spit it out!"

"I've told you all I know. Except the contract—did I mention the syndication contract?"

"Which you stole. Yeah, you mentioned it. Proves nothin'."

"Only that you and Mrs. Rosser stand to get very rich."

"She's already rich."

"You're not."

"What everybody wants, isn't it?"

"Ten percent of eight million—that's almost a million right there."

"Proves nothin'. Any Derby winner's gonna be worth millions. That contract's a legal document, and kosher."

"Kosher. Now there's a word you must have picked up somewhere. Up to now sitting here listening to you has been like listening to Toby. But kosher—" He shook his head.

Now Owen was not even trying to grin. In a low harsh whisper he said: "Now listen, listen good. I told the girl, I told her old man—things can happen. Lotsa things. And they *will* happen when I say so. I don't do the dirty work personal. I hire pros. They know their job. Did old man Cameron tell you what could happen to his daughter? Like she could have her cunt cut out?"

There was a pause. Clay realized that he must have moved a muscle, or something must have come into his eye, because now Owen's beard twisted into a grin again and he sat back and waited.

Clay did not move.

Owen said: "You love her, baby brother? Now ain't that sweet?" He was shaking his head. "No, you haven't changed after all. Well, go ahead, swing. Swing, so I can beat the livin' shit out of you, way I always used to."

"Not here, thanks," Clay said, astonished at his own voice and words. "I don't want to get suspended or barred from the track before the Derby. Also, as you say, I don't want to get the shit beat out of me. You scare me."

Now Owen grunted a satisfied laugh. "Yeah, you did change. Used to be you'd come for me anyway and take what you knew was comin'."

"I'm older now. I've learned that's not the way to fight."

"You know, I don't get you at all today. You still got somethin' up your sleeve, you won't play it—"

"Nothing up my sleeve, sorry. I know when I'm licked."

"Puking little coward, always have been."

"True."

Owen stood up and bent down, only slightly. "Clay, stay outta things don't concern you. This is the big time, the really big time, and you're outta your waters. I got you where the hair's short and I got Cameron by the balls too, and you both know it. You'd've gone to the cops long before this only you don't want the shit to hit the fan any more than I do. Now you waited too long to yell fire, so you both take what's comin'." He turned away as if he wanted to spit. "If that bangtail favorite wins, the girl's got hers comin' if it takes months, years. So put it in your pipe and—"

"Owen—"

"Yeah, what now?"

It was a hunch. It was a wild hunch, but it was the only card he still held, so he played it. "How'd Stuart Rosser die?"

A moment. Would the hunch pay off?

"He had a heart attack," Owen said, but his voice had changed. "Like it said in the papers. He had a bum ticker for years. Like the coroner said in his report."

"Don't get excited. I was only curious."

"Well, butt your ass out."

"I was curious, and now I know."

He did not even see the blow coming. It exploded along the side of his face and then he was on the floor, staring at Owen's Western boots. He tasted blood and then the pain began, but he knew. He'd hit pay dirt. He wasn't even shocked. Flat on the floor, with Owen's boots clumping toward the door, he knew: The fight was far from over, but he'd won this round. And he had a weapon now. Could he use it? How?

Oddly enough, although a toothache was setting in, his stomach did not twist—and he realized that he was not going to vomit.

"Hullo."

"Andrew?"

"Yes, Clay?"

"Has she come back?"

"Not yet."

"Christ."

"She gave the bodyguard the slip on Interstate 64. Led him a merry chase. I guess he didn't have a chance against that Peugeot of hers. The last he saw of her she was traveling west."

"Have you brought in the police?"

"Blake keeps insisting. What do you think?"

"It'd be front page news if you put out a missing-person bulletin on her—is that what's stopping you?"

"No, damn it, it isn't, whether you believe that or not."

"I believe it. Take it easy, Andrew."

"The reason I haven't, the reason I never have is that this isn't the first time she's disappeared."

"You'd better explain that."

"I'm not sure I can. With any expertise or precision. The truth is, Clay, she's subject to . . . what I call blank spots. Or spells. The tensions get too great and she . . . vanishes. When she comes back she says she doesn't know where she's been. At first I didn't believe her."

"And now?"

"Now I've come to."

"God."

"Clay, I've been down this street before. It's always the same—walking on thin ice. If you do one thing, such as asking the authorities for help, it might be just the thing to push her over, to trigger—" His voice broke off. "To trigger God knows what!"

"I think I understand, Andrew."

"Yes, I think you do. Well, did you see your brother?"

"I saw him. If he had anything to do with Kimb's disappearance, I'd know it. He hasn't. But he's still making threats. And don't fool yourself, he means them. How well do you know Mrs. Rosser?"

"Christine? I never really knew her well, and I haven't seen her at all in recent years."

"Do you know her well enough to . . . let's say invite her to dinner?"

"Ye-es—"

"She may or may not be involved."

"I can't believe that." But then he added: "I shouldn't say that after all that's happened. I don't know what to believe. Is that what you want me to find out—whether she's implicated?"

"If possible."

"Short of asking her outright—I'll try."

"If she's not involved, Andrew, we may be able to use her."

"I don't believe I understand—"

"I'm not sure *I* do. Yet."

"There's more you're not telling me, Clay."

"There is."

A long silence.

Then: "Clay . . . now listen. I don't know why, but I've come to trust you. There's a lot in the past that I don't understand and I may have done you a wrong—"

"Time enough for all that, Andrew."

"You're right. But if I've wronged you, I'm sorry."

Another silence. Then Clay said, "Later. Tonight, I need to know whether there's a way to stop my brother."

"It's my turn to advise *you* to take it easy."

"*You* take it easy, Andrew. You sound worse than I feel."

"Don't worry about me, Clay."

"Phone me at my motel. Good luck—"

"You, too."

She was no longer being followed. She had spotted the blue Chevy in her rearview mirror as she crossed the bridge into Indiana, and then she'd picked up speed on the superhighway, watching, and sure enough, he'd stayed behind, at a distance, but behind. And then when she'd slowed almost to a stop, as if she were going to turn into one of the scenic overlooks, so had he, a dead giveaway, so she bore down on the gas-feed then, almost enjoying the chase and cursing Andrew under her breath. Had the sonofabitch in a dark business suit and hat been behind her all the way from the Downs? Or possibly earlier, on her way *to* the track from the hotel just as dawn was breaking? Andrew had threatened to hire a bodyguard, and she'd warned him. Well, she didn't need one and now she'd lost him—what the hell kind of a bodyguard was that?

Her head continued to ache, though. She'd wakened, or come to, alone in the bed, with her head splitting with pain, her eyes blinded by it. If it weren't for the headache now she could almost enjoy the drive—the exhilarating sensation of speed, of power, of plunging ahead, like riding when you give your mount his freedom and then stay with him, as if you and the horse were one animal. Or it was like sailing—yes, sailing a boat, the wind strong, only this was better in a way, with all that power thrumming under you—a smooth gliding, skimming speed indicator inching toward the right, the tach needle reaching too, and the road, or river, rolling slightly in smooth waves, green banks rising on both sides now, little traffic, other cars and huge trucks whisking by on the right in blurs of color as she passed them all, held the left lane, the motor a hollow roar of power and intensity. If only her head would stop aching—

Click.

It had happened again. That curious snap in her head. That was the only way to describe it—like the sharp, distinct click of a camera shutter. It was a weird sensation and she hated it, but she was used to it by now. As though a shutter had snapped down in her brain, clicked tight. Just like that. As if she'd blown her nose too hard and was dizzy, lightheaded. Or as if she had dived into a swimming pool and had struck her head against the bottom. And now she was floating around, but without panic, in hushed green depths. She'd never known it to click so tight, though—as if this time she were locked in for good, forever. But, oddly enough, she was not frightened. She had left fear behind somewhere, in that other world, that outer real world that she had left, or that had left her. There was no pain, and no sound now. That other, outer world had become dead and dim and . . . strange. It was like watching a film and all at once having the sound track fail. But the figures on the screen continued to move, the trees kept sweeping by, a car on the other side of the parkway island approached and passed in a black streak in the opposite direction. But no sound. And she could feel the faint vibrations of her own car, of her own speed, but she heard nothing. The hollow thunder of the engine was no more. The whole world, although it continued to move, was soundless, like one of those old silent movies on television, but no piano sound. And nothing that she saw seemed to have actuality, vivacity, any true reality. As if she had somehow entered into some incredibly eerie world.

But she was not frightened. There was no urgency in her. She welcomed the weird quiet. All of this had happened too often—and more often in the last year—for her to be terrified, or even too dismayed. And there was no panic. Instead, a kind of soothing, spectral peace. Strange, yes, it would always be strange, but she gave herself over to this cloudless, vast detachment.

And no memories vivid and real enough to disturb and torment. And the other Kimberley, whose voice she hated, was not a part of this world.

Lulled by the rhythm of the smooth-sailing car, by the needles on the dashboard at various angles, some moving; tranquilized by the floating sensation of headlong speed, with fields flashing by, green and wavelike; calmed by the hush—she gave herself over to the sensation of unreal helplessness, paralysis, sweet harmony, all unwilled, all without commotion or conflict or decision.

Where was she going? Even that did not matter now.

Her headache was gone. Had she had a headache? She couldn't remember. And did not want to.

After Owen had paid over the fifty-five thousand in cash, explaining that he understood this did not cover the total due, and after he had described exactly what he wanted done, but before he could ask what this would cost, Miss Bette, whose blood was ice water, allowed herself a feminine, girlish shudder and then said: "Gruesome. You know, of course, that we are not talking about a horse now, but a person, so it's a whole new ball game."

Owen said, "I know that." And he waited.

He still could not believe that he was sitting on a park bench at dusk, talking to a girl who wore a printed blue granny dress to her ankles and who looked like one of the many young innocent-eyed

347

hippie-types who seemed to be everywhere—and discussing violence. On another bench diagonally across from them, two college-type young men in sports clothes sat talking together: the two who had escorted him to Miss Bette in the middle of the night, after the fire, one of whom had held a Lüger at the base of his skull. They seemed to have no interest in what Owen and Miss Bette were saying. But they were there; both looked like linebackers on a college football team, and their faces were blandly pleasant.

Finally, in the same sweet voice as before, Miss Bette said: "We're in the business to please, so we're willing to do anything. For a price."

Was it time to ask? "How much?"

"If you're so damned determined to win," she asked, ignoring his question, "wouldn't there be easier and less expensive ways?"

"You mean drugs?"

"I read somewhere about new ones that can hardly be detected." She smiled her sweet smile. "Not that we don't want the business."

"There is a drug called Sentanyl that can only be detected in a horse's blood by some new tests that've just been developed. But it's risky. I'll level with you, Miss Bette. If a drug is detected, it means you lose the race. It means losing your license to train, and in California, where some trainer tried to get by with it, it meant criminal charges too."

"You think your way's safer?"

Owen shrugged and pulled his Stetson down over his brows and tried to relax. "It's a gamble any way you look at it." How the hell long had it been since he'd really relaxed? Maybe when he got this over with—

"*You* gamble," Miss Bette reminded him. "We don't. We have others higher up to whom we have to answer. We can't afford to get caught, and our price reflects my estimate of our risks."

Jesus Christ, this one was too much. "There's not that much risk here."

"Bullshit. I'll determine that."

"Well?"

"You're kind of shaky, aren't you? Doesn't pay to get shaky."

"How much? Please."

"I'm thinking. If this got out, and I don't see how it could fail to hit the front pages, there'd be a thorough investigation this time, because we're not talking about snatching a horse. Our risk is that you might be questioned and that you'd mention me. Our deal."

"Not a chance."

"I'm only trying to calculate our risk—which is not that *we* might get caught but that *you* might and that then you . . . what's that old underworld word? . . . that you might *sing*."

"You already told me what'd happen if I didn't pay."

Miss Bette smiled, very faintly, and Owen remembered hearing that Indian squaws were crueler and more savage than any brave. He thought of those women in the old movie—sitting at the foot of the guillotine doing their knitting. "Sometimes," Miss Bette said, her voice distant and contemplative, "sometimes we make them deball themselves until they lose consciousness."

Get it over with, spit it out—*how much for the job?* Was she getting her jollies out of this?

"We expect to be paid whether your horse wins the purse or not. You know that."

"Yeah, I know that." He didn't know whether to push her, but his insides were crawling and—

"Considering the particular person involved here, we'll need three hundred thousand to pull it off. Half down."

Half down? Christine'd never cough up another hundred and fifty thousand. If Christine ever began to suspect he wasn't using the dough to pay off bets—

"You don't have it," Miss Bette accused, flatly.

"Not till Monday."

"Hmm."

"The whole bundle on Monday."

"Why Monday?"

He didn't dare tell the little cunt about the syndication deal. And she was smart enough to know that his share of the purse wouldn't cover—

"Monday's the day the results become official. After the chemical tests. That's when the purse is paid, official."

"The total purse won't cover this."

She knew, she was way ahead of him.

"And you don't collect the total yourself even if your horse wins. You only get a percentage."

"I'll have it on Monday. All of it." Take it or leave it, cunt.

"On Monday the total will amount to almost half a million dollars with interest."

"I'll get it."

"Win or lose?"

"Win or lose. I'll get it from my fiancé."

"Oh, she must be very rich."

"She owns Fireaway." And it came to him all of a sudden: If they were married, Christine couldn't testify against him if things went sour—

"Well"—and Miss Bette shrugged her frail shoulders and smiled at him again—"well, you must be confident. Knowing what will happen, inevitably happen, if you don't pay. Most people want to live, but when we're through with them, they want to die. You've got a deal. You know the stakes. It's your gamble."

She stood up from the bench and without glancing across started off. The two husky linebackers stood up too, also not glancing. And for the first time Owen saw Miss Bette walking.

She walked with a grotesque limp, as if one leg were actually six or seven inches shorter than the other.

"Yes?"

"Clay?"

"Yes, Andrew? Anything on Kimberley?"

"Nothing."

"Did you have a good dinner?"

"Delicious, thank you. But very puzzling. It's my opinion, for what it's worth, that Christine Rosser knows nothing of what's really been going on."

"Did you inform her?"

"No, I took my cue from something you said last time we were on the telephone. I planted some hints, or suggestions. Whether sufficient to fuel her suspicions, I don't know. She was pretty smashed through the evening, although charming nevertheless, and I gather that she's damned fond of that brother of yours."

"Everybody loved my father too."

"I don't think I quite follow that."

"Sorry. A sudden stab of nostalgia."

"You're in a strange mood, aren't you? How's your shoulder?"

"Thank God I've two of them. Forget it. What about Kimberley? Is this still part of the pattern?"

"It is."

"How much time are you going to give her?"

An audible, tired sigh. "I don't know. God's truth. You keep doing things, or failing to do them, or refusing to do them, and you keep hoping you're right. But you know it's only a hope. How long, Clay, how much time *should* I give her before doing what my attorney advises and bring in the authorities?"

"I can't answer that. How long does she usually stay away?"

"Two hours. Two days. A week. Ten days. There *is* no pattern when it comes to time."

"We're in the same leaky boat, Andrew. It is possible, though, that since she's pulled these stunts before, she's safer wherever she is than around here, bodyguard or no bodyguard."

"That does it, Clay. We wait till morning, anyway." A pause. "You know what's been going through my mind? Something outrageous, considering the man I've always prided myself on being and considering the circumstances—"

"Yes?"

"The idea of offering you a flat million, or more, to take her and go. Do what you'd intended to do seven years ago. The Derby's only another horse race, after all, and Hotspur and Starbright could run anyway. And the race can be watched on television."

"Is that an offer, sir?"

"Clay—my name's still Andrew, and it is *not* an offer. I know better. I know *you* better, now. And don't call me *sir* ever again!"

"Thanks, Andrew. For *not* offering. In your shoes I'd grab at any straw too."

"You must be exhausted, boy. If you want to reach me during the night, ring Mrs. Tyrone's rooms. Try to get some rest."

"I'll try, Andrew."
"Good night."
"Good night."

"What did you and your old beau talk about?"

Owen had been in this strange state of mind ever since she had returned. He had done nothing but ask questions. And while they sat and watched another old Western on television—how Owen did like his Westerns, whereas they bored her to tears—he would suddenly throw in another question—actually more a demand than a question. She was more than a trifle annoyed at him.

"I've told you, Owen. We discussed everything under the sun. The old days. People we used to know. Where they were. Who had married whom and which ones had died. Oh, Andrew and I were mostly reminiscing. We were both in that sort of mood."

And so she remained. It was like looking at the present and the past through a pleasant haze. She was, as the saying in her family had it, awash in a sea of gin, and the boat was rocking slightly, lulling her, and she knew that she should not have any more now, even if Owen offered to mix it—if she did, she might not enjoy Owen later. Owen and what he did to her. And for her.

"What I can't dope out is why he picked today to call you—"

"Oh, I've been half expecting it. And wondering why he didn't—"

"Did you and Andrew Cameron ever fuck?"

"I refuse to answer that—"

"Then you did."

"Not because . . . not for that reason, no, no. But because I can't bear that gutter language. I was with a gentleman all evening and—"

She did not finish. Could not. Owen was on his feet and he was stalking toward the sofa, two fists clenched, and when he stopped, towering above her, she had the distinct but unreasonable impression that he might actually strike her.

"I'm *not* a gentleman, is that it? I asked you a question. Did he ever fuck you in the dear dead days of long ago?"

"No. We used to dance, and drink a little, and enjoy each other and all the—" She sat up straight and looked into his pale flat eyes. "You don't have any right to act this way, Owen. You don't own me, after all."

"Did he fuck you tonight?"

"I'm not going to stay down here and listen to this." But his hard heavy body was in her way, so she could not even stand up. Suddenly she felt imprisoned. "I want to go upstairs, Owen."

She had never known him to behave like this before. Had *he* perhaps been drinking? He stood aside and then he turned his back to her—and she realized.

"Owen—" And when he did not turn, only stared at the television screen: "Oh, Owen, I don't believe it. Are you . . . is that it? You're *jealous*."

"Maybe." And then, as if he had made up his mind to admit it: "Yeah, jealous."

She rose and stepped toward him. Her body swayed slightly, but now she was warm all through, tingling and pleased. "Well, don't be ashamed of it, honey. I'm . . . I'm de-lighted!" She was close behind him now, so close that she could smell that familiar mingling of scents: cigar fumes and masculinity and even a suggestion of perspiration. It made her feel sexy. What did the young people say these days? It turned her on. She could feel a hot tightening in her loins. "You know," she whispered, "you know there's nobody but you now, Owen."

"What else did you talk about?" It was like an obsession with him; it was as if she had not spoken. "Besides old times?" He swung about to face her. "What did he have to say about today?"

"Us. He was interested in us."

"And . . . what did you tell him?" His tone was low, not hard, cautious. "Well?"

"I told him the truth. Yes, I admitted that we were having an affair."

"Jesus."

"Owen. Andrew's a man of the world. He . . . probably already knew. I'm sick of trying to hide it. Aren't you?"

Owen moved away in a semicircle, wondering, pondering. "What'd he say? About us?"

"Calm down, Owen."

"*What?*"

"Well, if you must know"—and now it was her turn to stroll, but a trifle unsteadily and keeping her distance from the decanter of gin—"well, he said he didn't blame me and that damn few people would. He said you were a rugged-looking man and handsome, and he could see how any woman . . . he could understand why I would love you."

"Love? Did he say love?"

"Yes, honey. He did." She halted, herself uncertain now, the word looming between them as it had not before. "All I told him was the truth." She heard herself laugh. With delight. "I didn't tell him you'd be jealous, though, Owen—because I didn't know you would. And you have no idea what it really means to me—that you are."

His beard twisted and his lips grinned. "In a goddam short time now I'm going to show you *how* jealous."

"I think I'll go up and take off my gown and . . . wait."

He stepped to her and kissed her, his arms encircling her so tightly that her breasts felt pain, and her back and ribs. His mouth forced hers open and his tongue plunged in, and she gave herself over to him.

But then, suddenly, he stopped, released her, stepped back.

"Owen, what is it?"

He did not answer at first but began to walk up and down in long thunderous strides. "So . . . so that's how they plan to play it. So that's what they're up to."

"Who?" Bewildered, she watched—startled again. "Who's *they?*"

"Andrew Cameron and Company, that's who!"

"Andrew wasn't *up to* anything, Owen."

"They're all against me, you know."

"All? Owen, you've got a morbid streak that I don't . . . I can't understand."

He did not glance at her, only strode faster, up and down, eyes half closed. "He fed you all the backside gossip, I suppose."

"What he *fed* me was delicious wild pheasant with—"

"He tell you about Eric's dog?"

"Eric's dog? No. *You* told me yourself that your brother killed the dog."

"Goddamn groom left the gate open!"

"It does strike me as odd now, though—your own brother and your own assistant's dog—"

He stopped pacing and wheeled about. "You're with *them*, are you?"

"Owen, what is this?"

"What else did he tell you?"

"Owen—"

"Answer me, goddamn it. What other shit did he ram down your gullet, the polite phony bastard!"

"Owen, please. Let's leave the TV on, and the lights; let's just go upstairs now and I'll show you how much I appreciate—"

"What'd he say about Vincent Van?"

"Vincent Van?" Now she was more lost than ever. "Harold Johnston's name came up. We both knew him and his first wife a long time ago. It *was* too bad—"

"What was too bad?"

"What happened to the horse. Oh, Owen, stop attacking me, I'm so tired and I—" But then she broke off. Because it had come to her why he was acting this way, this defensive way. He had bet and lost again. She drifted toward him. "Owen," she whispered, "you're in trouble again, aren't you?"

"Trouble? I'm not in any—"

"Don't think about it, don't *worry*, honey." She was smiling now, with relief. "Only promise not to bet any more until after the Derby. Will you promise me that?"

He again looked like the chastised child. And her tenderness turned to a suffusion of heat, in her mind and in her body. "Now . . . I'm going up. Don't be long. Please."

And then, when she was naked and in bed, waiting, dismay swept over her. Would Owen ever learn that he couldn't win by betting?

Would he, *ever*? She couldn't let those things that he had described happen to him—those unspeakable horrible things—but if he had to have another twenty or even fifty thousand, she could spare it. But she wouldn't tell him that. And when she did let him have the money, she'd make it very clear that this was the last time ever. But time enough for that tomorrow—would it be Friday so soon? Yes, tomorrow would be Friday. The Kentucky Oaks—

When he appeared in the doorway, he had not undressed. And his face still wore that haunted, tormented expression. But now his tone was casual as he propped himself with one arm raised against the doorframe. "Did he mention the fire?"

Andrew again. Had he? Oh, yes— "We talked about it . . ."

"And?"

"And what, Owen?"

"Don't lie."

"I don't lie." Her desire was gone now. So she said, "Owen, I've an idea. I've had a lot to drink and you're all upset—why don't we wait to make love till morning?"

"What else did he say?"

"Well . . . let me think back. Well, he didn't say it in so many words, but he did just sort of hint that he himself thought the fire might not have been an accident."

"Was *he* sloshed too?"

"He didn't say he *believed* it, only that he wondered—"

"You'd think a man like Cameron would have more sense than to go looking for niggers in the woodpile." He moved in and started to undress. "How well did Cameron know Mr. Rosser?"

"Stuart? They never met."

His chest was bare: covered with that thick reddish brown hair, which also ran down the backs of his muscular arms. "Then he didn't mention him—" He was taking off his boots.

"Well, he did say how sorry he was." She was watching him with the sexy feeling returning. "That's all."

"Nothing about how it happened—"

"Owen, please, can't we forget Andrew? He *knows* how it happened. It was in all the papers, on the radio, TV news—"

Owen stood up. "So no need to ask."

"That's right."

Owen peeled down his tight pants and underbriefs together and then stood a moment naked while she stared, beginning to shake inside. "He didn't, then?"

"No. No. Why should he ask?"

"No reason, baby." Owen sounded almost, but not quite convinced. "You may be bombed and I may be upset, like you say, but I'm never too upset to fuck."

But tonight it turned out that he was wrong. No matter what she did, no matter what *he* did, his cock refused to stiffen.

And finally she began to giggle, and he growled, "You think it's funny?"

"I think I was right: you're too uptight." The giggling increased. "I mean . . . I mean—not uptight enough to be up!" And she was half-sitting and laughing so hard that tears ran down her cheeks and she couldn't stop. She was reminded of a joke she had heard in California—what must have been an old joke, but the more the words repeated themselves in her mind, the more uncontrollable her laughter became.

"What's so goddamn funny?" Owen stood up from the bed, glowering down on her.

"Did . . . did you ever hear the one . . . the one about . . . trying to get an oyster into a slot machine?"

He hit her. She didn't realize it at first because it happened so suddenly, but then the scalding heat and fierce pain rushed into her face, into her mouth, and through the veil of her quick tears and the blur of the pain itself she saw his contorted face, gone pale with fury and then changing, regret rushing into his eyes, and he stood there, appalled and stricken, shocked. While her head seemed to have gone slack on her body at the open-palmed blow, and for a long moment she thought that she was really dead drunk and that this nightmare was an hallucination.

But she knew better.

And so did he.

Chapter Ten

S CENES and places and the faces of people, the past and the present, especially the past—Eugene's funeral in the rain that he had hated; Ancient Mariner's eight-length win in the Bluegrass and his wire-to-wire performance, looking Vincent Van in the eye, in the Wood Memorial; her son, Eugene Junior, who had died of pneumonia before his fifth birthday; her own father, her own father who had been dead for more than half a century; the days and nights at Brookfield Farms, the lovely parties and the music and the laughter—all this and oh, so much more drifted through Rachel Stoddard's mind in such a way that she could not really be sure whether she was awake and remembering or asleep and dreaming.

When Ancient Mariner, Eugene's horse, had died—had been put down—after the fire in the Derby barn, something vital and vivid and alive had gone from Rachel Stoddard. Not only because Ancient Mariner had been Eugene's horse and losing him was like losing Eugene again, but also because of some quality of spirit in the colt himself which she had always loved and admired and which would have made Eugene proud—that vibrant spirit that would not be defeated. The colt's life had been star-crossed from the night of his foaling. Always ailing, stiff and sore of joint by some strange curse of nature, with a chronic arthritic condition, surviving three falls and a wrenched back, he had been one of the very few colts, like Bold Ruler, ever to have battled back from cancer. Crichton himself had often compared him to Ruffian—a compliment indeed coming from a trainer like Crichton, who knew horseflesh as well as any man alive.

Alive.

Eugene Junior had been alive—so many, many years ago. And his father, the only man she had ever loved, who had left her so soon after Ancient Mariner's foaling—Eugene, in those few last days, had been convinced that Ancient Mariner would be Brookfield's first Derby winner. And herself—she was still alive. But lying in the spacious hotel bed in the dimness, hearing the rain pelting down outside, she thought of her age. Eighty-three years. Gone. All behind her. Full years, good years—but gone. Past. All lay behind.

Her Miss Mariah would run in the Kentucky Oaks tomorrow. Tomorrow? What time was it? Time, like itself, even memory, seemed to elude her now—was it tomorrow so soon or was it still Thursday night? And did it matter, really? Soon she would have to get up and dress and pull on her disguise—the tart-tongued, amusingly unpredictable, bluff and wise, respected and beloved great lady of racing—how long before she would have to stir herself into moving, acting, living? How long till morning? Perhaps it would never come—

I'm coming, Eugene.

She knew it. She was old, after all. Everything else was pretense—play-acting for her own benefit as much as for the entertainment of others. It was time. In some deep mysterious way she had already accepted that. Perhaps she had been accepting it ever since Eugene had left her. Tonight, or this morning, she accepted it fully. And without regret.

Soon, Eugene. God willing, soon.

"It's a private club," Andrew explained. "I have guest privileges when in the city."

Only a few chairs were occupied at this time of morning in the enormous hushed and vaulted room. The walls were of polished mahogany hung with gilt-framed portraits of elderly men with brass nameplates below and soft hooded lights above. The windows were framed massively with small mullioned panes. The long library tables were covered with neatly arranged periodicals; there were rows of leather-bound books, mostly in large matched sets, in the cases. The furniture was of soft leather, maroon in color, and arranged to accommodate individuals who wished to maintain their privacy as well as groups ranging in size from two to ten or so. Andrew realized that such a room might strike someone like Clay as formidable, so Andrew was doing his best to make the young man feel comfortable. Not to relax, because there was no relaxing today—at least not until or if Kimberley returned.

"Shall we sit here? I couldn't think of a more private place except the hotel, and after this many days I'm beginning to be a trifle bored by that sitting room. Coffee? Brandy? Tea?"

"Nothing, thanks. Only information."

"I'm not sure I can oblige. To your satisfaction, I mean." Andrew was studying Clay closely, carefully. Wearing a brown tweed jacket over a turtleneck sweater, he was the only man in the room without a tie, but he seemed to take his surroundings for granted and betrayed not an iota of self-consciousness. Andrew was gratified to note that Clay did not allow the muted elegance on all sides to intimidate him in the slightest. A small matter, really—social and trivial. But Andrew was pleased nonetheless. He had become aware of the changes in Clay Chalmers during the past few days—perhaps this simple graceful acceptance was part of that pattern. "You have a thousand questions, I imagine."

"Only a few, really. You've already answered some."

The events of the last several days had brought Andrew to such a state of confusion and apprehension that he had difficulty recognizing himself as the same man who had flown his plane into Louisville. But, having left Brigid only a short time ago, before she was stirring from bed, he did have that underpinning, that refuge to which he could return. Still, since he had not taken her completely into his confidence—why?—and since the Derby would be run tomorrow and the next day Brigid was booked to leave for New York, there to take a ship to England—he had the unpleasant feeling that things were approaching a climax that he both feared and anticipated. At fifty-three he was a man trapped in, lost in, a convergence of events and possibilities that had become a battleground in his mind and in his blood.

"You asked on the phone yesterday how long she might stay away—"

"And you said an hour to a week or ten days, yes. But . . . where does she go?"

"I don't know." Andrew was shaking his head. "God's truth, Clay. I don't know because *she* doesn't know."

"That's hard to believe, Andrew."

"So it is. I didn't believe it myself for some time. At first I thought she was playing games—that she simply didn't want me to know. But when she refused to consult a psychiatrist I arranged to see one myself. I described the situation and he told me two things: that psychological amnesia is not uncommon, but that it's only a symptom of a more deep-rooted trouble and that she should submit to treatment. Needless to say, she would not. It's reached such a point now that I hesitate to so much as mention the subject. If you have a hard time believing this, or accepting it, join the club."

"Everyone's heard of it," Clay said. "In fact, I experienced it once myself. When drinking."

"I recall," Andrew said, aware that neither of them wished, at a time like this, to hark back to Lord Randolph's demise. "And I've come to accept that too."

"The question now, though, is how long we should wait to do something."

"On the nose, Clay. And I can't tell you how good it is to have someone to share this with."

"Same here." Clay's dark brown eyes narrowed and a note of caution came into his tone. "If the authorities should be able to locate her, there'd be questions. And if she really can't remember, their questions might unsettle her even more."

"On the other hand, what if she has an accident, or is sick, or meets the wrong sort of—" He stopped speaking, knowing that his own words only echoed the young man's thoughts. "All those things, Clay, and more."

Andrew only hoped that he did not sound as tired, as burnt out as he felt all of a sudden, facing this head-on, discussing it, speaking of it—

"She's driving the Porsche, you know." And when Andrew nodded: "The damn thing will go at least a hundred and twenty-five an hour, maybe more."

"I'm afraid I know that too."

"Is there some way to get a report on car accidents?"

"Where? By this time she could be in New York. Where, incidentally, she has come out of it several times. Or she could be on her way to California or Mexico or Canada. When she comes to, she doesn't know, and not being able to recall scares her more than the thing itself."

"How long should we wait?"

"You tell me." He heard the harshness that had come into his voice. "How can a man know? If you look back later, if there's a tragedy, you could spend the rest of your life blaming yourself for failing to do the proper thing at the proper time. *But how the hell does a man know what and when?* And if the police should be able to find her—and I'm not at all that sure they'd try very hard, since no crime's been committed—but if they did and they approached her, as you said, might that fact alone plunge her deeper into . . . who knows, who knows?"

Clay, to Andrew's surprise, stood up from his chair. "Every way you turn, it's a gamble." Neither of them, Andrew realized, had mentioned Clay's brother, or his threats. "But I'd be for setting a time, an arbitrary time, and then putting out an alarm. If it takes a crime to make the cops get on to it, tell them we suspect a crime. We suspect kidnapping, you pick a crime, anything—she stole your car, anything. And face the rest when she's back here and we're with her."

Andrew gazed up into the younger's man's face. "I'll go along with that." He rose to his feet. "What is the current lingo? I'll *buy*

362

that, Clay." And then he added: "Shall we say at the end of the racing day? After the Oaks?"

"Settled. Except this: Shall we also say that it's a joint decision? The two of us. If it's the wrong one, we made it together."

Andrew, still capable of being startled, put out his hand, which Clay shook. What Clay was really saying was that if tragedy, of any sort, ensued, he and Andrew would share the responsibility—and the blame, if any. "Thanks, Clay."

Abruptly, but not for the first time, Andrew wished that he had had a son. A son like this young man whom he had hated for seven years.

A horse race is a horse race is a horse race, as Gertrude Stein did not say. She was writing of something more sweetly fragrant. It's eleven A. M. *Friday and here we are again, one day before the Derby itself and only hours before the running of the Kentucky Oaks. What is remarkable is that nothing remarkable has occurred—no stable fires, no horses injured or put down, no spectacular pileup since the Derby Trial on Tuesday. Whatever is occurring—and you could safely lay strong odds that something is occurring—it is taking place behind the scenes and is not for us mere mortals to know. All we can do is conjecture, and our wildest guesses will probably not equal the reality we are not privileged to witness. But heigh-ho, anyway, and a-waaay—*

Today—post time five-fifteen—is the one and one-sixteenth mile Kentucky Oaks, the prestigious event for fleet fillies of three years! Leave us—your curiosity being our command—leave us now to examine the nine young lassies entered and the probable odds at post time. Two three-to-one favorite ladies: Miss Mariah of Brookfield, Connecticut, owned by the greatest of racing ladies, Mrs. Rachel Stoddard, whose Ancient Mariner was destroyed only three nights ago; and favored alongside Miss Mariah, Golden Claire, owned by the world-famous Calumet Farms. Calumet has competition in this race, and, alas, no entry in the Derby on the morrow. Calumet, I might add for the noncognoscenti among us, spawned seven Derby winners in seventeen years, starting with the great Whirlaway in 1941 and ending with Tim Tam in 1958. But that does not take into account the winner-by-disqualification, Forward Pass, also a Calumet entry, in 1968. That was the Derby, you will recall, when Dancer's Image crossed the wire first but was later disqualified and placed in last position officially when chemical tests established that he had been illegally medicated. Today going off at seven-to-one is the spry little minx named Bitter Alma. Running from post position, Number One, today will be Marty's Laugh at odds of four to one, a lively stepper. Then, beginning on the outside, Number Nine, will be Lady Evelyn, pronounced, as in the Bible, Lady Eve-lyn, with odds of six to one. Also at seven to one, like the aforementioned Bitter Alma, is Merry M'Liss from Connecticut. And then there's an unpredictable disco dancer of a filly who could well come in to accept the prized silver trophy and the purse, which amounts to about ninety-five thousand dollars, one of two Florida high-steppers—by name Sorry Sally, with morning-line odds of eight to one. At ten-to-one, still most respectable odds, is Goodness Gracie, who could be a winner if she'd keep her mind on one subject at a time. And last, but starting dead center in the short field, is Silly Phyllis, Number Five, also from Florida, a low-rated twenty-two to one. But re-member: This is a horse race and anything—repeat, anything—can happen.

A wise handicapper, they say, is the one who doesn't bet. But if Count Wyatt Slingerland were betting he'd go for Miss Mariah and/or Silly Phyllis, who, at such long-shot odds, seem a bargain.

One vital element that makes Miss Mariah such a good choice is that she will be ridden today by the celebrated Pepe Benitez, he of the golden hands, who will be aboard the favorite, Starbright, in the Derby tomorrow. Miss Mariah has been steered by others, but Star-bright has had only one pilot—Pepe Benitez. Mr. Benitez is such a devoted jockey that on the morning of a race he personally walks the track to determine its condition to his own, and no one else's satis-faction. He also, it might be added, is one of the few who ride their mounts in the final morning workouts. Not many come down the pike to compare to the incomparable Pepe.

Winner's Circle

Speaking of tracks, today's is cuppy because of the persistent rains. That means that on a sandy track like this one the horse's foot slips back two or three inches with every step. Outside the press box now the sun is bearing down, hot and dry, so make your own decisions as to what a fast track might mean tomorrow—what it might mean to the likes of Starbright and Fireaway and Bonne Fete, who love such, and to Hotspur, who knows exactly how to splash about in the mud, as he proved in the sensational Derby Trial.

There's the field, folks, and a solid one. Not a lively lady among them to be sniffed at. Not what is known as a "rank outsider" in the lot. If you have any money left after the Oaks, there's always the Derby. Meanwhile, this is your obedient servant, Count Wyatt, reminding you that Lady Luck is a cruel witch, a word that is spelled with a B, especially by suckers, but never on the sacred air waves. Tallyho, one and all—

The doctors had been reluctant to release her from the hospital, but against Molly's insistence, the poor men had scarcely a wisp of a chance between them. It was a changed Molly, but Brigid had not yet been able to decide either what direction that change was taking (only yesterday morning the child had all but refused to speak of anything but home and how soon they could leave) or what had brought about this transformation—from a detached and anguished and silently withdrawn girl to a quietly determined young woman who had to see her beloved Irish Thrall. Whereas before she had hated the poor colt—despite all Brigid's reasoned arguments and despite the child's own nature—now she sat quietly in the front seat while Brigid drove, saying nothing, only glancing at her watch occasionally as if time, for her, were standing still. Her face remained pale and her manner had none of the liveliness that Brigid had so much loved.

In the car park she climbed out of the BMW awkwardly, one side sagging somewhat from the heavy cast, and made her way toward the Derby barn, going in the wrong direction until Brigid reminded her that the horses had been moved after the fire. At mention of the fire Molly had not blinked. She only stopped and passively waited to see which way Brigid would lead her.

Gregory McGreevey was smoking his pipe and waiting, and he greeted the lass without any show of emotion. Brigid recalled his concern not only for the girl's mood but about the colt's refusal to eat properly or perform even reasonably well in the morning workouts. At one stage Mr. McGreevey had advised that they withdraw the horse from the race because it would be a miracle if he could return to a racing state before Saturday—which was now tomorrow.

Molly did not pause when they reached the barn but went directly to the stall. And there, behold, was Irish Thrall, he with lackluster eyes and drooping spirit, looking now for all the world as if he gave not a whit whether school kept or not.

Until he saw Molly. But no, he hadn't seen her yet. His head came up and his nostrils quivered, as if he had scented her, or sensed her presence in some way that humans could not comprehend.

When she reached the stall, Kevin Hunter, who had visited her in the hospital twice with Gregory McGreevey, opened the gate and snapped a lead on the halter and extended it to Molly. She took it gravely, unsmiling, and led the gray colt from the stall.

With ears perked up straight Thrall's head ducked and lifted and ducked again, and then, when Molly had him out on the grass, he nudged at her bandaged shoulder, and she stepped quickly aside to stroke him, first on his forehead and then along his sides, long, sweeping soft strokes. Then he pawed the grass and then reared straight up, forefeet paddling the air; he lay down on the grass and tried to roll. He got up and reared again, then kicked and bucked, and then pranced in a circle, while Molly began to laugh, saying, "Quiet, quiet, quiet," her tone filled with love. And then he was standing quite still, noble head high, and making small sounds, neither whinny nor neigh, as of deep pleasure. He lifted one foreleg and lowered it, not stomping, only pawing at the turf, and when Brigid caught sight of his eye, from where she stood to one side, observing, it glittered with vitality, vivacity. It was as if he had returned to full and vivid life within the very few minutes that had transpired.

"I knew," Gregory McGreevey said, his lips moving around the pipe stem as he stared, "I knew. Agh, it's a miracle but it only took the doin' of it."

Was Molly forgiving the horse, or was she asking the horse's forgiveness? Brigid could not hear the words that the girl was speaking now, which were more a flowing purr than human speech. Kevin Hunter, far to one side now, watched with a faint smile.

"Poor Kevin," Brigid said. "The heartbroken swain."

"Heartbroken, is it?" And Gregory McGreevey removed his pipe to say, "Agh, sure now, he's found himself a tall blond drink of cool water, a hot-walker in barn nineteen with pale blue eyes and the manner of a queen. So much for young romance and broken hearts. Quite a few are bein' mended this afternoon, it appears." He gave her a quick scan from beneath the brim of his hat, as if wishing to inquire but never daring it as to her own heart.

And if he found the audacity to ask, what would she answer? That hers was a battleground of conflict and confusion. As if at her age, no child she, she knew even less of the direction her feelings were carrying her than she had known when Andrew came to her room that first night, after the fire, when they had only sat and talked together. How long ago that seemed now. The change in him after that upsetting and mysterious phone call yesterday—the savage bellow of "Shut your filthy mouth, shut up, shut up!"—a change that had carried into the night, their night together, had left her bewildered and saddened and in a quandary. The call had had to do with Kimberley, little doubt of that, and that fact alone had come down like a knife between them. He had not attempted to explain; nor had she questioned. The girl, present or absent, remained between them, and even the starved and touching intensity of his lovemaking did not shatter the wall.

"I've little fear now," Gregory McGreevey was saying, "that we'll have a different workout tomorrow dawn than we've had the last two. Even if the colleen won't be aboard him as he likes."

Irish Thrall was moving again now, shifting his hindquarters on legs that appeared to have had the life brought into them, tugging at the halter as if what he wished to do, damn you all, was *dance*! Gregory McGreevey couldn't spare a smile, but Kevin's lean freck-

led face was grinning. And now Molly's too was alight with joy—
the familiar Molly, the girl she'd always been.

"We'll give them all a run for their money now," Gregory Mc-
Greevey growled, moving off to the barn.

And then Molly was leading Thrall off toward a short young man
wearing a baseball cap, whose shoulder was heavily bandaged. He
was staring at her and at the horse as he waited for their approach.
The assistant to the trainer of Hotspur: Brigid recognized him at
once. She continued to watch as Molly seemed, for all the world, to
be introducing him to Thrall and Thrall to him. Brigid could not
hear the words, but she saw the young man, whose name was Bernie Golden, move alongside Thrall and begin to caress him with
the only hand he seemed capable of lifting. Brigid recalled Clay
Chalmers in the hospital waiting room that first morning: *Or rather,
he was attacked by a dog.* How strange she had thought his attitude,
his suppressed anger. Later Molly had reported that rabies had not
developed, but little else. And she had carefully refrained from
mentioning Mr. Bernard Golden.

All the more reason for added astonishment now when Molly,
not much shorter than the fleshy young man, leaned toward him
without the slightest betrayal of self-consciousness and kissed him
on the lips. Then she turned the halter over to Kevin, who had
moved in, nodding to Bernie Golden in a friendly sort of way, and
now Molly gave Thrall a final tap with her palm and came toward
Brigid, holding Bernie Golden's hand.

More perplexed than ever, Brigid acknowledged the introduction
by inquiring as to Bernie Golden's shoulder. He winced when he
shrugged and said, "Pleased to make your acquaintance, Mrs.
Tyrone. Shoulder's nothing to what Molly's been through."

"Scars of war," Molly said, and her voice now had that familiar
teasing fun-filled vitality that Brigid had thought might be gone
from her forever. "Now Bernie's going to take me somewhere and
get me some of that delicious chili and barbeque that they wouldn't
let us have in the hospital. Come with us, Aunt Brigid?"

"Thank you, no. Will you be back in time to see the Oaks?"

Molly darted a glance at Bernie. Suddenly she seemed shy and more girlish than Brigid could ever remember. "Bernie and I are going to see it from the guinea stand."

So . . . so that was the way of it. When Molly rose on her toes to kiss her quickly on the cheek, Brigid felt very much alone.

And when Molly said, in that same hushed and timid but excited tone, "You may thank Bernie that I'm here, Aunt Brigid, and so may I," Brigid suddenly felt that time and space were coming between her and Molly. Circumstance and happenstance and possibly a kind of inevitability. Brigid smiled at them both, but she could feel an emptiness settling inside her somewhere. Or—the emptiness, already there, expanding, claiming more territory.

Christine had been ill all night. She had never in her life been struck by a man—or woman either, for that matter. And between the excitement of the dinner with Andrew and then that strange scene with Owen, the open-palmed blow in bed and all the gin she had consumed, she had been sick. But the sickness was also in her mind, she knew. Or her soul—how very long it had been since she'd even considered that she might have a soul. But then Owen, overnight, had changed into another man altogether. He had gone to take the workouts and had come back to the house when she'd been only considering the necessity of getting up, overblown head or not, and he'd brought breakfast to her on a tray—a tray not only neatly arranged and laden with the foods she most enjoyed but decked out with flowers that he must have picked himself from the gardens. What a transformation. At first she'd refused to be taken in—after all, he had hit her, and for no reason really. She had been only teasing him: Any man had a right, if he was tense enough or upset enough, to fail a woman in bed. Stuart had done so many times, so many times that finally he had given up altogether. She had never held the fact, physical and/or psychological, against him. Nor would she have held it against Owen if he hadn't become abruptly violent. The left side of her face was swollen, but only slightly, and the pain had gone completely. In a way his almost shy contrition had amused her, had appealed to her in its own way. Much as she needed his strength and his masculinity and his exuberance, there was still another part of herself that was charmed by the man's almost boyish hesitations and remorse. He had not had to say it in so many words; she knew that he was as sorry as she was that her sense of fun—for that's all it had been, that and an impulsive, drunken lapse of restraint—had triggered such a quick and explosive response. He had not needed words.

He had made love to her. Slowly and with tenderness, without the use of those offensive words; he had been making love to her even during Count Wyatt's telecast and he had prolonged it unmercifully, with full control, and then finally, at climax, he had said what he had never put into words before: He had said, "I love you, Chrissie," and her orgasm had been shattering and complete.

His words, more than the act itself, his words and then the quiet aftermath were what had dissolved the hesitancies and uncertainties in her; had taken her mind from all those questions that had attacked her during the night.

On the way to the track now, the white Corvette edging its way through thickening traffic, he was singing again: "My father was a gambling man, my mother was a whore. No matter what my old man lost, my mother brought home more." Owen was himself again. And as usual his high good spirits infected her. She looked forward to seeing the Oaks, perhaps placing a reasonable bet on Mrs. Stoddard's Miss Mariah. She looked forward to being in the box and enjoying the crowd and the sunshine and the intoxication of racing, which had become such a part of her own nature by now.

"There's something I got to say before we get there with a lot of people around, Chrissie."

"I love that suit, Owen. It's so different from all the other men's clothes, yet it just seems to fit *you*."

"Listen, Chrissie—"

"I'm listening, darling."

He was staring straight ahead, chin lifted slightly. "I was jealous."

So she had been right last night. So . . . that *was* what it came to, all of it. "I don't mind."

"Men like Andrew Cameron—I can't help it. When it comes to you, I'm jealous, that's all."

She reached and placed her hand over his on the steering wheel, not removing her white glove. "I said I like it."

"I wanted you to know."

"I'll forget anything ever happened. And you have no *reason* to be jealous, Owen."

"I was even scared maybe you two did . . . make out."

She laughed. What a quaint phrase, and coming from Owen! He turned his head and grinned. "I'd of killed him if you did."

Delighted, she removed her hand from over his and adjusted her wide-brimmed hat, trying to see her reflection in the windshield. "I want to . . . make out only with you, Owen." And it was the truth!

"Well," Owen said, "you'd better get used to my being jealous, that's all. It'll be worse after we're married."

Naomi Yogi was no longer amused. Last night, when Mrs. Takashi, his employer's wife, had arrived unexpectedly and unannounced, and when she had, with quiet dignity, routed the two blondes (they were Hosomoto Takashi's third pair of the week) by opening the door and pointing gravely with her arm and finger, repeating only the one word "Out!" while her black eyes flashed, Naomi Yogi had been highly amused, although of course he did not betray this to either his employer or to his employer's wife. But he had lain in bed grinning for a long time and this morning he had wakened still grinning. The scene had been hilarious, really—almost as if it were in a comic play on the stage. But now he was no longer amused. On the way to the race course in the long black limousine he had been sacked. All his carefully laid plans for the future had been demolished: Now he could no longer wait for his opportunity and, after careful secret manipulation of the affairs of Mr. Takashi, take over Mr. Takashi's position. He remained certain that, given the time, he could have accomplished this and would then have established for himself a racing empire in the United

371

States to complement the financial and manufacturing empire in Tokyo. He was with Mr. and Mrs. Takashi in their box waiting for the start of what was known as the Kentucky Oaks, the sun was shining, the crowd was growing larger, and he dare not reveal the bitter depths of his disappointment, his cruel chagrin. *Twenty minutes to post time.* He had no choice but to smile and to bow and to continue to be polite. His future now, he knew, lay not in the legitimate business world but with the Yakuza, the vicious but somehow glamorous Japanese counterpart of the Mafia in the Western world. Until recently the Yakuza had had a taboo against trafficking in drugs, but now that this had broken down there was always a need for shrewd racketeers in the ever-growing gangs. It would not be easy; and it would be hazardous as well; but rising in the Yakuza could be swift, so that achieving a position as high as the one he had enjoyed with Yosomoto Takashi's world-wide enterprises would not require a great deal of time. What irked him, though, was that he had been sacked not because his employer had suspected his schemes and tricks but because Mr. Takashi's wife had insisted on his dismissal because he had procured the Caucasian blondes, who, unlike the Japanese geisha, were not acceptable to her. Oh, no need for Mr. Takashi to say this, for he never would, but Yogi knew. If the women's liberation movement had not invaded Japan, Mrs. Takashi would never have dreamed of coming all the way to the United States by herself. *Seventeen minutes to post time.* Yogi was sick. Accidents of this nature and ironies like this reached some sensitive part of him that was, he knew, vulnerable. They enraged him. Life should not be subject to such vagaries of fate, such disordered accidents, such capriciousness! And now Mr. and Mrs. Takashi were speaking as if he were not in the box with them. They had been comparing the racing facilities here—so casual and disordered and lacking in grace and cleanliness—with the businesslike formality and luxury of race courses in Japan and Hong Kong. Now their conversation shifted to a discussion of Anne Boleyn, the second wife of King Henry VIII of England and mother of Queen Elizabeth I, who had been beheaded in 1536 for failing to provide the monarch with a male heir to the throne. Yogi had, at his employer's insistence, researched the matter himself in the bookstores. Mrs. Takashi was vastly amused, tittering aloud at the allegation in some books of history that a woman had been so unfortunate as to have been born with three breasts. Yogi decided to take his leave.

Fifteen minutes to post time.

Conscious of Molly's absence in the box, acutely aware of Andrew's polite abstraction and the distance between them, which was widening for reasons still beyond her, Brigid was nevertheless, her nature being what her nature was, determined to enjoy the Oaks. The sun was shining brilliantly and the crowd had that excited and exciting sense of anticipation about it that still, after years of racing, stirred in her whatever it was in racing people that expectation of a good race stirred. Daniel had taught her that, had gifted her with that, and she had always been grateful. Without racing what would she have done, what would have become of her? Today, alas, she wondered that again—what did the future hold? *Leave it all to God*, her father might have said. God, is it? Brigid Tyrone, the bogman's daughter, had never been the one to do so.

While Andrew was chatting with his old friend, the redoubtable but universally loved Rachel Stoddard, whose stables had the favorite in the race about to be run, a Miss Mariah—who, according to the newspapers and the telecasts, had a personality of her own, as if all horses didn't—Brigid was being entertained by the attorney, Mr. Raynolds, whom she found mildly amusing.

". . . forgive me for mentioning my ailment, my dear Mrs. Tyrone, but I do so only to explain why I have taken the inside seat and why I do not rise when introduced."

"No apologies required, Mr. Raynolds, none whatsoever. I have seen horses with laminitis, or pony gout, as they call it, and I know it can be unbearable."

"Mine chooses to be unbearable whenever I attend a social function," Mr. Raynolds said in his comfortable drawl. "Do you suppose my inner nature is trying to communicate something to me?"

She was allowing her eyes to roam over the scene. On the race course final repairs were being made to the surface, and the infield crowd did not seem so large as it had been for the Derby Trial. This was, however, one of the outstanding races for fillies, and at least one, Calumet's Golden Claire, was being pointed, according to the sports columns, to the Arc itself. In spite of Andrew's loyalty to Mrs. Stoddard and her Miss Mariah, Brigid had placed fifty American dollars, roughly twenty-five pounds, on Golden Claire. Mrs. Stoddard appeared to have aged. And in such a brief time. Where had the fine flush gone, the mocking eager look of eye, the imperious carriage? In the box across the aisle she was nodding at Andrew, but there was a vacancy in her eyes and the flesh of her face seemed to have shrunken, as if she were ill perhaps. Or might the transformation, or deterioration, have to do with the loss of her Ancient Mariner?

". . . ever hear the term party-pooper in your country?"

"I can't say that I have, Mr. Raynolds." She did not add that it sounded vaguely scatalogical. "Is that what you've been accused of being?"

"Not accused of. That's what I most certainly am. At horse races, I mean to say."

Brigid could not imagine anyone not liking or appreciating a grand race.

Twelve minutes to post time.

In her mind she could imagine the jockeys in their fine silks mounting, and although she could not hear this on the loudspeaker here, she imagined she could hear "To your horses, gentlemen" and then "Riders up!" Her eyes took in the other boxes. She had not seen the Hautots for a day or so, and today the black owner, a Mr. Edwards, was not with his pretty young wife in their usual place. But the owners of Prescription were there, a family of four now, the boy with a luxurious black beard, and the daughter, as always, excited and trotting up the aisle to get soft drinks or place bets. The Japanese owner of Fuji Mist was at his familiar stand, but there had been a change in that box. Instead of the flashily dressed American blondes, a neat short Oriental woman, pretty and conservatively but fashionably dressed, was beside him, with the younger, taller man conspicuous by his absence. Always fascinated by the secrets of lives she would and could never know, she recalled Count Wyatt's broadcast of the morning—his hints at stories hidden behind walls, his suggestion of the human skein behind the public tapestry. And as she let her mind wander, thinking of Andrew's voice shouting rage on the telephone at his unknown caller, a line of Yeats returned to her mind: *The wrong of unshapely things is a wrong too great to be told—*

Then she became conscious of two others standing in the aisle. She had been introduced to them fleetingly in the excitement before the Derby Trial on Tuesday, and she recognized them at once: Christine Rosser, owner, and Owen Chalmers, the tall, handsome trainer of Fireaway. Mrs. Rosser was speaking to Mrs. Stoddard, and Mr. Chalmers was standing in the aisle facing Andrew, who had spoken in a friendly manner to the woman but who now only stared at Owen Chalmers. Andrew's face was a mask—a mask she had glimpsed before but one that always startled and slightly dismayed her.

Without offering his hand Andrew said, "Mr. Chalmers and I have met." That and just that.

"How are you today, Mr. Cameron?" Owen Chalmers's manner was one of reserved, cautious friendliness and his pale blue eyes were expressionless, as if waiting. His hand was extended. Mrs. Rosser was chatting with Mrs. Stoddard.

Unmoving, Andrew said flatly, "We also spoke on the telephone."

"Did we? I don't recall."

"We discussed my daughter, as I *do* recall."

"Must've been my brother." Owen Chalmers shook his head. "Not me, sorry. But it's a privilege to make your acquaintance, sir."

"Not to me."

And Owen Chalmers lowered his hand. Brigid became conscious of Mr. Raynolds beside her: His soft bulk of body had gone tense and he seemed to be breathing somewhat heavily now—as if he, at least, comprehended what was transpiring.

"Look, Mr. Cameron," Owen Chalmers said then in a low, heavy tone, "I don't know what you got in your craw and frankly I don't give a shit."

At this Mrs. Rosser straightened and turned. She was really a handsome woman. "Owen," she asked, "what—"

Joseph Hayes

But Andrew, stiff and unyielding, unflinching, interrupted: "I'm sure." He appeared, however, to be trying to make up his mind, and Brigid saw his hand at his side; it was tight, white—a fist.

"Well," Owen Chalmers said with a grin that looked genuine enough, "well, we both breathe the same air, *sir.* And we both get into our pants one leg at a time."

Christine Rosser's mouth was open and her brow was furrowed above eyes that were more baffled than angry.

"Although," Andrew said in a voice that until now Brigid had never heard, "I have lived my whole life in Virginia, I've never wished before that duelling had not been made illegal. If not, Mr. Chalmers, you'd be dead by now." And then he turned and bowed, quite formally, very stiffly, to her: "I'm sure Mr. Raynolds will see you back to the hotel, my dear."

But Owen Chalmers blocked his way. "Choose your weapons, *suh,*" he said, the note of mockery hard and sharp. "Pistols, swords?"

"I'm using the weapons that *you* have chosen, Mr. Chalmers. I think they've come to be known in recent times as dirty tricks."

Seven minutes to post time.

"Now step aside, Mr. Chalmers. I have to find fresh air."

And to her astonishment then, Owen Chalmers moved away, his beard, glinting copper in the sun, a tight hard mass of hair, and his eyes flooding with the sort of violent hostility that Brigid had rarely seen before.

Ladies and gentlemen, the horses are coming onto the track. The crowd rose en masse and a roar went up and in the infield a band began to play.

And Brigid was remembering Andrew driving his car to the hotel after the Derby Trial and whispering: "I can't talk, Brigid, I'm afraid to talk. I might shout. I'm afraid I might yell." And then, a few minutes later, hammering his fist on the steering wheel: "People like that shouldn't be in racing!"

Six minutes to post time.

*   *   *

376

Two minutes to post time.

The ferment and hubbub behind her and on all sides was mounting. But Rachel Stoddard experienced it not as something inside herself, as she always had before an important race like the Oaks; now the uproar and anticipation were outside her, not a part of her—and she did not seem to be a part of it.

Oh, she was conscious of the running about in the aisles, people going to place last-minute bets, returning. She was conscious of the tote board across the track, blinking and flashing, the odds changing even now. Miss Mariah no longer three to two, Miss Mariah now two to one and Golden Claire four to one. She saw all of this; it registered. But in an odd way—as from a distance. As if she were a detached spectator; as if Miss Mariah, sporting her green-and-black stripes, were not really hers, or Brookfield's, only another filly, sedately moving in the post parade down below, in a line of others, Pepe Benitez sitting straight, head high, dignity itself. Whether he and Miss Mariah won or lost, however, seemed now to have no significance.

If only the sun were not so bright. Reflected from the track and infield and off the glistening silks, it blinded her eyes, dazzled her mind. If only this would soon be over and she could get into the limousine and glide back to her bed at the hotel—

The horses have reached the starting gate.

Would Miss Mariah protest, as usual? Or would she enter with docile good grace? Marty's Laugh, Number One, was already in the gate. And two others. Rachel lifted her binoculars. But with effort; her arm was so tired, everything took so much effort. The assistant starters were all but pushing Miss Mariah into her slot. In a moment they succeeded. Should she lower the glasses? It would only mean that in a matter of seconds she must lift them again. Beside her Crichton's voice was saying something—something about having told Pepe to rate the horse for the first half-mile if possible. Crichton, dear Crichton, she must tell him how much she appreciated all he did, and not with the horses alone—how much his devotion meant to her personally. She must not wait too long to tell him—

They're at the post!

Joseph Hayes

The tumult quieted slightly; it was that expectant hush that was never quite a hush, the change in tone and temper of the crowd in that brief space of time that had always been what she enjoyed the most. As if the anticipation were even more excruciatingly satisfying than the race itself—

The clanging, the metallic clanging that she knew she could not actually hear at this distance, and then the loud metallic cry: *They're off!*

She became confused then. More confused. She was watching through the binoculars (thank you, Eugene, they're by far the best I've ever owned) when she should have been looking without them, but if she lowered them as the field passed the clubhouse she would have to lift them (that's the trouble, that's what takes the effort!) when the horses made the turn and then adjust them for the back-stretch run. It was too much; she couldn't do it, she couldn't force her stiff fingers and hands to—

The movement was a blur of speed in front of her, speed and color, the animals bunched together still, but with one—devil's red-and-blue silks of Calumet—moving out front several lengths, that would be Golden Claire or Bitter Alma—

Beside her Crichton was his stolid quiet self, observing, and in her box her friends, so many friends, were beginning to join in the shouting, the frantic urgings and cries that, always before, she had enjoyed so much, had relished—

Her arm was aching and her stiff, wrinkled fingers refused to move on the serrated adjustment cog of the binoculars and her whole big body felt slack and empty. Her eyes perceived the green-and-black of Pepe's silks, laying back on the turn, several lengths back, why, why didn't he let out the wrap, was it too soon—

And now they were on the backstretch, how fast it all seemed to go—had it always been this fast—so quick that she somehow couldn't really follow it, but now the track on the far side was in better focus and she could see the order: Golden Claire by two full lengths, then Number One, Marty's Laugh, her mind registered that, as she heard that steady, fast, loud metallic voice, syllable tripping syllable, she saw Pepe in third and staying outside, Silly

378

Phyllis moving up along the rail, and then the others, no matter the others now, she was shifting her gaze with the leaders as she always had, habit working, but the field glasses (oh, Eugene, I love them) were heavy (had they always been so heavy?), her elbow was cramped against her body, and now the leaders were approaching the far turn, her mouth was dry, her tongue seemed swollen and hot—

Crichton, at her side, was not shouting or cheering with the others. He always watched in stolid silence. But afterward he always knew every move, every change of position. There was something she had to say to Crichton, something important, vital, before it was too late, but she couldn't think, her mind wouldn't—

Pepe was making his move. On the far turn. She could see that clearly enough—the green-and-black colors charging steadily forward, and now, never mind the voice telling her, for a vivid moment she saw for herself: Miss Mariah challenging Marty's Laugh, edging to pass, with Golden Claire now three lengths ahead and straining toward the homestretch.

She dropped the glasses.

She could see nothing now. At least not until they came along the stretch toward the wire. Crichton had not noticed; she was grateful. It mattered to Crichton. Miss Mariah had to win, but not for her, for Crichton. What was it now that she must tell him—

The tumult increased, a thunder on all sides, a cavernous bellow from behind, overwhelming—

She would like to sit down. They must be on the stretch now— blue and red or green and black winning?—and the furious uproar threatened to crush her, to overpower her utterly—

Then . . . pandemonium exploded. In which she had once reveled. Which had once reassured her that she was alive and a part of something, a part of others, and their joy and—

But today she felt befuddled. Had the glasses broken, had the fine strong German lenses shattered? (I'm sorry, Eugene, I don't know how it could have happened.)

It was almost too much. She had to be careful now. She could not, dared not let it become too much.

Joseph Hayes

There was a crescendo, a climax of cheering and howling and shouting, and she knew it was over. She could sit now. No one would notice now if she sat down.

But the seat, although pillowed, was hard, unyielding. She leaned back, wondering what was happening to her breath. Why, she didn't even know who'd won! But she was grateful for the sound dying down and for a pause in the announcer's sharp voice after— what had he said? He must have announced the winners and she had not heard.

Then she became conscious of the hubbub's changed character, vehemence gone, pleasurable groans of loss and shouts of triumph. It was as it always had been. But she . . . she, Rachel Stoddard, she was not as *she* had always been.

Crichton's huge ugly face was smiling down on her and so she knew. "That Pepe," Crichton said, eyes glittering with admiration, "he held her in till the sixteenth pole, then he let out the wrap. Congratulations, Mrs. Stoddard."

"My . . . my binoculars," she heard herself say, but she was not certain that Crichton heard, for her voice was a low and hollow whisper and really not her voice at all.

But Crichton had heard. His great tall body stooped and his paw of a hand then held her glasses, which he turned to examine, even lifting the instrument to his own eyes before saying, "You'll use them for many more races, Mrs. Stoddard."

No. Of that she was certain. Not many more. A few, perhaps, perhaps. "Thank you, Crichton."

And then she was being kissed on the cheek, both cheeks, and the box was packed until all she saw was a jumble of happy, kind, excited faces and voices, one saying "Two full lengths!" and hands on her shoulders, on her back, and then Crichton—dear Crichton, she remembered now what she had to tell him—was helping her to stand, his deep, solicitous voice inquiring something, she could not hear distinctly, his face seemed to be floating in her vision, his words lost, but she nodded, knowing, they had to make their way to the winner's circle, that was it, of course.

"Do you feel up to it, Mrs. Stoddard?"

There. She heard those words distinctly! And naturally she felt up to it. It had to be done, didn't it? And now she had forgotten what she had to say to the man. She had forgotten *again.*

She allowed him to guide her, to make a path between waves of bodies and faces, up the steps—had she forgotten her cane? she had to have her cane, there it was, and Crichton had the glasses—and they were making their way through the labyrinth, down steps now, and onto green grass, and then it was as it had so often been: She was standing beside the horse—it was Miss Mariah this time, not Ancient Mariner, but she must not think of him now, because if she did, she would think of Eugene, and she was saving that thought, that memory, until she was safely out of this hubbub and back at the hotel, and alone, alone except for Eugene—

Other hands now were helping her up to the presentation stand and she saw Pepe Benitez standing beside the proud, prancing filly while cameras clicked and popped and whirred. Oh, that sun, it was terrible, that sun was enough to paralyze her—

She accepted the trophy, she nodded her thanks because her mouth and throat were too dry and she was saving her voice to tell Crichton what she had to tell him. Perhaps he would not go back-side this time but would stay with her and go with her in the limousine. She was certain that if she could be alone with him and Joseph driving and the commotion all behind, why then of course she would tell him how grateful she was for all he had—

She felt her legs giving way. She felt her heavy body beginning to collapse, she heard voices but not words, shouts of panic, her name over and over from all sides, and, hot, so very hot, she seemed to be sinking in air, sinking, she felt hands, a strong arm—

And then she was staring upward and there was Crichton's face.

His face turned into Eugene's face. It was framed in sunlight. She closed her eyes. And everything was mercifully quiet at last.

JD knew he was driving like a wild man. But nothing could go wrong now, nothing. He was so worked up that he hadn't even phoned Almeta from the backside. This he had to tell the chick in person! He had to see her face when he told her. Now he wished

Joseph Hayes

he'd gone to the drawing for post positions with her; instead, he'd watched on television. No matter what Almeta thought, no matter what Count Wyatt said about Almeta being pretty, he, JD Edwards, knew that her taking part was only window dressing—Almeta, his wife, the token black for the TV audience. Well, the hell with all that now. Just when he was ready to toss in the towel, thought he'd never be able to hire a licensed trainer for Also Ran, just when he'd got used to the idea that Matt Haslam had spread the word that JD had given him a raw deal, that the word had got out: "Don't work for that uppity nigger"—that's when the impossible had happened! The tall monster of a man with the unsmiling huge face, the trainer named Crichton, whose employer had died at his side in the winner's circle with the trophy in her hand—Crichton had come to *him*, had found him in a poker game with a groom and a couple of gallop boys in the tack room of barn 16. He'd asked politely whether JD could spare a moment and then, outside, he'd said, "I understand, Mr. Edwards, that you're having some difficulty hiring a trainer. Well, I'm available." JD hadn't known how to take it at first: Was the man putting him on? But Crichton had said, "Ancient Mariner's been put down, as you know, and Brookfield's Miss Mariah has already won the Oaks, so I'm free if you want me." Want him? Man, JD had almost burst into tears! "I don't know how to thank you, Mr. Crichton." And then, believe it or not, Crichton had said, "Don't thank me. Thank Matt Haslam. He asked me personally, as a favor to him." If that ain't a ball-cruncher! Matt Haslam? It'd take JD some time to get that one into focus. All he could think of now was that not only would the horse run but his trainer would be listed as Alex Crichton hisself! Crichton—one of the ten best in the league! "Matt Haslam has filled me in, so I'll just follow his pattern." Yeah, it'd take some time to absorb that. He came to a sizzling stop outside the motel room door. "Almeta, baby, come a-runnin'!" But she was not in the room. Goddamn my luck. He looked around, because the place didn't seem the same. It just *looked* different. The bathroom door was wide open but she wasn't there either. He looked into the closet enclosure alongside the wash basin. Only his clothes were hanging there. He knew even before

382

he found the note. He remembered: *If you do fire him, sugar, yours truly is going to take a long walk.* And then he sat down on the edge of the bed and read the note, his mind blurring: *I'm sorry, JD, but I've had it. I'll miss you. Good luck if your horse gets back into the Derby. Yes, I'm crying, sugar, and I'll miss you but I can't take any more. I'll miss you. I'll be watching the race on TV. I'm sorry.* He could feel the despair taking over his body. He was too limp even to stand up. She meant it. Bleakly he remembered what they'd had. He'd never be able to make the same magic with anyone else. Well, JD, you proud of yourself now, man? You fucked it up. You fucked it up, but royal.

Crack!

It almost knocked her down. It was as if her brain, her very skull, had exploded. It made her reel. Not a snap, not a click—loud, *shattering!* As if her head were splitting open.

Then, in an eruption of furious sound and battering sensation, she was on a street corner. And alone. And in a strange unknown city. Somewhere—

Where? How had she come here?

It had never been this awful before, this terrible. Everything came flooding back, rushing, roaring back—noise, color, light, the fury of everyday life, the smells of a crowded street. But what street? *Where?*

It was almost more than she could bear. It would settle down. She would adjust herself soon, but for the moment it was too much. She leaned against an upright pier of black steel that rose above her at an angle. It seemed to shudder with her weight. Faint, she looked up into a tangled structure of steel and tracks, and just then a train rumbled overhead, its rushing black belly between rows of flashing wheels. The noise was overpowering, everything shuddered around her, even the air—

She must not panic. Above all, now, she must not panic. This has happened before. It never happens in the same place or in the same way, but the trick now is to go slow. It's only a train going by above your head, take it easy, allow it to happen. Let it come back slowly. Above all, don't panic.

The train thundered away. She fled across the street. Brakes screeched, a horn barked, a voice called angrily. She found herself on a curb facing a row of ugly storefronts, shops, lunch counters. Where was she? How, *how* had she come here?

What was she doing here, in this strange hot city with people passing, rushing, with dirt everywhere, grime, with no one she knew, where no one cared?

The noise was deafening. The sun glinting at an angle against a plate-glass window stunned her eyes, pierced them. People jostled. She was choking with the exhaust, the smog, the stench. And she was tired—oh, God, what had she done to be this sickeningly tired? How far had she walked?

She knew what had happened in her head—that awful *crack* had been like the click of a shutter coming down before—when her head had gone the other way, the nasty way, that bad, dead way. It had just gone the right way now, and she knew a brief moment of exhilaration. She always had a time like this just after her head had erupted and she found herself hearing again, understanding again. After that first tremendous rush of noise and comprehension there was this good brief time of elation, almost relaxation, relief. She began to walk, blindly. Taking a strange pleasure in hearing and looking at everything she passed, in actually *seeing* again. The joy in knowing exactly what she was doing, even though she had no idea where she was.

Then panic struck. Even though she knew who she was—Kimberley Cameron, of course—and even though she had once again escaped from that dead, dreary mysterious world with the sound turned off, it was all happening too fast now. The silent film was gone and everything was overbright, clear, vivacious, almost blinding—the sound had returned full blast but the film was loose on its sprockets and running faster than her mind could possibly . . .

She had to learn, she had to find out where she was. It was a city, a city with an elevated train, a city of many people. How long had she been here? How had she got here? No cause for panic. How had she got here and where was the fast, new red Porsche that she had bought for Clay?

Clay. Had Clay brought her here? He was always trying to get her to go with him—but where, *where*? If she could only remember that much: *How . . . had . . . she . . . got . . . here?*

"Excuse me, miss—"

She was looking into the eyes of an old woman, rheumy worried eyes—but kind, kind. A shopping bag of groceries in her arms.

"I don't mean to trouble you, miss, but can I help?"

"No. It's all right, thanks. I'm just feeling kind of . . . giddy."

"It could be the heat, miss." Her eyes looked apprehensive, even frightened. "Sure you're all right?"

"Just dizzy."

"Well, if you're certain—"

The woman turned away. She couldn't let her go.

"Where . . . where am I?"

"Where? Why, we're on Monroe Street between State and Michigan. Do you want me to call you a cab?"

Monroe Street, State Street and Michigan. What city, where? *Where?*

"You take care now, miss. Chicago gets hot earlier than strangers know."

Chicago? The woman was going down the street now. Monroe Street. The old lady had told her the name of the city when she hadn't even asked.

How had she come here? How had she come to *Chicago?*

She was walking again. Every muscle, every nerve protested with pain. And now the headache had returned. And then she had it! She had been driving along a highway just after she had lost the man who was following her, the one Andrew had hired, she had been sailing along down a stream with green hills on both sides and there had been that curious snap in her head—

But when? How long ago? And where was her car?

Blank. A complete blank. And she knew now that no matter how hard she tried, no matter what tricks she tried to play in her own brain to recapture that missing time, she would never recall.

She had to accept that too. It was the worst part. The most terrifying aspect of it all. The part she could not bear, the mystery that she could never solve. Like a part out of her life that had not really been hers.

The poor woman, how sweet of her, how could she ever have known? Or did she suspect?

She arrived on Michigan Avenue. But of course, she and Andrew had been here only a few times, but the broad boulevard seemed, nevertheless, oddly familiar. Beyond was a maze of expressways, and beyond them the lake. She watched the stop lights carefully— had she almost been killed a few minutes ago?—and then walked to the far side. What was she wearing? Not her riding clothes, although now she did remember going to the Downs from the hotel in Louisville, visiting with Starbright, and speaking with Mr. Arnold. She was wearing flat-heeled shoes, a simple beige dress, panty hose, nothing else.

But there was something unfamiliar around her neck. She was no longer walking in that dazed way, but her legs felt as if they might collapse at any moment. She had never, never been this tired. Tired to the marrow. Because the tiny chain was so short that she could not see what was attached to it, she reached behind her neck and found the clasp, unfastened it with her thumbnail. She stared at it in her palm; it was not hers; it was not like anything she had ever seen.

Attached to the chain was a coinlike piece of metal, possibly silver, with the image of a robed figure kneeling, a suggestion of a light, or halo, over his head. A religious medal or symbol of some sort. The chain was flimsy and not silver. But . . . where had this come from? She had never seen it before!

She was walking again. There was grass on one side now, traffic on the other. Looking along the avenue she could see the Wrigley Building, the Tribune Tower, and looming above all the modern monstrosity of the Sears Tower.

Chicago. She hardly dared to think of it.

So far from Virginia. So far from Louisville.

Louisville. The Derby. The Kentucky Oaks. She had to be there for the Oaks. What time was it?

What day?

Simply that, if nothing else, what day of the week?

And what week?

The sun was going down behind the tall buildings. Twilight was in the sky.

But what day, what week, what month?

Oh, God, it was worse this time. Much, much worse. Just when she'd convinced herself it would never happen again. Just when she'd told herself that those dead moods, those strange and frightening spells, whatever they were, were getting better. They were, instead, coming closer together now—and possibly lasting longer. How could she know, find out?

She was in front of a handsomely proportioned building with a wide tier of steps. She had to sit down. If she did not sit somewhere—

Others were seated, in groups, mostly young people wearing jeans and long dresses and beards. Some carried paint boxes and sketch pads. Her body felt limp, her feet were sore, she was certain she had walked many miles, and her head throbbed with a steady, overpowering ache. But she had to ask, she had to know—

"I beg your pardon."

A well-dressed, middle-aged couple were descending the steps. They halted, turned politely.

"Yes?" The woman spoke and her tone was guarded, not quite hostile. "Yes, what is it?"

"Do you know what time it is?"

This time the man consulted his watch and spoke: "Twenty minutes after six."

Hastily she asked, "What day is it?"

The man and woman looked at each other—not perplexed, but knowing. "What date?" the woman asked.

"Yes." She could not find the strength to stand up. "Yes. And what day of the week?"

They were edging away. "It's Friday," the man said over his shoulder, and as they moved off and down the steps the woman said, "She's high on some drug or other."

High? She was far from high. Low. She was miserable. Wretched. Friday. She had been gone overnight. And the Oaks had

387

been run over an hour ago. And where had she left her car? And she had no purse, no money.

It came to her then, though: If she could find the strength, if she could summon the will power, she could find a toll phone and she could telephone Andrew collect. If he was not in his room, he'd be with the Irish bitch.

And then it all came flooding back, all of it.

All she needed was a dime. If she had a dime, Andrew would fly here to get her.

But she had no dime.

Don't panic.

You know how to get a dime, Kimberley.

So . . . so you're back too.

I've never been gone, Kimberley. I'm you, remember?

Then . . . then tell me where I've been.

You know I won't do that. I never do.

Then fuck off.

You're yourself again. *If* I told you, maybe you'd remember something that you would wish you could forget.

Go away. I hate you.

I can tell you how to get a dime, though.

How?

Any male, any stupid male—a smile, a teasing promise, a lie, you lost your purse, or someone snatched it—

Seated at the vanity—vanity, is it? that for certain—Brigid was thinking of Molly. Which meant that she was also thinking of Andrew. Because between the two of them her very sturdy and dependable world had been shaken. Not shattered—not quite yet. But the earthquake had occurred, at some deep and mysterious level, and soon she would be alone. As it was, when she was with Andrew, there was a third presence, and had been from the word go. And now Molly: the casual, intimate way she'd kissed that Jewish boy to thank him. Well, Bernie Golden had done what she, Brigid Tyrone, had failed, for all her love, to do: He had brought

Molly back to life. Molly would be grateful all her life, that much Brigid knew. And what is gratitude but a step toward love?

She examined her hair. It had lost only a glimmer of its brilliance over the years. And her face: That too had been unafflicted by the sad savageries of time. More vital, though, was the fact that she herself had also been brought back to the world of the living. If no more than that came of her affair with Andrew—how she despised that word *affair*! it did not *apply*—if only that emancipation from limbo came of the happy and tragic happenstances of the week she too would be forever grateful. And gratitude, as she had only just now reminded herself, was a step toward—

The telephone made its apologetic *burr* sound, and from where she sat she could lean to the night table to answer.

"Brigid Tyrone here."

"Miss Kimberley Cameron calling long distance. Will you accept the charges?"

"Yes, yes, of course, put her on, please—"

"Go ahead."

And then Kimberley's voice—or was it? "Where's my father?" The desperation was clear and sharp and alarming. "Is he there, please, *please*?"

"I'm sorry, Kimberley." And she was, for the child's need was frightening. "Did you try his room?"

"Of course, of course, of course! Tell him . . . please tell him I'm in Chicago and I—please, will you?"

"Naturally, child. But—" And then she recalled. "Kimberley, are you there?"

"I . . . I think so. Yes, I'm here!"

"He said something about meeting with Mr. Raynolds after the racing. May I . . . is there anything *I* can do, Kimberley?"

"No. No, nothing. There's nobody who can do anything."

There was a faint click and then Brigid was holding a humming telephone.

Chicago? And she had not left a number. But Brigid knew: It had been a distress call, a plea for help— Oh, God, please, nothing must happen to the girl. For Andrew's sake.

Had Andrew not known where she had been all this time when she had not made an appearance?

The voice had been as of one drowning. Helpless. Calling for help. Hopelessly calling across miles of deep waters.

Brigid dressed hurriedly. She must find Andrew herself. Now.

Odd, though—why did the girl call her father instead of Clay Chalmers?

Blake Raynolds had hobbled to the phone in the foyer of his suite and had taken the call. "Yes, your father and Mr. Chalmers are here with me." He did not say that they had again been debating what course of action to take as to her own damnable disappearance. "To whom do you wish to speak, Kimberley?"

A pause. No reply.

"Kimberley?"

"Yes. Andrew, please."

Coventry—it was the word that kept recurring in his mind. She treated him with utter disdain—no, worse: Janice Wessell had come to the point where she acted as if he did not exist. Her silent scorn was intolerable. And all he had to do was tell her what she wished to know or throw her the hell out.

"Where are you going?"

"Dinner. Why?"

Jealousy stabbed. Wyatt was hot all over, then abruptly cold, shivering. How had he allowed her to bring him to this?

He knew where she was going. After dinner, what would follow. He wanted to accuse her. He had no grounds, no claim on her. It was Friday and after tomorrow he would never see her again. Time was running out.

She had suspended her insolent disdain long enough to inform him that her editor, to whom she had read her story over the phone, had said he couldn't print it: "He loves innuendo and he thinks I'm onto something, but he called what I wrote nebulous. Conjecture. He even called it fiction." This had been her final plea. Now she was naked in front of the mirror and drawing on her sweater. It was the torment she had devised. *Don't touch the candy.* But he watched, with abject helplessness, inflamed. She was silent, haughty, really contemptuous.

"Why don't we do it together?" she had said. "Blow the whole kit and caboodle sky-high. Lift up the rock, report what's crawling there! Why not, Wyatt baby? The Kentucky Derby Story. Let the shit hit the fan for real."

"I gave my word."

"You what?"

"It's as simple as that, Jan. Yes, I gave my word."

"Wyatt, baby, this is the twentieth century. This is now. Ethics is a course in freshman philosophy. No one believes in things like that today."

"I do."

But did he? What was it to him? A fire had been set, a horse had been stolen, then returned, with his help—that's all she wanted. Facts. What any good reporter wants. Still, he could not. And he knew now that as soon as she left he would take off his clothes and masturbate. Again.

"You are really fantastic," she had said. "You are not to be believed. You are playing along with a cover-up on ethical grounds. Far out, man."

Dressed now, finally, at last, she gave her short brown hair a push or two with her hands and then, ignoring him, went into the high-ceilinged living room of Vilma Solotorovski's studio and picked up her shoulder bag. He followed. Like a fool. Like any other fool. As if the last sight of her going off to be with someone else—it didn't matter who—had to be witnessed, the bitter ignominy had to be swallowed to the last humiliating, poisonous drop.

But at the door she stopped and turned. "I never go dry, you know. Plenty there for all. By the time I come back, if you haven't jacked off enough to satisfy yourself, I'll do a blowjob on you."

"If," he said, sourly, sick inside, sick in every nerve and fiber.

"Naturally, baby. *If.*"

She was gone.

Shunning—he had read about this custom among the Amish. A man's whole community, his own family, could turn against him and punish him with silence—the cruel pretense that he no longer existed. In the name of religion, of course.

If . . . The promise had been there. The promise and the threat. Her contempt for him had some time ago infected his own bloodstream. Wretched, his body quiveringly alive and his mind flaring with visions of lubricious and unbearable paroxysms of ecstacy—it was the only word—he swallowed the dismal hatred of himself that he had come to know but could never accept, a self-contempt amounting to torture, and he went into the bedroom and took off his clothes.

In Andrew's private plane with Andrew at the controls not much was said en route to Chicago from Louisville, or on the return.

On the way, as a silver gray dusk gathered, they spoke of the weather. No matter what else, everyone speaks of the weather.

"Cirrocumulus above," Andrew had said, "and stratus below. No nimbostratus in sight."

But Clay had another way of judging. "Red sky at night, sailor's delight." But the sky was not red, it had a rosy glow, very soft: fair weather ahead.

"Good for Starbright," Andrew had said. "Not much good news for your mudder, Clay."

The official weather bureau had also forecast fair weather for the next forty-eight hours and highs in the eighties tomorrow. "Hotspur doesn't go to sleep just because it's not raining," Clay had reminded Andrew.

Andrew had tried to laugh—and had failed. "A friendly word of warning, Clay—"

"Shoot."

"If you can refrain, don't ask her too many questions. As I told you, she'll pull a blank, and what upsets her most is being questioned—as if she should remember when she can't. It's a delicate situation, I realize, but you're in this deep, you may as well know the worst. The blackouts terrify her more than any other aspect of the situation."

"I'll try," Clay had promised.

Now, on the way back to Louisville, himself next to Kimberley, who was huddled down in the seat behind the pilot's, Clay was recalling this. And he was also remembering the scene on the steps of the Chicago Art Institute on Michigan Avenue, where they'd found her waiting, as arranged. She had been sitting with her head down, and then she had looked up in a dazed way, almost warily, like a small trapped animal, and then she had stood and had gone first into Andrew's arms and then into his.

During the trip by taxi to Midway Airport she had been subdued, silent, almost withdrawn. Then, once in the plane, she had gone promptly to sleep before they had even left the runway.

Over the steady purr of engine and turn of props Clay was now remembering too how he had refused her gift. In a low voice he asked, "What about the car?"

Andrew shook his head and shrugged very slightly. "It may turn up."

"Are you going to report it stolen?"

"How do we know it was?"

"Well, are you going to ask her?"

"Clay, believe me. I understand your quandary. It wouldn't do any good to ask her. She honestly and simply won't know. It's happened before. The police find a car, abandoned or stripped or both, and trace it to us. I've already chalked the Porsche up as a loss in my mind. If it gets to the authorities it can only mean questions, if not a full investigation. It's thin ice, I tell you. I have to think of Kimb first."

Well, he had asked and now he knew. He did not continue to probe but stubbornly his mind kept refusing to accept, to believe totally. What his mind had to do was to sort it all out somehow—his position, his responsibility, his participation in all this, and what would be best for Kimberley. That above all. But what a hell of a time for airplane trips, for soul-searching! By tomorrow this time the

Derby would have been run. Was that the end then? Had he come only for that? Would it all be over?

Would it ever be over?

"In a picklement like that, you never know what's the right thing." Dutch Leon lifted his short, hard body up with the effort of a fifty-three-year-old man and went into the kitchen to get himself another beer.

Marie, his wife, continued to stare at the television without seeing. She'd been disturbed all day. And through last night too. *Had* they done the right thing?

Dutch had found this odd young woman walking, he said, like she was half-blind, or stoned. He also said, though, that he'd been on the beat for more than thirty years and he knew what a junkie was, knew how to handle a drunk, and this kid was neither one. But if someone didn't do something, she'd end up in a cell with them, and the hookers, and worse. So, even if he was on his way to the IC and off-duty by then and tired as hell, like he said, ready to come home and perch hisself in front of the boob tube in his own worn-out chair and maybe watch a ball game—the Cubs were playing at home—even so, he couldn't just pass her by, could he? He couldn't let a kid like that roam the streets of Chicago alone and in the condition she was in, especially on the South Side. This wasn't the old days; this was now. So he'd brought her home to Marie. God knows what'd happen to her if he didn't—a looker like that and in them fine clothes. He didn't like that sort of stunned look in her eyes—it wasn't what he'd call natural.

Although the girl had said she thought her first name began with a *K* but she couldn't recall her last name or where she lived or where she'd come from even, and to Marie she didn't seem to know where she was, Marie had given her some homemade soup, made with chunks of beef and fresh vegetables, nothing canned, and then she'd asked her to stay the night. If she didn't mind sleeping on the couch. It was an old house, and small, but clean, and it had only the one bedroom because Marie, in spite of her motherly instincts

394

and all her praying and novenas and masses said, had never been
able to have children. The girl had looked grateful and all tuckered
out—windblown and on the verge of taking a cold after all that rain
the last week, a cold or something worse, like the flu. Or even
pneumonia.

So . . . she'd stayed the night. Or most of it. Marie had looked
in on her around five, when the milkman delivered, and she'd been
sleeping. But at seven, when Dutch had to get up and shave and
put on his uniform again—pow, just like that, the girl had vanished. She'd been on Marie's mind all day. That queer look, that
lost little girl look, like a scared little animal, poised for flight—

"Maybe," Dutch said, coming back from the kitchen, "maybe
she's got folks. Maybe she'll be okay, Marie." But he didn't sound
convincing, or convinced in his own mind. "Maybe she only
needed that shuteye."

"Whoever she is," Marie said, "I hope she's still wearing that
medal I gave her." Saint Christopher, the patron saint of travelers.
Even is she wasn't a Catholic—she had said she didn't think so—St.
Christopher would look out for her. "If you ask me, she come a
long way from somewhere, not Chicago."

Dutch looked worried. "I can see you ain't gonna sleep too well
tonight, not knowing." He settled down. "Well, we done all we
could. She don't fit no missing persons photos, or ID's, and I even
got into the wanted lists. I even checked main headquarters personal. All we know, Marie, all we gotta *remember* is that we did
what we thought was right. After all, it was a private decision. I was
in uniform but I was also off-duty when I spotted her wandering
along."

"Just the same," Marie sighed, "I wish we knew."

"Maybe we'll never know."

"Probably. Probably never will."

She slept. The pallor showed through her tan. Her face looked
small and childish and vulnerable. And at peace. Clay carefully
drew the sheet up to her chin and sat staring at her. What had she
been through? Were the demons inside sleeping too?

Around her neck was the chain with the religious medal on it.
"What's this?" he had asked.

"It's mine."

"It's yours, but what is it?"

"I don't know. A good luck charm, maybe."

"Where'd you get it?" And as soon as he had asked, remembering Andrew's warnings, he had been sorry.

But all she had said was, "I don't know."

She had refused to eat, saying only that she was not hungry. Her mood—in the plane and en route from the airport to the hotel—had remained the same: meek, almost apologetic, contrite. And with a touching hesitancy in it. She had never seemed more a child—a somewhat miserable child, anticipating blame, or punishment, or both. He had weighed every word, every intonation.

In the bedroom, once Andrew had kissed her tenderly on the cheek and had gone, she had asked: "Aren't you going to take me?"

"Kimb, shouldn't you try to go back to sleep?"

"There's so little time, Clay—"

He had ignored that. What if he had said *There's plenty of time, all our lives*—how would she have responded?

"Are you trying to punish me, Clay?"

"There's nothing to punish."

"You don't want me."

"I always want you, Kimb."

"Then take me. Tell me you really do. And that you forgive me. Prove you love me."

He had had no choice then. But he had recalled his own words when he had warned Andrew that they could not risk anything, anything, that might push her over the edge, the edge of something that neither of them understood. So he had made love to her—against his better judgment. Not knowing, wondering. But even as he did, his mind was teeming with intrusive thoughts. Her illness, if that's what it was, gave her the power to insist on her own way. She had been less intense than usual, less violent, but even in her strange passivity there had been a kind of desperation. In silence, her head moving from side to side, she had come twice before he had, and then again when he had, with a cry that was almost a scream. And afterward, subsiding, she had whispered, "Only with you, Clay. It's only this way, this much, with you."

Now he was lying with her head on his arm, her face still and quiet and pale, eyes closed, and he was wondering: what now, what next? And was the decision his, or would the tyranny of threatened hysteria, unconscious as it might be, determine what was to come? He remembered Jason Arnold's words: *I think that the best thing that could happen to both of them, whether Andrew knows it or not, is if you'd tie her up, soon's the Derby's over, lose or win, and throw her into the back of that pickup of yours and take her off. Anywhere.* And he was recalling too Andrew's saying that he wished he could offer Clay a million dollars now to do what he'd tried to do seven years ago—and what Andrew now wished he had succeeded in doing.

Was she safe here now? Even if he was with her every minute? Even with the bodyguard back on duty? *It was a threat that if I didn't find a way to scratch Starbright, certain things would happen to Kimberley. Unspeakable things, which I do not intend to repeat.* Things which Owen had taken a sick delight in repeating. Clay's mind flinched from the possibility. And he remembered running into Owen backside after the Oaks and Owen's pausing to say, with a grin: "I know when I'm licked, little brother. Let's shake and forget the whole thing." Which, Owen being Owen, only meant the opposite: Owen was never more dangerous, never more brutal than when he offered peace. Once again Clay recalled two small boys behind a barn—the larger one fanning the other with a piece of cardboard on a hot day, then suddenly dropping the fan and substituting a fist.

Did the key lie somewhere with Mrs. Rosser? But where? *It's my opinion, for what it's worth, that Christine Rosser knows nothing of what's really been going on.* Then what if it were explained to her? Would she believe it? And if she could be forced to believe, could she prevent whatever Owen now had in mind?

What could she possibly do? *I hire pros to do the dirty work.* Even if she could be convinced, what could she do? And if she was in love with Owen, or herself involved—

Andrew's anguished words came back to him: *You tell me. How*

Joseph Hayes

can a man know? If you look back later, if there's a tragedy, you could spend the rest of your life blaming yourself for failing to do the proper thing at the proper time. But how the hell does a man know what and when?

What are you doing, Brigid Tyrone, pray tell—wandering about alone on this strange lawn festooned with lanterns and lighted by flaming torches while behind you there's a grand party in a grand house? Driven by your own furies, is it? Feeling sorry for yourself, are you? Feeling excluded and lonely? But not from the party—otherwise excluded, in a more important way. Music followed her, and incessant voices, and laughter—the Jordans' Derby party was known far and wide, and in Europe as well. The high fine house of many rooms and the gracious servants and the guests aglitter and aglow with fine wine and whiskies and, by now, with the dinner of pheasant and other game fowl. While overhead a pale sky made more lovely by the thin white clouds moving across a distant moon. Then why should you feel the intruder here? Certainly not because of any lapse of manners on the part of guests or hostess. No, because of something inside that felt strange and that bewildered.

All through the evening there had been the same question, asked in various ways: "Where is Kimberley?" Or: "Is Kimberley ill?" Or: "I trust Kimb's well, we haven't seen her tonight." As if on such an occasion Andrew and Kimberley should be, as usual, together. It was not, she told herself, jealousy that plagued her mind, peloothered her mood—no, it was rather a sad sense of hopelessness. But why hopeless? Because, although she had known all along that what she shared with Andrew was and could be nothing but what it was—a brief affair, however complicated—still, there was something old-fashioned and conservative in her nature that rebelled and protested: She was not a woman to have casual affairs. What had sent her out here alone had been her hostess at dinner: A somewhat hearty woman with a full figure now, blond hair streaked with sun, and a slightly weathered face. "One can never underestimate the importance of breeding, upbringing, background. Oh, you can have affairs, God knows I've had plenty, but you always marry someone

398

from your own environment," she'd said. Well, Brigid Tyrone had *not* had affairs. Until now. And without the stamp of permanence on it she indulged herself in the guilt of her own background, the bogman's daughter still. But she had known from the start, hadn't she? And tonight she had been reminded over and over that it was Andrew and Kimberley who were not only together at such dinner parties but were together in other more complicated and unknowable ways as well. Kimberley seemed always to exert her own particular tyranny, to intrude herself, even when physically absent.

"Do you welcome company?"

Andrew had followed her. *Did* she welcome company? Looking at him, standing straight and confident in his dinner suit, she was reminded again that this was to be their last night.

She drew the stole of Kenmare lace about her shoulders. "Yes," she admitted. She stepped to link her arm through his. "Yes, Andrew, I do."

"Are you not enjoying our tribal rites?" he asked gently.

She did not reply. She was thinking then of the toast proposed by their hostess and then the minute of silence in tribute to Mrs. Rachel Stoddard. "Rachel," Andrew had whispered, "was always such a vital part of these doings." That she could easily believe. She held Andrew's arm closer, knowing that he and Rachel Stoddard had been friends of many years' standing.

"You'll have to bear with us, Brigid," Andrew was saying as they strolled. "I hope our friend from Hollywood was not much of a bore."

"I'm from Ireland, remember? We take drunks for granted."

"I'm afraid it's the only way to take them on Derby Eve. Alcohol is the great leveler, as someone must have said sometime. Ambassadors, cabinet members, Wall Street tycoons, prime ministers and ex-dictators of banana republics—the Jordans can be depended upon to have them all. Not to mention the blue bloods of all shapes and sizes."

"Not to mention the Arab oil sheikhs—*without* wives."

His smile was in his tone. "They didn't drink, at any rate."

"They might have been more stimulating if they had."

"Our hostess has a more colorful background than you might

imagine. She's old-family Boston, which accounts for the clenched-teeth speech—what we sometimes refer to as Long Island lockjaw. For all her talk about proper breeding—her obsession seems to get stronger every year—she rebelled in her youth, worked as a show girl in cabaret shows and was even painted nude by some Communist artist in Mexico. They say the painting hangs over some bar down there even now." He stopped and faced her. "Now tell me, are you bored? Shall we make some excuse and go?"

"Don't mind me tonight, Andrew." She walked on. "I have Molly on my mind." It was an evasion—not a lie. "I have a feeling she's growing serious about a young man—if she isn't already serious."

"Molly? Little Molly Muldoon?"

"The young asistant trainer who was attacked by the dog."

They moved along. She waited. She had moved into the area of Clay Chalmers and this always puzzled her. And now Kimberley was back into their lives. As always.

"I don't know him personally," Andrew said. "But if he's Clay's assistant, I'm damn sure he's all right."

Startled, she found herself frowning. At least they were talking at last. Or were they really? "I'm . . . reassured," she heard herself say lamely.

"Clay Chalmers," Andrew said quietly but firmly, "is one of the few real gentlemen I've ever known."

She halted, faced him. "Now we're talking. Andrew, talk to me. It's not curiosity alone, believe me. I know it's late now, but you've shut me out. You know that, don't you? I warn you, Andrew: I won't be shut out. Talk to me."

Now, in the light from a torch that framed his head and glinted on his steel-gray hair, Andrew studied her with slow care, as if considering. Then he said: "As you wish, Brigid."

"I wish," she said simply.

"Very well. From the beginning." He continued to gaze at her as he began to speak. "I'll try not to leave out anything. Let's start with a horse named Vincent Van—"

*   *   *

By the time she wakened, Clay had escaped from the bed and had dressed in the bathroom and had gone into the living room. By this time too, several hours later, he had made up his mind. Thanks, again, to Andrew.

"Aren't you going to take a shower with me?" Kimberley asked from the bedroom doorway. Except for the chain around her neck she wore nothing. She stood waiting.

"Perhaps when we get back from dinner."

Her shoulders revealed her quick sense of rejection. Then her body stiffened with anger. "Do what you fucking like. It's our last night." She disappeared and in a moment he heard the shower gushing.

Their last night. Just like that. He was tempted at first to follow, to barge in, to demand what the hell she could possibly mean. But something held him. Some dread. Some sense that he already knew but was refusing to accept what she really did mean. He had a stiff drink and waited. He could handle the booze now. Small comfort, small accomplishment. Then an overwhelming sense of déjà vu came over him. Had he been here before, had he acted out this scene some other time in his life? He had had too much to drink that time, seven years ago, and then—

She came in, wearing a long sleek dinner gown, her shoulders bare, her head lifted defiantly; she was smoking a cigarette. "I'm starving. You can't go to the Jordans' dressed like that."

"I've never had any intention of going to the Jordans' dinner," he informed her, but with slow care.

"Oh, don't be silly. Mix me a drink. A strong one, please." She moved to the glass doors and flung them open. "It's suffocating in here!"

He obliged. "What I was about to suggest, Kimb, is that we leave."

"Leave?"

"Just the two of us. Tonight. Go any place where we can be by ourselves."

She was standing with her bare back to him. "The Derby's to-morrow—" Her tone was cautious. "We . . . we did come for the Derby, didn't we?"

He took the drink to her. "The Derby's only another horse race."

She whirled to face him. "Now you sound like Andrew!"

"I'm quoting Andrew. It was his suggestion."

She took the glass. "I don't believe you."

"Hotspur and Starbright can still run. There's not much more I can do anyway—and nothing you can do to make Starbright win. We can watch on television."

"Did . . . did Andrew suggest that too?"

"Matter of fact, he did. He thinks it would be a good idea—and safer for you now—if you and I did what we should have done seven years ago."

She threw the drink into his face.

He didn't move. Nor did she. Her green eyes had that familiar icy glitter.

Then she said coldly: "You're lying."

"It seems a good idea—to both Andrew and me. You'd be with me, and safe, and no horses need be scratched."

"Andrew hates you."

"I don't think so, Kimb."

"And you hate him."

"No."

"Liar, liar, *liar!*" She was screeching. Then she was moving in long catlike strides around the room and snatching another cigarette, lighting it, eyes avoiding his. "You haven't asked me where I've been."

"I was given to understand it would do no good. That you wouldn't be able to remember."

"Andrew's so easily fooled." She came to a stop and laughed. The sound was bitter, without mirth—scornful. "And so are you!"

"If you do remember, if you want to tell me—"

She strode to the bar, splashed whisky, the decanter clanking against the glass. "Did you ever read a book called *Looking for Mr. Goodbar?*"

"I didn't even see the movie."

"It's about a girl who's a nice schoolteacher—who spends her evenings picking up men, all sorts of men, in singles' bars, and then takes them home for the night."

He didn't speak. He couldn't. Did he believe what she was saying? Was it possible?

She quaffed the whisky, neat. Then she asked, "You still want me to go with you, Clay?"

Did he?

No.

He turned and went into the foyer, without turning.

He went into the corridor and closed the door behind him. He did not slam it.

So . . . so that was the game. The phony game.

So that was Kimberley Cameron, after all.

Now he had it all. He had it all the way. And the waste that lay behind loomed in front of him. Something had gone out of him. He didn't know yet exactly what it was. Possibly he never would. Probably he never would. All he knew now, tonight, was that it had gone, whatever it was, and it had gone forever in only a few minutes.

He decided to get drunk. He decided to get roaring drunk, like everybody else in Louisville the night before the Derby. Then he remembered what had happened that other time when he had gotten drunk. And he knew why the sense of déjà vu had come over him back there.

This time he was going to get drunk and it wouldn't matter. He knew what he had to do in the morning and he'd do it. But it was hours until the morning workouts. A century of hours.

In Andrew's Mercedes on the way to the hotel Brigid was silent. It had taken her time to assimilate all he had told her. Appalled but not incredulous, she had begun to wonder how the story she had heard, its lurid and violent details described in Andrew's quiet matter-of-fact manner on the lawn of the Jordan estate, affected her. Brigid Tyrone—where did she fit in? She understood Kimberley's phone call from Chicago now: It really had been a desperate cry for help, poor child. She understood so much now. But . . . where did it all leave *her*?

403

Andrew seemed relieved—as if the telling of it had released something within him, perhaps clarified some tangled riddle that he himself was struggling to unravel.

Without preliminaries he said now: "I've decided to accept your invitation to Ascot next month." Turning into the car park in the hotel building, he added: "And to be there when Irish Thrall runs in the Arc in Paris in the fall."

As simple as that. A statement. As of a decision made. A commitment?

In spite of everything else, all the uncertainties, she felt her spirits lift. A strange vivid excitement took over. And she realized that she had become involved; she had somehow been revived. She was a part of something. Irish Thrall's winning or losing, once so important, had lost significance. To be alive, to participate, to *feel*—this was vital. And Daniel's shadow, or ghost, seemed to be smiling. She could almost hear his delighted laughter.

As they went into the hotel, leaving the car to the uniformed attendant, she took Andrew's hand. It was heavy and warm and strong—his grip was so intense as to be almost painful.

And she loved it.

And him.

At last, yes—she loved him. She could love again.

Chapter Eleven

THE mare named Foxy Lady in barn 7 had a rooster for a mascot. Or good luck charm. Whatever. During the night he had been wakened once by a goose, which had nudged at his sleeping bag and honked once, probably begging food or only curious. It had not wakened Molly. Backside was really a strange place if you stopped to think about it—chickens, cats and dogs, goats in the stalls and wandering about, even a pig at some track or other down south. Bernie loved the backside area most especially in the early morning when it was just beginning to come to life. Someone's alarm shrilled.

The sky was only starting to pale a little, but enough so that he could see it was cloudless. And there was a heavy dew glistening everywhere in the dimness. The horses would not be yawning this morning. It would be a hot clear day. Sorry, Hotspur—a hard fast track, not even cuppy. Rotten luck for the big one.

Derby Day itself. He glanced at Molly; she still slept, the heavy white cast outside her sleeping bag. Her delicate loveliness, even with the bandaged forehead, brought a hollowness to his gut. Not desire, although desire was part of it sure as hell, but a sort of choking tenderness, an urgency or need to protect her, to care for her. He was eager to get up, to start moving. This is it, this is the day! Yet he was reluctant to move. That's Bernie Golden for you: at sixes

405

and sevens, always wanting two things at the same time, opposite things.

Occasionally through the night a van had arrived from another track to be unloaded. And in at least two barns a groom or vet sat up with an ailing animal. Now the action at the Fourth Street gate, which he could hear but not see, was increasing: trainers and gallop boys and girls, hot-walkers, and others arriving for the morning workouts. Behind where they lay on a slight slope of grass the barns were shadowy hulks, dark shapes, with moths circling the dusty bulbs and lights burning in some of the tack rooms, and coming on in others. He could hear an occasional whinnying and a muted stomping of hoofs here and there. Some of the horses would wake up to discover they were muzzled; they would know that today they were racing. The small houses across the narrow street in the distance were still dark. The crisp distinct smell of bacon frying mingled with all the familiar odors of backside; hay and dust and straw and the muskiness of horseflesh. Farther away he could hear the muffled tippety-tippety-tippety of hoofs thudding faintly on the track itself; some trainers preferred working their wards in the dark, anything to keep the official clockers from recording a fast workout. He had a few more minutes now before he would join Elijah and Zach and Clay.

"Hi." Molly had opened one eye; it looked dark and moist and beautiful.

"Top o' the morning," he said in a whisper.

And then she smiled, opening the other eye. "That's what *I'm* supposed to say."

"Isn't it true," he asked, "that Irishmen say that only in bad American movies about leprechauns?"

But she had not heard him. A cloud had come across her fine features and her eyebrows had become a straight black line. "I can't ride," she said. "The most important works of all and look at me."

"I'm looking, Molly."

"You're always looking, aren't you?"

"I can never look enough."

"Oh, you." She emerged slightly from the bag and stared about,

her mood changing again, as usual. "Do you know what this reminds me of? Gypsies. In caravans. That's what we are, isn't it, Bernie? All those vans and trailers—and us. Gypsies moving from place
to place, one track to another—"

It was true: That's what racing folk really were, of course. And
always in the morning—any morning but especially those before a
race—each day was a new beginning; each dawn brought new hope.
The girl had changed him—imagine Bernie Golden having such
thoughts! "Last night, before you dropped off to sleep, you started to
tell me something about the purse—what it means."

"The purse, is it? Oh, yes, yes. Well, in the olden days, the early
days of racing, that is, on the English moors, a bag of coins was
hung at the finish line and the first rider to get there grabbed the
purse. You see? Stay with me, lad, you'll learn a thing or two."

"I'd like to stay with you, Molly."

She frowned again. "Do you know, this is the first time I've ever
spent a night with a man."

"You didn't," he said.

"I know. It doesn't mean I won't, though."

"Molly—"

But she spoke quickly: "Mr. McGreevey will breeze Irish Thrall a
half-mile this morning and he'll do it in forty-seven seconds, no
fractions, and handily."

"The Spur will get his blowout and he'll eat it up. Three furlongs
hard and fast, flat out, to clean his pipes for this afternoon. And
he'll do it in thirty-four seconds and change."

"Will you be taking the works?"

"Me? The day of the big one? Listen, Clay Chalmers has to have
his blowout as much as the horse. The works are his morning fix,
the way some people use coffee, some use dope—Clay's life is right
here and the works are the best part of his day."

She smiled, very faintly. "You like him, don't you?"

"No," Bernie said, his tone grave and low, "no, I love him."

"Mmm. The way I love Aunt Brigid."

"Very like, Irish, very like."

"But not the way you love me."

"No. No, it's not the same."

"I know." She looked away, resting her weight on her free elbow. "I don't know how I'm going to tell Aunt Brigid—"

"You haven't told me yet. You've decided then?"

She faced him. With a direct, dark probing stare. "I've decided." And then the quick smile: "But not because of you."

"What then? Because you can't leave all the chili and barbeque in America—"

"Yes. Mostly that."

"A fat Jew—"

"Jesus was a Jew. And when I was a girl the mayor of Dublin himself. And Mr. Bloom."

"Who's Mr. Bloom?"

"Leopold Bloom, the man himself." She laughed aloud then. "A fat Jew in a book that I was forbidden to read, so I did."

"Molly—"

"Yes?"

"I believe in miracles after all."

"And why not? They happen all the time. And when are you going to kiss me good morning?"

"Now."

He was no longer drunk. Except with anger. And with that sensation of déjà vu that had stayed with him through the night of drinking, through the workouts—three furlong blowout, thirty-four and no change—and now remained in him like a cloud as he faced Kimberley. Probably for the last time.

"You said you were with a man in Chicago. Or was it several men?"

"Yes." She still refused to look at him. Or, really, to answer. Her tone was as flat and distant as her eyes.

"Kimberley, listen to me now. Where is the new Porsche?"

She didn't even shrug. "Some street somewhere—"

"You mean you can't remember."

"Yes."

"And that religious medal around your neck—" He saw her

touch it with one hand. "You can't remember where that came from either, can you?"

Her voice was bleak and hollow. "No."

"But you do remember picking up a man in some bar?"

She only shook her head.

"You lied, didn't you?"

Now she only nodded her head. As if it didn't matter. Almost as if he weren't there.

He had been certain. It had come to him while he was drinking—trying to blot it all out of his mind. Trying to blot her out. It had come to him in an exploding terrible moment of illumination. Maybe the drinking helped. The truth at last. And he knew.

"Why did you lie, Kimberley?"

But he knew that too. And he knew it was no good questioning her. Possibly she herself didn't consciously know. So he told her.

"You lied to me to drive me away."

Now. He had said it. He had said it because he knew it to be the truth. At last.

"I was getting too close, wasn't I, Kimberley? Insisting you go with me. Insisting you go off with me. I was getting too close, wasn't It?"

But it was no use. If he knew, if he had been so damn certain, then why had he come back? What could be accomplished by making sure she confessed?

"Well, it wasn't necessary to lie. If you didn't want me, why couldn't you have said it straight out? Why can't you say it? Why the hell do you have to be dishonest about it? Find excuses—"

He realized that his anguish was coloring his tone. He turned away and was tempted to pour another drink—why not, why not? But that's what he had done last night. And had stumbled across the truth. That's what he had done seven years ago, and that time he had not known what the truth was. He had almost allowed them, her and Andrew, to convince him that—

"It wasn't necessary to lie last night, Kimberley. And it wasn't necessary, seven years ago, to destroy a fine horse just to have an excuse for getting rid of me!"

Still, she did not turn. It was like talking to a statue. But she did not need to speak, to admit it. He knew. *How can I go with you now? After this? After what you did to Lord Randolph?* Kimberley had opened the stall, had unlocked the stable. She had done it so that—

"All you had to do, either time, was say: 'I don't love you, Clay.' " But she hadn't had the guts. The honesty—

"I . . . I do love you, Clay."

"Well, it's not enough!" he heard himself shout. "It's a kind of love I don't understand and it's not enough!"

Then the question that had been burning in his mind all night flared to life: Did *he* love *her?*

He did not have the answer to that. Yet. Possibly he never would.

"Good-bye, Kimberley."

He started toward the foyer, but, finally, she spoke.

"Is he dead?"

At first he was not certain he had heard. Had she asked whether his love was dead? He didn't know. Yet.

"Is he dead, Clay?"

He turned into the room again. She had stood up and now was framed in the balcony doors.

"Pepe," she said. "Is he dead?"

"Pepe?" he asked. "Maybe you'd better explain what you're talking about."

She was facing him now. Her face was a pale mask, without expression. Her eyes looked dazed. Empty.

"Is he, Clay? Is Pepe dead? I have to know."

Then she made a single simple gesture toward the sofa where she had been sitting. He stepped and picked up an envelope with two photographs. He examined them.

The first was a Polaroid shot of a pair of hands, in closeup. They were small and dark-skinned and on one finger was a ring in the shape of a diamond-crusted horseshoe.

He looked at the other one. His breath held and he went sick and hollow, every muscle and nerve tightening. The picture was of the same pair of hands—crushed, red with blood, grotesquely mangled, the fingers flattened and lifeless. The ring seemed to dangle from shrunken flesh.

He thought for a second that he was going to vomit.

And one word came to him.

"Is he dead, Clay? I have to know. Is poor Pepe dead?"

The word that had come to him was a name.

Owen.

Paul and Annabelle Hautot were taking a morning stroll. The streets were crowded, alive with people. It was the first time that Paul had left the hotel after his most unfortunate experience at the hands of the sadistic perverts whom he had met at the bar frequented by the lowest of their kind. He was able to walk now in a natural manner: very straight but giving the impression of a casual self-confident man of the world. Annabelle walked close to him, cautious not to hold his healing arm too tightly. During his painful convalescence, while he was being dutifully nursed with single-minded and tender devotion by Annabelle alone, they had agreed, between themselves, to certain resolutions of various kinds, each promise and commitment solemnly sealed by a glass of excellent wine that she had somehow procured from an import shop. For his part, he would never again become involved in homosexual affairs of any sort, and she, for hers, would refrain from experimenting with cocaine or other drugs; she would devote herself entirely to him henceforward and he to her, eschewing all others of both sexes; they would never again enter a horse, male or female, in the Kentucky Derby. Both were well aware that neither had any genuine intention of fulfilling any of the resolutions except the last one. And each knew of the other's awareness too. Meanwhile, though, it was their intention to enjoy the races of the afternoon, including the Kentucky Derby, to the fullest of their capacities. *Bonne chance, Bonne Fête!*

"It's Kimberley. Let me in. Please."

Brigid opened the door. It was Kimberley. It was always Kimberley.

The girl went directly to her father, ignoring Brigid.

"Andrew, I'm ready."

"Ready?" Andrew was studying her with a frown. "Kimb, sit down. You look—"

"I'm fine, Andrew. I've never been better." Her tone, like her face, was wan and forlorn—distant. "I'm ready to go now."

"Go where, Daughter?" he asked gently. "The race isn't until five-thirty—"

She shook her head. Her pale hair dangled loose, unkempt—as awry as her face. "I don't mean that. I'm ready to go home."

Brigid took several steps toward the bedroom, but Andrew shook his head and his eyes met hers, almost pleading with her to stay. She stayed.

"Kimberley," Andrew said, "we all know you've been through a difficult time. But you don't want to miss the Derby after—"

"Andrew, please. Take me home. That's the only place I want to be. *It's the only place I ever wanted to be.*" Then the words tumbled out. "Take me away from here. Terrible things happen here. Please, Andrew, if you love me, you'll take me away. You do love me, don't you. Don't you love me? I only want to be home, and with you, with *you*, Andrew, why can't you understand?"

Kimberley rose on her toes and kissed her father. On the lips. With desperation. Her arms went around him and one hand held his head from behind.

She was kissing him then as Brigid had never seen a daughter kiss a father. Her entire body was thrust against him, straining, passionate.

Brigid had to turn away. She left the room. Trembling. She had never seen a daughter kiss her father like that before and, shaking all over, and cold, she trusted that she never would see it again.

Something hard and implacable and dangerous in Clay Chalmers's eye told Christine that she should not try to close the door in his face. She stepped aside and he came into the high center hall.

"He's not at the track, so he's here," Clay Chalmers said.

"Sure I'm here," Owen said from the top of the curving stairway. Then he started down. "What do I owe the honor to, kid brother, and on Derby Day?"

"Is he dead?"

"C'mon, let's have a drink." Owen went into the sitting room as he spoke. "Is who dead, baby brother?"

Clay followed without glancing at her. She stood listening, unmoving. She wondered why she was not surprised. She wondered why she had the feeling that there was something inevitable about this scene. She had had too much to drink, but now she wished she'd had more. So that it wouldn't matter, so that so little would really matter. Curious, though, she called out, "Make one for me, Owen."

"Owen, I may as well warn you," his brother said. "Don't try to bluff this out. Straight shit now—*straight*." When she arrived at the door of the room Owen was pouring drinks, his back to his brother. "I'm here to find out and I'm going to find out. Now. Is Pepe Benitez dead?"

Pepe Benitez? The jockey? She had had too many after all. The jockey who was to ride for Andrew Cameron?

Owen extended a glass to Clay. "Your little friend Kimberley received my little gift, did she? It could happen to *her*, you know. Or worse."

Clay moved then. So quickly that she did not realize what he had actually done until she heard the mirrored wall over the mantel shattering and saw that Owen no longer held the glass. It had been struck out of his hand. The noise was ugly and tremendous.

"Is he dead?"

"I don't know what the hell you're talkin' about, little brother."

Clay hit him then. Fast. A solid blow alongside the cheek, fist against flesh, a terrible flat sound. It went through her mind in that instant that of course they couldn't fight. Not here. And Owen was so much taller, heavier. What a strange thing to think. But then this wasn't really happening—

"You shouldn't ought to've done that, Clay," Owen said, his tone quiet now, very low. Almost regretful. "You come here to tear ass, then goddamn it, let's get on it, let's tear ass." He spit a clot of blood to the carpet. He rubbed the back of his hand across his mouth. He hunched his thick shoulders. Then his right fist went out, very fast, but not fast enough. Clay swayed quickly to one side and shot out his left, not once, but several times, in quick sharp jabs, each one to Owen's face.

She couldn't believe this, she didn't—

"Forgot about that left o' yours," Owen said, and then he swung hard and fast, his fist smashing Clay's ear. As Clay went to one side, not falling, Owen moved in closer, but Clay straightened and flicked out his left again and again. It was like the tongue of a snake darting, and she realized that if Owen ever came in close enough to use his weight, Clay would be done for, and that Clay knew this too.

But it was not really happening, of course—

"Is he dead?" Clay asked, the left fist striking out in pistonlike jabs, Owen trying to back away, trying to get his face out of the way, arms lifted.

Blood was streaking down Owen's face now, and she wanted to scream, but she was mesmerized, trapped, fascinated. Clay's ear had begun to swell up, changing color, going purple. It was all really a dream—

"Is he dead?"

"Let the cunt fret," Owen snarled. "Do her good!"

He lashed out, missing with his fist, and then he charged, shoulders down and head forward, like a bull goaded to reckless fury, and he managed to move in close enough to grab Clay's jacket. Using it, he pulled his brother to him and delivered a blow in the stomach that caused Clay's eyes to open wide and his head to jut forward as he began to gasp.

Then they were on the floor, upsetting a lamp, rolling, Owen taking charge of the fight, his enormous strength and weight taking over now, and then he was astraddle the other man, his knees on the floor, but Clay reached and took a grip on Owen's beard, held and pulled until Owen's face was close to his, and Owen howled with pain for the first time as Clay's grasp tightened, his other hand finding the beard too, its fingers tangling in it. Their faces were almost touching, and now she became aware of other sounds: harsh breathing, grunting.

She'd wake up. Any second now she'd wake up—

Suddenly, as if he could stand no more, Owen reared back, trying to straighten, and then he bellowed again as the hair of his beard stayed in Clay's hands. With Clay prone beneath him he drew back his fist, but Clay rolled his face aside and threw the hair into Owen's eyes as Owen's huge fist plunged down.

It drove into the floor, and even though it hit the carpet, she could hear the bones cracking and crunching. Owen rolled away, holding his hand, and Clay scrambled aside and clambered to his feet, driving one boot into Owen's ribs as he lay there.

Now Clay shouted for the first time. *"Is Pepe dead?"*

His ear looked like an overripe fig and there were purple splotches on his face. He seemed to wait. Owen managed to stand, staggering slightly, crouching, cradling his injured right hand in his left arm. Both eyes were an ugly swollen purple color, one half-closed. They darted and then he picked up a straight chair with his left hand, and using it like a ramrod, its legs out in front, he rushed Clay, catching him and pushing his body backward, his chest and neck piniored between the legs, but Owen's grasp was uncertain, and as Clay backed into the wall he was able to kick out, his boot this time catching Owen in the groin. Owen dropped the chair and Clay stepped closer. This time he used both hands to grasp Owen by the back of the head, forcing his face down, and at the same time lifting his knee so that it exploded in Owen's face.

Owen, released, straightened and staggered stiff-legged backward, open to Clay's attack. Clay's left darted out again, flicking at Owen's crushed and blood-smeared face. As he jabbed he spoke: "This is for Vincent Van."

Again and again his arm flashed out, connected. And each time he spoke: "Mrs. Stoddard and Ancient Mariner! . . . Molly Muldoon! . . . Starbright in that goddamn barn! . . . Bernie! . . . and Kimberley, what you did to Kimberley!"

He paused slightly as Owen began to groan.

Then, flat and hard and merciless: "Is he dead?"

Owen growled savagely, "Fuck you!" Then, wildly, he lurched to the fireplace, picked up a poker from its stand and, whirling it like a saber, turned to attack again. The iron poker cut through the air with a whirring sound as Clay ducked away from each swing. Christine heard herself cry out for the first time. She was going to be sick—

Owen backed Clay against the sofa and now he was coming closer, his face a wild, grotesque mask of hate and murder.

What happened then was so unexpected and startling that it took Christine a moment to realize why Owen had stopped swinging the poker. Why he was standing straight and staring.

He was staring at a revolver that Clay Chalmers had in his hand, pointed at his brother.

In a voice she had never heard before Owen said, "You couldn't do it. You ain't got it in you."

Quietly but in a strange voice too Clay said: "I got it in me. *You* put it there."

She was staring at the gun now, nothing else. She saw Clay's thumb reach and pull back the hammer. There was a small sharp click. Which she heard even above the two men's breathless gasping.

"Throw the poker on the floor," Clay said.

Owen sounded bewildered, incredulous: "You . . . you really want to kill me, don't you?"

"Yes," Clay said. "Yes, I do." Then he snarled: "Throw that poker on the floor!"

Owen dropped it. He moved sideways, as if stunned, and then he spoke in still another tone: "You killed her. Now you want to kill me."

Her? His mother. He actually believed that then. Christine looked at him. For the first time she spoke: "Owen . . . tell him . . ."

Owen sank to the sofa, his shattered swollen hand cradled. His eyes looked stunned and filled with pain.

Ignoring Owen, Clay reached inside his rumpled, bloodstained jacket and produced an envelope, which he handed her. "In case you still have doubts," Clay said, his eyes on her.

416

She opened the envelope, trying to control the shaking of her hands. In it were two photographs. She examined them, first one and then the other.

Now she *was* sick.

In a broken, unrecognizable voice Owen said, "I never *killed* anyone—"

Clay Chalmers took the pictures from her hand, and the envelope. She couldn't speak. She couldn't move.

"Mrs. Rosser," Clay Chalmers said then, but his voice reached her across a vast echoing distance, "Mrs. Rosser, I never did tell you how sorry I was to hear about your husband. They tell me he was a good and decent man. Lucky for you and Owen the plane didn't actually crash."

Then, while she tried to arrange his words into some sort of order and meaning in her mind, he turned to Owen: "The only way Fireaway's going to win is if you juice the hell out of him."

Then Clay Chalmers was gone. Vaguely she heard the front door open and close. She heard a motor start in the driveway.

"I . . . I had to make sure, didn't I?" Owen asked. And when she only nodded: "I told you what they'd do to me if I couldn't pay up." And she nodded again. "Do you understand, Chrissie?"

Yes. Yes. Chrissie understood.

When Andrew finished telling his story to the doctor, whose name was Irving Stern and who looked very young but intensely, personally interested—he wondered whether he had told it all, what he might have left out. It was so much more complex than a few words could convey, so much more puzzling, but he had been careful not to leave out anything that he thought important, including the kiss that his mind flinched from describing but which he had described nevertheless, in every detail, making sure that the young man understood, as he now did, its implications. When he was finished, he stood up from the chair in the sitting room and said, "Well, you asked." What he had intended to say was something about this being a beginning, anyway.

Dr. Stern ran a hand through his bushy brown hair and nodded.

"It's a good start. Now, Mr. Cameron, I've been able to convince your daughter that I'm not what she calls a shrink. Only a general practitioner called in by the hotel. She wouldn't have allowed me to sedate her if she'd known the truth, but I think that, for now at least, we should obliterate things from her mind as much as possible. For now. There's no point in my telling you that she's a deeply disturbed young lady and not very communicative—not quite catatonic but definitely in a state of shock. The one thing she appears to fear most is acknowledging that she's . . . well, we don't like the words *brink* or *edge* or even *mental* or *emotional breakdown*, but they come in handy for the moment. Deep inside she senses how ill she is, but her mind rebels. That will cause difficulties, but it's not unusual."

At the balcony doors Andrew said, "I keep wondering: Was there anything I should have done, might have done, or something that I was too blind to do earlier—"

"Mr. Cameron . . . you'll excuse my saying that such over-the-shoulder thinking now can only torment you and can do nothing for your daughter." His voice behind Andrew approached. "It may be that you have been *too* devoted—probably to make up for your wife's negligence. Well, you can't spend a lifetime blaming yourself for that, can you? And if you had decided to withdraw the horse by one of the illegal devices you mentioned—drugs or faking an illness or injury or even causing an injury yourself—she would have suspected you'd done it. It might have turned out worse—or it may have precipitated this collapse sooner." And when Andrew turned, he said, intently: "Yes, sir, it is a collapse, and at this stage there's no way to make a reasonable prognosis until we know the depth and nature of—"

The telephone rang in the foyer.

"Excuse me," Andrew said and walked on legs that had gone weak, even unsteady, to answer it. "Andrew Cameron here."

"Andrew, it's Jason. I'm afraid I have more bad news. Pepe Benitez has had an automobile accident. His agent, Ansel Vendig, says it's a minor injury but mostly to his hands, so he won't be able to ride."

"Accident? I don't believe it."

"I told Ansel I didn't think you would. Well, that's the story that's going out to the press and public. The truth is that our old friend Pepe, it turns out, is a faggot. He was attacked coming out of a gay bar last night when he should have been in bed, night before the Derby. His friends, or enemies, stomped his hands, but Ansel's been able to cover it up. Pepe's in a hospital in Indianapolis on a DNP basis. That means Do Not Publish, so it looks as if they're going to be able to hush it up. It'd be one hell of a mess for all of us if it got out that one of the top jocks in the country frequents gay bars. The papers would have a field day, and it could only give the whole business a black eye. So it's still another whitewash, Andrew, but in this case I'm for it."

"Have you told Kimberley?"

"Not a chance, Andrew. That's your job, sorry."

"Who's going to ride Starbright?"

"Andrew, I took it upon myself. We could use any one of a number of hustling jocks, but no one but Pepe really knows the horse. So why not go for the best? I long-distanced Ansel's suggestion, and I think we can get the wonderboy, Herbie Martz. He's available, and eager as hell. Why not? He's only a kid but hot as hell right now, and if he could bring in a Derby winner, we'd stay with him into the Preakness and Belmont Stakes."

"Jason, contact Blake Raynolds. There's no space coming in here on commercial flights. Tell Blake to arrange for a pilot to take my plane—no, scrub that. Confirm it with the boy's agent and tell him I'll fly over to pick him up at La Guardia. Work out the times and let me know. I need something to do anyway."

"I'll get right on it, Andrew. Thanks. And I'm sorry as hell."

When Andrew turned into the room again, Dr. Stern was pacing up and down. "Mr. Cameron," he said, as if he had been thinking and not listening in the interim, "Mr. Cameron, when something like this happens to someone we love or cherish it's the universal tendency to look back and try to affix blame—usually on one's self. Looking back that way is a dangerous tendency and often leads only to anguish and distortion. What we must accept, sir, is that at the bottom there's mystery. The bottom line is that we cannot ever know."

Realizing how concerned and intense the young man had become in such a short time, Andrew also realized that Blake had again come up with the proper person at the proper time—a dedicated and conscientious man. Over the years he had underestimated Blake Raynolds. "Thank you, Doctor," he said, feeling oddly reassured. Then he explained the telephone call and waited.

"She'll have to be told, but she's resting now and there's nothing she can do. I try, as often as possible, to recommend telling a patient the strict truth, but I've discovered that the truth, as a principle, is often a risky road to take. But . . . forgive my ignorance . . . is the jockey who's been injured named Pepe?"

"Yes. Why?"

"Because one of the many things troubling your daughter is whether someone named Pepe is dead."

"Good God."

"My sentiments exactly. And since I have not fallen so low as to believe in ESP or the occult—although God knows I someday may—I can only conclude that Kimberley knows somehow that this Pepe has had an accident."

"When do you think she may waken?"

"I can't predict that to the minute. The nurse with her, a Mrs. Bates, is well trained and excellent. I shall instruct her to tell Kimberley that Pepe is alive, but only if Kimberley asks. Does that meet with your approval?"

"Doctor, you have been very kind. And helpful. I appreciate it."

"No need for thanks. You'll get the bill." The young man seemed embarrassed as he walked toward the foyer. "Only doing my job."

"Like hell," Andrew heard himself say.

"Try looking at the whole thing this way, Mr. Cameron. We all carry volcanoes around inside. The inner conflicts become too intense, the clashes too much, we erupt." He halted and faced Andrew. "What's disturbing you most, if I'm any judge, is that kiss."

"You're a judge," Andrew admitted.

"Well, sir, those latent impulses must have been in her for a long time. Circumstances and the pressures and what I've heard called the concatenation of events—they all came together and something

420

deeply concealed, even to herself, exploded into the light. Shocking as it may be to you, it might make my job easier—or whoever takes over from me. At least we have one element exposed. It may take a long time to reach the others."

"How long, Doctor? Do you have any idea?"

Dr. Stern shook his head. "After such a cursory examination, no way. Months, at least. Maybe years. I'd recommend hospitalization. Some private sanitarium here or elsewhere. If she were to continue to be my patient, I'd suggest it be as far from home as convenient to you. As to prognosis: Give us time, Mr. Cameron, give us time."

Months at least. "Doctor . . . do you have tickets for the Derby?"

Irving Stern grinned and again ran his hand through his thick brown hair. "I live in Louisville, but I never see the Derby."

Maybe years. "It'd be my pleasure if you and your wife would care to join us in our box this afternoon."

The young man considered, then shook his head. "I'm tempted, Mr. Cameron. And it's kind of you. But if your daughter will be there—and I'd recommend she go, since it seems so important to her—I don't think my presence would do anything but remind her that she's not well. But thanks, all the same."

After they had shaken hands and Andrew was alone, he stood a long moment in the foyer staring at the closed door. *Months at least. Maybe years.* It was like a sentence. A prison sentence. Kimberley, in her own way, was continuing to hold him, to demand—

His impulse was to go to Brigid.

Was being blind being responsible? How long had he been blind? Had he blinded himself because he'd been unwilling to admit—

No. He had had no idea. The doctor was right in this too. *It's the universal tendency to look back and try to affix blame—usually on one's self.* And he himself had felt no such sexual urges as Kimberley had now revealed. Never. *Looking back that way is a dangerous tendency and often leads only to anguish and distortion.*

He picked up the telephone and dialed Brigid's number.

"Yes?" Her voice. Her beloved voice.

"Brigid—"

"Yes, Andrew?"

"Brigid, what are you doing between now, this minute, and post time for the Derby?"

"I'm only . . . writing letters. I suppose, darling, I'm doing what most people are doing—very little of nothing."

"How would you like . . . how would you like to—"

"Andrew, are you there? You sound so strange. You don't seem yourself at all. Has anything—"

"Would you like to fly to New York?"

"New York?"

"With me. In my . . . in my plane."

But when she did not speak, he remembered: Brigid had not flown since her husband's death at the airport in Shannon. But he could not, he discovered, speak.

"Do you particularly want me to, Andrew?"

"Yes."

"Then . . . then I shall. Andrew, are you weeping?"

"Yes. I'll see you in ten minutes."

"I'm ready now. I'm here, Andrew."

He replaced the telephone and then he gave himself over, for the first time in many years, to tears.

All happy families resemble one another; every unhappy family is unhappy in its own fashion. Walter Drake, who had been married his last year in college, remembered the words but not the source or the author. Odd they should have stayed with him over the years. Well, today his was a happy family. They had not, to Margo's regret, remembered that a special breakfast was served at the Downs on Derby Day, but as they rode in a taxi past the blocked-off one-way streets on their way to the stable gate (they didn't want to miss any of the excitement) all four of them were about as happy as a man could expect his family to be. There had been times when Walter had wondered whether any family was ever really happy, but today he had come to realize that happiness is so elusive because you never really know it when you have it; before you know it, it's too late and you're only *remembering* being happy. Well, not today.

Terry, although his mother had not mentioned it, had had his heavy beard shaved off and he looked younger and somehow more boyish and innocent; and Margo spoke of today as if she had spent all her life building toward it and she didn't even mention her baby-to-come a single time. As for Susan, she was the laughing girl Walter had remembered. On the backside, which had a totally different and more sober atmosphere this morning, with only a very few newsmen and photographers bustling about and a general air of down-to-business now, she looked through the chain-link fence across the backstretch of track to the infield. The paper had said that spectators began to flood into the infield as soon as the gates opened at eight and that many had spent the night in long lines hoping to snatch the choice positions along the fence. Last night's carnivallike atmosphere continued there; you couldn't even see the grass for the swarm of people. They had decided to visit Prescription and then walk through the tunnel to the grandstand and spend the next six or so hours in their box or strolling around the gardens or watching the other races that would precede the Derby. By now Susan, who had lost her fear of the horse and had petted and stroked him as if she'd been doing it all her life, was convinced that Prescription would win. Walter was not, but he didn't say so. What he had decided, though, was that he was going to get into the racehorse business in a bigger and more serious way. Nothing in his memory had ever given his family such pleasure. And if you didn't win one year, there was always another horse and another year. Even if he lost today, Prescription could go on and take a few purses in stakes races here and there and finance the purchase of new horses— Hell, in time Walter'd have his own string, maybe his own stable. It was like finding a whole new life at age fifty! And look at Susie-Q—had she ever looked happier?

The lobby and parking area were busy and crowded, raucous with voices, some happy, some tense, some drunken. Clay parked his pickup himself and then was pushing his way into the lobby when he saw Andrew standing off to one side. Andrew was waiting for the young attendant to bring around his Mercedes.

"How's Kimberley?"

"Sleeping. With medication. You look as if you could use a little of both yourself."

"Will you give her a message for me, Andrew?"

"Why not give it to her yourself?"

Clay considered this and then shook his head. "No, I think I've taken my last ride on my trusty white charger. I'm doffing my silver armor." Then: "Tell her Pepe's not dead."

"Pepe? She'll be told that as soon as she wakes up. There's a nurse with her."

"Then I've had a little chat with my brother for nothing." But he changed his mind. "No. Possibly not. Besides, it had to come, sooner or later." Then: "So you know about Pepe—"

"Only part of it, Clay. It's all anyone ever knows, isn't it? Bits and pieces."

"Or less. Well, take this." He handed Andrew an envelope. "Open it after the Derby. Open it when you damn please. It'll explain something anyway. Well, so long, Andrew."

"Good-bye, Clay. I only wish we . . . it's a damn shame that—"

"I agree," Clay said. "I wish we'd had a better shot at becoming friends. And it's a damn shame too that we don't have more time now."

"One last thing, though, Clay—"

"If it's about Lord Randolph—"

"I'm afraid I know now who was responsible."

"So do I, Andrew."

"Will you shake hands and put it behind you?"

"I already have, I think."

"Well, good luck this afternoon. I wish I could say I hope you win."

"Starbright's a fine horse."

"I shudder to think what might happen to Kimberley if he doesn't take it."

Clay did not say how sorry he was or that that was Andrew's problem now. Instead he said, "Good luck to you too." He did not add that he had the feeling that Andrew would need it.

424

"You have something done to that ear, Clay. It looks like a bunch of grapes."

"What is it I'm supposed to say now? Something about you should see the other fellow."

"I wish I could. Yes, I think I'd like that very much, Clay."

Janice's contempt had become a poison that, while it lacerated and destroyed, nevertheless fed and nourished some sick need in him. It made no sense, but then his life had come to make no sense.

"Count Wyatt, the magnificent, the mighty! Listen, if you'd played ball with me instead of playing king of the mountain on that pile of bullshit—thinking you were protecting the holy sport of racing—my paper wouldn't have given me the ax! Instead I'd be walking out on *them*. You, you, *you*—do you know what you really are, Count?" Her face was grotesquely distorted by revulsion, *disgust*. She was smoking steadily and spittle dribbled over her lips and chin and she licked it away with a darting tongue, her eyes glazed with hate. "You are a phony and a prick! It made me sick every time I had to touch your soft, sloppy body. Every time you touched me, your splotchy, pudgy old hands made me want to throw up all over you! You have the idea you're a *bon vivant*, a *boulevardier*, a man about town—well, you are a tub of lard, a crock of shit! And old, old, *old*! Well, don't sit there, say something clever and witty and sophisticated. No, listen, *listen*—I've got it on tape, lover boy. All your barnyard grovelings and heavings and pantings, all of it, and I'm going to play it in the press room after the Derby. Fantastic! After that, you won't think your shit doesn't stink. Look in the mirror, lover boy. You're a walrus, a walking breathing obscenity—a funny-looking fat walrus with everyone sneering at you. All I know is that I'm glad I don't have to play any more games to make you get it up. Because even when you do, it's nothing. A little nothing and a large joke! So long, Count—from now on I only hope you can't even jackoff, you fucking pervert!"

425

* * *

On the plane en route to New York, with Andrew at the controls, Brigid discovered that the only fear she had was whether Andrew, because of whatever had happened to Kimberley, would tell her good-bye forever after the race. Then, as if—once again—he had uncannily read her thoughts, Andrew said: "Brigid, it appears now that I won't be able to join you next month for Ascot or the Irish Sweeps. But I will be there in the fall to see Irish Thrall run in the Arc in Paris. I'll be there, Brigid, regardless of anything or anyone. That's a promise." Then he added, his eyes looking across clouds: "There comes a time when a man, whatever his age, has to take a clean solid look at his life and decide what he himself wants and has to have, regardless of anyone else or any other demands. If that's selfish, put me down as a selfish man. October is definite. It's a promise."

"There does come that time," was all that Brigid said because, with the joy in her, she could not trust her voice to go on. She reached and placed one hand over his. She was young again. Very young. The schoolgirl in Galway with the world lying open ahead, dazzling with promise. For only the second time in her life she felt that she was giving herself over to a man.

And then, for the rest of the trip to La Guardia, they were both silent, enclosed in the small cabin high above the world and, for that short time at least, content to be detached from it.

Preparing for his eleven o'clock telecast in the cubicle at the end of the press room—which was almost deserted except for a few reporters at typewriters and a few with microphones and portable TV cameras and mint juleps in paper cups—Wyatt rearranged the typewritten pages and glanced at the teleprompter, which was unlit, careful not to look at the small monitor screen, which was lit and which contained his own image. He knew that picture too well; and now he would never be able to see it again without wincing inside.

Winner's Circle

The canted hat, the long ebony cigarette holder, the mocking eyes, the sagging jowls—the image filled him with nausea and self-contempt. He was not even sure that he could do the broadcast. Nor was he sure that the copy didn't sound empty and flat and as phony as the image on the screen. And after he did get through the ordeal—it had once been a pleasure and the highlight of his day— what then, what then? He must be careful not to be anywhere near the press room after the Derby. But where, where was there to go?

The red warning light came on.

Tallyho, yoicks, and all that, this is Count Wyatt coming to you from Ripoffsville, USA, on the banks of the sluggish and polluted Ohio River. Mint julep time has arrived! Your obedient servant is in the press room atop the clubhouse overlooking Churchill Downs, and from this Olympian aerie he is bringing you his final words of wit and warning. In forty-five minutes the first race of the day will begin and then, less than six fun-filled hours later, it will be post time for the Kentucky Derby itself, the one and only. The grandstands and box seats are not yet half-filled, the infield is already bulging with sweating humanity, and in all almost one hundred thousand guests are expected. But don't rush out and try to buy a seat. Except for general admission, only a few reserved seat tickets change hands from year to year. Most people watch from their homes, but many are relegated to watching on the television sets which dot the pari-mutuel areas. Bring your own folding chair! It's anticipated by the stewards and other hawkers that twenty-five thousand watered-down juleps will be consumed. No one has the gaseous gall to estimate how much beer will be ingurgitated, regurgitated, and urinated.

For it's almost time for the mile and a quarter classic, the Run for the Roses—although there's a rumor out that the roses are not roses but another flower dyed by hand this very morning. But a rose by any other name, to quote some romantic damn fool or other. The purse is worth approximately a quarter of a million dollars, and though owners and trainers will tell you that they run their horses for the glory, not the money, to date no purse has been refused. It's

427

inflation time now and every quarter million comes in handy at the supermarket. Regardless and notwithstanding, a Derby triumph is always the quickest brush with sports immortality. There's no gainsaying that this true American ritual constitutes the most dramatic, irretrievable two minutes in all sports.

In 1973 an editor of the Louisville Courier-Journal *dubbed the Derby, 'The nation's most prominent celebration of avarice.' But the late John Steinbeck wrote: 'The Kentucky Derby, whatever it is—a race, an emotion, a turbulence, an explosion—is one of the most beautiful and violent and satisfying things I have ever experienced.' So . . . somewhere in between those sentiments probably lies what we amusingly call the truth.*

But the truth is not on the track, not even in the grandstands, infield, or boxes. The truth lies somewhere out there in the city. Larger-than-life passions are poured into the Derby, but what those passions are, where they lead, how lives are changed, fates altered, lowly you and lowlier I will never be privileged to witness, behold, or participate in. What does happen behind the scenes, the polite facades? Love, violence, honor, madness—watch the horses and be satisfied, serfs!

The ill wind that has favored us here this year continues to howl and shriek. Yesterday, after her filly Miss Mariah won the Kentucky Oaks, Mrs. Rachel Stoddard of Brookfield, Connecticut, passed quietly to her rest in the winner's circle, holding the trophy in her hand. Now, alas, only two widows, not three, will vie to see which, if either, will drink a toast to her horse, Fireaway or Irish Thrall, from the sterling silver julep cup to be presented by the governor of the Bluegrass State.

The horse to beat remains Starbright, a Virginia gentleman bidding for superstardom here today. According to the morning line Starbright was a 2–3 odds-on favorite—meaning, gamblers, that he would pay less than even money. Take heart from the fact that only twenty-nine odds-on favorites have won and only ten have even come in second. And hold onto your straw boaters! In the last two hours the odds on Starbright have backed down to even money. Why? Because what started as a rumor has now been confirmed: The renowned and beloved Pepe Benitez, the only jockey who has ever ridden Starbright in competition, will not be up. He was involved, it seems,

428

in an automobile mishap—with, I hasten to add for his millions of fans, only minor injuries. But before anyone tears up his or her ticket or tears out his or her hair, hear this! Backside scuttlebutt now has it that Herbie Martz, the new wonderboy of racing, who looks like an angel and rides like a devil, will be aboard the great Starbright when he goes to the gate. Now . . . watch the odds change again and don't forget where you learned it first.

Of the three hundred and nineteen horses nominated for the Derby in February, only eight will go to the post. In addition to Starbright, Fireaway (at seven to two) and Irish Thrall (six to one), the field will consist of five other hopefuls.

Hotspur, the only owner-trained horse, is running at twelve to one. Smart money is holding down the odds because, while this little black speedster from Florida won the Derby Trial on Tuesday, that was only, some think, a fluke caused by a pileup on the backstretch, and today Hotspur will be running on a hard, fast track. This is not predicted, it is all but guaranteed. The latest weather bureau advisory shows no shower activity within a radius of three hundred miles.

Bonne Fete, a filly from gay Paree, is now showing odds of twenty-to-one. Prescription, Indiana-owned and Ohio-bred, is on the board at twenty-five-to-one. The third foreign entry, Fuji Mist, from Japan, is thirty-to-one as of this minute. And last, what could turn out to be a dark horse—apologies to JD Edwards, no racial offense intended—there is Also Ran, a gelding, at forty to one.

Make no mistake, friends and enemies and marks, every horse is dangerous, one to the other, every race holds some surprise, and odds on a tote board or in the newspaper or emanating from the jaws of your obedient servant can be deceiving—that's what makes the game a game. And today it's the only game in town! This is it and tally-ho!

On the way from the hotel to the track Clay pulled the pickup off the highway out of the endless line of traffic, and then he got out and vomited.

When he climbed in again, his body felt as drained, as purged, as his mind. An emptiness. A sadness.

And loss.

Yes, the loss was there. You couldn't spend seven years aching and yearning and hoping, only to realize that what you ached and yearned and hoped for was unreal, a creation of your own mind, a fantasy—how could you spend seven years with a dream without feeling the loss, the waste?

As he had known for hours now something had gone out of him. He didn't know yet exactly what it was. But he knew it was gone forever. And there was a yawning void where it had been.

How long would it last? Well, not forever. Or even, he suspected, for months or a year. What are voids? Only space. And space is something to be filled.

His ear was an incessant throb of pain. What had Andrew said it looked like? A bunch of grapes. Well, it didn't feel like a bunch of grapes. It felt like a pulsing two-ton bag of heat and weight and pain. An ear to go with his lopsided nose. Thanks again, Owen.

But the trouble was not in his ear, to hell with the pain. The trouble was in his mind. Or heart. Or in what once was referred to as the soul.

Finally, after crawling along a wide, crowded thoroughfare—all traffic moving one way today—he turned down a narrow residential street and arrived within a few city blocks of the Downs in a line of noisy, stalled, impatient traffic. He decided to walk the rest of the way. He parked the car cheek-by-jowl with others on one of the many front lawns converted into parking areas by homemade signs. Twenty bucks. He paid it to the owner of the small modest house and then joined the throng walking toward the track grounds.

In the crush of hurrying bodies he wondered why he did not feel different. Worse. So long, Kimberley. Damned if he was going to spend a life looking back over his shoulder. Good-bye, Kimberley, and good luck. I can't cry, sorry. No violins, no sad songs, no tears. Someday, Kimb, maybe you'll be as free as I feel now. I hope so, Kimberley—only the best. And don't think I'm not thankful. In some strange way that I haven't had time to dope out I wouldn't be here if it weren't for you. But I'm here, Kimb, the Derby itself, and thanks to you for that.

When he turned a corner and the twin steeples came into view, flags flying, he began to walk faster. Suddenly it was very important that he get to the backside, and fast.

Not that there was all that much to do this time of day. It was another six hours to post time of the eighth race. But backside was where he belonged. That was home. Well, it was as good a home as most—no, better than most. Sure, racing had as many piles of shit to try to step around as any of the shiny-desk, tie-and-button-down-collar jobs, eight to five with two weeks' vacation and retirement funds. But probably no *more* piles of it, if he only knew. The trick was to step around when you could, kick them out of the way where possible, above all to stay upright.

Walking, he could feel the old adrenaline begin to pump again. The past—Toby, Owen, his mother, Kimberley—all that was in back of him. Where it belonged. Where he would make sure it would damn well stay.

And the future stretched ahead—not a void but an open expanse to be filled. By him. To be filled by whatever he *chose* to fill it with. The future was his now—a challenge, an exciting challenge.

He arrived at the stable gate and walked through, nodding at the uniformed guard. There was a crowd up and down the chain-link fence. Peering in, curious and excited. The first race of the day was being run. He could hear the shouting from frontside and the in-field and when they were on the backstretch the hoofs of the horses and the shouts of their riders.

Who was it who had said, "I'd rather have me a bad day on the track than a goddamn good day off it somewheres else?"

He decided to watch the Derby from the guinea stand if he could make it back there between "Riders up" and "They're at the post!" Possibly during the singing of "My Old Kentucky Home." If Kimberley came to the track and if she caught sight of him in his box seat, it might disturb her. Even trigger some wildness in her. It's up to you, Kimb. Whatever happens to you now, you're the only one who can really decide it. Sick or well, the choice is yours, kid.

A slow hot exultancy flowed in his veins. He was a free man. At last. His own man.

A roar went up across the track. The first race had ended. He didn't even glance at the sky as he quickened his step. It's not going to rain, Hotspur, so it's up to you to do it on a fast, hard track. Nothing comes easy, a race or growing up, nothing. You don't choose your tracks, boy, you only decide how you run them. It's up to you.

Chapter Twelve

THE Derby that year was won by a horse from New Mexico named Fireaway, who came in ahead of the black Florida colt, Hotspur, by three full lengths. The race itself was not spectacular, but it was replete with the usual surprises. Fireaway, at odds of seven to two, took command almost from the gate and lengthened his lead on the clubhouse turn. He was never seriously threatened except by Starbright, briefly, on the backstretch, when his jockey, Herbie Martz, riding in place of the even more famous Pepe Benitez, made his move and let out a wrap. But the even-money favorite faltered badly on the far turn and lost ground disastrously on the stretch to finish in fifth place. Fireaway's time came close to threatening the great Secretariat's 1973 record of 1:59^2/s for the mile and a quarter but failed by two-fifths of a second. Another surprise was the accomplishment of a dark bay named Prescription; running at dismissive odds of twenty-five to one, he crossed the wire in third place, behind Hotspur by only a head. Fourth place went to Irish Thrall, with Fuji Mist, Also Ran and Bonne Fete finishing in that order.

There was an unusual public disturbance in the boxes when the Official sign lit up and the winners' numbers began flashing off and on. Miss Kimberley Cameron, the beauty known as the princess of that year's Derby, seemed to lose control of herself. Witnesses report

433

that after looking stunned she went wild and, screaming, tried to fight and claw her way down to the track, shouting obscenities and physically attacking anyone who attempted to calm her. She was restrained by police and she finally subsided in the arms of her father. It was conjectured that, like almost everyone else, she had been drinking, and when her personally owned colt, the much-vaunted Starbright himself, finished a weak fifth, it was too much for her. Unable to believe it—she was not alone in that—she seemed, spectators said, to explode. Supported by her father, she was escorted by police to a private stewards' room in the clubhouse. It was later reported that the distraught young woman was helped to a car in a catatonic state, her face wearing a faint and distant smile.

The race will go down in the history books, however, because of what followed three days later. The Kentucky State Racing Commission, after conducting a hearing, ordered redistribution of the purse, with first money going to Hotspur, second to Prescription, third money to the gray, Irish Thrall, and fourth instead of fifth to the big favorite, Starbright. Fireaway was set down to eighth, or last, place.

This action was taken because the chemical tests which are routinely run on the first four horses to cross the finish line revealed the presence of prohibited medication in Fireaway's system.

At the hearing Mrs. Christine Rosser stated that she was neither surprised nor shocked at the findings for two reasons: one, that Owen Chalmers had wanted to win so much that he had once told her that he would go to any lengths to do so; and two, that she had heard her trainer's brother tell him on the day of the race itself that the only way he could win was by "juicing his horse." In the hearing room at this point she turned to Owen Chalmers, whose face was clean-shaven and misshapen, as if he had had an accident of some sort, and said for all to hear: "That must have been what gave you the idea, Mr. Chalmers. I know it certainly made *me* think." Mr. Chalmers sat mute, as he had during most of the proceeding, except when he told the commissioners and stewards that he had been tricked. He was, he told them, not a fool. But when asked whether he had any more to contribute as to *how* he might have been tricked and by whom, he shook his head and said, "What'd be the use?" And then he lapsed once again into a brooding silence.

At the conclusion of the hearing Mrs. Rosser stated that she, as owner, would not challenge the findings by taking the matter to court as the owners of Dancer's Image did in 1968. She was, she said, quite satisfied with the decision of the Commission, even though it did mean that a certain deal for the sale of her horse could not now be consummated.

Eager to settle the matter quickly and with as little publicity as possible, the Racing Commission ordered that, except for the pari-mutuel payoffs (which had already been made on Saturday), the winner of the Derby be officially recorded as Hotspur and that both the purse and gold-cup trophy be awarded to its owner.

Subsequently the Thoroughbred Racing Protective Bureau, known as the TRPB, instigated its own investigation with a view toward criminal proceedings, but Mr. Owen Chalmers had mysteriously disappeared, although every racetrack has been alerted and is being watched, and he has not been seen or heard from since.

Interviewed on television later, Clay Chalmers, owner of Hotspur, refused to comment on the hearing and had only this to say: "The Preakness is next."